Barbara Comyns

Manchester University Press

'A marvellous biography – detailed, fascinating and meticulously researched, bringing to life this uniquely talented author in a highly compelling way. As well as winning Comyns a new legion of fans, the book looks set to raise some tantalising questions for existing devotees.'

JacquiWine's Journal

'Richly detailed, sympathetic and endlessly fascinating, this biography brings Barbara Comyns to life.'

Claire Fuller, author of *Unsettled Ground*

'A riveting account of the bohemian life of one of Britain's finest – and most underrated – novelists. It made me long to re-read her distinctive and original novels.'

Alexandra Pringle, Founding Director of Virago Press

'Avril Horner's beautifully written, thought-provoking and extensive examination of Comyns' life will hopefully garner some of the recognition this incredible writer so richly deserves.'

Jan Carson, author of *The Raptures*

'Finally, there is a definitive and fascinating record of this overlooked writer's wildly varied and adventurous life, told in prose as fast-paced and naturally riveting as that of Comyns herself.'

Emily Gould, author of *Perfect Tunes* and *Friendship*

'Thoughtful, thorough and completely engaging, the book delves into Comyns's work and life and brings both vividly to the page. I loved it.'

Kate Hamer, author of *The Lost Girls*

'An exemplary biography that sheds light on the life of a wonderful and original writer. Horner not only makes a case for Comyns's literary importance; she reveals someone human and impulsive and fallible – and all the more likeable for it.'

Brian Evenson, author of *Song for the Unraveling of the World*

'This is a riveting portrait of a writer more people need to read. I hope Avril Horner's book will be an introduction to the singular, savage, and sneakily complex world of Barbara Comyns.'

Richard Mirabella, author of *Brother & Sister Enter the Forest*

'Finally, a biography of one of Britain's greatest novelists! Avril Horner has written a wonderful biography of a "hidden in plain sight" genius and a vital examination of being a woman artist and writer in the 20th century.'

Camilla Grudova, author of *The Coiled Serpent*

'An important and valuable job in bringing Comyns into the light.'

Rosemary Hill, author of *God's Architect*

Barbara Comyns

A savage innocence

Avril Horner

MANCHESTER UNIVERSITY PRESS

Published by Manchester University Press
Oxford Road, Manchester M13 9PL

www.manchesteruniversitypress.co.uk

British Library Cataloguing-in-Publication Data
A catalogue record for this book is available from the
British Library

ISBN   978 1 5261 7374 4   hardback
ISBN   978 1 5261 8493 1   paperback

First published 2024
Paperback first published 2025

Typeset
by New Best-set Typesetters Ltd

For Nuria Leighton and in memory of Julian Pemberton

And for my family, with a special welcome for Charlotte, last but certainly not least!

In the back of my mind I was always sure that wonderful things were waiting for me, but I'd got to get through a lot of horrors first.

Barbara Comyns, Mr Fox

Barbara Comyns deftly balances savagery with innocence, depravity with lyric interludes.

Ursula Holden

Contents

Introduction

Barbara Comyns was a twentieth-century author whose life was as extraordinary as her novels. She was a woman of many parts, including commercial artist, keeper of chickens, dog breeder, antique dealer, piano restorer, imaginative house renovator, cook-housekeeper, landlord, painter, sculptor and eventually successful author. For many years she thought of herself primarily as a visual artist who tried her hand at writing from time to time. Her first book was published when she was forty and the ten books that followed established her as a unique voice in English fiction. Although she remained passionate about art, it was as a writer that she finally made her name. By the time she was fifty, she saw herself as an author who painted for pleasure rather than an artist who dabbled in writing, though her training as an artist certainly influenced the way she wrote. She had learned to look at the world very closely, a discipline that evolved into a wickedly sharp focus on people and their behaviour in her fiction – and her enthusiasm for surrealism as a young woman resulted in books that offer a strange and distinctive vision of the world, sometimes dreamy, sometimes nightmarish.

Barbara's education as a child was haphazard; like many women of her class in the nineteenth and early twentieth centuries, she was taught (on and off) by governesses at home and had only occasional spells at school. As an adult, she spent many years in London before moving to Spain in 1956 with her second husband, where they stayed for eighteen years, finally returning to England in 1974. She lived in more than thirty flats or houses before she died and, when moving, relished the challenge of turning a new space into a home. She had two husbands and many lovers – and she sometimes sailed close to the wind in relation to the law, especially when living with her racketeer partner, Arthur Price, in the late 1930s and early 1940s. When young, she was attracted to the *demi-monde* in London and found middle-class conventions and conformity dull and comical, preferring to mix with artists. Her first husband's relatives, the Pemberton family, were appalled by her behaviour and did not mince their words in condemning her when she had a child by a lover in 1935 while still married.

As a young woman, Barbara Comyns wanted to become an important painter and sculptor, but by the age of 29 she was a single parent with two small children to support at a time when there was little financial help available and plenty of censure of women in such a position. During her twenties she endured a feckless husband and a failed marriage; an abortion; a lover who did not stand by her when she became pregnant by him; a breakdown and a suicide attempt. In order to get through those difficult periods, she was sometimes impulsive and occasionally manipulative in a way that worsened her situation. It was not until she became economically self-sufficient and started writing seriously in her thirties that she was able to transform those bleak episodes of her life into compelling fictions of great energy and poignancy. The power of the novels derives from a life often lived on the edge. Most of her heroines endure spells of misery or poverty as young women – as she did – but Barbara Comyns' determination to survive and to make her mark as an artist or a writer gave her life a focus that they lacked.

From childhood, Barbara was a voracious reader. She loved nineteenth-century fiction, although according to her son, Julian Pemberton, her favourite novel remained Daniel Defoe's *Moll Flanders*, published in 1722. It is not difficult to see why: she had much in common with Defoe's heroine. They were both beautiful women who quickly drew admirers; they were also resourceful, intelligent and determined individuals who used their native wit to survive the many vicissitudes of their lives. They were both much occupied by money and knew what it was to live in penury. Barbara Comyns also admired Defoe's style; her precise and pellucid writing owes a great deal to his work. She might even have identified a little with Defoe himself, a merchant investor who tried his hand at many things and who was often in debt; a man who started writing novels relatively late in life and who was connected with the world of espionage, having been employed as a government spy in 1706. Barbara Comyns also knew something of that world: for some years she was good friends with Kim Philby, who worked with her second husband, Richard Comyns Carr, in MI6. How Barbara Irene Veronica Comyns Carr (née Bayley), born into an upper-middle-class family in a village in Warwickshire in 1907, became mixed up in the greatest spy scandal of the twentieth century is a story worth telling – as is her rise to fame as an author.

The novels of Barbara Comyns were regarded as extraordinary when they were first published and sharply divided readers into those who thought she was a brilliant new author and those who found her work peculiar or unpleasantly macabre. Mordantly witty and occasionally deeply chilling, her books reveal the horrors of family malice and grinding poverty while celebrating the beauty and the comic incongruities of life. Her first book,

Sisters by a River (1947), is mainly autobiographical, as is *Out of the Red, Into the Blue* (1960), which she later described in a letter to her agent as 'three-quarters true'.[1] Four of her novels are strange and disturbing works that could be described as her gothic quartet. These are *Who was Changed and Who was Dead* (1954), *The Vet's Daughter* (1959), *The Skin Chairs* (1962) and *The Juniper Tree* (1985). The five remaining novels, *Our Spoons Came from Woolworths* (1950), *Birds in Tiny Cages* (1964), *A Touch of Mistletoe* (1967), *Mr Fox* (1987) and *The House of Dolls* (1989), are more realist works, although even they include Chagall-like episodes. She also wrote a short biography, *Leigh Hunt in Italy*, and a novel entitled *Waiting*, both refused for publication and sadly now lost, although an early draft of the latter has recently been found.

It was her widely praised fourth book *The Vet's Daughter*, published in 1959, that established Barbara Comyns as a talented and unusual writer. The two novels that followed were reviewed less enthusiastically, however, and her reputation dwindled between the mid-1960s and the late 1970s. Never a member of authors' clubs or coteries, and living out of the limelight in Spain during much of that time, she fell into obscurity until Virago Press started reissuing her work in the 1980s. These reprints were followed by a new novel, *The Juniper Tree*, which was published in 1985, after a writing silence of eighteen years, to great acclaim. Yet in spite of the waves of praise her writing has attracted, Barbara Comyns has not received the attention due to her. While other mid-twentieth-century novelists such as Elizabeth Taylor, Elizabeth Jane Howard and Barbara Pym have been rescued from their previous obscurity, Comyns is still regarded as a rather marginal figure, despite her many admirers and the translation of her novels into French, German, Italian, Spanish, Polish and Chinese. Although her books have been praised by major authors, including Graham Greene, who quietly advanced her career when he could, she has yet to be fully recognized as an important twentieth-century writer.

Barbara Comyns was a survivor who transformed the events of her life into compelling stories which are a strange mixture of wit and melancholia, the mundane and the weird. Her early work is marked by a child-like, innocent view of the world that renders it amusingly odd and threatening. In her first book, *Sisters by a River*, the bizarre is woven into the everyday and life appears both dream-like and full of the comic macabre. In her second novel, *Our Spoons Came from Woolworths*, society's shortcomings as Sophia Fairclough's life sinks into poverty are conveyed through witty and offhand remarks. Comyns was a virtuoso when it came to shifts in mood and she could move seamlessly between witty asides and moments of great pain in her novels. She has been aptly described as standing 'with one foot in the plain-spoken world of early 20th-century England, and another in a realm of cracked-mirror fairy tales'.[2] But in her darkest books, the innocent become victims and the fairy tale transmutes into nightmare or gothic horror. Several characters die violent deaths in *Who was Changed and Who was Dead* and *The Skin Chairs* features furniture upholstered with human skin. In *The Vet's Daughter*, Alice Rowlands is able to levitate, an act that allows her – if only in her mind – to escape the constraints and ill treatment she experiences at home, although her father's exploitation of her gift results in her death. In *The Juniper Tree*, Comyns' use of a German myth lends the novel an air of the mysterious and the terrifying, despite its being set in the late twentieth century in a wealthy middle-class area. But while her gothic novels exude a potent strangeness, they also illuminate the injustices of the real world, shedding light on the abuse of the vulnerable and the cruelty often meted out to women and children. At the same time, her deadpan humour and the inclusion of lyrical interludes temper the darkness of her work, which offers an intriguing combination of savagery and innocence.

The novels of Barbara Comyns are perhaps best regarded as 'autofiction' – a useful though contentious term often used to describe a particular sort of writing that draws on the author's life while featuring fictional characters and episodes. 'L'autofiction, c'est comme le rêve, un rêve n'est pas la vie, un livre n'est pas la vie' ('Autofiction is like a dream, a dream is not life, a book is not life'), wrote Serge Doubrovsky in 1977.[3] Falling somewhere between a dream, a nightmare and a lived reality, the novels of Barbara Comyns both entertain and disturb. Behind the naivety of many of her female characters is a knowing author whose fiction offers a savage indictment of a society in which casual cruelty is commonplace. And while the female characters in her novels are not Comyns, they often represent aspects of her personality and her experience, albeit in condensed and exaggerated form. The biggest temptation facing a literary biographer is to raid the writer's work for evidence of the writer's life, thereby reducing the books to loosely disguised memoirs. I have tried to avoid this by drawing on Comyns' novels only when I have proof (as provided by her family and others) that certain episodes in them were inspired by events in her life. When I discuss her books, my aim has been to pay close attention to them as works of art in their own right. I hope that, in *Barbara Comyns: A Savage Innocence*, I have managed to get the balance right – although, of course, a life is always sea-changed in the telling, whether in memoir, fiction or literary biography.

1

From Bell Court to Amsterdam

Barbara Irene Veronica Bayley, who was later to become Barbara Comyns, was born to Albert Edward Bayley and his wife, Eva Margaret Mary Bayley, on 27 December 1907, on a night when Bidford-on-Avon in Warwickshire was softly coated in snow. Having two girls already, her parents had hoped for another boy, but Dennis Darby Bayley, born in 1904, was to remain their only son. Two more girls were born in the following years, so Barbara became the middle sister of five girls. Her two older sisters, Constance and Margaret, were affectionately called 'Molly' and 'Nan' in the family but the two younger ones, Kathleen and Chloe, were known simply by their names.

Their father was a resourceful self-made individual who, once he set his mind on something, always saw it through. In 1893 he was a handsome and ambitious young man of nearly thirty who sported a luxuriant, black, down-turned moustache. He came from a hard-working Wesleyan Methodist family who lived in West Bromwich near Birmingham; his father ran a building contracting business and his mother was a pawnbroker. His three brothers made their livings in coal merchandising, oil manufacturing and commercial travelling, and his two sisters stayed at home to help their mother. Albert had set his sights higher. He was the best educated in his family and he was determined to make his way in the world. In the 1880s he had been a commercial clerk, but by 1891, according to the National Census, he was a brewer's chemist. One day, calling in on a cottage owned by his parents which was rented by a widow called Annie Fenn, he noticed her young daughter skipping in the garden. She was a pretty child of ten and he watched her for a while before telling her mother that he would marry Eva when she was old enough to cook. Family memory also has it that Albert Bayley wrote off a large sum of money that Annie Fenn owed his parents on condition that she would later let him wed her daughter.[1]

Albert Bayley did indeed marry Eva Margaret Mary Fenn, much to the disapproval of the Darbys, her mother's family, who thought Eva was marrying beneath her because Albert's family were all 'in trade'. The wedding took

1 Barbara's maternal grandmother, Annie Fenn (née Darby)

place on 2 July 1903 in Ilfracombe, Devon, and was followed by a brief honeymoon there. It was far enough away from home to avoid any gossip – for Albert was 39 and Eva was already pregnant at 20 years old with their first child, who would be born just four months later. During the first few years of their marriage, Albert and Eva, by then known to her family as 'Margaret' or 'Marjie', lived in the Bayley family home in West Bromwich, an ugly house full of dark wood furniture and heavy curtains. Margaret hated it there and was desperate for a home of her own. Albert worked hard to achieve it: energetic and inventive, he patented a procedure which

2 Barbara's father, Albert Edward Bayley

significantly improved the brewing process. This brought him a considerable sum of money with which he bought a brewery near Birmingham, and the profits from this business made him wealthy enough to buy a house in the country by the time his eldest daughter was four years old. Sometime in 1907 Albert, Margaret and their three children moved to Bell Court, a beautiful riverside house in the Warwickshire village of Bidford-on-Avon. Margaret's mother, Annie Fenn, came to help them settle in but ended up living with them until she died in 1923.

* * *

Bell Court, where Barbara Bayley was born and grew up, was one of the oldest houses in the village, parts of the building dating from the fifteenth century. The front faced Bidford High Street and the back looked over the

3 Barbara's mother, Eva Margaret Mary Fenn, as a child

river Avon, sometimes referred to as 'Shakespeare's Avon', which winds its way from Naseby in Northamptonshire to Tewkesbury in Gloucestershire and through several of Barbara Comyns' novels. Having been enlarged in the nineteenth century, Bell Court was also one of the biggest houses in the village, with three large rooms downstairs as well as three kitchens, several bedrooms, a billiard room, a nursery, an engine room, pantries, cellars, a saddle room and a boot room (which doubled as a punishment room for the children). The garden consisted of three large lawns running down to the river which were used for tennis, croquet and bowls. There was also a two-roomed coach-house, where the girls had their lessons, and a cottage that provided accommodation for the resident governess. Old photographs show that when the family moved into Bell Court – fictionalised as 'Shellford Court' in Barbara's memoir *Sisters by a River* – it also had a beautiful veranda running along the back of the house, its roof supported by intricate ironwork arches, to one of which a swing was attached. This was to prove a hazard for Barbara, whose irrepressible energy often got her into trouble: one day she swung so high that she crashed into a glass door and smashed it to bits.

Bell Court was also home to many animals: dogs, cats, parrots, rabbits, a monkey (which was her mother's special pet), ducks, hens and a peacock called Phillip, which was devoted to Barbara's father. 'Home' meant a menagerie as well as a family, and consequently, as an adult, Barbara was rarely without pets, however little money she had. As befitted the owners of such a large house, Barbara's parents had some pretensions to social standing, holding tennis and dinner parties for the local dignitaries from time to time. Her father regularly invited the vicar and the two village doctors – Dr Hobbes and Dr Crawford (who appear as the 'Old Doctor and the handsome Doctor' in Barbara's memoir *Sisters by a River*) – for a game of billiards during which, drinking whisky and eating ginger biscuits in the billiard room, they would be spied upon by Barbara and her giggling sisters.

In the first few decades of the twentieth century Bidford-on-Avon was a thriving village surrounded by farms and market gardens. With well over a thousand residents, it had plenty of shops and shopkeepers who were

4 Bell Court, from back of house

happy to deliver orders to the door by horse and cart or pony and trap – the main form of local transport. But life in Bidford was less easy for the poorer villagers. There was no electricity or mains water in most houses; light was provided either by gas, which had been installed in the village in 1850, or by oil lamps; water was taken from either wells or the tanks into which it had been pumped. Very few cottages had bathrooms or toilets and their inhabitants relieved themselves in soil lavatories at the bottom of the garden. Strips of newspaper did for toilet paper and a 'middy man' came round at night to empty the toilets, shouting 'Muck, muck, bring out your muck'.[2]

Life at Bell Court was very different: there were maids as well as a governess, a nursemaid and Palmer, the gardener/odd job man who doubled as butler when the occasion demanded and who was responsible for burying the afterbirth under the walnut tree each time a new baby arrived. There was a clear domestic hierarchy, with the governess considering herself far superior to the maids, who were not allowed to use the flush lavatory in the house and who had to trek to the outside 'lav' situated a hundred yards away, tucked between the dog's kennel and the pen for the pullets. The 'middy man', Coddy Bennet, would empty the maids' 'lav' bucket during his nightly round. The hierarchy also applied to life outside the home: Barbara and her siblings were not allowed to play with the village children,

5 Barbara with her four siblings (Chloe not yet born) and her mother in the garden of Bell Court. Left to right: Kathleen, Barbara, Nan, Dennis, Molly and Eva (now known as 'Margaret' or Marjie) Bayley

6 Left to right: Nan, Molly and Barbara in May Day costumes

although this did not stop them getting into mischief. Barbara often led the way when they decided to bang door knockers before running off, or throw bits of coal at the windows of village houses – and her lively imagination sometimes got her into trouble. One of her father's proudest possessions was an Edwardian wind-up gramophone with a large green trumpet horn. As a small child, Barbara was fascinated by it and the music it produced. One day she broke up a biscuit and carefully fed the crumbs into the horn. When her furious father asked why she had done this, she replied that she thought the people singing inside the gramophone would be hungry.

Weather permitting, the children spent much of their lives outside: family photographs – most of them taken by Albert, who developed his own photographs at home – show Barbara with her siblings, either playing in the garden or paddling in the shallows of the river Avon. Often left to their own devices, the children spent a lot of time with the family pets and climbing the fruit trees. They also conducted dubious experiments on the garden's creatures, including – according to Barbara's memoir – riding rabbits until they 'squashed' and ceremoniously hanging caterpillars 'on gallows made of cotton and match sticks'.[3]

* * *

Barbara was a pretty and spirited child with widely spaced dark eyes and thick curly brown hair who enjoyed playing with her older siblings, Molly, Nan and Dennis, until they were sent away to boarding school. After that, she grew closer to her two younger sisters, Kathleen and Chloe, although the three of them remained very fond of kindly Nan (who was later to become 'Beatrix' in *Sisters by a River*). Nan was the only musical Bayley child and played the violin and the piano to a good standard, sometimes even to dinner guests. Her brief spell at Malvern Girls College, while doing little for her intellect, turned her into an enthusiastic Christian. Later, she fell hopelessly in love with a priest and converted to Catholicism; she was seen as nervy and highly strung by the rest of the family, but Barbara retained her affection for her.[4] Kathleen was a beautiful but eccentric child, whose imagination sometimes ran riot, prompting her occasionally to adopt alternative identities including that of an owl when she was about 12 years old. The three youngest sisters regarded their eldest sister Molly as bossy and prosaic, traits which became more pronounced as she grew older. All

7 Dennis, Nan, Barbara and Molly playing in the shallows of the River Avon

the sisters regarded their brother Dennis as rather stuffy. He did indeed turn into a respectable and conventional young man who earned his living as a senior sales manager for International Paint, a company that manufactured high-quality products for yachts. As an adult, he was always anxious to avoid any hint of scandal and was later to be challenged by Barbara's unconventional behaviour more than once. Chloe, the youngest of the family, was in time to become Barbara's favourite sister. She contracted rheumatic fever at the age of 11 and was seriously ill for one year and convalescent for the next: Barbara was later to recollect that 'she sat all drooping and lifeless in her bath chair like a snowdrop'.[5] The illness resulted in a weak heart and she was to become the invalid of the family, contracting polio in her late twenties, which left her with a pronounced limp. Barbara and Chloe became very close as they grew older despite an age difference of five years. As young adults they were adventurous and determined to break away from provincial English life; they also both experienced bohemian poverty and then a failed marriage. More importantly, unlike their other siblings, they were both risk-takers.

The Bayley children found it easier to relate to their father than their mother. Albert was not keen on babies but became fond of his children as they grew older and was happy to spend time with them, teaching them how to ride a bike and how to row on the river. He was always pleased to have the children home again after their spells away at boarding school and was more openly affectionate than their mother. He also had a good sense of humour, which Barbara inherited. He was, however, very moody. In 1980, when writing a fresh introduction to the Virago Press edition of *The Vet's Daughter* to be published the following year, Barbara described him as 'an impatient, violent man, alternatively spoiling and frightening us'.[6] Provoked by the financial worry of having to support a large family and its entourage of servants, his bouts of temper became worse as he grew older and drank more heavily. *Sisters by a River* contains vivid accounts of Barbara being horsewhipped by her father and of her mother being beaten by him, appearing at breakfast the next day with a dreadful black eye and bruised arms. Nor was his temper confined to Bell Court. On one occasion, wearing a pale suit, he was sitting on a bus next to a man who had a joint of meat in a box on his lap. Blood began to leak out of the box on to Albert's trousers; he was so furious that he frogmarched the man off the bus, shouting abuse as he did so. On another occasion, attending a Sunday morning service at the village church of St Laurence's where the Bayley family had a family pew, Albert noticed that only the second-best hassocks had been put out. Enraged by this slight to his status, he threw one at the vicar, who quickly reassured his parishioner that they would be replaced immediately by the best hassocks.

Barbara's father claimed the billiard room, built as an extension to the main house, as his own private space. There he would retreat from family life and its irritations, write letters in peace, and drink whisky. The servants and the rest of the family knew he was not to be disturbed and the room was cleaned only on Mondays, when he travelled by train from Broom Junction Station to Birmingham in order to oversee his brewery business. By the time he was 45 he had made enough money to give up full-time work and was listed as 'retired chemical manufacturer' in the 1911 National Census. The weekly trips to Birmingham were merely to keep an eye on things. Nevertheless, he dressed fastidiously for these excursions, sporting highly polished shoes and a buttonhole carefully chosen to impress his staff. He was a rather vain man according to his daughter's memoir.

Barbara's mother, Margaret Bayley, resented being trapped by so many children and, while making sure they were well dressed and well fed, neglected them emotionally. Although she lived until 1935, as they grew up the Bayley girls learned to turn to each other, rather than to their mother, for comfort and support; Barbara and Chloe in particular became each other's confidantes for many years. This is reflected in Comyns' novels, which are marked by the absence of loving or effective mothers. The kind mother in *The Vet's Daughter* is terrified of her abusive husband; ill and downtrodden, she is unable to protect her daughter. A young mother in *The Skin Chairs* neglects her baby so that it almost dies. Although the last novel, *The Juniper Tree*, ends with a reconciliation between a mother and a daughter who have been emotionally estranged, it is narrated in such a barbed manner that the parent is condemned in the same breath: 'Mother was becoming the kindest of women and seemed to like me more now I was going insane; perhaps I had been too independent before.'[7] As a child, Barbara was not close to her mother, whose attitude to her children veered between sentimentality and impatient rejection. In her introduction to the 1981 Virago edition of *The Vet's Daughter*, Barbara was to recall her as a rather remote figure:

> I remember her best lying in a shaded hammock on one of the lawns, reading and eating cherries, which she was inordinately fond of, or in the winter sitting by the morning-room fire and opening and shutting her hands before the blaze as if to store the heat. Her pet monkey sitting on the fender would be doing the same.

Margaret was a tall and attractive woman despite her protruding front teeth, and she had a fine head of thick long dark hair that was wound up in a bun on the top of her head. Like most upper-middle-class women of her time, she dressed carefully and had outfits appropriate for every occasion, including one for punting on the River Avon. She always wore beautiful shoes, even for picnics in the garden, and she liked to dress in white, a choice that must have kept the maids perpetually busy with laundry and ironing. A slightly eccentric and self-absorbed woman, remembered by the adult Barbara as having 'a kind of gypsoflia [*sic*] mind, all little bits and pieces held together by whisps',[8] her emotional remoteness became even more pronounced when she went deaf at the age of 29 after her last child was born. (This was probably caused by otosclerosis, an inherited condition in which there is abnormal bone growth inside the ear that can suddenly worsen during pregnancy due to changing hormonal levels.) From then on, Margaret communicated with her children through sign language, although she would turn her head away if they tried to convey something she did not want to hear, saying 'I won't look at your hands. I hate you all.'[9]

Barbara's mother enjoyed painting and begrudged the fact that having six children had deprived her of the time and freedom to develop her gifts: she seems to have seen herself as a bohemian at heart who had become unfairly trammelled by domestic responsibilities. Some of her creativity was diverted into dreaming up elaborate menus for dinner parties and for special occasions such as Christmas, when she spent a great deal of time making the table look beautiful. She had her own book of recipes which comprised loose sheets of paper, burnt at the edges through being left too close to the heat, which were tied together with string. She would consult this book when planning special meals or river picnics and, in a loud voice, would give the cook and kitchen staff directions about how the food should be prepared. The staff could hear Barbara's mother all too clearly but, because of her deafness, she could not hear them, so communication frequently broke down, causing frayed tempers in the kitchen. Barbara, like her mother, enjoyed good food and would later become a very competent cook herself. Her love of painting when she grew up was also no doubt partly due to her mother's influence, as was her love of cities. Living in a village in Warwickshire, Margaret yearned for city life – perhaps because she had been brought up near Birmingham. Trips to London (which Barbara's father hated and avoided) and to Birmingham for Christmas shopping demanded much planning and created a great deal of excitement. As a teenager, Barbara visited London at least twice with her sister Nan and her mother, who took them to plays and musical comedies, despite her deafness, as well as to silent films. Margaret loved having visitors at Bell Court, particularly if they were intelligent and interesting, as were the archaeologists who excavated the eighth-century Saxon burial ground in Bidford in 1921. Her growing frustration with her husband frequently resulted in threats to leave Bell Court and live with her mother's Darby relations in the Warwickshire village of Hillmorton, which she associated with gentility and wealth.

Margaret Bayley's growing sense of having married beneath her derived in no small part from the Darbys, her mother's family. Annie Fenn, Barbara's maternal grandmother, was born a Darby and, like all her relations, was very proud of her horse-breeding ancestors who had mixed with high society. Born in 1853 in Shepherd's Bush to Anne Darby (née Lucas) and George Darby, Annie and her family claimed kinship with the illustrious Darby family of Ireland, the owners of Leap Castle, about 85 miles west of Dublin. George Darby, Annie's father and Barbara's great-grandfather, who was a dealer in high-class hunters like his father John Darby,[10] lived for several years in Drumcondra, near Dublin. From there he supplied fine horses to his brother, already established in Rugby as an important horse-dealer.[11] His horse-loving children, Annie and her younger brothers George and John, spent part of their childhood in Ireland and became excellent riders; John even rode with the Ward Union Hunt, a famous club based in Finglas in North Dublin.[12] George Darby senior and his children probably visited their supposed Darby relatives at Leap Castle but it is doubtful that the two families were actually related. (A recent DNA test taken by descendants of the Irish line and the English Darby line found no genetic link.)

Even when young, Barbara's grandmother had a strong, lively personality and was an exceptionally gifted rider – so much so that Queen Victoria, whose royal household bought fine hunters from Annie's father, was said to admire the girl's riding abilities. In the mid-1860s, when Annie was about 12 years old, Alfred de Prades, a popular society artist who specialized in sporting subjects and hunting scenes, painted *Portrait of Master George Darby, Miss Anne Darby and Huntsman Charles Davis, following the Royal Buckhounds in full cry*. Charles Davis, the Queen's Royal Huntsman, is shown on the right hand side of the picture, resplendent in his white breeches, red hunting jacket and black hunting cap. Streaking ahead of him is Annie Darby, dark-haired, wearing a long green dress and riding side-saddle, with her younger brother, George Darby, precociously in the lead having just jumped a ditch.[13] Horse-riding dominated Annie's life and, always headstrong, she later ignored advice about not riding with the hunt while she was pregnant and lost twins early in her marriage. According to family memory, having miscarried the babies at home, Annie wrapped each one in a leg of a pair of bloomers and told the gardener to bury them in the garden. About two months later, a policeman arrived at the door to inform her that it was illegal to bury bodies on private land without permission and that the death of the twins needed to be properly registered. The babies were then exhumed and given a conventional burial.

By the 1870s Barbara's maternal great-grandfather George had settled his family, including his daughter Annie who was then in her early twenties, in Hillmorton House, a large farmhouse that had stables and some attached farmland (which in due course increased to over 300 acres). Hillmorton was then a pretty and prosperous village near Rugby in Warwickshire. George and his brother John (who had the better business brain) became commercial partners in horse-trading and George was able to continue his career as a distinguished horse-dealer. Hillmorton was thus associated, for Barbara's mother and for her grandmother Annie, with wealth, success and social cachet. The fact that Annie Fenn had become impoverished and ended up renting a small cottage near Birmingham – after the sudden death of her mining engineer husband Arthur at the age of 37 – only made Hillmorton seem more glamorous and the Darbys more socially polished than they had appeared when she was a young woman living at home. It was an attitude tinged with snobbery that rubbed off on her daughter Margaret, who was always acutely aware of social class.

By the 1920s the main focus for family visits to Hillmorton – fictionalized as 'Hillersdon' in *Sisters by a River* – was the home of Barbara's great-uncle, John ('Jack') Darby, who was, like his forebears, a dealer in high-class hunters. According to the National Census of 1921, at this time he and his wife and four children lived in a grand 14-roomed house that had several stables attached, in Upper Street. Barbara did not much enjoy visiting her mother's wealthy 'uncle Jack' because she was often left with her dreary older cousins while the adults of the family went hunting or shooting. She preferred to spend time with the grooms in the stables; chatting to them and helping with the horses provided a welcome change from the affected behaviour of her Hillmorton relations and the polite manners demanded by her mother when staying with them.

Although growing up in a beautiful house in rural Warwickshire might seem the perfect setting for an idyllic childhood, the increasingly volatile and sometimes violent nature of their parents' marriage did not provide a psychologically secure world for the six Bayley children. Barbara's memoir, *Sisters by a River*, features several accounts of the high drama that resulted from rows between Albert and Margaret Bayley. The children found it difficult to escape from the arguments that raged at home; they were not allowed to play with the local children when young and, as they grew older, their parents discouraged their adolescent offspring from becoming too friendly with other families in the village. As his relationship with Margaret deteriorated, Albert's outbursts were sometimes accompanied by physical attacks on his wife. He was often remorseful after such episodes but the remorse did not last long, and his anger was exacerbated by his binge-drinking, which became more frequent during his fifties. By the early 1920s, when Barbara was entering her teenage years, her parents' marriage had begun to deteriorate further, fuelled no doubt by Albert's worries about his increasingly precarious finances. Breweries were no longer the gold mines they once had been: the reduction in licensing hours since 1914 and pressure from the Temperance Movement during the First World War had badly affected the sale of beer. Increased duty on beer, together with new local regulations passed in 1916 forbidding the buying of 'rounds' in Midlands pubs, had also hurt local trade considerably. By the time Barbara was 14, she felt an air of doom about Bell Court; her father was drinking more heavily and would sit in the morning room biting his moustache in anxiety until roused to fury by a remark made by his wife. Her mother, too, seemed afflicted by depression and apathy, with the result that the house began to look neglected.

Like her sister Kathleen, Barbara was a highly imaginative child whose response to her disturbing home life sometimes took the form of sleep-walking episodes and nightmares that frequently featured her father. The desire to escape the increasingly toxic atmosphere when her parents argued was also no doubt responsible for Barbara's conviction as a child that she could perform paranormal feats and literally rise above reality. There is a moment of apparent levitation in *Sisters by a River*, when the narrator and her sister Beatrix seem to fly in the air on a 'magic stick'. The phenomenon continued to fascinate Barbara and would eventually inspire the extraordinary closing scene of *The Vet's Daughter*, in which Alice Rowlands rises above a milling crowd on Clapham Common, an event orchestrated by her abusive father who hopes to make money from it. Many years later, Barbara confided to a friend that she and her sister were convinced as children that they could walk on water if they tried hard enough: 'I would get into the middle of the river, not able to swim, put one foot down. I would quickly change my feet and think I'd almost done it.'[14] Even when she was an adult, Barbara remained fascinated by the paranormal. In 1947, aged almost forty, writing to a friend who had recently moved to Spain, she asked 'Have any Flying Saucers come to Spain yet? I'm always looking in the sky for them but haven't seen any so far.'[15]

A more conventional means of escape when her parents were arguing was to lose herself in the countryside around Bell Court. The Avon, in particular, was a constant and consoling presence in her life. In winter and spring, everyone marvelled at the occasional floods and the children would walk through the water on stilts made by Palmer the handyman; in the summer they spent hours messing about on the river and enjoying family outings on a large green punt. When, in the early 1920s, the atmosphere at home sometimes became dark and oppressive, the Avon provided a soothing escape. The narrator of *Sisters by a River* often rows up the river very early in the morning, soothed by the singing of the larks and by the sight of gentle cows standing quietly in the shallows: 'everything would seem so good and clean, I felt I wanted to cry with so much happiness'.[16] It seems likely that Barbara drew on her own experience when writing this passage. But despite the growing tension between their parents, life was often enjoyable for the Bayley children. Picnics, tennis parties and Christmas – and especially the food prepared for them – provided happy interludes, as did the twice-yearly arrival of the Fair on the Big Meadow and making 'houses' of hay during harvest time.

*   *   *

The other consolation and beacon of stability in Barbara's life – at least when she was young – was her grandmother, Annie Fenn, who enjoyed looking after babies and small children. Unlike Barbara's mother, who quickly lost patience with her brood, 'Granny' was happy to spend hours playing imaginative games, including 'shops' in the garden: 'if she said a bay leaf was a humbug, and an oak leaf a pound of tea, the leaves seemed to turn into a humbug and a pound of tea in front of our eyes'.[17] Granny kept a watchful eye on the children and as an adult Barbara credited her with saving them from danger and drowning more than once. Annie got on well with her son-in-law, who was only eleven years younger than her, but less well with her daughter, with whom she frequently quarrelled. Granny's strong opinions, jutting chin and apparent ability to hypnotize people made her a formidable individual. She was also highly superstitious, claiming that she often heard restless spirits crying at night. Proud of her Darby family lineage, Granny would tell the children tales of her childhood years spent in Drumcondra in Ireland, which included stories about the haunted Leap Castle owned by the Irish line of the Darby family. She treasured a corner cupboard and a small carved chair with a heart-shaped hole in its back that she had brought to England and that she claimed came from Leap Castle. As a child Barbara would go to this chair when she was miserable. She would sit on it with one arm through the hole and lay her head against its curved back; it seemed to give her the comfort she was unable to elicit from her mother. Later, both the corner cupboard and the chair went with Barbara wherever she made a home.[18]

As a child Barbara heard many times the tale of how the fifteenth-century Leap Castle passed from the Irish O'Carroll family, who owned it until the seventeenth century, to the English Darby family. Despite having little basis in historical fact, this exciting and romantic story was recounted by descendants of the Darby family well into the twentieth century. The tale was that in 1558, during the Tudor re-conquest of Ireland, the O'Carrolls captured an English captain by the name of John Darby and imprisoned him. They sent their beautiful daughter, Finola O'Carroll, to push food through his prison bars and the two fell in love, eventually marrying and living in the castle.[19] Said to be inhabited by at least two ghosts, the castle was (and still is) most famous for 'the Elemental'. Whereas the other ghosts and strange sounds were associated with specific past events, 'the Elemental', or 'The Thing', was a vague and malevolent presence that took an animal-like form and reeked of death: Mildred Darby described it in her story 'Kilman Castle, or the House of Horror' as

> about the size of a sheep ... Its face was human, or to be more accurate, inhuman, in its vileness, with large holes of blackness for eyes, loose, slobbery lips and a thick saliva-dripping jaw, sloping back suddenly into its neck. Nose it had none, only spreading cancerous cavities, the whole face being one uniform tint of grey.[20]

Barbara was both riveted and terrified by her grandmother's tales of ghosts and hauntings, especially those associated with Leap Castle. Many years later, in the 1950s, she wrote a short story, set in Ibiza (where she lived with her second husband for two years), entitled 'Something to Celebrate'. An unpublished piece, it features two terrifying 'elementals' that appear in a dream to a young wife when she and her husband are living on the island:

> I dreamt of elementals. Two came into our home, one was a fearful brown thing resembling a kiwi crossed with a rat, and it clung to me. In my dream I ran down stairs I'd never known and threw the creature into the street and dogs waiting outside set upon it but, although mauled and bleeding, it doubled back – screaming like a young child it leapt onto my shoulders and gnawed my hair. I tore it away and threw it to the dogs again and when I shut the heavy doors I could hear the most horrible sounds coming through the key-hole. I went up the unknown stairs again and there was a dirty unknown flat and my husband Guy was standing at the sink washing dishes. He didn't appear to see me although he slowly moved away from the sink and stood looking down at the tiled floor with vacant eyes. I went to the sink and continued with the washing-up. Quite soon the greasy grey dishcloth in my hand changed into a fluffy animal with long hair parted down the middle of its back. It was growing larger all the time and in its mouth there was a fearful set of human false teeth with pink gums. We stared at this creature and were so afraid we couldn't speak to each other – we just stood together while the creature grew and snapped its false teeth. Suddenly Guy seized it from the bowl and rushed onto the roof with it, and I could hear fighting sounds coming through the ceiling. When Guy returned to the kitchen he was not the same any more. He could not speak properly and was wearing a soiled yellow dressing-gown and with a large straw hat on his head, although he had been dressed in a suit a few minutes before. He smelt of vinegar and on his face and hands there were squares of light brown paper. He had become all vague and his eyes were pale.[21]

The nightmare seems to indicate several fears: of having to deal with a creature/child that terrifies her (by the time she wrote this passage, probably in the late 1950s, Barbara had had an abortion and had given birth to a baby with congenital abnormalities); of living a degraded life ('dirty', 'greasy', 'soiled') and of seeing a partner suddenly incapacitated by terror. The mention of 'vinegar' and 'brown paper' brings to mind the traditional nursery rhyme 'Jack and Jill went up the hill', in which Jack's head injury is treated with a 'plaster' made of vinegar and brown paper. The overall effect of the passage is one of grotesque horror modulated by comic incongruity and by the mundane (the washing-up). It resonates strongly with Barbara's novel *Who was Changed and Who was Dead* written a few years earlier, in which Granny was transformed into Grandma Willoweed.

The weirdness of that novel and of the story 'Something to Celebrate' suggests that Granny played an important part in shaping Barbara's imagination as a child. Indeed, she had a great influence on all the Bayley children, who saw her untidy bedroom – full of toiletries, feather boas and strange home-made medicines – as enticingly forbidden territory. But Granny could on occasion be irritable and unreasonable and grew more so as she aged. She was, according to her granddaughter's memoir, also fierce with the maids and sometimes fell out with both daughter and son-in-law, on one occasion provoking Albert to such anger that he tried to shove her out of her bedroom window. She was saved only by the width of her hips. During the last few years of her life, Granny took to her room, her bloated feet and legs probably a symptom of heart disease, her only consolation a glass of whisky. She hated being left alone and members of the Bayley family took it in turns to sit with her and rub her back. During the last few days of her grandmother's life in 1923, Barbara read *Tom Brown's Schooldays* to her and listened to her reminiscences about how she was not allowed to read novels when young. Rebelling against this stricture, the young Annie Darby and her sister would hide in a four-poster bed with the curtains drawn in order to read in secret Emily Brontë's *Wuthering Heights* and Bernardin de Saint-Pierre's *Paul and Virginie*, both of which would have been considered highly unsuitable reading for girls during the 1860s.

*   *   *

Barbara inherited her grandmother's rebellious nature and her love of reading, as well as her belief in the supernatural and her gift for creative exaggeration. Like many authors, she started writing when young and was producing her own illustrated stories by the age of ten; 'I don't know which I enjoyed most, the writing or drawing', she later noted in her introduction to the 1981 Virago edition of *The Vet's Daughter*. But her education was haphazard. Whereas Dennis, the only boy, was sent off to boarding school from an early age, the girls' education was a more random affair. Apart from a term at a local private primary school set up by parents in Bidford-on-Avon, and 'a year at a small school at Henley-on-Thames', which she later described as 'a boarding school for the Daughters of Gentlemen',[22] Barbara was taught in the coach-house, which doubled as the schoolroom, by a series of poorly qualified governesses who would be vividly memorialized in her writing. A stubborn and independent child, Barbara often resisted the discipline her governesses tried to impose on her. According to her memoir, she spat at Miss Tucker when she tried to drag her through a field of cows and she protested against Miss Vann's decision to put her to bed early, as a punishment for being naughty, by kicking her downstairs. At the age of eighty, Barbara vividly recalled that episode: 'She had all these petticoats of different colours … and long, long knickers. She landed in a big brass pot with her legs sticking up the stairs.'[23] In the 1940s the adult Barbara was to write a gothic short story, reminiscent of Sheridan Le Fanu's work. Unpublished and entitled 'The Governess Arrived in a Carriage', its main character, an elderly governess, dressed in black and resembling Miss Vann of *Sisters by a River*, turns out to be a vampire. Writers have their own way of wreaking revenge.

Barbara's education finished at the age of 15 and she then spent her time reading, looking after the family dogs and passing days with a married woman friend in the village who bred Sealyham terriers – pedigree dogs that had become popular during the First World War and were associated with the British Royal family and Hollywood stars. She also went to local dances with Nan and occasionally stayed with Uncle Jack and his family at Hillmorton. There was no suggestion that the girls should find work and their father's retreat into alcohol and their mother's drift into vague apathy provided no encouragement to do other than live a leisurely life, despite the financial cloud gathering over Bell Court. In the spirit of Jane Austen's Mrs Bennett, Margaret Bayley was anxious for her daughters to marry young and showed little interest in helping them to develop their talents or think about how they might earn a living.

The question of how to earn a living was suddenly to confront the 18-year-old Barbara when, in May 1925, her father suffered a cerebral haemorrhage, He died within a few hours and soon Bell Court was full of relatives, including the Darbys from Hillmorton, who were the first to arrive. Albert Bayley was buried near Granny's grave in St Laurence's churchyard in Bidford-on-Avon. With the family in shock, the relatives officiously took things in hand, advising the older girls that they would now have to find work since their father had left nothing but debts. This was not quite true: Barbara's father left £4,884 6s. 9d. – £352,915 in today's money.[24] A certain amount was reserved for Harry Keene, his accountant, who had become a good friend, but the bulk of Albert's money, as well as a life interest in Bell

Court, were left to his wife Margaret and his son Dennis. There was still a mortgage on the house, however, and Albert's pension died with him; there were also several thousand pounds' worth of outstanding bills to be paid to creditors. What Albert had left his wife was not enough to fund indefinitely the upkeep of Bell Court, which included servants' wages and maintenance bills as well as mortgage repayments. The house was not sold immediately, however; Barbara's brother Dennis lived there until 1931, when Bell Court was put up for auction. The sale of the house and its contents – which included some 'fine Queen Anne, Sheraton and Chippendale furniture' – was announced in the *Warwick and Warwickshire Advertiser* on 4 July 1931.[25] The girls were each to receive £200 (about £14,450 today), either through an insurance policy or war savings certificates, on reaching the age of 21.

The Bayleys' interfering relatives all impressed upon Barbara's mother that she should live somewhere else more cheaply and that her daughters should get jobs as soon as possible. After the relatives left, the Bayley girls embarked on a short period of mild domestic anarchy, with Molly going off to live in a caravan in order to work on a nearby farm while Kathleen and Chloe refused to be taught by the governess any longer, thereby putting an end to their education at the ages of 14 and 12 respectively. Nan went to live with a relative near Birmingham and enrolled at a secretarial college. In the meantime a rented cottage was found for Barbara's mother, although once she had recovered from the shock of her husband's death, she embarked on a house-buying spree with her legacy. By 1928 Margaret Bayley was living with her daughters Barbara, Kathleen and Chloe in Rodney House, Bridgefoot, Stratford-upon-Avon. Barbara attended art classes at the Stratford-upon-Avon School of Science and Art for a few months, an experience that confirmed her resolve to become an artist.

However, Barbara realized that she needed to earn some money in order to become independent, which she wanted very much. She rejected the idea of training as a typist like her sister Nan, having no intention of leading a dull life in an office. Instead, she thought hard about how her main interests – painting, reading, keeping dogs, messing about on the river and observing people – could be put to good use. Spirited and adventurous, she also wanted to travel and see the world, so she decided to apply for a job as a kennel maid. This episode in Barbara's life is briefly referred to near the end of *Sisters by a River*, when the narrator applies successfully for a job in Cornwall, although it is more accurately reflected in a later novel, *A Touch of Mistletoe*, published in 1967. In this book, Barbara's fictional counterpart, Victoria ('Vicky') Green, travels to Amsterdam to look after some aggressive snarling bull terriers, housed in kennels called 'The Hounds of Pleasure' that belong to a Mr and Mrs Groningen. Vicky is miserable there: the house is cold, the food poor and she is forced to work long hours. She finally flees the Groningens and is helped to return home by a benign Dutch man who has British ancestors and is fluent in English.

Barbara's experience as a kennel maid in Amsterdam seems to have been very similar to that of her character Vicky Green, even down to the experience of being in pain with a septic finger. Indeed, many years later Barbara wrote to a friend, 'If you read my Mistletoe book it might amuse you to know that the Dutch and sisters in a bed-sitting room parts are true, the rest is pure fiction.'[26] On 24 January 1929 a Mr Mackay wrote a letter from his home at 46 Fredericksplein, Amsterdam, addressed to 'Mrs Margaret Bayley' in Stratford-upon-Avon. After thanking her for her letter of 22 January, Mr MacKay proceeded, in his slightly fractured English, to gently admonish Barbara's mother for allowing her daughter to venture abroad alone at such a young age:

> That I have assisted your daughter as much as possible was quite clear. She looked, and still is, so young and then to be a foreigner, not able to speak or understand the Dutch language and without money!
>
> You are quite right that you will never allow her or her sisters to go abroad unless you know the family perfectly well where they are coming. It is always difficult for English girls to go abroad because they mostly do not know foreign languages.
>
> That I met your dear daughter here seems to have been the Will of Providence. My intention was to take another street where I could impossibly have met her but I felt something which forced me to go to the left instead of going straight on.
>
> I am certainly very pleased to hear from you that the finger is much better. She will be very happy to be at home again under the protection of her mother which is the best in the world a girl can have.[27]

So, at the age of 22, Barbara was rescued from the misery of working as a kennel maid and from the streets of Amsterdam by a kind-hearted passer-by in an episode that might have come out of a novel by Charles Dickens. Mr Mackay, a Dutch man of Scottish descent, continued to write to her after she returned to live with her mother in Stratford-upon-Avon, sending numerous letters in his distinctive spiky handwriting. He was not to know that Barbara's mother was incapable of offering her daughter the sort of warm unconditional love that he envisaged a good mother would give her child.

Now safely back in England, Barbara needed to consider her future. Displaced from what had seemed to be a secure upper-middle-class background and shaken by her first experience of the wider world, she no doubt felt vulnerable and uncertain. However, having turned 21 in December 1928, she could now claim £200 against the insurance policy her father had set up in her name. She decided to use it to pursue a career in art. By chance – probably while reading *The Studio: An Illustrated Magazine of Fine and Applied Art* – she saw an advertisement for the Heatherley School of Fine Art, an independent art college in central London. She immediately applied to 'Heatherleys', as it was more commonly known. Her life was soon to change dramatically.

2

Portrait of the artist as a young woman

In 1929 Barbara went to study at the Heatherley School of Fine Art, then housed at 11–13 George Street, off Baker Street. Despite being accommodated in a rather ugly building, Heatherleys had much to recommend it, including a sceptical attitude to traditional teaching methods. Teaching was focused entirely on portraiture, figurative painting and sculpture, which suited Barbara's aptitudes. It was also then the only London art school where students could draw from life without having to spend their first year using plaster casts as models. Men and women students were admitted on the same terms so that both drew from nude models in one room – unusual in art schools at that time. Past students included Dante Gabriel Rossetti, John Everett Millais, Walter Sickert, Roland Penrose and Kate Greenaway. It particularly attracted those who went on to be writers – Samuel Butler, William Makepeace Thackeray, Baroness Orczy and Evelyn Waugh all studied there.[1]

Mr Henry Gibbs Massey, Heatherleys' eccentric principal in 1929, had bought the art school in 1907 and directed it with his wife Gertrude until his death in 1934. In photographs taken in the 1920s he appears as a cheerful figure with a short white beard and a bald head. (He was later to inspire the character Mr Wracker in *A Touch of Mistletoe*.) Massey had studied in Paris in the 1880s and had been much influenced by the French emphasis on life classes, so Heatherleys advertised itself – and still does – as being based on the traditional French atelier system with students from all levels sharing a life model.[2] Massey also believed, however, that the college should provide a practical education for students rather than filling their heads with ideas about abstract art and 'isms'. 'Art defies convention but artists should know where to draw the line', he once said.[3] Pretentiousness was not tolerated: 'Abandon swank all ye who enter here' was pasted on the door leading into the studios.[4]

Barbara was full of optimism, both about living in London on her own and about realizing her ambition to become a sculptor of renown. She hoped to study at Heatherleys for two years, and on 31 January that year

8 1929 Heatherley's Year Group. Barbara is third left in the second row down. Henry Massey, principal, is second from right in the front row.

she paid the fee of 12 guineas (about £940 now) for the first term's teaching, which ran from 4 February until the end of April.[5] She soon found somewhere to live in central London – probably a women's hostel off Baker Street – and in February embarked on her course. For new students, the emphasis was solely on drawing; only the more advanced students were allowed to enter the painting studio. Barbara was happy at Heatherleys, enjoying the eclectic mix of students, which was very different from that of other more selective London art colleges, such as The Slade or St Martin's. Indeed, Gertrude Massey proudly declared that at Heatherleys one could find:

> students of all ages ranging from sixteen to sixty and of all nationalities ... a well-known painter is working next to a girl straight from school; nearby is an ex Vicereine of India working near an Indian student. Here is an eminent surgeon standing beside a widely-read author. In front of them work one of London's best-known architects, a noted naturalist and a woman journalist ... All are equally at ease, united in the study of the mysteries of art.[6]

Coming from a small village in Warwickshire, Barbara found being part of such a mixed community in the middle of London exciting and stimulating. Free and carefree, she knew then that she was at heart an urban creature.

* * *

Soon after Barbara started at art school, her two younger sisters, Kathleen first, then Chloe, came to visit her. Chloe, 17 in 1929, had returned to live with her mother in Stratford when her brief 'mannequin' course in Mayfair finished, but was desperate to move back to London and become independent. Tall, slim, with long dark hair, and strikingly beautiful, she had high hopes of becoming a model. At just over 5 foot 4 inches, Barbara was three inches shorter than her sister but also slim and beautiful, with dark, wavy, shoulder-length hair and limpid brown eyes. She wanted to make her living through art but, like Chloe, was prepared to compromise her ambitions in order to stay in London. Looking for somewhere cheap to live, the sisters found a large bed-sitting room in a Victorian house in Mornington Crescent on the border of Somers Town, then a somewhat seedy area sandwiched between Euston and St Pancras stations. Their flat was in a 'decaying, gritty district but central, and it pleased me to know', Barbara wrote many years later, 'that Dickens had once lived there, also several of the characters in his books'.[7]

In the summer of 1929, finding that she was running short of funds, Barbara had to abandon her plan to study at Heatherleys for two years. Although Chloe was managing to earn some money, it was not enough to support them both. Neither sister wished to return to live with their mother in Stratford-upon-Avon. Barbara loved visiting the free London art galleries, especially the Tate, and, discovering public lending libraries, became an avid reader. She was determined to make up for her piecemeal education as a child (although spelling was always to remain a challenge) and devoured dozens of nineteenth-century novels. Inspired by her reading, she began writing short stories and even embarked on a novel, although it remained unfinished. Like her father, Barbara was resourceful; desperate to stay in the city, she soon found a job 'in a small advertising agency, drawing, typing, writing simple copy and visiting clients',[8] while Chloe managed to get work occasionally as an artist's model. Shortage of money meant that they had to shop very frugally and eat sparingly – an experience that later fed into *A Touch of Mistletoe*, in which Victoria and Blanche buy their food in Camden Town and survive on shrivelled oranges, broken biscuits, cocoa without milk and cut-price offers from the local grocer's shop. In the novel, sausages and kippers are an occasional treat that are cooked on a gas ring in their bedsit.

The money problems faced by Barbara and Chloe worsened the following year. By 1930 the Depression, which had rocked the United States in 1929 when the Wall Street stock market crashed, hit Britain. Although the north of England, with its manufacturing and mining industries, bore the brunt of the Depression, London and the south felt it too. In London unemployment suddenly shot up to 13.5% and in 1930 soup kitchens were set up in the capital to feed the poor. In Somers Town, then a working-class area of London, Barbara and Chloe saw evidence of poverty all around them, including hungry children on the streets. In this climate of economic gloom, Barbara held on grimly to her job in the advertising agency, putting up with long hours, many tedious tasks and not a few unwanted advances from older male colleagues.

The sisters managed to have fun nevertheless. Barbara loved clothes and would continue to love them throughout her life, often buying new things even when she could not really afford them. But in 1930 she and Chloe had hardly any money left after paying their rent and buying food. Creative and imaginative, they made their own clothes, often out of brightly coloured remnants, cheaper to buy than material from a roll. With their dark hair, large earrings and eye-catching vivid dresses, they were amused to be mistaken occasionally for young Spanish women. Barbara's friends from Heatherleys sometimes invited her and Chloe to parties, where their beauty quickly drew male admirers. At one such party, a smart young man wearing brand new shoes with rubber soles asked Barbara to dance – but she told him in no uncertain terms that she could not possibly dance with someone whose shoes squeaked. Undeterred, he disappeared, reappearing 15 minutes later having sliced off the soles of his shoes. She was quickly learning that her beauty was an asset in more ways than one, not least because it gave her power over men.

Barbara's life changed later that year when Chloe took a live-in job as a lady's companion. Unable to afford their large bed-sitting room on her

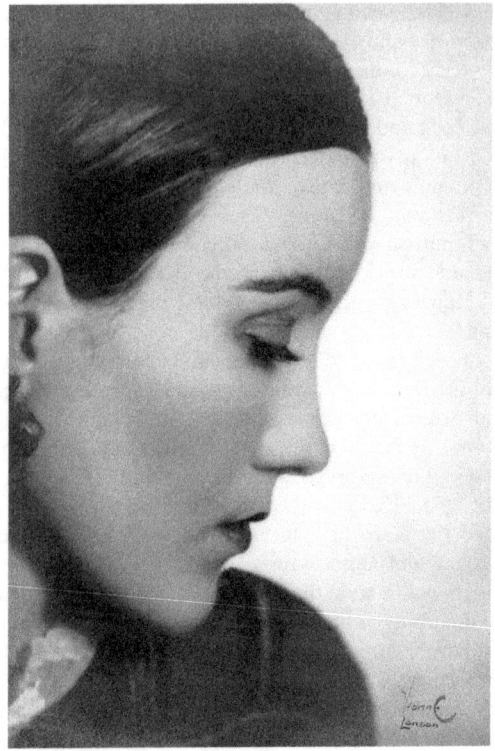

9 Barbara in her twenties

own, she took a cheaper smaller room in Oakley Square in the Kings Cross area. Although her new bedsit was tiny, there were compensations. The plane tree outside filtered the sunshine so that on sunny days her room was full of dappled faint green light. London Zoo was only just over a mile away and when her window was open she could sometimes hear the lions roaring and the seals barking at feeding time.

*   *   *

The year 1930 was to bring yet another change in Barbara's life. John Francis Pemberton, whose home was in Stratford-upon-Avon and whose family knew the Bayleys, came to London to study art. Some years later, when writing *Sisters by a River*, Barbara was to describe him as the boy who had arrived with his father in Bidford-on-Avon to visit the Anglo-Saxon archaeological dig there in 1921: 'both were dark and very delicate looking … I remembered the boy for a long time, he had such sad, shining brown eyes and a huskey [*sic*] voice … some years later I married him.'[9] Photographs of John Pemberton in his twenties show a slim man of medium height, with a pale complexion and thick dark hair parted on the side and brushed back from his forehead. Finely shaped eyebrows emphasized his dark eyes and he had a long, slightly pointed nose and a full but rather small mouth. Barbara liked his lanky gait and was impressed by his intensity and his wide knowledge of fine art. Born in 1910 to Guy Pemberton, an architect, and his wife Emily Muriel (née Allday), John came from a successful middle-class family. The eldest of three, he had a brother, David Alwyn, born in 1912, and a much younger sister, Elizabeth ('Buffy') born in 1920. Previous generations of the Pembertons, who had all made their money from the family brass foundry business in Birmingham, were good businessmen but also prided themselves on being cultured, with many family members sharing a passionate interest in acting and the stage.

Guy Pemberton, John's father, born in 1883, was an attractive, sociable man who belonged to several local clubs in Stratford-upon-Avon, including

10 Barbara pretending to be drunk

the tennis club and the Shakespeare Amateur Dramatic Company. He and his wife Emily – known to the family as 'Muriel' – were respected in the county of Warwickshire and were socially ambitious. Because his older brother, Thomas, had taken over the family brass foundry business, Guy had been free to choose another career and had become a successful architect. Ambitious for his children, he had sent both his sons, John and David, to the recently opened Stowe School in Buckingham. Its headmaster, J. F. Roxburgh, was a man with progressive liberal views on education who wished to establish a school that focused on the talents of the individual child and that would break with some of the traditions associated with public school education in England at this time, including flogging and bullying. Despite the school's relatively enlightened ethos, John Pemberton had been unhappy at Stowe. He was not an academic child but an artistic dreamy one; when he was young, Barbara and her sisters used to call him 'Little Johnny Head-in-the-Air', after the character in *Struwwelpeter*. However, John proved to have a talent for art and his parents allowed him to pursue it, hoping he would be able to make his way as a society portrait painter. His father set up a monthly allowance so that John could live in London while apprenticed to an established artist, working alongside him in his studio. He was placed with a successful Royal Academy portrait painter and found himself a bedsit at 25 Harrington Square which, either coincidentally or by design, was only a few minutes' walk from Barbara's flat in Oakley Square. Like Barbara, he was delighted to leave provincial England behind and excited by the prospect of living in London.

The reality of living at the age of twenty in a large city with no friends was daunting, however, and John felt very alone. Barbara was also lonely now that she was no longer sharing a flat with Chloe. Not surprisingly, then, John and Barbara soon began spending time together, strolling around London discussing their enthusiasm for various artists and movements. Gradually, companionship turned to love. Infatuated by each other, they decided to marry, despite John's initial reservations about marriage; he wanted no truck with what he saw as bourgeois institutions and values. They continued to rent their separate bedsits until their wedding day – perhaps for the sake of appearances – but some weeks before their marriage they moved into a semi-basement garden flat at 50 Gondar Gardens, Hampstead, one of an elegant terraced row of four-storey large Victorian houses. Although the exterior of the building was imposing, they had to make do with second-hand furniture and cheap cutlery – hence the title of Barbara's second novel, *Our Spoons Came from Woolworths*. In the spirit of the Arts and Crafts movement, the couple rejected Edwardian heavy furniture and thick curtains, preferring bright, light, uncomplicated rooms, like the poet hero of *Ragged Banners*, a then popular novel by the left-wing writer Ethel Mannin:

> He liked this bare room with its tall window and pale walls and bookshelves and the divan with the hand-woven blue and yellow striped linen cover, and the weathered oak chair with the rush seat, and the blue-painted table and the rush-mat ... It somehow reduced the business of living to the simplicities ...[10]

Adopting this bohemian template, John and Barbara lived cheaply, simply and colourfully. They painted their second-hand furniture in shades of green and blue and transformed the walls of the dull rooms with light colours, painting one of them yellow. Inside *The Tragic Life of Vincent Van Gogh* by Louis Piérard, a book that John bought for Barbara as a gift just before they were married, he wrote 'To my darling Barbara, from John to commemorate decorating our "Sun Flower" room'.[11]

Although John and Barbara were very happy together, their families were appalled by the news that they were about to marry. Barbara received a telegram from her brother Dennis who, having heard of her plans, ordered her to do nothing until he arrived. The Pemberton family reacted with outrage and a delegation arrived in London to try to prevent the marriage. John's father and mother, who had recently separated and rarely spoke to each other, cooperated in the hope of saving their son from Barbara. However, despite these attempts to sabotage it, the wedding took place at St Matthew's Church, Oakley Square on 30 May 1931, not much more than six months after John had arrived in London. He was 21 years old and Barbara was 23. Just before she married, Barbara destroyed everything she had written while living in London, thinking it was 'imitative and self-conscious'.[12] From now on, she decided, she would focus entirely on art, like her husband.

Barbara wore a tweed suit for her wedding, not being able to afford a new outfit, and she took her pet newt, concealed in a damp handkerchief in her pocket, to the ceremony (choices which later fed into *Our Spoons Came from Woolworths*).[13] The wedding was witnessed by Barbara's sister Nan, who was now living in London and working as a journalist for women's magazines (she later became a publicity officer for Madame Tussauds Waxworks Museum and then for the Royal Opera House). The second witness was Madge Lee (née Pemberton), John's aunt, who was living in Chelsea and who would come to feature more vividly in Barbara's life than either woman might have imagined in 1931. John's parents attended the wedding, but separately. His father Guy had started an affair with his young secretary, Christine Fischer, in the late 1920s and his mother Muriel had taken a lover about the same time. In 1930 Guy had moved out of the family home and into a house he had bought in the Cotswolds, much to the scandalized interest of the respectable burghers of Stratford-upon-Avon. Christine soon joined him, ostensibly as his housekeeper (to save her reputation), and they were to marry in 1935. Even though John was nearly twenty when his father left the family home, he had been deeply upset by the breakdown of his parents' marriage. Possibly because in 1931 Guy had both his mistress and his wife to support, he decided to stop his son's monthly allowance, telling John that if he was old enough to marry, he was old enough to support a wife. It was not a very promising start to wedded life for Barbara and John.

*   *   *

The Depression years, when even wealthy people cut back on their spending, were not good for artists, and although John Pemberton sold a painting from time to time, he earned very little. Their main steady source of income was Barbara's work at the commercial art studio. John would meet Barbara there at the end of the day just as Eugene, the fictional character based on John, meets Victoria after her day's work at the Pimlico studio in *A Touch of Mistletoe*: 'There he would be, very black and white and his long, long legs in their narrow trousers, looking so wonderfully different from everyone else.'[14] Their income was supplemented by an occasional cheque that came their way – sometimes payment to John for a painting commissioned by Aunt Madge or Aunt May who were sharing a house in Chelsea, or sometimes money for Barbara from the sale of the furniture at Bell Court. John would stay at home in their flat and paint, occasionally using Barbara as his model. Once, inspired by Pierre Bonnard's *Nu dans le Bain*, John decided to paint her in the bath. They did not have much money for the meter, with the result that Barbara was immersed in lukewarm water which rapidly turned cold. Not surprisingly, she brought the project to a speedy end. But despite their relative poverty, Barbara was happy; John was gentle and attentive and life in London was exciting for young artists. Her only real frustration was having so little time to sculpt and paint; her own creative work came second to John's and had to be fitted in either after a full day's work or during the weekend. It was a pattern that would come to dominate her life, even after her later success as a novelist.

Although they had separated in 1920, John's aunt Madge was technically still married to Rupert Lee, president of the important exhibiting society, the London Group. John and Barbara thus had an immediate entrée into London artistic circles. While the group was ostensibly comprehensive and tolerant, in fact there were often tensions between various factions; Walter Sickert had resigned in protest, for example, at the inclusion of Wyndham Lewis's work in the exhibition of March 1914. The early 1930s saw the beginnings of another lively tension – between those members of the London Group who, in the footsteps of one of its most influential members, Roger Fry, still revered the work of Cézanne and the Post-Impressionists, and those who were increasingly drawn to the work of the surrealists in Paris and other major European cities. Unlike France, where in the 1920s André Breton had published two manifestos defining and promoting surrealism, there was no surrealist movement in Britain during that decade. But by the late 1920s and early 1930s artists were looking towards Paris, which was then dominated by the surrealist movement.[15] These artists included Paul Nash, who had been deeply impressed by the 1928 London exhibition of the surrealist Giorgio de Chirico's work and by a visit to Paris in 1930, where he had seen many modernist and surrealist paintings. He was a close friend of Rupert Lee, and Barbara and John would certainly have met him. The avant-garde magazines, *transition* and *This Quarter*, which carried articles about surrealism were sold in a bookshop in Charing Cross Road and provoked much discussion in artistic circles. It is hard to say exactly when Barbara first realized that surrealism offered her the lens she needed to distil her vision of the world, but the strange conjunctions, dream-like scenarios and the sheer weirdness that came to mark her writing and her painting probably originated in her first encounters with surrealist art during the early days of her marriage. In time, John also came to embrace surrealism; the National Galleries of Scotland hold an accomplished and surreal picture of a pier entitled *Since the Bombardment* that he painted in 1948. Both he and Barbara were to carry forward the legacy of surrealism, albeit in different ways.

The excitement of meeting artists who fervently discussed tectonic shifts in the world of art did much to compensate for the fact that Barbara and John had little money. In fact, they wore their relative poverty as a badge of honour, claiming to despise material wealth and middle-class conventions. They were proud to belong to bohemia, 'an incongruous, eccentric club of artists, some rich, some poor, talented and untalented, who believed in friendship more than family and who by their very differences proclaimed themselves to be part of a confederacy'.[16] Social class was (supposedly) not an issue in such an environment; art was everything. Barbara was thrilled to be part of such a milieu. She began to dress in an arty way and wore her thick hair parted in the middle and pushed behind her ears so as to show her elaborate earrings. The Café Royal in Regent Street, where Augustus John held court, and the Eiffel Tower in Percy Street where the Vorticists used to gather, were both restaurants that attracted a bohemian clientele, including – when Rupert Lee treated them – John and Barbara.[17] For a cheaper meal, Bertorelli's in Charlotte Street would provide a large bowl of thick bean and pasta soup for sixpence.[18] Rupert Lee also introduced them to the drinking places of Fitzrovia, an area where artists, writers and intellectuals met in various taverns. The Wheatsheaf in Rathbone Place was popular, as was the Fitzroy Tavern on Charlotte Street, the latter especially with artists and writers born in Wales; these included Dylan Thomas and Nina Hamnett, later known as the 'Queen of Bohemia'. In 1931 Hamnett was finishing her memoir, *Laughing Torso*, which focuses on her life in London and Paris; published in 1932, it quickly became a best-seller in Britain and the United States. Hamnett was already drifting into alcoholism when Barbara first met her. Ten years later, in 1941, Barbara wrote to a friend, 'I think Nina Hamnett is an awful warning not to drink too much, she has often put me off having another pink gin, poor thing.'[19]

Through Lee and his connections, Barbara and John quickly came to know many London artists. Victor Pasmore, then a young man in his twenties who was working at the Public Health Department at County Hall in London and able to paint only in the evenings and at weekends, often came round for a meal. At this time he was attending evening classes at the Central School of Arts and Crafts.[20] Within a few years he would become a founding member of the Euston Road School of Art, which opened in 1937 and flourished until the war forced its closure in 1939. The three young artists had much in common and talked excitedly over bottles of wine about impressionism, cubism, fauvism and surrealism. A much older and rather different sort of artist, James Pryde, in his mid-sixties by 1931, also enjoyed spending time with Barbara and John. Having had a successful career in graphic art and design as one of the famous Beggarstaffs during the 1890s,[21] he later became interested in the theatre. In 1930 he had designed the sets for *Othello* at the Savoy Theatre in which Paul Robeson played the lead role – the first black actor to play the part since Ira Aldridge in 1825. Pryde's conception of a giant thirty-foot high four-poster bed as the centre-piece of the production drew much comment and some scorn from reviewers. Barbara sometimes visited Pryde in his studio, which contained a huge four-poster bed that sported a large ostrich plume at each corner – probably the very same bed (or a cut-down version of it) used in the production of *Othello*. The plumes were so full of dust that they hung down heavily and disconsolately, but Pryde refused to have them removed and cleaned. When visiting Barbara and John, he rejected wine and drank only brandy, which he said was less likely to 'swell him up'. He has been described as 'the Edgar Allen [*sic*] Poe of Painting' – a true bohemian who was deeply interested in the underworld and the macabre.[22] Barbara's memories of life in London's artistic circles would later inspire several episodes in *A Touch of Mistletoe* when Victoria Green mingles with famous painters, writers and sculptors.

About this time Barbara lost her job at the commercial studio, probably because she was now a married woman. The 'marriage bar', which was to remain in place until the mid-1940s, was frequently applied during the Depression and was justified as a social policy aimed at preserving work for men with families. As the main breadwinner in her marriage, Barbara was desperate for another job and managed to find one with a small film company, where she worked on the animations for a screen version of *Gulliver's Travels*. The film, if indeed it was ever finished, was never released. Barbara and John were now only just scraping by financially but, young and carefree, they were still enjoying life in London. Indeed, in bohemian London at this time it was almost *de rigueur* to be a borrower if you were an artist or a writer because it signalled your rejection of middle-class values and conventions. Poverty and indebtedness were to be embraced as outward signs that you were committed to your art and that you despised the bourgeoisie.[23]

*   *   *

This cheerful bohemian existence was to change quite suddenly when, within a few months of marriage, Barbara found that she was pregnant. Although Marie Stopes and others were pioneering contraception in the 1920s, it was not until 1930 that the government began to take the initiative on 'family planning', as it was then called, and started to encourage local authorities to give birth control advice in welfare centres. While it was possible to buy contraceptives over the counter, only the urbane and the well-informed knew what to ask for. It seems likely that John and Barbara were as carefree in their attitude to birth control as they were to life in general; it is also quite possible that Barbara knew little about contraception. Her ignorance would not have been unusual at this time: right up until the beginning of the Second World War, many young women went to the marriage bed knowing little or nothing about sexual intercourse or birth control. Although Barbara had mixed feelings, including panic, about becoming pregnant so soon in their marriage, she was later to use it to comic effect in *Our Spoons Came from Woolworths* when Sophia reflects that she had no idea what birth control meant: 'I had a kind of idea if you controlled your mind and said "I won't have any babies" very hard, they most likely wouldn't come. I thought that was what was meant by birth-control.'[24]

John, only 21 years old and certainly not expecting to be made a father so soon, was appalled by the idea of parenthood. By the autumn of 1931 their cheques in the dresser-drawer had all been cashed and they had no reserves for the baby. He managed to get a job designing patterns for a wallpaper manufacturer, but when he was asked to produce unattractive designs for the cheaper wallpapers so that customers would be more likely to buy from the expensive range, he refused to compromise, both ethically and aesthetically, and was sacked. Barbara's feelings about having a baby included both dreading the responsibility it would incur and happily fantasizing about becoming a young mother. One thing she did enjoy was choosing an unusual name for her child, at one point deciding to call the baby 'Diagram'. The name came to her during a fainting fit in which the Holy Ghost, perched on a spectral mattress-like object, floated into the room of her mind and told her that she would have a son 'and he shall be called Diagram'. Coming round after the faint, Barbara was convinced that the vision had been sent from the supernatural world, if not from God himself. She announced to John and family members that the baby would be called Diagram, at which point a very unholy row broke out, with various relatives expressing disbelief and consternation at the thought of a Pemberton child being given such an outlandish name.

The baby was due in late April 1932 and Barbara's pregnancy was normal. There was no statutory maternity leave or maternity pay scheme at this time and no state provision of nursery care. Before the advent of the National Health Service in 1948, the task of finding out which hospital would provide delivery care either free or cheaply was very important for a young woman with little money. And if she wanted a doctor (as well as a midwife) to attend her during childbirth, she had to pay a fee upfront; she also had to pay for any prescribed medicines. Moreover, between the wars, pregnant women were usually asked to resign from their jobs. When, in the autumn of 1931, Barbara told her boss at the studio she was expecting a baby, she was asked to leave by Christmas.

Luckily, through John's artist friends, she managed to obtain occasional work as an artist's model. She was often given lunch by the painters who employed her, a welcome bonus as by now she and John were running very short of money and both frequently went hungry – not that this would have been noticed during her pre-natal check-ups. The hospital treatment of expectant mothers was at this time briskly regimented, very basic, and little was explained to the women themselves. If helpful advice from hospitals was lacking, there was no shortage of articles about childbirth and motherhood in popular women's magazines, the vast majority of which peddled the idea that motherhood was the natural state for an adult woman and that a baby would bring unqualified joy into her life. For Barbara, whose marriage was spiralling down into poverty, the prospect of having a third mouth to feed cast a very long shadow. John was not interested in money. As long as he could afford his daily supply of cigarettes and paint peacefully at home, he did not bother his head about it; indeed he would later accrue a reputation as a borrower who rarely repaid his loans.

In the spring of 1932 Barbara and John decided to go to the funfair on Hampstead Heath, which arrived at Easter every year. That year Easter

11 John Pemberton with his portrait of his friend Francis Codd

Sunday fell early, on 27 March, a month or so before the baby was due. Barbara loved fairs; they reminded her of the funfair that was set up twice a year on the Big Meadow in Bidford-on-Avon during her childhood. Often she and John were accompanied by their friend Francis Codd, a tall athletic young man with blonde hair and blue eyes who had inherited the printing works that produced Hansard and who went climbing at weekends. He never failed the 'Strong Man' challenge and always brought the mallet down hard enough to ring the bell. Barbara would spend the rest of the evenings after the fairs festooned with the cheap and tawdry soft toys he had won.

On Saturday 26 March, setting off for the fair on Hampstead Heath with John and Francis, she no doubt felt the same sense of rising excitement that she used to have as a young girl running across the bridge over the river Avon, hearing the fair music and smelling the mixture of grease, candy floss and toffee apples that filled the air. Partway through the evening, she and John decided to try the 'Wobbly House' attraction, the floor of which shook violently from time to time. Losing her balance, Barbara fell heavily. The fall triggered premature labour; she felt ill on Easter Sunday and her waters broke in the evening. Experiencing strong contractions, she persuaded John to call a taxi and they arrived at University College Hospital in the middle of Easter Sunday night.

After a traumatic 24 hours, during which Barbara was offered little pain relief and was subjected to the usual harrowing procedures undergone by women in labour in the early 1930s (which included having her legs put in stirrups), she gave birth to a boy on 28 March 1932. Her baby was small and had red hair like his great-aunt, Madge Pemberton. Many years later, Barbara told her son that his father remarked at the time that he had 'looked like a skinned rabbit'. Her anger at the insensitive treatment she received in hospital, and her outrage at having to pay for it, would later be reflected in Sophia's experience of childbirth in *Our Spoons Came from Woolworths:*

> We did get two pounds from the insurance people I had been insured with when I had worked in the studio, but we had to give the hospital that. I can't help feeling if we are all the King's subjects the least he or the Government could do is to pay our birth expenses.[25]

Over fifty years later, when the novel was reprinted in the 1980s, Barbara was to express surprise that none of the reviewers 'mentioned how awful it was having a baby before the National Health Service'.[26]

Barbara had just read Aldous Huxley's newly published *Brave New World* – a novel she greatly admired – and wanted to name her son 'Aldous'. Either family pressure or sudden doubts about her choice resulted in the baby being named instead after Aldous Huxley's distinguished brother, the scientist Julian Huxley. The baby owed his second name to the fact that, having been involved in a minor accident, King Gustaf V of Sweden had recently been in the news. Barbara was taken with the unusual name. Although 'Diagram' had been well beyond the pale for the Pemberton family, 'Julian Gustav' proved acceptable. Barbara received little practical and no financial support either from her own mother or from John's family, who regarded her rather disparagingly. John's sister Buffy was later to recall caustically that Barbara 'called herself a sculptor in those days'.[27] Barbara, in turn, thought little of the Pemberton family; she saw them as pretentious busy-bodies who had inflated ideas of their social standing. She certainly did not feel inferior to them and dismissed them as 'waddy' – by which she meant silly or small-minded and conventional. She was proud of her independence from both her own mother and John's relatives and rather enjoyed shocking them.

But John found the responsibilities of fatherhood onerous; he was too young and self-absorbed to want to spend time with a baby. Rather than look for work to support his wife and child, he continued to stay at home, painting all day and awaiting the occasional commission. Barbara had been the breadwinner before the arrival of Julian and she resumed that role a few weeks after his birth, taking the baby with her when she went to pose as an artist's model. Fortunately, Julian was a healthy and good-tempered child who was easily settled in a play-pen while his mother posed. In the autumn of 1932, when the London art colleges reopened for the academic

12 Barbara holding Julian as a baby with John Pemberton, her first husband, 1932

year, Barbara was offered more work. She and John were coping reasonably well until, in early 1933, Barbara's modelling stints became less regular and commissions for John dried up completely. It was difficult to survive, let alone plan, with such fluctuating incomes. They lived on a very meagre diet, saving most of their milk and eggs for Julian, whose meals were supplemented with lumps of bread and jam that were sometimes blue with paint at the edges. John, although more reconciled now to the idea of being a father, continued to be very self-absorbed and Barbara began to feel a dismal sense of disappointment in her husband.

Later in 1933 things started looking up socially and financially, if not emotionally. Barbara was offered modelling work at various art colleges and John received a few commissions. On the strength of their improved income, they moved to a slightly bigger flat at 50 West End Lane, West

13 Barbara holding Julian, c. 1934

Hampstead – an area popular with artists and musicians. Fired with fresh optimism, Barbara began sculpting again. She and John were even able to go to impromptu parties held by artist friends in the evenings, when either Barbara's sister Nan or a couple in a neighbouring flat agreed to keep an eye on Julian. The social life of London's bohemia was spontaneous, informal and fuelled by drink, music, dance and a sense of artistic fellowship. The wealthy and well-born mingled with poverty-stricken artists, the former often willing to act as patrons for the latter. Parties were sometimes themed ('Masked parties, Savage parties, Victorian parties, Greek parties, Wild West parties, Russian parties, Circus parties ...')[28] and frequently went on till dawn.

At one such gathering Barbara met Barney Seale, a painter and a sculptor. He was well-known in London art circles and had exhibited at the Leger

Galleries in 1931 alongside Augustus John and James Pryde, among others.[29] His famous large-scale architectural works, such as the 38-foot high group of a man, woman and child made for the British Pavilion at the Empire Exhibition in Glasgow in 1938 and a 16-foot long Royal Lion sculpted for the New York World Fair in 1939, were yet to come. In the early 1930s he was looking for a beautiful woman to model for him and he chose Barbara. Transformed into 'Bumble Blunderbore' (the surname evoking the giant of Cornish folklore) in *Our Spoons Came from Woolworths*, he is described in the novel as a Humpty Dumpty sort of man who is afflicted by constant wheezing. Nevertheless, Seale, overweight and sporting a neat moustache, was a kind and generous man who often treated Barbara to delicious meals in good London restaurants. By current standards, he also paid her generously, offering £2 for a two days' sitting session (about £166

14 Pemberton family. Left to right: Guy Pemberton, his mother Mary Pemberton (née Townley) Julian Pemberton, John Pemberton, 1934

today), which would have been a very welcome addition to the small income of the Pemberton family. Barbara was glad to sit for him, both in his London studio and at his home in Walton-on Thames in Surrey, where she sometimes spent weekends, taking Julian with her. Barney's wife, a mild-tempered woman, knew the relationship was entirely platonic and so was happy to welcome Barbara and her son into her home. Seale never finished his sculpture of Barbara, much to her disappointment, but they remained good friends and she continued to visit him occasionally in his London studio.

Although their financial problems had eased slightly, John and Barbara were growing emotionally distant from each other. The strain of having a child when so young themselves, coupled with anxieties about money, had taken its toll. John had not wanted a child in the first place; he had come to London to be a free spirit and to live a bohemian life. Barbara was disappointed in him as a father and frustrated that she was unable to fulfil her own artistic ambitions. The marriage was becoming very strained.

3

Lovers and others

The Pemberton marriage came under yet more strain early in 1934 when Barbara found that she was pregnant again. John was horrified at the prospect of a second child, and Barbara, now deeply worried about their financial situation, knew that finding enough money to feed another mouth was impossible. She would later refer to this period in her life as 'the poverty'; it took on a horror that she would never forget and that she would always associate with John and his inability to provide for her and Julian, now almost two years old. She was the main source of income for the three of them and without it they would surely starve. The only solution was to get rid of the baby. In an undated letter to a friend written a few years later, Barbara confessed, 'I admit I have had an abortion.'[1] Although it is impossible to date this event precisely, it seems highly likely that Barbara had an abortion in early 1934. Until the Abortion Act was passed in 1967, abortions in England were illegal, but, despite this, they were not uncommon. Wealthy women could afford to have their abortions privately, often in clinics euphemistically referred to as 'osteopathic' practices where a rich woman would pay £100 or so for the operation (about £8,500 in today's money).[2] Poorer women would first try homespun 'remedies' such as drinking port with quinine or gin with castor oil or climbing into a scalding hot bath. If none of those worked, finding a backstreet abortionist was the next step. There were always working-class women, recommended by word of mouth, who would perform the procedure cheaply, but having a backstreet abortion was often terrifying. The operation was done without anaesthetic, with unsterilized instruments in poor light (usually on a kitchen table) and performed by women with no medical training. The experience frequently left women in agony and sometimes resulted in dangerous complications.

There were also a number of doctors in London who found carrying out illegal abortions to be a lucrative practice. Although she had little money, Barbara did not want to risk her life. It seems likely that she and John managed to raise enough money by borrowing from friends to pay a doctor to perform the operation. There is no record of Barbara's experience, but her descriptions, written years later, of the effects of abortion on Sophia Fairclough in *Our Spoons Came from Woolworths* and Victoria Green in *A Touch of Mistletoe* suggest that it was traumatic for her. Sophia eventually recovers physically following complications but the experience leaves a deep psychological scar: 'my mind didn't recover at all'; Victoria feels 'disgusted and degraded afterwards and for days imagined I smelt of dead birds however many baths I had'.[3]

Rather than bringing John and Barbara closer, her abortion pushed them further apart. Although they continued to live together, they gradually started to lead separate lives. John began staying out late at parties and sometimes did not come home at all; from 1934 he was unfaithful with a number of women. When he wasn't painting, he spent most of his time in Soho clubs and bars. When the Shim Sham Club (named after a popular Harlem dance routine) opened in Wardour Street in 1935 and began to attract both tourists and black Londoners, it became one of his favourite haunts. He was fascinated by the capital's African American and Caribbean working population – dancers, boxers, waitresses, musicians, chefs and bouncers – and would often ask if he could paint them. He was not the only one: the 1920s had seen black entertainers, including the dancer Josephine Baker, become extremely popular. By 1934 the legacy of black art in all its variations – from jazz to blues to painting and sculpture – was being celebrated. An article headed 'Negro Art', published in *The Burlington Magazine for Connoisseurs* in April 1920, had created particular interest among artists and writers. Its author, André Salmon, suggested that Western artists needed to divest themselves of their prejudices about what does and what does not constitute 'good' art and that they should look afresh at the African and Polynesian sculptures to be found in places such as the Louvre and the British Museum, where they would see 'in the grandiose and savage fragments of antique negro sculpture the very principles of art'.[4] John Pemberton's interest in 'negro art' and in using black Londoners as subjects during the mid-1930s thus came at the tail end of the movement. Nor was his enthusiasm for his sitters entirely academic. He was sexually attracted to many of them, and one in particular, a tall African American dancer known to Barbara only as 'Marie', became his regular companion.[5] Although little is known of her – apart from a vague family memory that she had a minor role as a dancer in the 1937 film of *King Solomon's Mines* – she clearly signalled John's decision to break away from convention and from his marriage. He was beginning to carve out a life for himself that had little to do with Barbara or with fatherhood.

By the spring of 1934 Barbara and John accepted that their marriage was failing. There were no furious rows and, in true bohemian style, they still slept together occasionally. However, Barbara was beginning to see things with clearer eyes. She became more critical of her husband, and her earlier faith in his artistic talent was fast waning. She also now realized, angrily, that he would never provide her with the emotional and financial security that she so desperately wanted. While he enjoyed his new-found freedom, she saw him as selfish and irresponsible. She knew, however, that she would face a bleak future as a single mother. Understandably, then, she too looked outside the marriage for support and companionship. About this time she had an affair with John Banting, the artist and writer.[6] Banting was now based in London, where he produced commercial and decorative designs; he also exhibited with the London Group, so Barbara might have met him through Rupert Lee. Banting's visit to Paris in 1930 had inspired an interest in surrealism, and for Barbara this added to his attractiveness. It was a short-lived but passionate affair. Francis Codd was another admirer. Originally one of John's friends who had spent a lot of time with the young couple over the previous few years, he was now becoming romantically attached to Barbara. He was a tall handsome man with blonde hair who had no trouble attracting women. However, although Barbara valued his practical nature and appreciated his reliability, she found him dull and prosaic. He lacked the charisma, imagination and sophistication of her ideal lover.

* * *

That ideal lover turned out to be not only sophisticated, but a very talented artist and considerably older than Barbara. Just to complicate matters, he was also her husband's uncle by marriage. As a young man, Rupert Lee looked remarkably like the American film star Cary Grant. By the time Barbara first met him in 1932, he was in his mid-forties and rather gaunt with thinning hair, but he was a highly intelligent, cultured and still attractive man. He was also witty and 'a superb raconteur'.[7] Born in India in 1887, Lee had been sent to England to be educated and lived with his grandparents in Lewisham while at school. In 1911 he enrolled as a student at the Slade School of Art, where he met Paul Nash, who was later to become famous as a war and landscape artist. Nash was intrigued by Lee from the first time he saw him and later described his fellow student's unusual appearance in his autobiography:

> A conspicuous figure at the Slade at this time was a personage known as the Man from Mexico, so-called from his habit of arriving each morning in Gower Street riding an elderly bicycle and wearing some sort of equestrian leggings and a wide-brimmed hat. He was not, however, a person to stand for ridicule as the Slade wits soon found out. He had a power of caustic reprisal and was capable of aggression [...] his face had an intellectual structure and his finely modelled features a serious, half-sarcastic expression.[8]

15 Rupert Lee, c. 1912, two years before he married Madge Pemberton

Having introduced himself, Nash was invited to tea by Lee, who lived at this time in two small top-floor rooms in a Victorian house in Fulham. Unlike Nash and many of his other contemporaries at the Slade, Lee had no private funds and needed to earn money or win scholarships just to make ends meet. He survived on a very frugal diet: 'Bacon in the morning, peanuts at lunch, and sardines at night'.[9] Shocked by Lee's apparent poverty, Nash was nevertheless greatly impressed by his intellect and by his extraordinary musical ability.[10] The two men soon became good friends.

In 1912 Rupert Lee enrolled at the Royal College of Art and during that year he met 26-year-old Madge Kendal Pemberton, who strongly supported the Suffragette movement and who was one of Guy Pemberton's younger sisters. Like many members of the Pemberton family, she was very keen on the theatre and was working as secretary for Ellen Terry's son, Edward Gordon Craig, the modernist theatre director/stage designer.[11] Paul Nash, who met Madge in 1912, thought that she 'was very intelligent and had a rather mordant wit'.[12] She was also aunt to two-year-old John Pemberton.

Following a strange one-sided courtship in which Madge seems to have manipulated Rupert into becoming engaged, they married in 1914 and began life as a couple in a small flat in Chelsea. The marriage was a disaster from the start; Madge did not enjoy sex, later frankly admitting that she found it 'disgusting', and adding that she would shoot herself if she became pregnant.[13] Nevertheless, she refused to divorce her husband even though they started to lead independent lives within a year or so of their marriage. In 1916 Lee joined the Queen's Westminster Rifles and, having completed his training, was sent to France in December of that year to fight in the First World War. Weakened by influenza and suffering from symptoms of shell-shock after the March retreat of 1918, he was sent to the Seale Hayne Military Hospital in Devon for treatment, where he documented the horrors of the trenches in cubist and vorticist-inspired paintings and woodcuts. Although he had not been seriously wounded physically, his experiences left deep psychological scars, and after the war Lee was a more emotionally volatile man than he had been before it. His time in France had changed him in other ways too: a visit to a Parisian brothel had taught him that sex could be a joyful, liberating experience. In 1919 he celebrated it in a fluid and erotic oil painting entitled *La Belle Suzanne*.[14] He now understood fully why his marriage to Madge Pemberton had been doomed to failure.

Invalided out of service in 1919, Lee began to work closely with Paul and John Nash producing wood engravings for publications such as the *Sun Calendar Yearbook*; by 1920 he was recognized as a key figure in the wood-engraving revival in England. In the same year, after an explosive row during the summer, followed by a vicious campaign in which Madge blackened his name to all their mutual friends, Rupert and his wife separated. Rupert left their flat to live alone in a rented house in St Ann's Terrace in St John's Wood. His sexual experiences in France had made him less tolerant of their sterile marriage and he now wanted the freedom to pursue relationships with other women. Meanwhile, his artistic reputation was growing; he regularly had work accepted for exhibitions organized by the London Group and also by 'The Friday Club', founded by Vanessa Bell. His sensitive drawings and carvings of animals were being bought by eminent collectors such as Arnold Bennett and Roger Fry. In 1921 Lee took charge of the London Group's hanging committee and in 1922 he was elected a full member. The London Group, a body of artists that had grown out of the Camden Town Group, had championed all forms of modernism since 1913, from post-impressionism to cubism, and it now played an important role in the London art world.[15] Its luminaries included Vanessa Bell and Roger Fry (with whom Rupert Lee was good friends), David Bomberg, Jacob

Epstein, Harold Gilman, Lucien Pissarro, Paul Nash, Duncan Grant and Mark Gertler. In 1926 Lee, now regarded as an extremely successful artist, was elected president of the London Group, a position he was to hold for ten years. By the time Barbara moved to London in 1929, he had become an influential figure in the art circles of London.

* * *

It was through the London Group that Rupert Lee met Diana Brinton, who was also to play an important role in Barbara's life. Born on 29 March 1897, she was the eldest of four sisters and one brother. Their father was Reginald Brinton, a wealthy carpet manufacturer, and the family home, Croft House in Kidderminster, was a lively place, often full of guests, including school friends who came to stay during the holidays. A young visitor there remembered the Brinton girls as 'spoilt, clever, attractive, extrovert, rich and afraid of nothing and nobody'.[16] By her late teens, Diana, or 'Dinnie' as she was known to her immediate family, was fluent in French and Spanish and very knowledgeable in art history; by her mid-twenties she had worked her way up to become sub-editor at *The Burlington Magazine*. Roger Fry relied on her excellent knowledge of languages when reading articles submitted from abroad, including Salmon's essay 'Negro Art', which Diana translated for publication in the magazine in 1920.[17] Although she was not classically beautiful, her independent spirit and her fine intellect attracted many male admirers, including the writer and theatre critic Harold Child, who wrote love letters to her for many years.[18] She was also a superb organizer and in 1922 became the secretary of the London Group, which she rescued from its parlous financial situation by arranging frequent events and exhibitions. Rupert Lee and Diana Brinton soon found that they enjoyed each other's company and began to meet in the evenings for dancing lessons. By 1925 – by which time the Group was flourishing – she and Rupert were 'insepa-rable', despite the fact that he was still married to Madge Pemberton and that rumours abounded concerning his many affairs.[19]

A striking photograph of Diana, taken by Rupert in 1925, shows an interesting looking woman, her short dark hair combed fashionably back from her high forehead to form a neat cap on her head. Diana's facial features were strong rather than pretty and her firmly set mouth suggests a serious nature. Her large and rather protruding eyes were very distinctive. In other photographs taken by Rupert at this time she poses almost nude *en plein air*, appearing confident and at ease with her body.[20] This outward appearance of strength and confidence in fact hid an empathetic and complex personality. Diana Brinton was deeply attached to Rupert, whom she considered highly talented, and she ignored the malicious gossip which

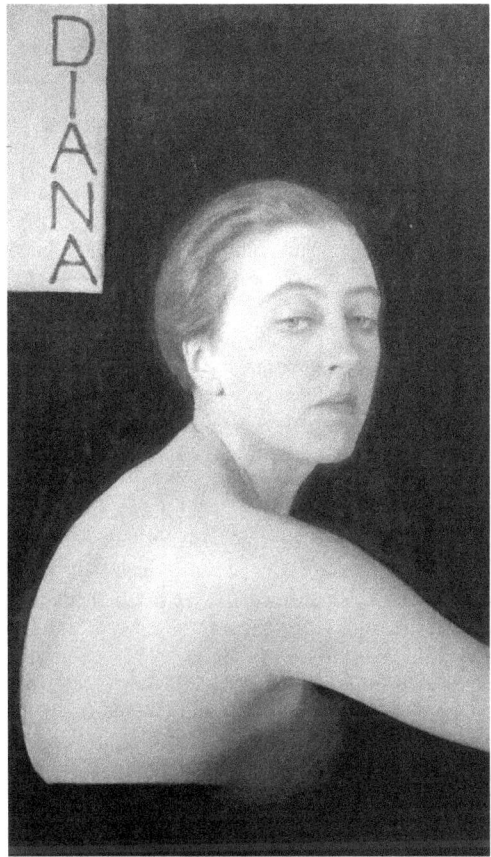

16 Diana Brinton, c. 1925

suggested that he only wanted her for her money. Her family also liked him, despite having been warned about his reputation. Although she was not prepared to live with Rupert, she was prepared to endure any disapproval of their relationship, hoping that they would eventually marry when he became free. Indeed they were brought closer by the malice of his wife Madge who, while refusing to divorce her husband, continued to campaign against him, spreading spiteful stories. These included the accusation made in 1925 that Rupert had seduced an underage girl, a claim that resulted in his suspension from his post at the Westminster School of Art, where he was teaching sculpture, at which he now excelled. He was reinstated later that year when the accusation was proved false. He vented his bitterness in a poem about Madge, two lines of which refer to her same-sex desires:

> My wife, who lived in secret vice, was eaten up by rats and mice,
> But as you know, oh gentle readers, rats and mice are dirty feeders.[21]

Rupert and Diana worked well together professionally as president and secretary of the London Group and were responsible for organizing many memorable London Group events and exhibitions, including an important sculpture exhibition held on the roof gardens of Selfridge & Co. in Oxford Street in 1930, which Barbara, given her ambition at that time to become a professional sculptor, would probably have attended. The exhibition featured sculptures by Henry Moore (then aged 32) and Barbara Hepworth (aged 27), whose pioneering work Rupert Lee had warmly encouraged at a time when large open air sculpture was seen as strange and puzzling by the general public. By 1930 his reputation as an innovator and leader in the art world was secure.

However, Rupert 's private life was still painful. Madge remained adamant that she would not grant a divorce, a decision that deeply distressed him and prevented his marriage to Diana. Even though their marriage had collapsed in 1920, Madge wished to retain her married title, presumably for reasons of social respectability. In desperation at his wife's refusal to divorce him, Rupert met a Dutch lawyer in February 1930, who advised him that he had a good case for desertion since, to all intents and purposes, his wife had left him permanently during their summer holiday in 1920. He assured Rupert that, once he had fulfilled the necessary residency clause of living in the Netherlands for at least three months, he would be able to file for divorce through the Dutch courts, which would prove easier and quicker than obtaining a divorce in England. In fact, the whole process took much longer than expected because of Madge's obduracy, and Rupert ended up living in The Hague for well over a year, having moved there in October 1930. He returned to London occasionally in order to fulfil his role as president of the London Group, which Diana was running on a day-to-day basis, but he spent months at a time in the Netherlands (which was why he had been unable to attend the wedding of his nephew, John, to Barbara in May 1931). Throughout this time of isolation and occasional depression, he leaned heavily on Diana for emotional support.

At the time of Barbara's marriage to John Pemberton in 1931, Madge – then in her mid-forties – was still legally Rupert Lee's wife. Her fictional counterpart in *Our Spoons Came from Woolworths*, 'Aunt Emma', is an imposing figure and – according to Barbara's son Julian Pemberton – was clearly inspired by Madge:

She was a very tall woman with red hair and she wore a cloak and three-cornered hat. She wrote, and was altogether very intellectual and interested in women's rights, but she disliked children, babies in particular, but perhaps that was because she had never had any and couldn't very well now Simeon, her husband, had run away.[22]

In January 1932 Diana Brinton bought a large elegant house in St Quintin Avenue, between Ladbroke Grove and Shepherd's Bush. Confident that their plan to marry would succeed, Rupert and Diana chose furniture for it together and Rupert oversaw the installation of an expensive hot water system.[23] By this time their relationship was based more on shared interests than physical desire: Diana was far less interested in sex than Rupert and turned a blind eye to his occasional affairs with other women, who would soon include Barbara. The relationship was underpinned by their shared love of art and their involvement in the London Group, but there were also other factors that held them together. For Diana, Rupert was a witty and gifted companion who was admired and respected in London art circles; for Rupert, Diana's wealth offered a secure and comfortable life with a sophisticated woman, suggesting that his memories of poverty still influenced his choices in life. For sexual fulfilment he looked elsewhere. Nevertheless, confident that their marriage would bring them happiness, Diana continued to support Rupert both emotionally and financially in his attempt to divorce his wife. The Dutch court granted Rupert a divorce from Madge in June 1932, but she was allowed three months to appeal against the decision. He returned immediately to England and he and Diana announced their engagement in the autumn. The champagne flowed; there were many celebrations with friends and family; in October *The Star* printed an article under the headline 'London Art Group Romance' and the *Daily Express* carried a piece entitled 'Romance Among the Artists'.[24]

The celebrations were premature for in September 1932 Madge Lee appealed against the Dutch court ruling. Against all their expectations, Madge's appeal was successful and the divorce ruling was overturned in June 1933. During this difficult period, Diana found out about Rupert's recent affair with Elizabeth Japp, one of his models.[25] Rupert admitted the relationship but reassured Diana that he wanted her as his wife: 'our life together is planned and nothing else will be'. Persuaded of his love for her, Diana stuck by Rupert and constantly assured him of her devotion. The couple exchanged many passionate letters up until Christmas 1933, at which point the relationship became strained. Rupert, feeling angry and deeply frustrated that the divorce strategy had failed, lashed out at Diana and turned again to other women for comfort. In a particularly nasty twist of the knife, he confessed to Diana that he had loved Elizabeth Japp for three years. In a short account of her life at this time entitled 'Synopsis', Diana charted with some pain the way Rupert blew hot and cold during 1933 and 1934 about his commitment to their relationship.[26]

*   *   *

If 1933 and 1934 were difficult years for Rupert Lee and Diana Brinton, they were even more problematic for Barbara. In early 1934 her marriage was disintegrating; she was also desperately worried about her future and no doubt still feeling weak and miserable after her abortion. Another blow came in March, when her mother, aged only 51, died in the Radcliffe Hospital in Oxford from peritonitis and a heart attack, complications resulting from appendicitis. Although Barbara had never been close to her mother, the news was nevertheless a shock and threw her into depression. She began to confide in Rupert Lee, who seemed a sensitive listener and who encouraged her to express her feelings. Now aware that his nephew's marriage was falling apart and always drawn to beautiful women, Rupert began paying close attention to Barbara. He asked her to sit for him as his model and she spent a lot of time in his Soho studio, grateful both for the fees he paid her and his company. When he set out to seduce her, she was – perhaps not surprisingly – flattered and receptive. They quickly became close and by June 1934 they were lovers. Barbara was ravished by Rupert's brilliance and his importance in the London art world. After living on the breadline with John, she enjoyed being treated to good meals and mixing with the well-known artists whom she met through Rupert's position as president of the London Group. She was also physically drawn to this lanky and highly talented man and was moved by his apparent vulnerability. Rupert Lee was, in some ways, a more successful version of John Pemberton – both men were highly creative but dependent beings who sometimes acted irresponsibly and found it difficult to make decisions. They were drawn to strong women, preferring to let their female partners become the dominant force in the relationship. They both hated confrontation, seeking to avoid it at any cost – but Barbara was to find this out only later. After John's casual selfishness, Rupert's kind and thoughtful nature gave her much pleasure; she enjoyed his company and was flattered by the urgency of his desire. His insistence that she was outstandingly beautiful and very witty restored her confidence and – understanding little of the complex bond between Rupert and Diana – she began to believe that he loved her and would choose her over Diana.

But loving a man whose partner was his main source of income would not resolve Barbara's financial situation. Now that Julian was two, Barbara needed someone to look after him during the day so that she could work, but she could not afford to pay for childcare. John was contributing nothing

to the household expenses and certainly did not want to be responsible for
his son, but he offered a temporary solution: Julian could stay for a while
with his relatives who lived in Wombourne, a Staffordshire village in the
countryside near Wolverhampton. Barbara reluctantly agreed and Julian
was driven to the home of his great-uncle, Douglas Allday, a younger brother
of John's mother, Muriel Pemberton (née Allday). Douglas Allday was a
wealthy man, having made a fortune through the family firm of Alldays
and Onions, a Birmingham-based company that had very successfully made
stylish four- and six-cylinder cars during the first few decades of the twentieth
century. He and his wife Marjorie had a daughter, Judith, aged five. Barbara
knew the Alldays were rich and that Julian would lack for nothing, but
after a while found that she was missing her son badly. Rupert could see
that she was miserable and offered to take her to visit Julian; he did not
own a car but he was sure Diana would lend him hers. Rupert later wrote
that Barbara sat in the car for the first twenty miles 'looking like Cassandra
until I staged an engine failure by a nice pub in Warwick and after two gins
she relaxed'.[27] We can only guess what happened when they arrived at the
house of John's relatives, but an episode in *Our Spoons Came from Woolworths*, when Sophia Fairclough goes to visit her small son who is being
looked after by relatives living near Evesham, gives us some idea. In the
novel, Sophia arrives to find her two-year-old son pale-faced and over-dressed,
with his beautiful auburn curls completely shorn. Deeply upset by the visit,
Barbara spent the journey back to London planning how to reclaim Julian.
This was only the first of several periods he would spend away from his
mother and each of them made Barbara feel miserable and guilty. The
following morning Barbara wrote a brief thank you letter to 'Miss Brinton',
for the loan of the car. That short note was the first item in a correspondence
between the two women that would continue intermittently for several
decades.

※   ※   ※

By the autumn of 1934 Barbara was convinced that Rupert would leave
Diana and that they would make a new life together. However, she had
no one close to her with whom she could share these hopes. Her favourite
sister, Chloe, to whom Barbara told all her secrets, was no longer living in
England, so Barbara had lost a valuable confidante who might have warned
her against such soaring optimism. During the summer of 1934 the 22-year-
old Chloe had her own romance. An attractive woman, always elegantly
dressed, she had many admirers and knew plenty of young officers, some
of whom had simply struck up conversation with her on a train because
they were so taken by her beauty. In the summer of 1934 she became

engaged to 27-year-old Charles de Lacy Wilbraham Ford, a lieutenant in
the West Yorkshire regiment who had been born into a military family in
India. He was at home in England on leave from service in India when he
met Chloe. For her it was a match of convenience rather than love; she had
watched Barbara's marriage spiral down into poverty and misery and was
determined not to make the same mistake. Barbara thought the engagement
unwise; despite her own poverty, she disapproved of marrying simply for
money. But her strong misgivings about her sister's marriage did not stop
Chloe from becoming engaged to Charles Ford, as he was more commonly
known, and agreeing to sail out to India to marry him.

On 15 September 1934 Chloe Elizabeth Bayley travelled out second-class
to Bombay (now Mumbai) on a P&O ship called *Viceroy of India*, her fare
no doubt paid for by her fiancé, since she certainly would not have been
able to raise the money herself. This was a luxurious ship with 'a built-in
swimming pool surrounded by Pompeian reliefs' and a smoking room designed
to look like the great hall of a castle, 'complete with hammer beams, baronial
arms, a large fireplace and crossed swords on the wall'.[28] On the ship's
register she is listed as travelling with a group of other young women; they
would no doubt have had a lot of fun during the voyage, despite bouts of
sea-sickness. Chloe was a risk-taker but her decision to change her life so
dramatically by sailing to India would not have been uncommon in the first
few decades of the twentieth century. During the period of British rule, many
young women travelled to India – usually having a contact already there (a
brother in the British Army or an aunt who had lived in India for some
years, for example) – in order to find a husband. The arrangement was one
of mutual benefit: there were many thousands of serving officers in the British
Army and young men in the Indian Civil Service who desperately wanted
wives, but it was hard to find the right woman during their short leave
periods in England. The young women who travelled out to India, either to
look for a husband or to marry a man they had recently met in England
(like Chloe), were known as the 'Fishing Fleet'. Chloe is described in the
ship's register as 'having no occupation' and as having previously lived at
119 Greencroft Gardens, West Hampstead, London NW6. She and Charles
were married in Bombay, on 4 October 1934, soon after she disembarked.

Chloe Bayley certainly managed to avoid poverty by marrying Charles
Ford, and she was soon enjoying a rich social life. When the cold weather
started in India in mid-October, 'it was the signal for four months of non-stop
gaiety – race weeks, polo weeks … horse shows, race meetings, gymkhanas,
paper-chases, moonlight picnics, garden parties and constant dinner and
cocktail parties'.[29] There were, however, other aspects of living in India that
took some getting used to. Barbara would wait eagerly for the occasional
letter from her sister but was sometimes shocked by what she read about

daily life there. With three-quarters of each railway platform reserved for Europeans, hundreds of Indians would be squashed onto the last quarter. When the train came in, there would be a surge towards it and some Indians would fall under the train wheels and die a horrible death. Chloe reported 'lumps of meat' being carried out of the station but it took her a while to realize, she wrote, that these were the remains of the unfortunate victims. She also never quite got used to the fact that when you used the lavatory at home, there was no flush; instead, if you looked down after defecating, you would see a pair of brown hands removing the bowl beneath and replacing it with a clean one. She found this experience particularly unnerving at first.[30]

Barbara's early intuitions proved correct: the marriage was not a happy one. Chloe did not love her husband but she did enjoy his wealth. Within six months she had spent all his money, including his savings, and had embarked on an affair with another man who was so desperate for her love that he threatened to go into the jungle and shoot himself if she left him.[31] By early 1935 Chloe's life in India had become very complicated and she was not available to listen to Barbara's hopes and dreams.

* * *

While Chloe's marriage was disintegrating abroad, Barbara was feeling emotionally buoyant and was immensely optimistic about her future with Rupert Lee. In the autumn of 1934 relations with her husband John were reasonably amicable, and the three of them rubbed along well enough together; Barbara and John still lived in the same flat and Rupert even invited John to share his studio in Soho. Barbara would later write of this period that Rupert 'made love to me in the afternoons while John had me at night'.[32] Julian, now two and a half, had been returned by John's relatives and was back in Barbara's sole care. She was able to take him with her when she worked as an artist's model because she was sitting for Rupert and his friends, who understood the situation. Rupert seemed to like small children and had no objection to Julian coming too, so long as he and Barbara could find enough time for their love-making in his flat in the afternoons. Their relationship was beginning, at least to Barbara, to feel comfortably secure, despite the presence of Diana Brinton in the background. Indeed, the fact that Rupert had been unable to obtain his divorce from Madge led Barbara to believe that he would never be able to marry Diana, who would not live with him unless they were married. Diana's mother had died in a motorcar accident, caused by a burst tyre, in 1921 and from then on Diana felt that she had to set a good example to her three younger sisters – so she would not contemplate having a live-in lover. Barbara, on the other hand, had no qualms about living with Rupert and was confident that he would soon abandon Diana and choose her as his lifelong partner.

She was also beginning to sculpt again, using clay either provided by Rupert or donated by artist friends. She was pleased with the results. Although she could not afford an armature, she would improvise, using Julian's toys to make a support frame. Photographs of Barbara's work at this time show that, like Sophia Fairclough, she focused on female heads: 'The face was rather Burmese and I left the eye sockets hollow, which sounds gruesome, but, in fact, was most effective.'[33]

Julian was also beginning to show some artistic talent, albeit in a somewhat unorthodox manner. One Sunday morning, waking up in his cot to find he had had an accident, he made an impromptu collage by sticking loose feathers from his pillow to the wall with the excrement from his sheets. He thought it worked well and was pleased with the effect, recording in his memoir many years later:

> I enjoyed the golden glow of the thinnest part of the shit appliqué in the sunlight on the white washed wall. I was feeling quite pleased with myself when Barbara came in to get me up. She let out a most frightening cry, probably disgust and rage. I was stuck in the bath while it was cleaned up and no one was nice to me for ages.

Like most artists of the 1930s who considered themselves interestingly unconventional, Barbara had taught Julian to call her by her name rather than 'mummy' or 'mother'. Romilly John, the son of Augustus John, called his mother, whose name was Dorelia, 'Dodo'; Vanessa Bell's children, Julian, Quentin and Angelica, all called their mother 'Nessa'. Julian Pemberton was in good company. 'The culture of deference had no place in Bohemian families', as Virginia Nicholson has remarked.[34]

Rupert Lee encouraged John and Barbara to submit work for the London Group Thirty-Second Exhibition, to be held at the New Burlington Galleries between 12 and 30 November 1934. Rupert was listed as a member in the catalogue, Barbara and John as non-members. They were in august company: the exhibition comprised 302 items and featured work by many famous artists, including Duncan Grant, John Nash, Vanessa Bell, Walter Sickert and Eileen Agar. John showed a painting entitled *Still Life*, which was priced at 15 guineas (over £1,300 today). Rupert exhibited three sculptures, all studies of women with whom he was or had been intimate: they were listed in the catalogue as *Elizabeth* (Elizabeth Japp), *Miss Jeanne de Casalis* (who had starred alongside Anna Neagle in the 1934 film *Nell Gwynn*) and *Barbara*. Barbara, it would seem, had replaced Elizabeth Japp and Jeanne de Casalis as Rupert's muse. All three pieces were priced at £50 each (the equivalent of about £4,250 now). Barbara's sculpture, entitled simply *Kathleen*,

17 Head sculpted by Barbara in 1934

18 Bust sculpted by Barbara in the 1930s

19 Head of Barbara, sculpted by Rupert Lee in 1934

was a bust of her younger sister, now living in London and engaged to marry Edwin ('Teddy') Catford, who was later to make his name as a cinematographer. It was priced at £21 (about £1,780 today) and did not sell; nor did John's painting. However, Rupert's head of Barbara, cast in bronze, did sell, although its whereabouts now is unknown; all that remains is a photograph of the life-size plaster bust he made before the head was cast in bronze. Barbara's thick wavy hair is brushed behind her ears and her fine bone structure and beautiful facial features are evident even from the rough cast. There is no doubt that Rupert Lee was very fond of Barbara at this time and that she adored him.

In November 1934, the month of the exhibition, Rupert confessed to Diana that he had been having an affair with Barbara since June. Diana suggested that Rupert should stop seeing Barbara but he refused. Not only that, he openly showed Barbara affection in public, which left Diana feeling deeply hurt and distressed, especially when their London Group friends began to quiz her about the situation. She found herself in a quandary for, far from regarding Barbara and her 'unfortunate husband and child' as enemies, she liked them and thought Barbara 'kind-hearted and sensible'. Mulling over how she should react, Diana drafted a document listing her options. She wondered whether she should move abroad but decided against it. She considered asking Rupert 'to behave like a man' and explain to Barbara that his relationship with her (Diana) was 'not one to cause any jealousy' – a phrase that seems to confirm that sex was no longer an important element in their partnership. She must at least insist, she decided, that she and Rupert stay friends, whatever else happened.[35] Unaware of Diana's agonized reflections, Barbara remained infatuated with Rupert and was living very much in the present moment. This was all to change early in 1935, when she discovered that she was pregnant again.

4

Desperate measures

Barbara calculated that the baby would be due in mid-October. John assumed that he was the baby's father but this time he did not try to persuade Barbara to have an abortion, perhaps remembering what she had been through the previous year. However, Barbara was certain that Rupert was the father and told him so. Rupert liked small children and had said he regretted not having any of his own – so Barbara naturally assumed he would be delighted that, in his late forties, he was going to become a father for the first time. She also assumed that he would now make good the many promises he had made to her that he would leave Diana and that they would move away, possibly even abroad, and start a new life together. She was determined to have the child, whatever the difficulties. However, when she broke the news to Rupert in the spring of 1935, he was strangely evasive and non-committal, although he still talked vaguely about their being together in the future. Deeply disappointed, Barbara grew very anxious. Although she still saw Rupert as the love of her life, he showed no sign that he would step up, either to support her financially or to acknowledge that he was the father of her second child. Meanwhile, John continued to think that the baby was his and grudgingly adjusted to the idea. He and Barbara even moved to a bigger flat in Belsize Park so that they would have more space for their expanding family.

In the early summer of 1935, Diana Brinton and Rupert Lee went on holiday together, probably to Spain, a country they both loved. They returned as 'Mr and Mrs Brinton Lee' and told friends and family that they had married quietly while abroad. As Rupert had not been able to obtain a divorce from his wife Madge Pemberton, this would not have been possible unless he had committed bigamy. No marriage certificate has ever been found and it seems likely that, instead of marrying, Diana simply changed her name to 'Brinton Lee' by deed poll.[1] Sensing the real threat that Barbara posed to her long relationship with Rupert, Diana seems to have decided to checkmate her rival with a clever move. Soon after their return, Rupert moved in to live with Diana at 7 St Quintin Avenue, and they presented themselves to the world, to all intents and purposes, as man and wife.

Barbara, now four months pregnant, was devastated and finally had to face up to the fact that she was on her own. While John seemed fairly equable about her pregnancy, he was now leading his own life and often away from home, spending a lot of time with his bohemian friends and with his girlfriend Marie. Moreover, he was not capable of earning enough money to keep a wife and two children and constantly stressed his need to be free in order to pursue his art. Barbara could not afford childcare and would not be able to work without it. Although a Child Tax Allowance had been introduced in 1909, this benefited mainly middle-class parents. There was no Family Allowance, Family Income Support or easily accessible child support maintenance system in 1935. A single mother could apply for an affiliation order against the father, but before the days of DNA, it was often very difficult legally to prove his identity. Furthermore, the burden of proving the father's identity, chasing him up and collecting payment fell solely to the mother. And, given Rupert's 'marriage' to Diana, it now seemed impossible to rely on her lover for financial support.

It was probably her fear of sinking into poverty again that made Barbara decide to ask Diana who, like most people, assumed that John was the father of her child, for help. Responding generously, Diana offered to pay for a good doctor to attend Barbara before and during the baby's birth. This doctor – who was later to become president of the Royal College of General Practitioners and to be made a dame for her pioneering work in medical research – was Dr Katharine Annis Calder Gillie, who was then working from a practice of three women doctors based in Porchester Terrace in Westminster. The Brinton family, who all used her and affectionately called her 'Gillie', had complete confidence in her. Her fees would have been way beyond what most women could afford and Barbara realized how lucky she was. After her first appointment, she wrote to Diana to thank her and to let her know that the baby was due on 14 October. She added, 'This child kicks about so much I hope it isn't twins. I do hope you don't see three any more'[2] – a playful comment which suggest that the relationship between the two women was relaxed at this time.

As the due date for the baby's birth drew near, there were discussions as to what could be done with Julian. By this time he was three years and seven months old. Small for his age, he was an attractive, elfin-like child with hazel eyes and a mop of thick curly hair which was so vividly auburn that strangers would comment on it. He was also a curious and inventive boy and took pleasure in turning household items into toys, sometimes with disastrous results. His Catholic aunt Nan, Barbara's sister, was upset to find that he had taken down the numerous crucifixes on her walls and, leaping from sofa to chair, was using them to stage battles between enemy aeroplanes. It was a while before she volunteered to look after him again. John and Barbara had nicknames for Julian's hands, 'Picker' and 'Stealer', because he was always into something; one of his favourite tricks was to collect knives and forks and stick them into a loaf of bread so as to make an interesting object or figure. His parents would move things out of his way for safety, piling them up in the centre of the dining table where he could not get at them. He would peer over the edge of the table, muttering to himself, able to see a world of fascinating objects that were just out of his reach.[3]

Although they were by now leading separate lives, John offered to look after Julian while Barbara had the baby and until she was strong enough to cope with both children. Barbara was grateful and looked forward to a rest and to spending more time on her own and with Rupert – who still wanted to see her, despite now being obviously committed to Diana.

*   *   *

Caroline Georgina arrived over a fortnight late. She was born on 2 November 1935 at 32 Glenloch Road in Hampstead, a private maternity home. The birth was not registered until 13 December and the birth certificate named the father as John Pemberton, 'Artist (Painter) of 49a Belsize Park'. At this point John did not know that Caroline was Rupert's child, and Barbara seems to have hedged her bets, a strategy reflected in Sophia's behaviour in *Our Spoons Came from Woolworths*:

> The baby took a long time coming and when it did come I was so tired I didn't care what kind it was or if it was alive or dead; but after I'd been asleep I felt more interested, but didn't like to ask to see it in case it was like Peregrine, or in case there was some mark on it to let people know it wasn't my husband's child.[4]

Caroline was a healthy and pretty baby with dark hair. When Barbara was strong enough, she returned to the flat in Belsize Park with her daughter and Julian was returned to his mother. Barbara managed to care for the two children by using her savings, but by early 1936 she was running out of money.

Guy Pemberton, her father-in-law, thought it was time that John earned some money to support his family and offered to help him market his work. In March he drafted a letter, as if written by his son, to an influential patron of the arts. The patron was politely invited to view John's paintings in the hope, presumably, that he would buy some. Nothing came of this venture, however, and John himself did nothing to promote his art commercially.

20 Photograph of Barbara taken by Rupert Lee in 1936

Meanwhile, Barbara clung to the idea that Rupert would soon acknowledge Caroline as his child and would support them. She continued to visit Rupert in his studio, often taking her son and small daughter with her. He still had his flat and she would also take the children there sometimes, pushing Caroline in her pram. Julian was excited by Rupert's radio equipment which consisted of copper wires strung across the ceiling, as well as small lights that glowed, and needles that moved of their own mysterious accord. Occasionally crackling, whooshing noises erupted into the air; it was like nothing he had seen or heard before and the small boy was happy to be left to play with a few spare wires and bits of old equipment while Caroline slept and Rupert and Barbara made love.

About this time Rupert took some striking black and white photographs of Barbara. They all show her wearing a simple dark dress and a fine jewelled headband in her shining dark hair, which is parted in the middle and swept behind her ears. In one photograph she is seated at a dinner table with a cat on her lap, holding a napkin in one hand and an empty wine glass in the other. Behind her the curtain is drawn and she is softly silhouetted against it. She is smiling in a relaxed affectionate manner and is looking at the photographer. In another shot, she is lying on a bed or a sofa, looking away and leaning against cushions with some sketches in front of her. These images, reminiscent of Cecil Beaton's famous society profiles, show Rupert's skills as a photographer – and also suggest the love between him and Barbara.[5]

Sometimes Caroline would be the model. Rupert was very taken by the child, whom he would often draw; he also produced a beautiful sculpture of her head. However, there was no sign that he would acknowledge Caroline as his daughter, fond though he was of her. Indeed he had other things to think about. In January 1936 there was unrest in the London Group and a small faction plotted to oust him as president and install Walter Sickert (then in his mid-seventies) in his place. Some of the group's dissatisfaction with Rupert resulted from his many lengthy absences from London when he had been trying to obtain a divorce from his wife Madge – but there was also some disenchantment with the way the Bloomsbury Group members, Duncan Grant, Vanessa Bell and Roger Fry, had dominated the London Group's ethos and activities for the last ten years. In the end, both Rupert and Diana were unseated:

> Although Sickert was not ultimately elected President, the activities of the 'enemy' did enough to undermine Lee and Diana's positions and during the middle of January 1936 they were outvoted by 26 to 20 at the London Group meeting. Vanessa Bell stood up at the end of the meeting and publicly thanked Lee and Diana for their distinguished service to the Group over many years and insisted that a formal letter of thanks be written to them.[6]

Rupert's despondency is evident from the telegram he sent on 18 January to Diana, who was in Barbados escaping the English winter that always exacerbated her asthma. It simply stated: 'Sunk all hands president secretary outvoted 26 20'.[7]

Despite having lost their influential roles in the London Group, their reputations ensured that Rupert and Diana remained important in the London art world, and they were soon swept up in the organization of the International Surrealist Exhibition, which was to be held at the New Burlington Galleries in London between 12 June and 4 July that summer. Roland Penrose and Herbert Read set up an organizing committee and the first meeting took place on Monday 6 April 1936 in Penrose's home in Hampstead, with Rupert as chairman and Diana as secretary. The first two of the eight organizing meetings comprised mainly British artists, including Paul Nash, Henry Moore and David Gascoyne. Later, contact was made with European artists such as Paul Eluard and André Breton in France and E. L. T. Messens in Belgium, who all quickly became involved.[8] About the time of this meeting, Rupert told Diana that he was the father of Barbara's second child, having finally, it seems, accepted some responsibility for his daughter. Diana wrote immediately to Barbara, who was relieved to learn that the truth was out, but also very worried about what might happen next. She replied to Diana the next day with a rather wild and whirling letter:

Dear Diana,

I was glad to get your letter as I thought you must hate me. Rupert said you didn't, but I thought he might be being polite, anyway I'm glad you don't.

I don't know what is the best thing to do about all this and I can't bear to think of you being unhappy, perhaps the thing to do would be for you to live in another country with Rupert, and perhaps you would both be happy. I couldn't forget about him, now I have Caroline, but I could pretend to myself he was dead.

I shall be alone all Easter so I shall have time to think. I am glad you know about everything. I have told so many lies and been so miserable this last year but I can't help loving Caroline although she has caused so much trouble.

I hope I see you after Easter.

Goodbye,

Love from Barbara

Despite the shock she must have felt, Diana dealt calmly with the news that Rupert was Caroline's father. She was used to sorting out the complications of Rupert's love life and 'seemed to take some pride in turning potential enemies into life-long friends'.[9] The two women would indeed become good friends eventually, but there were some difficult times to get through first.

* * *

Rupert and Diana were very busy during the spring and early summer of 1936 with the International Surrealist Exhibition. It was a huge project that included over 390 items by more than seventy artists, including Giorgio de Chirico, Salvador Dalí, Marcel Duchamp, Max Ernst, Dora Maar, René Magritte, Joan Miro, Henry Moore, Meret Oppenheim, Pablo Picasso and Man Ray. Both Rupert and Diana had work accepted for the exhibition. He exhibited a pottery piece entitled *Vase with Tropical Fruit* and a sculpted mobile called *Plus Jamais, object-scenario*. In the spirit of surrealism, which valued the child's unselfconscious interpretation of the world, Diana exhibited a book of drawings she had made between the ages of nine and eleven.[10] The exhibition attracted huge press coverage, not least because of the accompanying events and enactments. André Breton, clothed in green, officially opened the exhibition, soon after which:

Sheila Legge made her way through the crowd in a long white satin dress with coral-coloured belt and shoes, her face completely covered with roses. In one hand she held a pork chop, in the other an artificial leg, but the pork chop had to be abandoned on account of the heat. Dylan Thomas was going round with teacups full of boiled string, politely enquiring 'Do you like it weak or strong?' at the same that a lecture was being held that was being constantly interrupted by an electric bell.[11]

Several talks were given on the nature of surrealism, including one by Salvador Dalí who, dressed in a deep-sea diving suit (to suggest how surrealism plumbed the depths of the unconscious) and holding two borzoi on a leash in one hand and a billiard cue in the other, gave a lecture on 'Authentic Paranoiac Phantoms', in which 'he described a student who had eaten a wardrobe over a period of six months'.[12] After he had been talking for a few minutes he started to suffocate and had to be rescued by his wife Gala, who unscrewed the helmet.[13] Several photographs taken before and during the exhibition feature Rupert and Diana alongside the most important artists who took part. Although both press reviews and the reactions of the general public were mixed, the exhibition made an enormous impact and attracted over 23,000 visitors.

21 Group photograph taken at the International Surrealist Exhibition, London, 1936. Left to right: Rupert Lee, Diana Brinton Lee, Edouard Léon Théodore Mesens, Roland Penrose, Nusch Eluard, Stellan Mörner, Eileen Agar, Herbert Read, Paul Eluard, Edward James, Salvador Dalí

Its effect on Barbara, who had watched its evolution from the sidelines, was profound. Almost thirty years later she was to record its similar impact on a depressed Victoria Green in *A Touch of Mistletoe*:

> I felt numbed most of the time, but can remember being tremendously impressed with the Surrealist Exhibition at the Burlington Galleries. Someone had given me a free pass and I visited it over and over again and it was as if I had been given an extra eye to see with and ordinary objects took on new shapes.[14]

What has been described as surrealism's 'poetics of displacement and estrangement'[15] no doubt spoke strongly to Barbara's feelings of detachment and anxiety during 1936. Her initial interest in surrealism in the early thirties was invigorated by the 1936 exhibition; from then on her painting and writing began to show its influence. That 'extra eye', in Barbara's case, was to develop into a writing talent that would defamiliarize the everyday and exploit the uncanny – and sometimes comic – nature of strange conjunctions. But in the mid-1930s she still thought of herself as an artist rather than a writer and nursed dreams of becoming an important sculptor. She continued to sculpt clay heads when visiting Rupert's studio; the work gave her a quiet satisfaction and an identity beyond that of motherhood. Rupert gave Barbara free passes not only to the International Surrealist Exhibition but to many other exhibition previews, and he sometimes accompanied her. In this way she kept in touch with the London art scene during 1936 and briefly became friends with Leonora Carrington, who was then studying at the Ozenfant Academy of Fine Arts. Carrington's carefree existence provided a sharp contrast with the responsibilities of motherhood that Barbara now carried, but the two women shared a belief that the mysterious and the magical are always present just beneath the surface of everyday life. They also shared a passion for surrealist art. Carrington, with her wild imagination, lifted Barbara's spirits, but she was to leave London in 1937 to live with Max Ernst in Paris. Barbara must have envied her friend's freedom. In time, both women were to become experimental artists, one in paint and one in words, blurring the boundary between the everyday and the fantastic.

Barbara sometimes went with Carrington to exhibitions but more often she went on her own, always taking Caroline and Julian with her as there was no one with whom she could safely leave them. Julian was old enough to enjoy looking at paintings and he also liked going to the parties and soirées held by members of the London Group, although he sometimes had nightmares afterwards. In one of them, the party guests, who were talking with great excitement to each other, had masks over their faces. Many years later Julian recorded the dream in his memoir:

> If I looked carefully I could see the edge of the mask on all of them. I felt horribly afraid and went to Barbara and told her what I had seen, she leant down to comfort me and as she did, I suddenly saw the edge of her mask just

above her ear where it met her hair. I woke up in absolute terror to find myself
in the dark in bed.

Then aged four, Julian was becoming sensitive to those around him and
was perhaps intuitively aware that his mother, beneath her bright social
façade, was depressed. For the usually resourceful and cheerful Barbara
was now feeling despair at the turn her life had taken and was beginning
to suffer from insomnia and exhaustion. During the Surrealist Exhibition,
she wrote to Diana:

> I do want all this awfull [*sic*] business finished one way or another, as things
> are I'm just so miserable all the time, I can't even seem to look after the
> children properly. Perhaps it's just as well I haven't come this afternoon because
> I'm in such a state I can't think properly. But can't we all talk this over when
> this exhibition is over.

The feelings of confusion and inadequacy Barbara expressed in this letter
suggest that perhaps she was suffering from post-natal depression – although
she would have had good reason to be depressed anyway, given her
circumstances.

Exhausted by their work for the Surrealist Exhibition, Rupert and Diana
decided that they would take a holiday after the exhibition closed on 4 July.
Diana loved Spain, which she had visited every year since 1932, and wanted
to travel there in 1936 despite evidence that the country was on the brink
of a civil war between the conservative Nationalists, led by Franco, and the
left-leaning Republicans, led by Azana and helped by the International
Brigade. She was interested in journalism and, like George Orwell, wanted
to record what was happening at first hand. Her ambition was thwarted,
however, when she and Rupert were told they could not enter Spain. Instead,
they holidayed that summer in Malta and the West Indies.[16] Although they
did not manage to visit Spain that year, the Brinton Lees were well versed
in what was happening: in November 1936 the English Surrealists issued
a 'Declaration on Spain' which was published as an insert in *Contemporary
Poetry & Prose*, a magazine inspired by the International Surrealist Exhibition.
The declaration, which the Lees signed, warned against the tyranny of
fascism and criticized the British government's non-intervention policy in
the war; it also called for arms for the people of Spain.

It made Barbara even more depressed to see Diana leading such a full
and politically active life when she was feeling trapped at the age of 29
with two small children. She was also jealous of Diana's holidays with
Rupert. Diana, who still regarded Barbara as a friend and could see that
she was very low, arranged for her and Caroline to have a fortnight's holiday
in Ostend. It was decided that Julian would be looked after temporarily by
his paternal grandmother in the Cotswolds while his mother was away.

Barbara and Caroline left for Belgium in late June and the trip seemed initially to lift her spirits. She wrote to Diana from Ostend:

it's quite nice really as long as one keeps away from the English people who are awfull [*sic*] and wear silk lace evening frocks and rimless glasses, this hotel is full of them but I'm leaving here tomorrow to go to a tiny place with an enormous room with only a bed in it, but plenty of hot water, not in the bed. The cafés are nice and I drink lager and Caroline gets off with the waiters. Her pram is always surrounded by small boys and she loves it, she has bathed in the sea every day except today when it was too cold and wet. The weather has not been too good. I had hoped to get as brown as Madame Breton.

During the first week of Barbara's holiday, her sister Chloe visited Ostend with her latest boyfriend, Charles Marsden. Having left her husband, Chloe had travelled from India to England through Palestine, where she had an affair in December 1935 with John Faraday, an Assistant Superintendent in the British Gendarmerie. In May 1936 her husband Charles Ford sued her for divorce, citing Faraday as co-respondent. Chloe – footloose and fancy free again, although still in touch with Faraday – was now living in a flat at 153 Abbey Road in north London in a house owned by a roguish landlord called Arthur Price. Chloe and Charles persuaded Barbara that she should not accept the situation she found herself in and that she should remonstrate with Diana. Convinced by their arguments, Barbara wrote to Diana on 7 July:

I have told Chloe and Charles everything and they think it's too dreadful and can't understand that Rupert who loves me so much could be so cruel to me and you encourage him. They say of course Rupert must live with and look after Caroline and me, that it is his duty even if he didn't love me, how can he expect John to keep his mistress and child.

All this is true and you must see it. How can you think it right for Rupert to stay with you who he doesn't love, at least he says he doesn't, when he loves me and is responsible for me, he is so weak and you sent him away when I needed him so much. You must see how the thought of him just going away for his holiday and leaving me in all that misery he brought on me, I keep thinking of it all the time. You must see how wicked and selfish you are being by keeping us apart. I have asked Rupert to spend a week with me here but I expect you will stop him, if you think it's right for him to go away and leave me it's right for him to be here with me.

I am writing to John and telling him the whole story and asking him to divorce me. I can't go on living with him loving someone else and the scandal doesn't really worry me. I shall have to live in Chloe's flat as I have nowhere to go to now [...]

I am writing this at about 5 in the morning, I haven't been to sleep yet, I feel so ill and funny from the lack of it all these weeks. Do you know Chloe and the family knew Caroline was Rupert's child because of the likeness, but

they didn't know I loved him or that you know. It was rather nice of them
not to talk to me about it.
    I am writing this by the light from the street lamp. I don't want to wake
Caroline.

Barbara, who in her fragile emotional state was easily influenced by others
at this time, was simply pouring out her feelings on paper. The only clear
thing to emerge from the letter, apart from her anguish, is that she had
decided to divorce her husband.

Quite what Diana would have made of being accused of being 'wicked
and selfish', when she had been footing Barbara's medical bills and had just
paid for a fortnight's holiday for her, can only be imagined, although, of
course, Diana's generosity was never disinterested. She was intent on keeping
Barbara indebted to her as a means of control: the last thing she wanted
was a scandal that might wreck her life with Rupert.

* * *

On her return from Ostend in mid-July, Barbara contacted John immediately,
announcing that she wanted a divorce. The Pemberton family, especially
Guy, John's father, were horrified by the news and rallied to John's cause
with a plan to separate Julian from his mother. On a sunny day in early
August, John collected Julian to take him to a children's fancy dress birthday
party being held at a house in Church Street, near the Thames in Isleworth,
owned by his friends Helen and Andrew Wordsworth. Julian was happy
enough to go, although upset that his 'Red Indian' headdress was not made
of proper feathers but of printed cardboard. After a few hours of high
excitement, when the other children were being retrieved by their parents
at the end of the afternoon, Julian asked for his father. The Wordsworths
then patiently explained that no one would be collecting him: instead he
was to stay with them for a while. It was not a happy time for Julian.
Resentful of their four-year-old visitor, the two Wordsworth boys, Jonathan
and Giles, found ingenious ways of taunting and hurting him. On one
occasion Julian was forced to stand on an ant heap while the boys whacked
him in the mouth with a cricket bat so that his teeth cut his lips and his
tears sent the blood splashing onto his shirt. When, after a few weeks, Julian
was eventually collected from Isleworth by his father, he was not taken
home to his mother in London, but driven to stay with the Allday relatives
who had looked after him when he was two. By this time his paternal
grandmother, Muriel Pemberton, had sold her house in the Cotswolds and
was living with her younger brother Douglas Allday and his wife Marjorie
in their home in the rural Midlands.

Once again, Julian suddenly found himself staying in the Alldays' grand country house in Staffordshire with its extensive grounds and many servants, whose quarters were carefully separated from the main house by the traditional green baize door that marked the boundary between 'upstairs' and 'downstairs'. He and seven-year-old Judith, the Alldays' only child, got along well most of the time. However, life was blighted for the small boy by the family's very formal meals. Everyone sat at a long table in the dining room, with uniformed staff serving food that Julian disliked and refused to eat. He was finally banned from the dining room and had to eat with the nanny. There were consolations though: Julian's uncle, David Pemberton (John's brother), was also staying in the house, as was his younger sister Elizabeth, aged 16 and known as 'Buffy'. David, tall, handsome and 24 years old, was the opposite of his brother John. He was a pilot in the RAF, a responsible and highly capable man but also great fun. He quickly gained Julian's affection by pretending that the radiator fan in his car made it fly, and that the engine had to warm up before the car could taxi and take off. Julian was so small that he couldn't see much through the windscreen except the sky and so half-believed that the car was flying. He also enjoyed watching the tortoises in the garden, which he loved feeding. He was well looked after in a wealthy household but he missed his mother and his little sister. Time seemed to stretch out endlessly before him.

Meanwhile, his father John was being encouraged to spend less time in London and more time in the countryside. John's aunt May, of whom he was very fond, wrote to him from Broadway in Worcestershire on 24 August, inviting him to stay for a few weeks and expressing her great faith in his talents – especially his work 'on the negroes' – and her sorrow at the breakdown of his marriage: 'If the loneliness is more than you feel you can bear ... ring up and say you'd like to come here ... you'd find nothing but sympathy, I assure you.' She also reassured him that his son was being well cared for: 'Julian was *so* good and attractive when he came the other day – we all love him.'

At the end of August 1936 Julian was sent to stay with his grandfather, Guy Pemberton, and his second wife. They lived in Chipping Campden, a pretty Cotswold village in Gloucestershire. Their house, 'Guild Cottage', was much grander than its name implies and certainly much larger than a cottage, having six bedrooms. Guy and Christine Pemberton immediately enrolled Julian in a private primary school nearby. The boy was not happy in Chipping Campden: his grandfather was an impatient man and not good with inquisitive and lively children. The last straw for Guy was an incident concerning his precious grandfather clock. Fascinated by the chain and the swinging pendulum, which he could just glimpse through the glass door, one day Julian hauled himself up the front of the clock so that he could see them better. Although he wasn't heavy, his weight was enough to unbalance the clock and send it over with an enormous crash. Guy was furious. Later, when reunited with his mother, Julian told her that his grandfather used to make him eat his meals in the kitchen with the maid because he was too noisy to join the adults and would not sit still.[17]

*   *   *

Meanwhile, Barbara had become homeless. On her return from Ostend in July 1936, when she told John that she wanted a divorce, they decided that they would no longer live under the same roof. In mid-August John began the business of formally initiating divorce proceedings through the Pemberton family solicitor, naming Rupert as co-respondent and denying that he was Caroline's father.[18] It was agreed that Barbara should move out as soon as possible, although she had nowhere to go. Staying with Chloe was a possibility, but only in the short term. Barbara had temporarily lost her son, her marriage had collapsed, she now knew that her dream of living with Rupert would never be realized – and she had no money. Almost fifty years later, when writing *The Juniper Tree*, Barbara must have looked back on this time when describing Bella Winter's breakdown: 'I had headaches and found it difficult to eat, the food seemed to stick in my throat; but the worst thing was the depression, sometimes really black and terrible, and at other times just under the surface waiting to pounce.'[19] Barbara was at her lowest ebb and one evening she tried to kill herself. There is no detailed information available about this attempted suicide – it is merely included in a list of 'sins' in a letter she later sent to Diana – but, like Bella, she probably took sedatives with alcohol. Dr Gillie was called in immediately, which suggests that Barbara was staying with Diana and Rupert. Diana assured Barbara that she could live with them at 7 St Quintin Avenue until she and Rupert had worked out a plan for her future. It was a kind act, considering the vituperative letter Barbara had written from Ostend, although no doubt Diana's generosity was once again linked to her desire to control the situation in order to avoid a scandal. There were scenes in which harsh words were exchanged and the two women wept. Rupert, hating confrontation, seems to have kept a low profile.

On 29 August, when Diana and Rupert were out and Barbara was alone in the house, she typed a letter – on Diana's typewriter and on Diana's headed notepaper – to Reginald Brinton, Diana's father, who lived in Kidderminster and who was still chairman of Brintons, the carpet manufacturing business. Inspired by mixed feelings of despair and desperation, the incoherent and misspelled letter must have come as quite a surprise to the 66-year-old businessman:

I am indeed sorry to be writing you this letter as I am afraid it will be a great shock to you, but you are now the only person who can help me or at least put my life in some kind of order.

Rupert Lee and Diana are not married, he has never been divorced from Madge Pemberton who is my husband's aunt and anything he has said to the contrary is quite untrue. Rupert has been my lover for the last two years and I have a child by him, we had one because we both wanted one very much, she is nine months old now. He asked me to go away with him since [sic] she was born and said he would look after me but now he won't because of Diana although she knows about our child and that untill [sic] a month ago we were still lovers.

My husband is divorcing me now and I have no parents, relations except for sisters and only ten shillings and nothing I can sell. I have lost my little boy through this and the only person I know well and love is Rupert and of course my children, he loves me but thinks it's his duty to stay with Diana now although up to a few weeks ago he was asking me to go away with him, and I know we could have been happy together and that he could get a job abroad if only Diana would let him. I am writing to you to ask Diana to give him up, she has a home, money and friends and in any case her so called marriage will be wrecked by this divorce. Rupert, Caroline and I are a family and we must be together and I do love him so much even if he is weak and awful, I can't bear to see him doing no work and being kept by a woman.

I have been staying with Diana the last few weeks and Caroline too as I have been very ill and have no were [sic] else to go, it is very kind of her to have us but I can't stay any longer now I have sent this letter and I do feel so awful being here and taking so much from her under the circumstances. It is hardly fair to expect her to keep Rupert, his mistress and his child.

I am sorry for all the trouble this letter will cause you and the only reason I am writing it is because I feel you are the only person who can now have any influence with them.

I expect you will be surprised to hear that in spite of all this I am very fond of Diana and always shall be.

Barbara Pemberton

The letter suggests that Barbara was at her wits' end and that her illness was mental rather than physical. She was no doubt egged on to write to Diana's father by her sister Chloe, who was continually urging Barbara to fight for her rights. Chloe had also contacted their brother, Dennis, who was alarmed by Barbara's plight and ready to help, so long as no scandal touched his own family. The letter to Diana's father, not surprisingly, did not have the effect Barbara intended. Reginald Brinton dealt with its tone of high drama with considerable *sang froid*. He replied immediately, agreeing that Barbara's situation was 'deplorable' but that he did not intend to intervene: 'The solution must be worked out by the parties; and I really do not see my way to take any action.' He also sent Barbara's letter to his daughter, who wrote to him the same day, giving her side of the story. Thanking Diana for her explanation, he responded, 'Of course the letter is slanderous and libellous, but I am sure you do not want to take any legal action. I won't say a word to anyone', and signed off 'Your loving father'. Instead of alienating Reginald Brinton from his daughter, Barbara's letter had only succeeded in uniting them against what they saw as her irrational behaviour.

The failure of her plan to get Diana's father on her side threw Barbara into even deeper despair. On 2 September, still living with Caroline in Diana's house, she wrote another extraordinary letter, again typed on Diana's typewriter. This time it was addressed to Diana. In it Barbara explained why she had disappeared for several hours the previous day: she had been trying to contact John about the divorce but she had also been deeply upset by the fact that Diana and Rupert were about to go away together again and felt she needed to be on her own:

> You see I couldn't bear the thought of Rupert going away with you for the week-end, I had told Rupert but I didn't want to tell you in case there was another scene where everyone says awful things to each other. I suggested that Rupert could come away with me to my brother's the following week-end, but he said he couldn't because of you, he never cares how much I am hurt as long as you are not, yet he still says he loves me.
>
> It was very kind of you to have me in your house but after all you and Rupert have brought all this trouble on me, if you had been willing to share him more none of this would have happened in any case you should have let Rupert go away with me when he first wanted to when Caroline was tiny, we could and perhaps one day now will be very happy together. This letter isn't a bit what I meant it to be but Caroline is screaming [...]
>
> I expect you will never forgive me for writing to your father, but I hope he will make you give Rupert up when he knows you are not married and that we have a child. You said to Chloe that it wasn't certain that Caroline was Rupert's child – that is absurd, only Rupert had made love to me the previous month and no one did for at least ten weeks after she started, anyway we can always have a blood test [...]
>
> I am leaving here mid-day, I have nowhere to go as you know so I suppose I should go to the workhouse but I can't do that so I shall go to the Eiffel Tower. I know Mr. Stulick and some of the people who stay there.
>
> I don't expect I shall ever see you again but in spite of everything I am very fond of you and I could have been very happy in your house under different circumstances [...]
>
> I have had to give my beautiful Caroline up so I have nothing at all now.

Barbara clearly fully intended to leave Caroline behind when she left St Quintin Avenue, as she wrote on the back of her daughter's birth certificate, left with the letter, 'Thank you very much for having me but I have gone now. B.' Her plan to fling herself on the mercy of the owner of the Eiffel

Tower in Percy Street in Fitzrovia – an expensive restaurant patronized by better-off artists and bohemians – never materialized.[20]

Barbara did not in the end abandon Caroline because Rupert and Diana returned earlier than expected, discovering the letter and a distraught Barbara before she had a chance to put her plan into action. There was an angry and tearful scene between the two women. Despite feeling distressed, Diana moved swiftly into action. She immediately gave Barbara some money and a suitcase full of food for Caroline, of whom she had grown very fond. She also suggested that, in the short term, Barbara should stay with Frank Slater, an artist friend of hers who lived in Portsdown Road (now Randolph Avenue) in Maida Vale. She reassured Barbara that she would not be penniless: she would arrange for an allowance of £3 a week (about £254 now) to be paid into her bank account for four months. Once Barbara had left St Quintin Avenue, Diana wrote to Frank Slater confirming what they had arranged by telephone, but adding, 'It is to be understood that this allowance will cease at once if I find she has been talking or writing unwisely about Rupert and myself, or if a writ is served on him in connection with her divorce.'

Diana then contacted a private detective agency and asked them to watch John Pemberton's every move for evidence of adultery. She and Rupert had decided that Barbara's decision to divorce her husband, naming Rupert as the father of her daughter in the process, would inevitably embroil them in gossip and scandal. It might even bring to light the fact that they were not legally man and wife. However, if the divorce could be taken forward by proving that John was an adulterer, then she and Rupert could be kept out of it. The agency submitted several reports during early September, in one of which the private detective described John Pemberton as leaving a flat in Percy Street, off Tottenham Court Road, in the company of a woman 'undoubtedly of the negress type […] about 28 years of age' with 'large dark eyes, long bobbed black hair' and wearing 'large ear-rings'. This was no doubt Marie, John's girlfriend, whose flat in Percy Street was now his second home. The private detective seemed to derive puritanical pleasure from noting how often John visited the Wheatsheaf pub and the frequency with which he and his friends were 'all slightly under the influence of drink'. His ignorance of the artistic world, however, led him to spell the name of one of these friends, Dylan Thomas, as 'Dillon'.[21]

Diana's arrangement with Slater lasted only a few days. Once he fully grasped the nature of the relationship between her, Rupert and Barbara (who no doubt spilled the beans to him), he took fright and wrote to Diana saying that he did not wish to be 'involved in an affair so essentially intimate and personal'. Barbara was now homeless again and turned to Chloe for advice and comfort. Chloe knew that her landlord Arthur Price was currently converting 16 Kilburn Priory, a large semi-detached house on the edge of

Kilburn and Maida Vale. Within a short time Barbara had rented the basement flat there. Returning her key to the front door of 7 St Quintin Avenue, she wrote to Diana:

> I have no feeling at all for Rupert any more except a longing never to see or hear about him again, he was quite a different man yesterday – all the things I loved him for had gone, I expect I just imagined he was marvellous and never understood him at all. You said I wouldn't love him if I saw enough of him you were right. I feel quite lost and vague not loving him anymore, as if I was walking on snow or all the world was made of cotton wool, but I'm not happy or unhappy.

She signed off by offering to let Diana and Rupert have Caroline to stay with them in St Quintin Avenue for the occasional weekend. In her reply, sent the next day, Diana wrote:

> I hope you won't feel too bad about R. You mustn't think now that his feeling for you wasn't genuine. He was immensely flattered by your conception of him and in that way you gave him something that no one else did. When he was with you he perhaps unconsciously tried to be what you liked, but he knew he wasn't really what you needed to build your life on. You see I like the other side of him as well. We have been through so much together, and if some of his life has been rather embittering, I have shared it.

She also confessed that she intended to do everything she could to stop the divorce proceedings that Barbara was about to initiate because they would involve Rupert in a scandal:

> I hope you won't think it horrid of me to try and stop/oppose this divorce. I know you must get free if you are to re-marry, but I think it would be much better if it could be with the person concerned. This is the usual thing and is neat and tidy and doesn't upset anybody. I don't believe you realize what a nasty mess and scandal there will be if everything is made public and the Pemberton feud re-opened. It is bound to affect their attitude to you and you can't be independent of them as long as Julian isn't and John you know is weak and will do anything for money. Naturally they will try to ruin R and I don't blame them or you, if you feel that way, but neither can you blame us if we are forced to defend ourselves. Also we are interested in you and Caroline and want to help you but if R has to pay J damages and costs we shan't be able to and it won't do you any good.

Diana's 'interest' in Caroline was more than that; by now she had become very attached to the child who was, after all, Rupert's daughter. She signed off by saying that she and Rupert would very much like to have Caroline occasionally because she missed her so much and that she hoped Barbara would 'find it a comfort to be free'.

Installed in her new flat by 12 September 1936, Barbara certainly felt much happier now that she had her own things about her and some independence: 'I even enjoy washing up', she wrote to Diana. Meanwhile, Nan, desperately worried about Barbara's situation, had visited Diana together with Francis Codd (who still nursed an unrequited love for Barbara) to ask her for more support for her sister. Diana responded by suggesting that she could help Barbara set up a small business of some kind that would allow her to become independent financially. Having heard about this plan from Nan, Barbara wrote to Diana expressing her gratitude and telling her that she would soon be going to stay with some friends in Stratford-upon-Avon. There was more than one reason behind her decision to take a holiday in that area. She desperately wanted to see Julian, who was still living with his grandfather in Chipping Camden, not far from Stratford. She also felt in need of some peace and quiet away from London. Finally, Arthur Price, the landlord of her new flat, had promised to finish some work on it, and they had agreed he would arrange for it to be done while she was away.

Barbara also took the opportunity to be frank with Diana in a letter that suggests her complex feelings about their relationship:

> you are the only woman outside my family I'm not shy of and all the time I knew you I have had to try and stop myself liking you. Now I don't love Rupert any more I have no bitter or unkind feelings for you at all. Rupert said the last time I saw him how well you had behaved over all this and how badly I had but I was fighting a loosing [*sic*] battle for the thing that meant more than any other thing, except perhaps the children, in the world to me. I suppose I feel about Rupert now like religious people must feel when God goes back on them but I know I never want to see him any more ever.

In some respects, Barbara had indeed behaved badly – using emotional blackmail to try to manipulate both Diana and her father, for example – but arguably her first husband and her lover had behaved far worse. Moreover, the combination of numbness, apathy and rage that Barbara felt at this time suggests a woman under great mental and emotional strain and possibly suffering from severe post-natal depression. At times she had felt hopeless and alone, with her life spinning out of control. Like Bella Winter in *The Juniper Tree*, whose 'poor disordered mind' leads her to act very strangely,[22] Barbara's behaviour at this time was out of character. Now that she finally had somewhere to live that was her own, she began to feel independent and calmer, despite the fact that she relied on Diana for an allowance to pay her rent. The next step was to reclaim Julian.

5

The Pemberton persecution

In early October 1936 Barbara went to Stratford-upon-Avon, taking Caroline with her. She stayed with Frederick Wellstood, a friend of John's father. A local historian who had published several books, he was secretary and librarian to the Shakespeare Birthplace Trust, which was housed in the sixteenth-century building in Henley Street where Shakespeare had been born. The house was now a museum and library for which Wellstood was responsible. He and his family lived close by in the Custodian's House (which came with his job) at 19 Henley Street, a pleasant half-timbered building with mullion windows.[1] Barbara did not mention any of her past troubles to Wellstood: she had fled to Stratford in order to get away from London and clear her mind. Wellstood and his family welcomed her and did their best to make her feel at home. Seeing how thin and tired she looked, they plied her with food and urged her to rest.

Barbara felt she had found a temporary refuge in the Wellstood home; she began to relax but the respite from anxiety was not to last. Within a few days her peace was shattered when Wellstood received a letter from Guy Pemberton concerning his son's relationship with Barbara. In August, John had initiated formal divorce proceedings but, before leaving for Stratford, Barbara had persuaded her husband to drop them, at least in the short term. This change of heart was the result of Diana's urgent request that the divorce should not be pursued in case any scandal should touch her and Rupert. As Diana was her only hope of financial aid, it was in Barbara's interest to agree, despite her desire to end her marriage legally. John was easily persuaded and went along with the change of plan, telling the family solicitor, Mr O'Kelly, to stop the proceedings. However, John's father soon got wind of the situation and immediately wrote a four-page letter to his friend in Stratford-upon-Avon railing against Barbara and describing her as 'an adulteress and a wicked woman'. He had hoped that John would be able to claim punitive damages from Barbara – an award of money that is meant to punish the defendant for egregious bad behaviour – and that he and his wife would gain custody of Julian. He was furious that this now seemed unlikely and claimed in the letter that Julian had forgotten all about 'that dreadful woman his mother', firmly declaring that Barbara would never see her son again.[2]

Far from persuading Frederick Wellstood to throw Barbara out of his home, Guy's letter had the opposite effect. Shocked by his friend's outburst, Wellstood assured Barbara that she could stay with him and his family as long as she wished. Although touched by their concern, Barbara still felt uneasy and wrote to Diana: 'Caroline sleeps in the birthplace garden and eats vegetables from Ann Hathaway's. These people are so kind to me and never stop making me eat, but I am so worried it doesn't seem to make me any fatter, it seems as if there will never be any peace for me.' That day, Barbara telephoned John who said he knew of his father's intentions; he agreed that she had a right to see Julian but he was adamant that their son should continue living with his grandfather. It would be in their son's best interests he said – and would also guarantee that the allowance his father was now sending him would continue, although he did not tell Barbara this.

Barbara wrote the same day to Diana about what she called 'the Pemberton Persecution'. She knew that Guy Pemberton and his second wife Christine had no legal right to keep Julian against her will, and was particularly upset that they had enrolled him at a local school without telling her. Conscious of Diana's deep affection for Caroline, Barbara included a short bulletin on her daughter's progress: 'She is so marvellous, Diana. Her eyelashes quite an inch long and her face so rosy, she is almost mobbed every time she goes out. She is so good and never cries except between the spoonfuls of her food, she has her meals in a high chair and eats quite grown-up things now.' She also asked if Diana would be kind enough to transfer some money into her bank account so that she could buy a train ticket to London and pay the next month's rent on her flat. She concluded: 'I don't expect to be happy, I don't mind as long as I'm not unhappy but dreadful things seem to never stop happening all the time, there is no space between them.'

*   *   *

On her return to London, Barbara learned that not only John's father, but also his mother, Muriel Pemberton, were now pressing him to restart divorce proceedings. Muriel had decided that she would make a more suitable guardian than her ex-husband Guy, and that Julian, of whom she was very fond, should live with her and the Alldays in Staffordshire. She was even threatening to contact Diana's father in the hope of forcing him to intervene, unaware that Barbara had already written to him. Clearly there were now tensions within the Pemberton family as to how to proceed. In the light of this complication – of which she was informed by a well-wisher – Barbara decided that divorce was the best way forward after all if she wished to be free of the Pemberton family. Acting on that idea, she went to Belsize Park, hoping to see John so that she could explain why she had changed her mind again. She was shocked by the state of the flat, describing it to Diana as 'such a disgusting place even the walls are covered in cats' messes and mould growing out of the floor, no sheets on the bed – and the smell!' John was not there but she noticed an open letter on the kitchen table. It was from Guy Pemberton to his son and had been written on the same day as the letter he wrote to Frederick Wellstood:

Dear John,

It is very good of you to say that you do not wish me to be worried with your affairs or to put me to any expense, but you overlook one factor, it is not only your 'your affair' but a family affair. The family name is very much involved and my reputation and Julian's future depends entirely on your action now.

You say you are dropping this Divorce because they will contest it, that it will be costly and that your evidence is slim, is it not also a fact that you are fearsome as to what would come out about yourself as well? Barbara is spreading the most terrible rumours about you both by letter to your Mother and by mouth to the Wellstoods and others in Stratford on Avon, about your infidelities and connections with black women, it is all too foul – you must do something to stop it.

If you only have a separation the following clauses must be embodied in it.

1 That she admits you are not the father of Caroline and are not responsible for her maintenance in any way, and that she does not go by the name of Pemberton, she must be Caroline Bayley. This is of the greatest urgency, we none of us want Rupert's bastard called by our family name, you will be cut off by everyone in the family, myself included, if you allow this.

2 You must have sole control of Julian and it must be stated that until you have a proper home of your own he lives with me and I will keep and educate him. I am not going to do this and then for Barbara to suddenly be able to get him away, I must be protected if I am going to do it.

3 You cannot make yourself responsible for any payments to Barbara as you could not keep them up and if you failed to keep them up you would be put into Court for non-maintenance and thus play into their hands entirely. Rupert must be made to find the maintenance [...]

We all want to help you but you must realize your responsibilities to us and especially to Julian and not just regard it as your own affair.

Of course we have all guessed, your mother and Aunt included, all along who the swine was, Diana's paid stallion, the greatest Womanizer in London, filthy brute, how you could introduce such a man into your family passes my comprehension.

You must see Mr. O'Kelly on these points, I have written to him on similar lines. I will pay all expenses if you will do this properly but not unless.

Christine took Julian to Birmingham in the week and bought all his winter clothes, he has started school and loves it.

Write and tell me you are acting on these lines and I shall be much happier, all this is thoroughly upsetting my work and health but I cannot sit down and do nothing when I see you being bamboozled and the family name being dragged in the mud.

Love from

Dad

Barbara was furious. She immediately wrote to Diana, enclosing Guy Pemberton's letter and vowing that Caroline would always be called 'Caroline Pemberton': 'After this I will never change her name although I hate it.' As far as John's 'connections with black women' were concerned, she was not at all judgmental but thought that his frequenting 'black clubs' till four in the morning was not a good idea. Still fond of him, she worried about his health, but 'if I say anything he jumps at me and says I am narrow minded and says he had such a boring time with me and the children he is making up for it now' – words echoed later by Charles in *Our Spoons Came from Woolworths*, who declares to his wife 'I am very fond of you, but I loathe this domestic life. The children are quite beautiful, but they don't mean a thing to me.'[3] Aware that Diana always wanted news of Caroline, she mentioned that her daughter was well – 'but I feel as if I would give ten years of my life to play with Julian for one day'. She was still thinking about how to reclaim her son, although her one-roomed flat at 16a Kilburn Priory was certainly not big enough for all three of them. Now she suggested that a possible solution would be to lease or own a house and let out furnished rooms, providing breakfast for her tenants; would Diana consider financing such a venture? This would mean she would not have to pay childcare costs and 'everything would be so bright and clean people would never want to leave me. I have been to see a lot of houses but nothing quite right yet and I would like to talk to you about it first.' The letter finished with the wish that 'all the Pembertons except Julian would drop down dead'. In a postscript she spelled out how important it was that any money given or loaned to her should come directly from Diana, not Rupert, otherwise her position in future divorce proceedings would be compromised.

Diana replied that she would be happy to discuss the possibility of Barbara running a guest house. She also suggested that Barbara should see a solicitor about the breakdown of her marriage. The solicitor Barbara saw advised her that a court would look kindly on the case, given John's irresponsible behaviour, and that it would certainly allow a divorce in her favour so long as John admitted to being the guilty party. He also stressed that Guy Pemberton had no legal right to prevent Barbara from seeing Julian. In fact, he went further and suggested to Barbara that she should reclaim her son

by forcibly removing him from his grandfather's home. Barbara seized on
the idea immediately. She could not, this time, ask Rupert to be her driver,
so she asked Francis Codd to help her out.

They set off for Chipping Campden on a bright day in October, Barbara
feeling very nervous. On the way, they decided to go straight to Julian's
school, rather than to Guild Cottage. They found it easily and arrived just
as the bell was ringing to signal the end of the day. As Julian came out of
school, the Pembertons' maid appeared to collect him. Intervening smartly,
Barbara grabbed Julian's arm and pushed him into the car. Once he had
recovered from the shock of being effectively kidnapped, Julian clung to his
mother and begged her not to send him back to his grandfather, who called
him 'shrimp' and was constantly telling him to be quiet. Later that day, and
during the following days, numerous telegrams from Guy Pemberton arrived
at Kilburn Priory demanding the return of his grandson and threatening to
withdraw all funding if this did not happen. Barbara ignored them all. Having
won this victory over the Pembertons, she decided to send Julian away again
so that he could not be snatched from Kilburn Priory by either John or his
father. Having been briefly reunited with his mother and sister, Julian was
soon returned to the Alldays and Muriel Pemberton in Staffordshire, who
promised not to allow her ex-husband Guy anywhere near her grandson.

Retribution was swift. John turned up at Barbara's flat the next evening
and demanded custody of his son – even though he was in no position to
look after him properly – because his father had threatened to cut him off
financially if he did not do so. Tempers flared and Barbara said she wanted
a formal separation because of his inadequacy as a husband and a father.
John retorted that no one would believe her side of the story as he and his
relatives had been telling everyone that she was mad and, indeed, one of
Guy's telegrams had threatened to have her certified as 'insane'. In a letter
to Diana sent later that evening, Barbara wrote:

> I wish you would get Gillie to write to John and tell him that if someone tries
> to distroy [*sic*] themselves after five years of acute poverty and strain and an
> unhappy love affair on top of it all it doesn't mean they are mad and he has
> no right to go about saying such a dreadful thing without any authority.

Despite their differences concerning Julian, John and Barbara managed
to keep talking and finally agreed to an amicable separation. They decided
they would see a solicitor and ask for a document stating that so long as
Barbara could provide a home for Julian, he should live with his mother.
The document was also to stipulate that John was not responsible for
Barbara's debts, but that he should pay for Julian's education and could
have access to him whenever he wished. There would, in addition, be a
clause allowing Julian to spend a month each year with his grandmother,

Muriel Pemberton – Barbara liked John's mother and knew she was good with children – but the clause also stipulated that he was not to stay with any other of John's relatives without her permission. It seemed an adult and sensible way to solve the current difficult situation. The divorce could come later. By this time John was so sick and tired of the constant arguments, both with Barbara and with his family, that he was willing to sacrifice any financial help promised by his father for some peace. He was also very tractable: in a letter written to her solicitor in mid-October, Diana wrote, 'John Pemberton will usually agree to anything suggested by the last person he sees.' However, when John told his father what he and Barbara had agreed, Guy Pemberton was furious and threatened to intervene. At that point, Diana suggested that Barbara and John should use her solicitor to draw up the separation agreement, rather than Mr O'Kelly, the Pemberton family solicitor.

This was a disaster for Barbara. If the Brinton family had chosen a good doctor in Annis Gillie, they had certainly chosen a good solicitor in E. S. P. Haynes, a leading divorce lawyer, whose practice was based in New Square, Lincoln's Inn. A friend to several well-known authors, including G. K. Chesterton, John Buchan and H. G. Wells, Haynes had advised many famous people during their divorce cases, including Evelyn Waugh, who probably drew on him when creating the character of Uncle Lionel in *Scoop*. Diana's solicitor was a colourful and slightly eccentric figure who took three-hour lunches and who would urinate in a chamber pot, his back turned to astonished clients, rather than trudge up a flight of stairs to the ancient lavatory.[4] He had a sharp mind, however, and campaigned tirelessly for reform of the divorce laws in England. In 1936 obtaining a divorce was a complex and messy affair: it could be granted only on the grounds that one party had committed adultery and that the other party was entirely innocent – and that there had been no collusion between the two. The King's Proctor, a government lawyer, had the power to invade private lives in order to investigate any possible collusion and could order detectives to question anyone associated with the unlucky couple, however briefly, from hotel owners to chambermaids to railway guards. For the sum of five shillings, any member of the public could demand that the King's Proctor investigate the claimants in a pending divorce case. Barbara was worried: she knew that Guy Pemberton would waste no time in having her past investigated so as to reveal her affairs with other men, including Rupert. And Diana had already hired private detectives in the hope of proving John's adultery. But if both parties had committed adultery, it was in the court's power to refuse a divorce. As John and Barbara had both had affairs and there was evidence of collusion – because John had pleaded with Rupert in front of witnesses to take Barbara away[5] – they were in a difficult position.

And even if they did manage to procure a divorce, the proceedings would inevitably tarnish one, if not both, of their names.

Barbara was easily manipulated by Diana and Haynes, who was clearly puzzled by Diana's generosity in paying all Barbara's legal fees. He advised Barbara that, for the time being, she and John should shelve the idea of divorce and await reforms in the law which he knew would be introduced in the near future.[6] Privately, Haynes urged Diana to persuade Barbara to hand over Rupert's love letters to her, in which he had made many rash promises. If Barbara had been able to afford an independent lawyer, no doubt she would have been advised to apply for an affiliation order against Rupert for Caroline's maintenance. But Barbara's only legal advice came from Diana's lawyer, and it was to his advantage to act in the interest of his client Diana Brinton Lee rather than Barbara Pemberton. Although she sometimes felt that his advice was not impartial and occasionally complained tearfully about it, Barbara did what he asked her to do.

Needing to keep Haynes fully informed, Diana wrote to him on 19 October, telling him that she was making Barbara an allowance of £3 a week (about £254 today), at least until the end of the year, and also that she had promised to set her up in some kind of business, 'but this is merely a friendly arrangement without prejudice on either side'. In exchange, Barbara promised to give Diana the letters from Rupert. Diana was anxious to get hold of them because they provided written evidence that Rupert had been Barbara's lover and was Caroline's father. If Diana could destroy them, then not only would any scandal be avoided but Barbara's chances of ever claiming financial support from Rupert would be diminished. The deal was done and Barbara gave Diana the letters, but, on learning that Diana had burned them, she wrote: 'you don't seem to realize how hurt it makes me feel that Rupert is so ashamed of having a child by me, he can't bear anyone to know, I have had no happiness since the day she first started but it doesn't stop me loving or being proud of her'. In July, just before her suicide attempt, Barbara had written a confessional document citing Rupert as her daughter's father but, as Diana took care to point out to Haynes, this was written 'at a time when her own doctor and a mental specialist wanted to certify her', so it would be worthless in a court of law. She no doubt concealed the fact that the doctor in question was Annis Gillie, the Brinton family doctor and therefore hardly unbiased. Diana was doing everything she could to protect Rupert and her relationship with him while simultaneously feeling compassion for Barbara and her children.

An extraordinary relationship was developing between Diana and Barbara: a genuine affection between the two women and a shared concern for Caroline's welfare was offset by a power struggle that involved manipulation and the use of emotional blackmail on both sides. Whatever the motives for her generosity, Diana's records show that she spent at least £350 on Barbara in 1936 (almost £30,000 today) – and she was about to spend more by investing in a property that Barbara could manage. Diana was a woman of independent means, her wealth deriving from her dividends in Brinton Carpets, but she was not fabulously rich. The financial arrangements between the two women were the result of a complex blend of personalities and circumstances that benefited them both, although they constrained Barbara in several ways, and at times her resentment at what she saw as bribery spilled over. In a letter written in late October she declared that she would pay Diana back every penny of the £3 a week she had received so far and wanted it no more: 'You imagine that you are being noble in letting me have £3 a week and expect me to be grateful and that I will "stay put" for life because for a few weeks you have helped me.' The alternative, though, was returning to 'the poverty', the mere thought of which terrified Barbara. By the end of October, she realized that Diana was the only person who could help her – and the more she turned to Diana, the colder she felt towards Rupert, admitting to Diana that: 'he never loved me really, only liked making love to me, all the things he said to me and when he made love to me after Caroline came he never meant it all, he was only just using me like a prostitute'. It had been a bitter lesson.

* * *

It was perhaps no coincidence that the first house Barbara found that she thought suitable for renovation and conversion into flats was in Greencroft Gardens in north London, where her sister Chloe had lived before she left for India. Diana and Rupert sifted through the builder's estimate very carefully, but decided the project was too expensive. Within a few days, Barbara came up with another suggestion – obviously at Chloe's prompting, since she and Barbara now shared the same landlord, Arthur Price. He was, according to a letter Barbara wrote to Diana in early November, 'a nice honest man', and he was willing to sell on the lease for the whole of 16 Kilburn Priory so that Barbara could manage the house and collect the rents from the other flats in it. This seemed the ideal solution to Barbara's predicament: it would mean she could look after the children at home and would not need to go out to work. Price put together paperwork which outlined the business plan for 16 Kilburn Priory and Barbara immediately sent it to Diana on 3 November.

Barbara was used to Diana answering her letters straight away but she heard nothing. This threw her into a highly emotional state and after six days she wrote an angry and incoherent letter to Diana in which she said she regretted trusting her. Her friends and two solicitors had told her she should have applied for an affiliation order during the first year of Caroline's life (Caroline had just had her first birthday, so it was now too late). She assumed that Diana's silence meant that she was not willing to fund the Kilburn Priory project but – since she had already told Price she would go ahead with it – she would now, she claimed, be forced to turn to prostitution to raise the money.

Diana responded the following day, explaining that she had simply been too pressed to write. They had people staying with them and she and Rupert (no longer president of the London Group but still on its Working Committee) had been so busy helping to set up the group's 34th Annual Exhibition that they had not had a spare minute. Diana and Rupert were clearly still living a life packed with challenge and intellectual stimulation, from which Barbara was now excluded. Diana had every intention, she wrote, of asking Price to come over one day the following week to discuss the matter, 'but' she added, tongue in cheek, 'if, as I gather from your letter, you intend to embark at once upon a career, of course I suppose I mustn't do this'. Her letter then took a more sober turn:

> Seriously, I do wish you wouldn't get so worked up the whole time about everything, it makes it so difficult to help you. If I were just out to do you down, it would be easy, it is only because I have your welfare at heart that there is any problem at all. Otherwise, I should just hand your two last letters to the police and call it a day. I wish you would get it into your head once and for all that you have no hold over me except in so far as I have decent and kindly feelings and am fond of you and Caroline. I had a suspicion when I got your earlier letter that someone was trying to get you to blackmail me. If so, they are being criminally foolish. You say you are 'advised' not to trust me! I don't know who your advisers are and if you don't trust me by now I certainly can't make you but I think you might remember that I am the only person connected with this case who has been perfectly consistent and has made personal sacrifices from a sense of what was right. One of my great difficulties has been that there was nobody else who seemed to care a damn what became of you or was willing to put themselves out in any way [...] I won't discuss threats or any nonsense of that sort. I know that left to yourself you are an honest and generous person and you know that I am, so there.

Diana was almost certainly right in thinking that someone else was behind the veiled threats in Barbara's letter. It might have been Arthur Price, but it was more probably Chloe, who was still urging Barbara to get as much as she could out of the Brinton Lees. However, 'Price', as he was more usually known, was indeed becoming more than just a landlord and was beginning to present himself to Barbara as someone who had her best interests at heart.

In her reply Barbara hotly denied she was blackmailing Diana and that there was anything 'criminal' in her letters:

> but if you want to hand them to the police I will write all the criminal things I have done now so you really will have something to take to the police if you want to. I admit I have had an abortion and tried to kill myself and have got a revolver and no licence in case a tramp got in the window at night, and I've pulled flower roots up out of empty house gardens and I expect there are lots of other things too.

She tried to explain how she loathed being dependent on Diana and wrote remorsefully, 'I can't see how you can be fond of me because I always take a pleasure in showing you how awful I can be.' She was lonely, she said, and finding it hard to concentrate on sculpting or reading, both of which used to give her great pleasure. The only other person who seemed to care for her, apart from Diana, was Francis Codd, who was taking her out that evening:

> I can never feel grateful enough to Francis for still thinking I'm worth loving after the way I've treated him and my sordid life, I never talk to him about Rupert and everything because I don't want him to think of me with all that mess around me, but however grateful I am I can't ever love him.

Francis, her long-suffering admirer, was obviously hoping that his persistence might win the day.

A short while after this highly emotional exchange of letters, Annis Gillie sent Diana a formal document stating:

> This is to certify that, in my opinion, Mrs Barbara Pemberton has been in a mentally unstable condition at intervals, for some months. This was unusually serious in July 1936, when she could not be held responsible for many of her actions or statements with regard to herself or other people.

In an accompanying note, Dr Gillie warned Diana not to expect Barbara to behave rationally:

> We doubt if very much permanent improvement is to be hoped for, the history is so long, and the attitude to life is so definite. I enclose a certificate here. I think that it is so important that you should have it. Keep the document for a real emergency but do feel free to use it then [...]

The note offered a harsh prognosis, suggesting that Barbara's mentally fragile state when she attempted suicide was likely to continue indefinitely. Her mood swings and bizarre behaviour would today no doubt be seen as symptoms of severe post-natal depression, but this condition was not medically recognized until the mid-1990s. More sympathetic to the Brinton family than to her patient, Dr Gillie clearly wished to protect Diana against any future claims that Barbara might make. It is possible that Diana initiated the certification; she could be calculating as well as kind. The certificate would certainly have been useful to flourish in court had Barbara tried to make legal claims on Rupert.

*   *   *

The Kilburn Priory plan gradually moved ahead. In December, Price – through his solicitor – offered the lease for the whole of number 16 to Diana and she bought it for the sum of £300 (about £25,370 today). She paid £250 outright and Barbara agreed to pay the remaining £50 over the next two years at a rate of three pounds and three shillings a week. She would collect the rents from the other flats, paying most of the money into Diana's account while keeping a percentage for herself as income out of which she would repay Price. This meant that, after the purchase of 16 Kilburn Priory, Barbara became Price's assignee and she was in his debt to the tune of £50. The arrangement was designed to put Barbara on her feet but it kept her financially indebted to Price and emotionally indebted to Diana. However, now that she had a guaranteed, albeit small, income, Barbara could legitimately ask the Alldays to return Julian to her. By December 1936 she had Julian and Caroline living with her once again. Barbara was delighted that both her children were with her for Christmas, a time she loved. Before the New Year, Diana made Barbara an allowance of £42 for 1937 (about £3,500 today) and took out a life insurance policy for Caroline that contained a 'Special Education Option'; this meant the policy could be cashed in when Caroline was 14 in order to pay for her education. Things were looking up and Barbara felt in much better spirits: 'I am very well and quite glad not to be dead now', she wrote with wry humour to Diana.

By the spring of 1937 Barbara had decided she would enrol Julian, now five, in a kindergarten school and would pay someone to look after Caroline during the day so that she could work as a photographic model for advertisements or as a crowd extra. She had by now abandoned the idea of making money as a freelance artist or sculptor while at home with the children, as it had soon proved unrealistic. And collecting the rents at 16 Kilburn Priory was not proving as profitable or as easy as she had hoped: the flats were small and basic so tenants tended to move on fairly quickly – and if they did a midnight flit without paying, Barbara was left high and dry. She also wanted an independent source of income so that she would not be entirely reliant on Diana if money became tight. Her aim was to earn at least £3 a week (about £250 in today's money) so that she could afford Julian's school fees and childcare for Caroline; by this time she had given up expecting any financial help from John although they remained on friendly terms.

Francis Codd continued to court her and helped with practical matters, doing all the heavy moving work required in the flat. He was generous and liked to bring her presents; using his printing works he provided her with elegant thin blue writing paper headed in red with her name, address and telephone number. He even dug a fish pond in the garden when Barbara mentioned that she would like one. Despite the fact that she often found Francis rather boring, she enjoyed their social life together, especially the parties that they hosted in his London studio. She even travelled down to Rye with him to visit his family occasionally. While she was emotionally biding her time, Francis was working hard to appear indispensable.

Diana, meanwhile, was busy in the art world, helping to organize a retrospective exhibition of paintings by Andrès de Santa Maria, a Columbian artist, at the New Burlington Galleries which was to run from 20 May to 5 June. She had also taken on a considerable amount of voluntary work, partly to fill the void left by her former job as secretary to the London Group. By 1937 Spain was in the grip of civil war: Malaga had been taken by Franco's forces in early February and Guernica had been bombed in late April, with many civilian casualties. Diana, who was appalled by the war, became heavily involved with the Aid Spain movement and spent much time helping to organize huge meetings in the Albert Hall in aid of the Basque Refugee Children, at which famous artists and writers, such as Picasso and Heinrich Mann, were speakers.[7] In 1937 she also became secretary to the Mass Observation Movement, a social research organization set up that year by the anthropologist Tom Harrisson, the poet Charles Madge and the film-maker Humphrey Jennings. Her reason for joining the movement, she wrote in answer to a questionnaire, was because 'one of my most passionate interests in life is to find out what people really do with their lives, and why'. Perhaps not surprisingly, given the relations between herself, Rupert and Barbara, she added, 'Obviously the most important line of investigation is sex, and I do not see how this can be undertaken.'[8] But after over a year of emotional turmoil, she and Rupert had weathered the storm of his relationship with Barbara and they were very close again. When Diana was away having her eyes treated in Bath, Rupert wrote to his 'precious one' telling her how much he loved her and that his life was 'just blank' without her; in another letter he signed off 'Wish you were here. Hate living without you my darling lovely one.'[9] With Barbara apparently settled and watched over by the conscientious Francis Codd, Diana no longer worried about her, and the two women exchanged friendly letters updating each other with their news. Occasionally she would send Barbara a pretty dress or a useful item of clothing for Caroline. Diana's life was back on track.

Although Barbara was interested in what was happening in Spain, her main worry at this time was finding someone suitable to look after Caroline while she worked. The first woman Barbara employed was the 'awful' Mrs Graham, who clearly did not see eye to eye with her employer. Barbara was convinced that she was filching money and described her in a letter to Diana written in May as 'a dreadful, dangerous woman'. The next carer did not fare much better: 'Molly isn't a fit person to be left alone with Caroline, she is the kindest person in the world and very honest, but no brains, forgets everything and a bit dirty'. Barbara finally decided against employing someone to look after the children: 'the ones I can afford are so awful we will just have to live on 35/- somehow. I wonder if we would be better in a cottage in the country, if I could get a cheap one with a bathroom.'[10]

Barbara was to get her cottage in the country, but not for a while. In May 1937 all plans were put on hold because she suddenly fell ill with scarlet fever, the symptoms of which include a sore throat, headache, high temperature, an itchy red rash and swollen glands in the neck. The disease, which had broken out in Doncaster in January, had spread to London by the spring. Today the illness is easily treated with antibiotics, but in 1937 it was regarded as serious and killed many small children. In *Our Spoons Came from Woolworths*, Sophia Fairclough catches scarlet fever and is hospitalized; three days after she is admitted, her small daughter Fanny, who also has the disease, dies. When, as a young adult, Barbara's daughter read the novel, she recognized Fanny as herself and exclaimed, 'But you've killed me!'[11] Caroline Pemberton did not die from scarlet fever as a child, but Barbara did base her description of Sophia's miserable time on her own experience.

In 1937 anyone who caught scarlet fever was sent to hospital and kept in an isolation ward for about six weeks. Ambulance staff would fumigate their home bedding in the street to stop the spread of the disease, and hospital visitors, if they were allowed at all, were often forced to communicate with their sick friends or relatives through a glass screen. Patients were fed a diet of milk puddings and junket and were subjected to heat treatments; once they began to improve, they were wheeled out into the fresh air during the day.[12] Barbara was subjected to all this and more, as were her children. Julian had to stay with his aunt Molly, Barbara's eldest sister, for two nights while their flat at Kilburn Priory was fumigated. He was then packed off to stay with Andrew and Helen Wordsworth in Isleworth, and Caroline was looked after by Andrew Wordsworth's mother, a bishop's widow who lived in the countryside near Salisbury, until Diana was able to have her to stay at St Quintin Avenue. Being in hospital for several weeks gave Barbara time to reflect, and she decided that, once discharged, she would not go back to Kilburn Priory. Price had still not finished converting her flat to make it bigger and it was just too small for her and two children. She was convinced that living there had made them all ill.

Diana paid for Barbara to stay in a private hospital and she also paid Dr Gillie's attendance fees. Always anxious about her own health, she visited Barbara in hospital only when she was no longer contagious, but she did send in magazines which Barbara greatly appreciated: 'it's marvellous to read anything in hospital and *Vogue* and the *New Yorker* are always lovely'. Another diversion was horse-racing; Barbara backed two horses in the Derby but neither won. John visited – but only to ask loudly for money in front of the other patients, which greatly embarrassed Barbara. His paintings of London's African American and Caribbean residents, on which he had been working over the past few years, were soon to be exhibited at the London Palladium theatre to accompany the 'Cotton Club' show there – and there were costs to be met.[13] The ever-faithful Francis Codd came regularly, bringing Barbara flowers and fresh supplies of elegant notepaper.

Chloe did not visit as she was soon to move abroad and was worried about catching the disease. Early in the summer, in leafy Surrey, Chloe had married John Faraday, a Crown Agent thirteen years her senior and the co-respondent in her divorce case. They were to sail to Port Said in Egypt on 16 July and would not return to London until 1939. Faraday would soon be seconded from the Palestine Police Force to become brigadier of the Arab Legion under Glubb Pasha, the British soldier who was its commanding general. Chloe was embarking on another exciting spell of life in a hot climate and would no longer be around to offer Barbara advice and support.

Meanwhile, Price kept an eye on things at 16 Kilburn Priory and collected the rents: 'He is an awful crook really but he has behaved very well to me and gone to a lot of trouble', Barbara wrote to Diana. Price's kindness was not entirely disinterested, however: he found Barbara very attractive and was beginning to hint that he could offer her an easier life. Despite her better judgement, Barbara was drawn to the flamboyant Price. He was a striking figure of a man: tall and well-built with thick auburn hair. He was occasionally prone to severe bouts of conjunctivitis when he would wear a black eye patch, which lent him a somewhat piratical air.

The pirate was quite capable of masquerading as a good angel, however. While she was in hospital, Barbara wrote to Diana that 'Someone who has heard about the awfull [*sic*] conditions we have been living in is buying the next door house for me in March. If this comes off we will all be quite happy for once.' As Price lived at 14 Kilburn Priory, the semi-detached next door to number 16 where Barbara lived, this announcement raises the question of the identity of Barbara's mysterious benefactor. It is vaguely possible that Francis Codd had made the offer, but it seems unlikely. John was certainly in no position to buy anything. The most plausible explanation is that it was Price's idea. But Diana would not have approved of Barbara

22 Barbara and Caroline, c. 1937

becoming closely involved with Price, of whom she was deeply suspicious, which would explain why Barbara was deliberately vague about her benefactor's identity.

In mid-June 1937 Barbara was told that she would soon be discharged on condition that she went away for a week's holiday in order to convalesce. After six weeks in hospital, she greeted the news with mixed feelings: 'I have liked being here – it has been so peaceful', she wrote to Diana. After a week in Southwold on the Suffolk coast, where she enjoyed browsing the antique shops and bought some lustre china, she travelled back to London, her heart sinking. She now realized that the Kilburn Priory project was not financially viable: 'I can never pay £3.3s a week here when I've only about 35/- a week coming in', she wrote to Diana. She returned to find Kilburn Priory uninhabitable: 'the woman has left the flat in the most hopeless and

23 Left to right: Teddy Catford, Arthur Price (sleeping), Barbara and Caroline

heart-breaking mess and every cat in Kilburn has used it as a lavatory', she complained in the same letter. Instead of moving back in, she went to stay with her sister Nan. But there was no room for the children there and they were due to be collected soon. She was in despair. It was at this point that Price stepped in and offered her temporary accommodation by way of a rent-free flat at 14 Kilburn Priory if she would undertake a few housekeeping jobs for him. He also promised that he would help her find her dream cottage in the country.

6

Mr Fox

Arthur Sherborn Price, or 'Price' as he was generally known, was soon to become Barbara's lover and would influence her life for the next six years. He was also the inspiration for her novel *Mr Fox*, written in the 1940s but not published until 1987. It was from Price that Barbara learned how to become truly independent. He taught her how to be resourceful and transformed her risk-taking tendencies into business skills. Price was brought up in Ashley Road in the Montpelier area of Bristol. His father, Stanley, was a printer cutter and his mother, Alice, worked as a draper and shopkeeper. Price's unusual middle name came from his maternal grandmother, Mary Albertina Sherborn. His parents already had two daughters aged 24 and 21 and two sons aged 18 and 14 when Arthur was born in March 1908. By 1911, when Price was only three years old, both his sisters, Florence and Alice, were married and his eldest brother, Reginald, had joined the army and was living in Salisbury. Only one brother, John, was still living at home. Price's urban childhood was very different from Barbara's relatively privileged, if chaotic, early life in a large country house in an English village.

Price's father died in 1921 when Price was 13. That same year, Price added a year to his age and joined the Merchant Navy as a cabin boy, perhaps feeling that he ought to earn his own way in the world now that his mother had been left a widow. He had a taste for adventure and no doubt enjoyed seeing the world – but, by the age of 16, he regarded himself as a merchant seaman and was growing impatient with the way he was still expected to do all the lowly chores on board. One day early in 1924, when his ship was moored off the coast of West Africa, he rebelled. Faced with the washing-up yet again, he lost his temper and noisily threw the dishes out of the porthole window into the sea. This small mutiny resulted in his being paid off and set ashore in Portuguese West Africa, now known as Angola. He knew nobody there but, luckily, he found himself in the port of Lobita, where men were being recruited to work on the Benguela Railway, designed to connect Lobita with the Belgian Congo. Progress on the much-needed railway had been interrupted by the First World War and now there was a sense of urgency about its completion. Price signed up as a labourer and was soon working hard in intense heat. It was here that he learned the rudiments of engineering and mechanics that were to stand him in good stead later. During his third year in Africa, however, Price contracted blackwater fever, a complication of malaria that often led to kidney failure. Once he had recovered sufficiently to travel, he decided to return to London. He sailed from Beira in Mozambique on 8 December 1927 on an ex-troopship, the *Grantully Castle*. Described as 24 years old on the ship's list, he was in fact only 19. Life had not been easy for him and he had grown up quickly, learning to count on nobody but himself.[1]

Price had earned good money when in Africa and, once settled in London, he decided to invest his capital in the car business. This was a shrewd move; the early 1930s saw a huge demand for motor cars. An item in *The London Gazette* on 23 June 1931 announced that Barrett & Price, a motor car dealer based at 111 Regents Park Road, NW 1, had now been dissolved and that the business would in future be run by Arthur Sherborn Price alone. Price, who was then living in a small flat in Adelaide Road in Hampstead, was clearly doing well. He was to do even better during the mid-1930s, by which time cars were no longer confined to the wealthy and were much more affordable than they had been in the 1920s. Suddenly, every middle-class family wanted a car – and not just any car. The boxy family saloon was now seen as old-fashioned and many buyers aspired to more upmarket vehicles that were sleeker and faster.[2] Price, who loved beautiful cars, caught the mood of the moment and began to specialize in second-hand glamorous cars; within a short time he had become a well-known London dealer in Bugattis, Lagondas and Delages.

Always financially shrewd, he decided to diversify and, with the profits from his car business, began to invest in property. By 1936, when Price first met Barbara, he gave every appearance of being an extremely successful man: he was still running his car business and owned several large houses in London that he had converted into flats. Among his properties were 153 Abbey Road and 8 Belsize Avenue as well as 14 and 16 Kilburn Priory. According to Barbara's son Julian, who was very fond of Price as a boy, he was also a very handsome man, not unlike the young Harrison Ford. His deep auburn hair, his neat red pointed beard and his cunning inspired Barbara to call him 'Mr Fox'. Price would wear old scruffy clothes when working on his cars, although when out on business he would sport a stylish hat and a well-cut Crombie overcoat. But Price was no gentleman investor; he was a rough diamond who could be very crafty when making business deals. He was known to carry a gun when he visited Warren Street, off Tottenham Court Road, then a famous venue for used car dealers, some of whom operated from showrooms while others sold dodgy cars parked on the pavement.[3] Being a sharp operator, Price was quick to spot any chicanery and the gun was a warning to local pickpockets (he took a great deal of cash with him on his trips to Warren Street) and to any second-hand car dealers who might try to cheat him.

Barbara and her children moved in temporarily with Price at 14 Kilburn Priory in early July 1937. Her own flat, at 16A Kilburn Priory next door, was almost immediately taken by her younger sister Kathleen and her husband, Teddy Catford, who was still working as a cinematographer. Barbara was pleased to have them close by, especially as her favourite sister Chloe was now in Egypt. Kathleen, with all her eccentricities, became Barbara's neighbour and confidante and Teddy provided practical help when she needed it, running her about in his car if Price was unavailable. Julian was thrilled to have his aunt Kathleen living next door. Having imitated owls as a child, she was now convinced that there were cats with furry wings to be found in remote parts of the Scottish Highlands and Ireland, and would spend hours painting pictures of them, which enthralled Julian. He, Barbara and Caroline went to watch his aunt and uncle move from their first floor flat in Bayswater and Julian peered up excitedly as their furniture was piled up on the balcony and then carefully lowered on to the waiting cart, from where it was horse-drawn to Kilburn Priory. Kathleen and Teddy were to live in Barbara's old flat until 1949, so they clearly found it more congenial than she had. The flat was big enough for two, and Teddy was often away filming. Having no children of her own (she found the sexual side of marriage distasteful and once remarked to Barbara that she 'had no idea that men were so rude'), Kathleen was fond of Julian and Caroline – and they enjoyed her wild imaginings.

Many years later, when revising her novel *Mr Fox* for publication, Barbara was casual about chronology but preserved many episodes that drew closely on her own life. In the book, Caroline Seymour, who is separated from her husband and has failed to make a living as the landlady of a large house, moves with her young daughter Jenny into an attic flat in a large property owned and lived in by a Mr Fox. Like Price, Mr Fox has a temper and is irritated by small things, such as Caroline forgetting her front-door key, 'but we had nowhere else to go, so we had to go on living with him'.[4] Mr Fox, like Price, makes his money by selling used cars and is always full of schemes to make more; his income is volatile and his fortunes veer dramatically between poverty and comparative wealth. And, just like Price, Mr Fox has a fine red pointed beard which he sometimes shaves off so that his creditors will not recognize him. Caroline does small jobs around the house and looks after Mr Fox's dog when he is at work, and in exchange he lets her live rent-free in his flat. Caroline recognizes that they are very different and that Mr Fox is nothing like her arty friends, but she likes him: he amuses and interests her. Mr Fox is a scoundrel who is happy to go to Brixton prison rather than pay his rates, but he is a generous man who likes to shower Caroline with presents: 'odd junk from antique shops, goldfish from Woolworth's, boxes of chocolates and sometimes rather frightful books and magazines that he thought were suitable for women to read'.[5] While Mr Fox is an exaggerated version of Barbara's lover at this time, the character accurately captures the aggression, warmth and energy of Arthur Sherborn Price.

Missing from the novel, however, is Barbara's move to a country cottage in Nash Mills, Hertfordshire, in late July in 1937, where she and her children lived for six months. The house, which was rented by Price on a short lease, was a pretty stucco Gothic Regency cottage called Tudor Lodge, close to a canal and with a large garden. It was Price's way of realizing Barbara's dream of living in the countryside. Although he remained in London near his various businesses, Price drove out to Hertfordshire frequently. As the house was only partly furnished and contained no bed, he and Barbara slept on a double mattress on the floor.

Diana Brinton Lee kept in touch with Barbara and sent her cheques from time to time as well as clothes and toys for Caroline. In a letter written to Diana in late August 1937, Barbara expressed her sympathy about the head injury Diana had suffered in a car crash near Broadway earlier that month that had kept her in hospital for a week.[6] It was the second car crash that year for the Brinton Lees; Rupert Lee was not the most careful of drivers. Barbara also sent Diana news of the children in the letter: Julian, now five and a half, was attending the local primary school and Caroline, at 21 months, 'can walk at last but still prefers going on her bottom, she talks a lot – much better than Julian could at her age. Both children look wonderfully well since we have been here and eat enormous meals.'[7]

True to the Bayley family tradition, the cottage at Nash Mills soon became a haven for animals, including Price's dog, a Great Dane, although – as Barbara explained to Diana in her letter – one animal suffered an untimely demise after eating a packet of Price's cigarettes, which he had left on the floor next to the mattress:

> I had not been here long before two tabby kittens arrived at the house, then a Bedlington bitch walked in and a baby rabbit which became quite tame and used to sleep in my bed and sit by the fire. I always took it to London with me but it ate a packet of cigarettes and died which made us very sad. There is also a Great Dane boarded here, I am hoping one day a cow will come into our field and we will have free milk.

Julian loved living in the countryside and exploring the fields with the more adventurous of the two cats. On one occasion he found an interesting looking puffball fungus and took it home. Unsure what to do with it, he hid it in a large kettle standing on the floor. Barbara habitually filled kettles through their spouts and that evening made a cup of tea for herself and Caroline. For the next few days she and Caroline were laid low with a nasty bout of diarrhoea. When Barbara discovered the by now slimy fungus at the bottom of the kettle she gave Julian a very stern lecture, pointing out that he could have killed them both. His punishment was the confiscation of his beloved tricycle, which was confined to the garage.

Julian's remorse did not cramp his spirit of adventure, however. He vividly remembered being taken by Price to the Royal Tournament at Olympia in the summer when Barbara was in hospital with scarlet fever, and decided to re-enact some of the spectacles he had seen there, including a Roman chariot race and motorcyclists riding through rings of fire. He piled some wood on to the embers of a bonfire in the garden and managed to get a good blaze going. Then he retrieved his tricycle from the garage and rode it as fast as he could into the bonfire, expecting to shoot out the other side with great élan. Sadly, the little trike got stuck in the firewood. Julian escaped the flames only mildly scorched, although the tricycle was badly damaged and its burning tyres gave off a horrible smell.

Undaunted, Julian tried next to emulate the Roman chariot race. He commandeered Caroline's pram – which was an expensive large bouncy vehicle on big curved springs, the sort pushed by nannies in London parks – and tied the Great Dane by its collar to the pram handle with some old rope. He then climbed into the pram and gave the dog a sharp flick with an improvised whip. It shot off at great speed, the pram lurching in all directions, and Julian soon fell out as it tipped madly sideways. The dog, however, kept running, panicked by the pram, which was by now bouncing along on its side with the cushions, blankets, mattress and flooring having been scattered all over the field among the clumps of thistles and brambles. Julian dreaded what was to come but – to his surprise and great relief – Barbara and Price were not as furious as he expected them to be. They simply told him that his punishment was the loss of his tricycle which would not be replaced – and that it was time Caroline started walking properly anyway, so the pram would not be replaced either. Forced to walk rather than ride majestically in her pram, Caroline grizzled continually on all their local rambles.

While Barbara was pleased to see the children enjoying the freedom and fresh air of the countryside, she was at heart a city person and missed London. She travelled in with Price once or twice a week, ostensibly to check on and collect the rents from 16 Kilburn Priory but also to view buildings with Price and learn about buying and selling second-hand cars.

While he understood what needed to be done structurally to a house and had plenty of contacts in the building world, Price realized that Barbara had a much better eye for interior decoration than he had and that she knew how to transform a room cheaply. She despised flowery wallpaper and could quickly visualize how a coat of primrose distemper and some colourful fabrics would make a room look light and interesting. She was also good with furniture, able to convert a second-hand dowdy chair into something elegant with a few coats of paint and pretty upholstery. An inveterate opportunist, Price suggested that they should become informal business partners.

When in London, Barbara also saw her sister Nan and had lunch with friends, including Diana and Francis Codd. Barbara concealed from Diana the nature of her changing relationship with Price, however. In a letter written in late August she asked Diana to chase Price up on a number of jobs, including repairing a cracked lavatory in the basement flat, so that 16 Kilburn Priory would comply with London Council County regulations. She claimed that Diana could deal much more effectively with Price than she could: 'You see no one is frightened of me and when you wrote before he did start those alterations although they were never finished, so maybe if you write a really snotty letter something will be done this time.' The request gave the impression that she and Price had little to do with each other, but this was far from the truth. Indeed, Julian felt that the four of them became a family at this time. Barbara was juggling two relationships that were both necessary to her, and was trying to keep them separate. Diana, who disapproved of Price, was still subsidizing her, and Barbara needed her financial support – but Price's suggestion that they should work together seemed to offer a way out of that financial dependency. And there is no doubt that Barbara and Price found each other sexually attractive – and that they made each other laugh.

*   *   *

The idyll (at least for the children) of living in a cottage in the Hertfordshire countryside lasted only until the end of 1937. By that time Barbara was once again in debt. In December she wrote to Diana telling her that she could no longer manage: 'I have lived very carefully the last year, but Kilburn Priory only brings in £2.10 per week when it's all let up so it's a wonder I'm not more in debt.' The only solution was to return to London to find work in order to pay off the money owing on 16 Kilburn Priory: 'It seems a pity when the children are so well and happy here but it can't be helped.' In order to become solvent again, Barbara's plan was that she would live

in a one-room flat: this would be much cheaper than renting a larger flat
to accommodate both her and the children. John had promised to pay for
Julian to go to boarding school in London, and she intended boarding
Caroline with a childminder during the week so that she could work. The
children could come home at weekends. Although this might sound callous
– particularly bearing in mind Barbara's protestations about her need to
have Julian and Caroline with her – it was not unusual at this time for
women, especially if they were single parents, to board out their children
during the week so that they could work full-time.

Barbara's letter, for whatever reason, did not reach Diana, so she wrote
again at the end of December, thanking Diana for the Christmas presents
she had sent for the children and underlining the gravity of her situation
now that Price had apparently reclaimed 16 Kilburn Priory:

> Now I have no money at all and have had to sell all my furniture etc., I haven't
> anywhere to live and just stay with whoever will put me up for the night.
> Julian is in a very nice school and seems quite happy. At the moment Caroline
> is at that home in Hendon she went to before, they charge £2.2s a week, so
> she is ticking up like a taxi. I'm afraid Rupert will have to have her now as
> I have no home or money to feed her on and cannot carry her about with me
> to look for work. I told the people in the home you will come and fetch her
> next Monday afternoon. I cannot fetch her myself as I have no money to pay
> them with.

The letter ended with Caroline's address – she was boarding with a Mrs
Betts, who ran a school and nursery in Sunningfields Road, Hendon, in
north London – and the information that Barbara could be contacted through
her husband John, who had by now moved from the Belsize Park flat to
36 Fitzroy Street. Price had no intention of seeing Barbara homeless of
course; rather, his plan was to use Barbara to squeeze more money out of
Diana. Still receiving no reply from Diana, Barbara wrote to Rupert on 5
January 1938, telling him that he should be glad to have 'his own little girl'
with him as he had always said he wanted a child; the letter ended with a
plea to 'do what you can for Caroline'.

By mid-January 1938 Barbara was writing to Diana from 153 Abbey
Road, a property owned by Price. She had probably moved into Chloe's
empty flat in the house – or perhaps she and Price were living there together,
as Price also wrote letters from Abbey Road at this time. The man whom
she claimed had taken possession of her flat in Kilburn Priory had in fact
provided her with another place to live. Unable to find work as an artist's
model or in a graphic design studio, Barbara revealed in a letter to Diana
that she had managed to find a job in a nightclub, working from 11 p.m.
to 5 a.m. It did not last long – she clearly hated it and was shocked by the

easy slippage between the role of 'hostess' and what we would now call 'sex worker' – but it did provide useful material for a comic episode in *Mr Fox* when Caroline Seymour gets a job in a nightclub called the 'Rose Bower'. Having been told to dress elegantly, she digs out 'a striped arrangement with no back to speak of and a very long skirt' with a train that hobbles her. Caroline imagines it to be a very glamorous way of earning a living but, when she arrives, the nightclub turns out to be a sleazy affair with 'paper roses climbing up pea-green trellis work […] and wretched little coloured lights in the ceiling'. She soon learns that there will be no salary but is assured that men will stuff money into her handbag; she is also told she must persuade the male 'guests' to buy her the exorbitantly priced chocolates, flowers and cigarettes available for sale – but that she should hand them back to the management at the end of the evening. When the club opens, the band suddenly starts to play 'and the girls became bright and talked to each other with great animation; it was as if someone had put a penny in the slot and the waxworks had come to life'. A businessman from Manchester, who looks 'like a bulldog crossed with a hot-cross bun', takes a particular fancy to Caroline and asks her out to dinner the next evening. When she arrives at the Italian hotel she discovers after the meal that he has hired a suite for the night. On learning that Caroline will not have sex with him, he rolls energetically about the bed so that it will look as if they have slept together and he won't lose face with the hotel management. 'I didn't let him know how funny he looked rolling about because I know men don't like being laughed at unless they are being funny on purpose; dogs are like that too', Caroline thinks to herself. Despite the protests of Mr Fox, who calculates that she might be able to earn 'twelve pounds a week free of income tax' (about £970 today), Caroline leaves her job after only a week.[8]

Barbara also left her job after only a few days. Despite the occasional desperate comment she had made to Diana about being forced to go on the streets in order to survive, Barbara was horrified at how easy it was for a woman to slip into prostitution when money was tight. A bout of illness ended her work at the nightclub and she was confined to bed for several days. Nan, thinking of her sister's spiritual welfare more than her physical well-being, asked an Irish Catholic priest to visit her, but Barbara was intensely irritated by his droning over her bed. It was a small price to pay though for having escaped work as a nightclub hostess.

Both Julian and Caroline were boarding at Mrs Betts's school in Hendon by this time. Although Julian did not want to be sent away from home again, the school was well run and he soon settled in. Many years later, he recorded in his memoir, with some guilt, how he inadvertently made Barbara cry on one of her visits there:

We sat in a little room and looked at each other. It felt like a very long time since I had seen her. I said after a bit 'What have you got for me?' Barbara burst into tears and said 'Nothing'. She said that she had nothing because she had no money.

Cheque counterfoils reveal that from January 1938 Diana began to pay half the cost of boarding Caroline with Mrs Betts, and that she also sent monthly cheques to Barbara for £2 (about £160 today) despite being worried about her own financial affairs. Diana knew that in 1938 she would not receive the usual annual dividend from her father's carpet firm; the spectre of war with Germany was already having an impact on businesses and profits were plummeting. And Diana was beginning to lose patience with Barbara. In mid-January she sent her a long stern letter:

> I don't want to reproach you and I wish you wouldn't make things more difficult by reproaching us. I am particularly sick of sneering references to Rupert's 'being kept' and not having 'looked after you'. Rupert works very hard, and if he doesn't earn as much as I get without working, at any rate he doesn't spend it on drink and n***** night clubs. If we have given you help on a scale commensurate with my income rather than his, it seems to me you should be the last to complain. It is a pity you don't appreciate that we both made very real and considerable sacrifices, and went far beyond anything anyone could have expected us to do, in order to help you to be independent and have both children with you. We were definitely told (by Francis and Nancy) that this was what you wanted, and that once it was done we should not be approached again.

In the same letter Diana offered several solutions to Barbara's financial problems. The first was that Barbara should assign her the lease of 16 Kilburn Priory, at which point Diana would pay off the arrears and administer the income for Caroline's benefit while replenishing her own account out of any surplus money. Secondly, she suggested that Barbara should take a job as a housekeeper, as Barbara's eldest sister Molly had done, so that she could keep Caroline with her rather than boarding her out: 'I am all against children being kept in homes; even if they are taken out on Saturdays. They want *constant* affection.' The third suggestion was that she and Rupert should adopt Caroline and bring her up as their own daughter. She assured Barbara that, with them, Caroline would have 'a real home and a future [...] If she was ours we should of course treat her in every respect as our own child, whether we had another or not'. Barbara ignored the adoption offer; while she had no compunction about sending Caroline away temporarily, she was determined not to give her up permanently. Angered on her behalf, Price persuaded Barbara that they should send a slightly threatening note to Diana's solicitor, Haynes:

Mr Price says that Mrs Pemberton (under his advice) would not assign the lease unless Caroline's income were assured, insisting that a clause be made in the trust that if we lose the house, Caroline's income be found out of other funds. If this is not done, he says he then knows what to advise Mrs. P to do.

Although it is clear that Price wrote the note, Barbara – driven by fear of poverty again – clearly went along with it, drawn into Price's schemes rather too easily. In the meantime, Diana's solicitor wrote to Diana (who had sent him a copy of her letter to Barbara), suggesting that it was 'a mistake to write long letters to a woman who has made the threats she has done', and that from now on it would be best if he handled all correspondence with Mrs Pemberton. Diana ignored his advice and wrote to Barbara on 20 January reporting a telephone conversation she had just had with Price in which he had told her 'that he intended to have the house himself and that he could not be bothered to tell me anything, and that as far as he was concerned I and my lawyer had no status'. She expressed her growing anger with Price and, implicitly, her disapproval of Barbara's relationship with him:

Mr Price stated on the telephone and also in your presence the other night that he was acting as your adviser, and if this is so I am afraid he has made it impossible for us to go any further on the lines suggested in my previous letter. Of course if you have copies (as you should have) of the missing documents and are willing to get my lawyer to represent you, we might at any rate enquire into the position as regards the mortgage. I think you should appreciate that, whatever his personal feelings may be, Mr Price, as mortgagee, has interests opposed to yours.

Her patience now sorely tried, Diana wrote to Haynes the next day making it clear that 'the man Price' should be excluded from all negotiations and expressing her frustration with Barbara: 'Though I do not think Barbara has any intention of dishonesty, the history of the last year does show that she is not exactly to be trusted. She is not very good at managing money, and is besides impulsive and unscrupulous in following her impulse of the moment.'

A few days later, Rupert Lee also wrote to Haynes, agreeing that the best course would be for him and Diana to pay off Barbara's debt of £50 (about £4,000 today) to Price on the mortgage for 16 Kilburn Priory and suggesting that the lease should be assigned to Diana, with £75 being paid annually to Barbara for Caroline's upkeep. After an exchange of many letters and several difficult meetings with Diana's solicitor, it was agreed during February that the mortgage lease for 16 Kilburn Priory, which had been set up in Barbara's name, should be transferred to Diana. Price continued to behave in a cavalier manner, writing to Diana in March to apologize for having borrowed almost eight pounds (about £650 today) from the rents at Kilburn

Priory which Barbara had asked him to collect on her behalf. He took it, he added, to solve a cash-flow problem, but Barbara had been horrified and had 'nagged' him to pay it back immediately. He promised to repay the money as soon as possible, 'as it is causing friction in the nest as the cook and unpaid housekeeper has gone on strike'. Barbara was presumably the said cook and housekeeper.

Although Diana loathed Price, she did not want to lose contact with Barbara, whom she saw as having fallen under his bad influence. Neither did she want to risk losing Caroline, of whom she had grown very fond and who was, after all, Rupert's child. Once the transfer of the lease for 16 Kilburn Priory to Diana had been agreed in principle, Diana felt more affable towards Barbara, whose willingness to look after her pets when she was away was very useful. At the end of March Barbara went to live at 7 St Quintin Avenue for a week to care for the cats while Diana and Rupert visited Germany. The trip was partly a holiday but also had a more serious purpose: Diana wanted to see for herself what was happening in the country. It had been clear since 1935 that Hitler's plans went further than overseeing Germany's recovery from the impact of the First World War and that he had imperial ambitions. On 12 March 1938 Hitler had annexed Austria in an *Anschluss* (incorporation) in direct contravention of the terms of the 1919 Versailles Treaty. The world was watching anxiously to see what he would do next. On her return, Diana wrote an article entitled 'The Uniform State', which was published on 23 April 1938 in *Time and Tide*, a political and literary review magazine. In it, she described a country that seemed to be preparing for war: she and Rupert had seen soldiers everywhere, citizens performing the Heil Hitler salute on the streets and the population being 'exhorted to collect metal and save fats for armaments'. An art gallery run by a Jewish friend had been closed down and she had 'disappeared'. On the train to Leipzig, Diana and Rupert overheard two businessmen having a conversation about art in which they violently attacked the work of 'der Jude Epstein', who was one of their friends. Diana came to the conclusion that Germany was now 'a country where the apostles of intellectual liberty may have to face a violent or a lingering death'.[9] Her analysis was prescient.

While Barbara and Diana appeared, at least on the surface, to have resolved their differences, Diana was nevertheless beginning to distance herself slightly from Barbara because she disliked Price so intensely. By May, Barbara was able to pay Diana £50 in full and final settlement of her debt. Diana was actually owed £62 in total but accepted the lower sum because, as she commented to her solicitor in a letter, 'I think it very unlikely that she will ever have so much money again.' Diana was wrong. Barbara had accrued a good sum of money from her share of the sale of 14 Kilburn Priory when Price sold it. How she came to have a 50 per cent share in the house is not clear – but it seems to confirm that she was in business with Price. From this time on, Barbara's dependence on Diana receded and she threw in her lot with her lover. In May 1938 the lease of 16 Kilburn Priory was legally transferred to Diana and her payments to Barbara and to Mrs Betts for the care of Caroline stopped. In November Diana cashed in the life insurance policy for Caroline, on which she had paid two premiums. She did not like Price or trust him and did not see why she should continue funding Barbara while she was living with him. She no doubt also thought that, as Barbara's protector, he now ought to take full responsibility for her finances and for Caroline's welfare.

*   *   *

In the summer of 1938 Price and Barbara moved with her children and the Great Dane into the basement flat of a handsome late Victorian house in a tree-lined road in Carlton Vale, Maida Vale. It was close to Kilburn Park tube station and not far from Kilburn Priory, so very convenient for Price's landlord activities. Price had a mews garage nearby which would take six cars, where his second-hand bargains were repaired and given a face-lift before being sold. By this time Barbara was fully involved in Price's car and property businesses. He trusted her to make deals and she went frequently to auctions with a mechanic to advise her. Her quick wit and her beauty would no doubt have worked to her advantage in such a male-dominated trade. She found that she enjoyed the cut and thrust of the auction room and bought only glamorous cars with large engines. Her best customers were actors who wanted something flamboyant; they would buy when they were in work and being well paid and then sell the cars back to her when they were 'resting'. Julian often went with her to the auctions and spent a lot of time in the mews garage watching the cars being prepared for sale. He was particularly intrigued by the man who would cut deep grooves in almost bald tyres to make them look newer than they were – a practice that was later made illegal. Barbara also went to view properties with Price; he knew she always had a good sense of how the building could be converted into small attractive flats and he valued her opinion. She had little time to paint and sculpt during this period of her life, and Price was not at all interested in art – but if there was some cement left over when he was converting a building, she would sometimes sculpt a small figure to decorate the brickwork. Her love of newts and lizards had not left her and she would often sculpt a lizard in cement to adorn a workaday drain hopper.

Barbara and Price embarked on yet another business venture at this time, buying a grubby greasy spoon café in the mews where Price rented his garage. Barbara saw how its interior could be transformed into something more exciting by using light and vibrant colours, and she persuaded John to paint a large mural of a jolly cook frying eggs and bacon behind the counter. They also provided games, such as dominoes, which customers could play with each other while eating their meals. Price employed a good temporary chef to improve the menu with the result that delicious food was soon being served at a reasonable price; it was not long before queues were forming outside the door. When Price and Barbara sold the café a year or so later, they made a very good profit.

Whatever Diana thought of Price (and it wasn't much), Barbara's children adored him. While he could be shark-like in business matters, he was warm-hearted, generous and funny when with them. Barbara might have been ambivalent about Price's social standing but Julian and Caroline had no such reservations: he seemed to them a source of strength and protection who provided fun and adventure. Julian, in particular, loved spending time with Price, who became a much-needed father-figure to him. Price was able to give Julian something his own father had never been able to provide: time, attention and affection. He would often take the six-year-old boy on outings that left an indelible impression on the young child's mind. One involved Julian's sailing boat which had a folding steel hull that looked splendid – but the boat always drifted sideways no matter how the sails were arranged. Price asked him if he would like to sink it with a real gun. Julian was greatly excited by the idea and the two drove to the pond near Jack Straw's Castle on Hampstead Heath where a number of children were already sailing their boats. Once Julian's was afloat and drifting away, listing to one side as usual, Price got out his revolver and helped Julian aim and shoot. The second shot holed the boat and they watched it go down until it disappeared beneath the surface. The other boat enthusiasts stared at the man and boy, shocked, but said nothing: Price was not someone with whom you would want to pick a fight.

While she did not entirely approve of such antics, Barbara was pleased that Price and her son enjoyed each other's company and she loved the family outings that Price would organize on the spur of the moment. He was not above playing tricks on her, though. Once he suggested a picnic outing even though the day was stormy and rain was forecast. They drove some miles into the countryside, but the sunshine that Price had promised was nowhere to be seen. Suddenly the heavens opened and heavy rain began to beat upon the car. Price suggested that they have their picnic in a farm barn, attached to a farmhouse. He went off to explore and returned having found the house itself empty and the back door open; why shouldn't they have their picnic there? They crept into the farmhouse kitchen and sat at the big wooden table to eat, Barbara feeling like Goldilocks and looking anxiously about her in case the owners returned. After half an hour, during which Barbara jumped every time she heard a noise, Price explained that he had the key because he was considering buying the farmhouse, which was no longer occupied.

Not to be outdone, Barbara also played practical jokes occasionally. One day, on her way to meet Price at a party, she stopped to buy some 'trick' soap from a street vendor. The white soap would, apparently, turn people's hands black as soon as they used it. She carefully put a bar wherever there was a sink in the house and waited expectantly – but was disappointed to see that when she and Price left, late at night, all the guests' hands looked perfectly clean. She then realized that she had been outwitted by the street vendor – who had sold her the white soap at twice its normal price – and acknowledged that Price was the superior practical joker.

Price's sense of fun and his love of practical jokes were, however, offset by a dark side. While he was always gentle with the children, he was a volatile man whose temper was never far beneath the surface; when it broke, he could be violent. Barbara was well aware of this and even the children caught glimpses of it occasionally. On another spontaneous outing, this time to the Forest of Dean in Gloucestershire, for which Price borrowed a glamorous Delage D8 from the garage, he met a car coming the other way on a narrow lane. There was no room to pass; the two cars stopped and the drivers climbed out. In both cars a worried mother and children peered through the windscreen to see what would happen next. There was a curt exchange of words and the other driver made the mistake of smirking at Price, who instantly punched the man hard in the chest. The driver sank slowly to his knees, a look of horror on his face. He then got up slowly and reversed for some way so that Price could pass. Price did not like to be crossed or confronted, as yet another man found out to his cost when Price borrowed Barbara's bicycle one day. Not only was it a woman's bicycle but it had a wicker basket on the front. He was riding down Kilburn High Road when a man standing outside a pub shouted 'Queer!' Price immediately jumped off the bike, thumped the man and then nonchalantly pedalled away, leaving the offender groaning on the pavement.

While Barbara and Price were happy in the Carlton Vale flat and Julian and Caroline were enjoying playing in the large garden and growing plants from seeds, clouds were gathering across Europe. In 1938 Hitler turned his attention to the Sudeten German-speaking area of Czechoslovakia, which he planned to reclaim for Germany. This would destabilize the newly created nation, allowing him to invade it, ostensibly to restore order. There was talk of war between Britain and Germany if the Führer actually invaded Czechoslovakia, and people in Britain were uneasy. This uncertainty affected businesses; both companies and individuals were less likely to spend or invest if they thought war was imminent. Buying a glamorous car was now considered frivolous, given what might happen in the near future, and Price's car business began to suffer. London was considered particularly vulnerable to Nazi attack if Germany decided to bomb England, and many of Price's flats were emptying as their tenants moved further out for safety. The Munich agreement, made between Chamberlain and Hitler in September 1938, seemed to avert the threat of war, with the English prime minister agreeing to the separation of the Sudeten Germans from Czechoslovakia in exchange for Hitler promising not to invade the country. Chamberlain returned home promising 'peace in our time', but others were not at all sure the Führer would keep his word.

The happy times in Carlton Vale lasted only a year or so. Price stopped paying the rent, probably because a high brick garden wall had collapsed when Julian was playing with his toy cars nearby. Fortunately Julian was not hurt but Price was incensed by what might have happened and had a furious row with the landlord, who promptly gave them notice. Price and Barbara ignored the notice and slipped further into rent arrears, with the result that bailiffs turned up to repossess the flat and confiscate all the furniture. Writing about this episode in his memoir, Barbara's son Julian remembered that

> There were two of them. They were both quite heavy men who spent a lot of time with their jackets off in waistcoats and shirts with springs around their arms just above their elbows. They drank an awful lot of tea made for them by Barbara. After a few days Price and Barbara reached an agreement with the bailiffs. We took all our nice furniture out of the flat and put in really awful shabby things instead.

This miserable event provided useful material for the episode in *Mr Fox* when Caroline Seymour faces eviction. The two fictional bailiffs 'with glowering eyes and bulging muscles' arrive, and she locks them out, only to find that they are 'pressing their faces to the kitchen window and their noses and fat cheeks were squashed into strange shapes against the glass' in an attempt to take an inventory of the furniture by peering into the flat. When Mr Fox arrives home, he subsides into 'a cunning kind of thoughtfulness' while drinking his tea, and tells Caroline to mark all the possessions and furniture she wants to keep with white bits of paper. Having crossed their palms with silver, Mr Fox comes to a deal with the bailiffs that they will return the next day. In the meantime, a removal van arrives to take Caroline's valuable possessions away, which Mr Fox replaces with wobbly old sticks of furniture.[10]

Arthur Sherborn Price left no mark on history, but he inspired a memorable character, the attractive rogue and charismatic rascal who gave his name to the novel *Mr Fox*. Although Barbara had reservations about much of Price's behaviour and had no intention of marrying him, she admired his resourcefulness and found him physically very attractive. They had fun together. And, despite her better judgement, she was fascinated by the way he managed to live on the edge of the law.

*　*　*

Following their eviction from Carlton Vale in the early summer of 1939 Price, Barbara and Caroline moved back temporarily into a flat in 153 Abbey Road. Julian was still boarding at Mrs Betts's school in Hendon and saw his mother and Price only at weekends. By this time, the prospect of war seemed very real. On 15 March German tanks had moved into Prague and it was clear that Hitler was set to occupy the whole of Czechoslovakia, thereby breaking the Munich agreement. The future looked grim: 'The war came nearer and nearer and there was no escaping it, you could almost see it coming like a great dust-storm.'[11] On 27 April Chamberlain introduced conscription for young men aged 20 and 21, who had to sign up for six months' intensive military training before joining the Territorial Army or special reserves. Call-up proceeded in waves from then on, until by June 1941 all men up to the age of 40 had been conscripted.[12] On 22 May 1939 Hitler and Mussolini signed an alliance dubbed the 'Pact of Steel' by the Italian leader; the skies were growing darker. Even John Pemberton, Barbara's husband and a most unlikely recruit for war, enlisted in the Royal Artillery in 1940.[13]

Preparations for war had begun in Britain well before September 1939. In 1938 the government drew up plans for moving children out of major British cities and there were evacuation rehearsals during the summer of 1939. Gas masks were issued during the year to all adults and children over the age of four. Julian left his in the Kilburn branch of Woolworths one day and Barbara had to apply for another one; he was roundly ticked off and told to look after it more carefully in future. Children under four – which included Caroline, who was three years old – were not issued with gas masks; their parents were advised simply to 'wrap them tightly in a blanket'.[14] A character in Barbara's novel *A Touch of Mistletoe* swears that if he ever has to wear his gas mask, he will 'soak the nozzle in whisky first to drown the rubbery smell' – the sort of thing Price might have said.[15] By 1 September, two days before war was declared, children were being evacuated from London to safer rural areas. By 3 September 1.5 million evacuees had left the capital.[16] Many adults – at least those who could afford it or who had relatives elsewhere – were moving to the countryside. London was emptying; the face of the city was changing:

> As war came nearer we saw long crocodiles of children with gas masks humped on their backs; the streets seemed to be filled with them. Then suddenly there was hardly a child left in London and, although the sun shone and shone, the

> parks were almost empty except for people digging long, straight holes, some
> said for trenches and others for mass graves [...] I thought about the horrible
> gasses that were coming, people said they would eat through the roof and eat
> into wherever we hid and there were death rays coming too ...[17]

Some people built Anderson shelters, distributed by the government between February and September 1939, in their back gardens and then covered them with earth. Others decided they would take refuge in their basements or under stairs or tables during the predicted air raids.

Barbara and Price had earnest conversations about whether they should move out of London, taking the children with them so that they would avoid the inevitable bombing of the capital if war was declared. Barbara had already decided that she would rather keep Julian and Caroline with her than have them evacuated. Price, now aged 32, would certainly be eligible for general conscription. He was hopeful that his engineering experience in Africa and his knowledge of car mechanics might help him find work in an aircraft factory. Britain was desperately short of planes and there was a dearth of skilled men to work in the factories that made them. Importantly for Price, such work was regarded as a reserved occupation, which meant that he would be exempted from conscription. With the help of a friend who provided a fake reference attesting to his work as a factory engineer, by midsummer 1939 Price had a job as a riveter at the Fairey Aviation Company in Hayes, Middlesex. He surrendered his mews garage and closed down his second-hand car business, keeping only a modest Austin Seven for his own use. He drove each day from Abbey Road to Hayes, about an hour's journey, and came home tired and bad-tempered in the evening. Barbara was left on her own with the Great Dane for company during the day as both children were now boarding with Mrs Betts. The school in Hendon was seven miles north of the Abbey Road area and therefore less likely to be bombed than central London. However, Price soon grew tired of the round trip of 33 miles a day and in August mentioned that there were some empty houses on a new estate near the factory. Would Barbara consider moving there with the children? He would certainly find life easier if he lived near the factory. She promised she would think about it.

7

Becoming a writer

'Thank God I don't live there!', thinks Caroline Seymour, the narrator of *Mr Fox*, when she sees the small town of 'Straws' from the train.[1] Barbara's response to Hayes in Middlesex, which she visited in August 1939 to look at the new houses that had been built near the Fairey Aircraft Factory, was much the same. It was a feeling shared by George Orwell who, having been brought up in Hayes, described it as 'one of the most godforsaken places I have ever struck. The population seems to be entirely made up of clerks who frequent tin-roofed chapels on Sundays and for the rest bolt themselves within doors.'[2] In Barbara Comyns' novel the sight of the main streets full of 'mean little shops filled with cheap rubbish' dismays Caroline, but the woods and fields beyond momentarily lift her spirits. As war now seems certain, most builders have been reallocated to more urgent work, so the estates remain unfinished and the place has the air of a building site. Having spent the day looking at small houses with small rooms covered in ghastly wallpaper, Caroline finally settles on one of the 'Happy Orchard Homes', despite her misgivings:

> It was a really dreadful little house and seemed as if it was made of asbestos and cardboard. There were only four rooms, scullery and bathroom – with white tiles on the walls, but they only came half way up. A boiler in the dining-room heated the water. At the back of the house there was a garden, but it was a mess of heavy brown clay strewn with rubbish; but I hoped that perhaps the garden of our house might be better – there could even be an apple tree left over from the orchard.[3]

Like her fictional counterpart, Barbara made her choice and gave a week's rent as deposit on a Honey Development house. Having weighed up the pros and cons of moving out of central London, she had decided it was the best thing to do. It would make life easier for Price, who would no longer have to drive to work if they lived in Hayes and – as the house had two bedrooms – the children could be with them and they would enjoy the freedom of the countryside nearby. It might also be safer there, she thought, than in London. She was right: despite its aircraft manufacturing business,

Hayes did not suffer any serious damage from wartime bombing raids until 7 July 1944, by which time Barbara and the children were back in London.

By early September 1939 the much-anticipated war had become a reality. In response to Hitler's invasion of Poland on 1 September, the prime minister, Neville Chamberlain, declared war on Germany at 11.15 a.m. on Sunday 3 September. Soon after the radio broadcast, London's air raid sirens began to wail; it was merely a rehearsal but it threw everyone into a panic. The mad scramble for shelters and safe places features in *Mr Fox*, in which a woman with 'a bowl filled with cake mixture and [...] a man with nothing on except a bath towel' rush for safety.[4] Price was at work, even though it was a Sunday, and Barbara suffered the indignity of not being allowed into the basement in the Abbey Road house because she had the Great Dane with her, an episode also included in the novel. The tenants

> started yelling that I was to turn [him] into the street because he would go mad and kill them as soon as the bombing started. I told them I didn't want to go in their beastly old gas-proof room: it most likely wasn't gas-proof after all. I said I preferred to sit at the bottom of the stairs with the dog.[5]

In London in September 1939, city-dwellers who did not have pets did indeed sometimes turn on pet owners, their self-righteousness fuelled by a government announcement on 26 August that all pets in urban areas should be sent to the countryside, but that if this was not possible then they should be destroyed. Many pet owners followed this advice; at least 400,000 pets were put down in the week the war broke out and people who kept theirs were regarded as irresponsible, particularly as the government made it clear that dwindling food supplies should not be wasted on domestic animals.[6] A keen animal lover, Barbara had no intention of having the Great Dane destroyed. Everything seemed to confirm her decision that the sooner they moved out of London, the better.

Two weeks later, in mid-September, Price borrowed a large car, and he and Barbara moved their furniture to Hayes. Germany had many more fighting planes than Britain at this time and the government was urging all aircraft factories to increase their output. Fairey Aviation in Hayes, which built naval aircraft and also bombers for the RAF, was under particular pressure to increase productivity. This meant long hours for the men who worked on the factory floor, including Price who, when he came home, was exhausted – so the job of turning the small house into a home for when the children arrived was left to Barbara.

Price collected the children from Mrs Betts's school in Hendon a week later, and by the end of September 1939 they were all living together in what Julian called 'the Honey House'. In the 1939 England and Wales Register, they are entered as resident at 61 Bedwell Gardens in Hayes, and

Price is described as an 'aircraft riveter, heavy worker'. Barbara is entered as 'Barbara Price', with her personal occupation listed as 'unpaid domestic duties', which suggests that Price regarded her as his common-law wife. (A later amendment to the Register altered Barbara's surname, probably at her request.) Most of the families who lived nearby were poor and the sight of debt-collectors banging on front doors was common. The local primary school had closed in mid-September on the assumption that many children in Hayes would be evacuated to more rural areas, so Barbara decided to home-school her son and daughter. It was not a great success. She was not a patient teacher, although she did spend many hours taking Julian and Caroline on country walks when she would point out trees and flowers. She also read to them and encouraged them to draw and make things at home. Nevertheless, Julian spent a lot of time with his friends roaming on the land opposite their house, despite Barbara's reservations about the local children, whom she thought scruffy, badly behaved and none too clean. Where there should have been another row of Honey houses, there were half-finished foundations, incomplete walls and piles of planks and scaffolding. Julian, now seven years old, loved his newly acquired freedom and enjoyed being in a gang, which was an education in itself. Out of the rubble he and his mates made a headquarters where they would plot their next adventure. One plan, drawn up to test the loyalty of gang members, required each boy to choose a much-loved possession and bury it in a large hole along with the gang's other treasures. Julian decided to give up his favourite book, *Hansel and Trudi: A Story of the Austrian Tyrol* by Averil Demuth. After a few days, Barbara noticed it was missing and asked where it had gone. Frightened that he would be ridiculed by his gang mates, Julian promised to tell her so long as they went to dig it up after dark. The book was retrieved, creased and muddy, and Barbara roundly expressed her disapproval. This was not the only time Julian was strongly reprimanded by his mother while they lived in Hayes. Playing with the local children enriched his vocabulary considerably. On one occasion he tripped at the bottom of the staircase at home and, having banged his knee, loudly shouted 'Fuck!' Two doors opened immediately, Barbara came out of one and Price out of the other like figures on a weather clock; they both smacked him hard and said he must never repeat that word.[7]

As well as worrying about the children, Barbara was growing anxious about money again. Price earned just over £4 a week at the factory (about £320 today), slightly less than the average weekly wage of £4.45 at that time.[8] It was not much on which to keep a family of four, particularly as the gas and electricity meters seemed to swallow innumerable coins when the weather turned cold. Barbara soon realized that they would be unable to manage on Price's wages and they began pawning their possessions, including some of her jewellery. Price took it to London where it raised more money than he would have been offered locally. After a few weeks they were unable to afford any more coal and were reduced to burning a couple of chairs. The winter of 1939/40 was the coldest for forty-five years; the Thames froze over and many villages were cut off by deep snow. Barbara dreaded not being able to keep her children warm. She went out during the day to collect dry branches which they would burn in the fireplace in the drawing room, and in the evenings, under cover of darkness, Price would carry home wooden scaffolds from the building site. They had no saw with which to cut them up so they would place one end of a scaffold in the kitchen boiler, with the other end poking out into the hall. They would gradually move the huge lump of wood forward as it burned brightly. The days when Barbara and Price drove glamorous cars and ate out in London restaurants seemed a very long time ago.

As well as having to endure the bitter cold, the family also had to cope with several minor illnesses. Julian developed long scabs on his limbs which Barbara bathed with salted water and Price suffered several bouts of severe conjunctivitis that necessitated yet more bowls of warm salty water. He took to wearing his black eye patch for days at a time. He also suffered from a tooth infection and rheumatism. Worn down by these ailments and by working long hours in the factory, he lost his former jaunty buccaneer spirit and became a bad-tempered man. Having to work nights made him even more irritable and, on one occasion when Caroline – now aged four – woke him up by clumping about the house (she was a heavy-footed child), he lost his temper and hit her. Caroline went white with shock and Barbara was appalled. Price was full of remorse but for Barbara it was a warning that she was living with a man who could become violent when angry – something she had seen in her father. She began to fantasize about a new life elsewhere, with or without Price.

Christmas brought some cheer: the local shops suddenly looked colourful with their decorations and festive lights glowing warmly through the cold winter greyness. The large pond in a nearby village froze over completely and Barbara and the children learned to skate, which they found exhilarating. Nevertheless Barbara began to think seriously about how she could leave Hayes. Having already introduced petrol rationing, the government announced that bacon, butter and eggs were to be rationed from 8 January 1940 and that further food rationing would follow. This depressed Barbara, to whom food was important; it had been difficult enough providing reasonable meals for the four of them even without rationing. She also felt that the children were running wild and that it was time that Julian, who would be eight in two months' time, went back to school.

Barbara dreamed almost every night and always in colour. She believed deeply in the significance of her dreams and thought of them as windows into the soul. One dream was vivid enough for her to share with Price and the children the following day at breakfast. In it she was standing naked on a small sand hillock on a tropical desert island, surrounded by a turquoise sea and a deep blue sky. Around her some beautiful pink flamingos were dancing slowly and rhythmically, moving their heads and wings up and down. As they circled round her, she noticed that they were starting to pull at their chests with their beaks. Horrified, she watched the birds continue to mutilate themselves until their beaks were tearing at great bleeding holes. The flamingos danced until they all dropped down dead, wrecked and ruined, in an awful bloody circle around her. The dream perhaps indicates something of the helplessness that Barbara felt in early 1940 and her anxiety that everything around her was disintegrating. Its echoes of the pelican myth, in which the bird tears at its own chest in order to feed its young, might suggest her fear of being unable to feed her children adequately at this time.

Whatever its meaning, the dream seemed to harden Barbara's resolve to leave Hayes. It had occurred to her that, if she could find a job as a house-keeper, her food would be supplied – and it might even be possible to take Julian and Caroline with her. In early January she and Price had several long conversations, and they decided that she should advertise her services as a cook-housekeeper in a national newspaper. Price did not want her to leave but he could see that life in Hayes was becoming difficult for her and the children. Barbara's own ambivalence about the move would later be reflected in *Mr Fox* when Caroline Seymour has mixed feelings about taking a post as a housekeeper:

> I hated the idea of that kind of work and living in someone's house and being bossed about by some frightful woman, but I thought that at least it would be a new start in life and would keep me going until something wonderful happened. In the back of my mind I was always sure that wonderful things were waiting for me, but I'd got to get through a lot of horrors first.[9]

Barbara received several replies to her advertisement and, in preparation for the next step in her life, she sold her remaining jewellery and bought some aprons and overalls. She decided on a Mrs Walton, who lived in Welwyn Garden City in Hertfordshire, as her future employer. Mrs Walton – who had a seven-year-old daughter – stipulated that Barbara could bring Caroline with her but not Julian. She explained that her daughter was a gifted and delicate child who would not enjoy the antics of a noisy boy – but Caroline would be most welcome to play with her. Barbara agreed to this condition and found a small private school on the south coast where Julian could board; it is unclear who paid the fees for this.

After the bleakness of Hayes, the tree-lined boulevards and well-planned centre of Welwyn Garden City cheered Barbara enormously and seemed to confirm that she had made the right decision. Mrs Walton welcomed Barbara into a large house full of polished oak floors; there were no mats or carpets to be seen in case dust should trigger her daughter's allergies. The small, cream-painted room at the top of the house, which she was to share with Caroline, was perfectly adequate. Barbara began to feel optimistic – but she soon discovered that Mrs Walton and her daughter were strict vegetarians and although there were plenty of dairy products in the kitchen, she was forbidden to touch their butter ration. Nor was there any tea or coffee in the house; Mrs Walton and her daughter drank only water and herbal teas. The house was also cold. Mrs Walton believed in fresh air therapy so windows were thrown open even when it was freezing outside, and in February they would often eat their lunch of eggs or vegetable stew in the summerhouse in the garden. Like Caroline Seymour in *Mr Fox*, Barbara did not find this ascetic life congenial: 'We had watercress and grated carrot and bread and peanut butter for "tea" and the table had American cloth instead of a tablecloth. I expect it was more hygienic. It was so cold I felt like crying.'[10] It soon became clear that Mrs Walton was a mean-spirited woman who was obsessive about diet and hygiene, and that her daughter was very spoiled. Barbara and Caroline often went hungry and Barbara supplemented her child's diet in whatever way she could, sometimes rifling the kitchen cupboards for anything tasty – 'Eat these, they will do you good', she would say to Caroline as she handed her some dates. After a few weeks, Mrs Walton informed Barbara that as well as being cook and housekeeper, she was also to be responsible for the shopping and for the wooden floors, which had to be polished once a week, as well as for wash-day on Mondays, the only day on which there was running hot water in the house. Barbara was allowed one half-day off each week, although she and Caroline were under strict instructions not to go shopping in Woolworths or see a film at the cinema in case they brought home germs. Their favourite treat was to sit near the fire in a local tea-shop, drinking tea and eating buttered toast.

*   *   *

Although the Blitz did not begin until September 1940, everyone knew that London would be a prime target for the Luftwaffe once the Germans started bombing England seriously. By the early spring of 1940 Mrs Walton was growing increasingly nervous about living only 20 miles from the city and made arrangements to move with her daughter to Scotland. Barbara was told peremptorily that her services were no longer required and so she set about advertising herself as a cook/housekeeper once again. This time she was luckier. Her new employer, Mr Turnbull, was a widower with two daughters at home: Sarah was 24 years old and Lucinda, aged 18, had a pilot boyfriend in the RAF. Their brother lived away and came home only occasionally. Barbara was assured that her two children would be welcome at 'The Manor', which was a great relief as Julian was very unhappy at his boarding school, where the toilets were filthy and the teaching poor; at the age of eight he was still unable to read. They were to live in the cottage that was attached to the main house but was quite separate with its own front door. Barbara was thrilled at the prospect and was not disappointed when she arrived.

Weston Manor House in the village of Weston in north Hertfordshire was a large and beautiful red brick house, built in the seventeenth century and added to throughout the eighteenth and nineteenth centuries. It had a splendid yellow front door, and an imposing high brick wall surrounded the land on which it stood. Owned by the Pryor family of Weston Park, its current tenant, Mr Turnbull, was a tall, well-built man who was good-natured and generous. He spent most of his time in London, where he worked as a senior figure in the police force, but, when home, he wore a cap and tweed plus-fours and became a country gentleman. His daughters were cheerful young women and the atmosphere in the house was relaxed and happy. The family's many animals reminded Barbara of Bell Court: there was a small dog that would perform tricks for a biscuit; a white pedigree giant poodle; a goat that devoured any paper left lying around (it had recently eaten a ten shilling note and a ration book); and, finally, a large and very fierce parrot that lived in the scullery and was free to fly out of the window when it fancied perching in the fruit trees in the garden for a change. The house was surrounded by 14 acres of land which were dotted with tall redwood trees. There was a duck pond and a kitchen garden looked after by 'Old Ives', who could neither read nor write but who was expert at growing asparagus and was shrewd with money. He was also responsible for the gun dogs, housed in outside kennels. He no doubt reminded Barbara of Palmer, who had looked after the Bayley dogs when she was a child – and he was to become the inspiration for the character of gentle 'Old Ives' in *Who was Changed and Who was Dead*.

Barbara had to decide each week's menus with the eldest daughter, Sarah, and was responsible for cooking and serving up meals; she also had to oversee Joan, the maid, who came in on weekdays. The two daughters were very different from each other. Sarah was gentle, serious and practical, whereas Lucinda was slightly eccentric – she once knitted a jumper out of the white poodle's fur and dyed it yellow with boiled onion skin juice – and she was always 'up for a lark'. She painted, and had a small studio outside which was crowned by a large animal skull meant to keep intruders at bay. Both sisters were kind and always patient with the children. Just before Christmas 1940, Lucinda invited Julian and Caroline to help her stamp out 'Happy Christmas' in giant letters in the snow outside. Within a few minutes her RAF boyfriend was circling over The Manor and dipped his wings before he flew off.

The Turnbulls were not only kind; they were also well read. The house had a dedicated library room with books up to the ceiling and a ladder for reaching those on high shelves – and even the upstairs lavatory was lined with bound volumes of *Punch*. Barbara was given free rein of the library and immersed herself in novels during the evenings, reading and re-reading books by Dickens, Trollope and the Brontës, and losing herself in the dark world of the great Russians – Tolstoy, Chekhov and Dostoyevsky. She was not the only one who enjoyed curling up with a book in the evenings. Wartime Britain saw an unprecedented boom in reading. New books sold out within days of release and libraries countrywide were denuded by borrowers. The classics were particularly popular – and when Russia entered on the side of the Allies in 1941, the popularity of Russian novelists soared. During the grim days of the war, reading offered both escape and consolation.[11]

Everyone's lives had been changed by the war. Barbara's sister Kathleen's husband, Teddy Catford, was now working for the Crown Film Unit, part of the Ministry of Information, which made films for the general public, many of them relating to the war effort. Barbara's favourite sister, Chloe, had returned from Jordan to London in 1939 with her husband John Faraday, who had resigned that year from his post as a brigadier in the Arab Legion in order to fight in the war against Germany. To his great disappointment, he was considered too old at the age of 40 for active service in his former regiment, the Irish Guards, and instead became a Provost Marshall and later a flight lieutenant in the RAF. Having contracted poliomyelitis while abroad, Chloe came home with a bad limp and needed to use sticks for support. She chose to wear trousers or long skirts to disguise her disability and got about locally on an adult-sized tricycle that had special holders for her sticks.[12] She and John lived in a fine Georgian house in Church Street (now Old Church Street) in Chelsea, close to the Chelsea Arts Club. On her weekend visits to London, Barbara would stay with Kathleen in her old flat in Kilburn Priory and visit both Chloe and Nan. She also saw many friends, including Diana Brinton Lee; the two women were now on good terms again (probably because Diana assumed that Barbara and Price had separated) and Diana was always anxious for news of Caroline. Now a volunteer driver for the Women's Army Auxiliary Corps, Diana was still working and writing for the Mass Observation organization.[13] Rupert Lee had become a major in the Home Guard and commanded the North Kensington Division, cycling 16 miles a day to carry out his duties.[14] Barbara's long-time admirer, Francis Codd, had become a British auxiliary and was serving on the fireboat *Massey Shaw* with the London Fire Brigade; he had taken part in the evacuation of Dunkirk in May 1940, sailing to France three times to pick up British soldiers from the coast. They all had stories to tell, especially Francis who, having returned to Ramsgate from his second trip to Dunkirk, set out to visit his mother who lived nearby but was seized by two members of the Home Guard. Seeing his blonde hair and scruffy appearance, they thought he might be a German spy and hauled him off to the local police station. On his final return trip from Dunkirk, Francis saw a ship blow up about a mile away; sailing closer he saw the sea full of screaming men, some of them badly injured, a scene that would haunt his memory for many years.[15]

During her London trips Barbara also spent time with Price, who was still devoted to her. He wrote to her regularly and even visited The Manor once, although he arrived hot and bothered because a puncture had resulted in his driving half the journey there on a slowly deflating tyre. His anxiety about his car – and the journey home – only added to the discomfort he felt during his visit, during which he shifted his feet nervously in front of the two sisters. Debonair and confident on the surface, he was still at heart a working-class boy who felt ill at ease socially in the company of the upper middle class – a vulnerability that manifested itself either in truculence (as with Diana) or in nervous mannerisms (as with the Turnbulls). During his visit he told Barbara that he was thinking of investing in a London property and would she move in with him if he did? She refused, determined to remain independent.

Unlike her friends and some of her relatives, Barbara was not directly involved in the war effort – women with children under 14 were not expected to take on such work – but she did see its impact on London, including buildings collapsed into vast holes, buses upended like toys, and people sleeping under blankets on Tube station platforms. The bombing raids frequently resulted in huge fires that swept across areas of London, and firemen fought in vain with inadequate water supplies to contain them. On one visit in September 1940, Barbara was shocked by the devastation of World's End, an area of Camden in north London, after a bombing raid by the Luftwaffe. The experience later fed into *A Touch of Mistletoe*. Seeing 'torn houses exposing people's pathetic belongings' and 'the ARP [Air Raid Precaution] men digging out dead bodies or carrying the living wrapped in grey blankets', Victoria Green can hardly believe 'the extraordinary things that had happened to the streets where we had walked the previous day'.[16] The Blitz had begun. London and other cities were bombed relentlessly from 7 September 1940 for 56 nights. England's capital had become a place 'with no street lights, no traffic and no pedestrians to speak of; just an empty, dark city, torn with great explosions, racked with ack-ack fire, lit with lurid flames, acrid smoke, its air full of the dust of fallen buildings'.[17] More than 40,000 civilians were killed by Luftwaffe bombs during the Blitz, almost half of them in London. Barbara was relieved that her children were over thirty miles from its centre. Much as she loved the city, now was no time to return to it. In any case, Julian and Caroline had no desire to go back to London; they were very happy at The Manor in Weston. The village, which surrounded a green with a pond, was small and safe. The local police station was an ordinary house where the village policeman lived; he was a big man who spent a lot of time digging his garden with his shirt sleeves rolled up and his braces hanging down either side of his trousers. Every now and then he would put on his uniform and cycle slowly around the village making sure that everything was as it should be. Pugh's shop sold daily essentials, including wonderful bootlaces that were cut to demand from a large sheet of leather. Near the church another shop sold bread, cereal, pearl barley and tinned food. Opposite was the Post Office. All other shopping needs could be met by catching a return coach to Hitchin once a week on market day.

Julian spent a lot of time outdoors, climbing trees, feeding the ducks with Ives the gardener and making dens in the hay bales in a neighbour's barn, where he once inadvertently caused a disastrous fire by taking an oil lamp into his straw retreat. With the village children he played marbles, hopscotch, hoops, raced buggies made from old prams and scrumped apples from local gardens. But best of all was the 'cow shit game'. The boys would take it in turns to shin up a tree where they would perch on a branch, using a smaller leafy branch as a shield; the other boys would scoop up cruddy lumps of cow dung and hurl them at the victim in the tree. The winner was whoever could stay up in the tree longest. At the end of the battle they would all troop home to certain punishment. Julian was always told firmly by his mother to undress outside and get straight into the bath.

There were more risky games, however; one of Julian's friends had an air rifle, which the small gang of boys practised using in turn. A favourite pastime was shooting at bluebottles on the ceiling. The aim was to hit the insect exactly, a feat that – if successful – resulted in a hole bizarrely surrounded by the fly's legs. The more dangerous side of gun play became evident one day when a boy was accidentally shot in the groin. When he dropped his trousers the others could see the pellet as a blue shadow under the skin. They decided to operate themselves rather than tell the adults and have the rifle confiscated. The shaken victim was exhorted to be brave while one of the gang dug into the blue spot with the tip of his penknife. The slug popped out leaving surprisingly little damage, and the gun games continued. Another gun was used for shooting rabbits. This was a challenge because it was important to hit the head so that the rabbit died immediately, rather than retreating wounded into its burrow. It could then be taken home for the pot which, given that the government had halved the meat ration in January 1941, was very welcome. The boys sometimes also used a ferret to catch them. After netting a few rabbit holes, they would put the ferret down one entrance and watch for a rabbit to emerge from another, at which point the boys would dive and seize it. Julian found it all very exciting.

Caroline spent more time indoors than her brother and became devoted to Sarah and Lucinda. She was especially fond of red-haired Sarah, who would spend hours playing games with her and who looked after both children when Barbara spent weekends in London. Affectionately called 'Mrs P' by the two sisters, Barbara was by now also responsible for the horse and walking the dogs, extra duties that she enjoyed. Early in January 1941 she enrolled Caroline at the local primary school. During the same month, Julian became a pupil at a small private school in the nearby hamlet of Clothall, his fees paid by the generous Mr Turnbull. A kind and patient Australian teacher took a shine to Julian, describing him as 'decidedly impish' and 'full of good humour' in one school report.[18] She saw his potential and gave him extra tuition in reading. The boy was suddenly liberated into a world of fantasy and imagination; by Christmas 1941 he was avidly reading Andrew Lang's *The Green Fairy Book* and thereafter anything that took his fancy in the library, including Bunyan's *Pilgrim's Progress*. He even spent hours sitting on the hard wooden seat in the upstairs lavatory devouring volumes of *Punch*. Barbara was delighted, although she had not been unduly anxious about Julian's illiteracy. Her own education had been extremely haphazard and she did not think that she had been damaged or disadvantaged by it; in fact, she thought that too much education could inhibit the imagination.[19] She believed – like many of her former bohemian contemporaries in London – that creativity and good manners in children were more important than academic success.

Barbara's days were busy, but at weekends and after school hours she and the children went skating in the winter and sometimes had picnics in a nearby field in the summer. There, a horse would bare its lips, eager for Marmite sandwiches. She made her own friends in the village, including Mr and Mrs Cockeral, whose children she gave painting lessons. Life was pleasant enough, although it was hardly what she had wished for when she first moved to London, full of dreams of becoming an important artist. Her nostalgia for city life at this time was later to feed into *Our Spoons Came from Woolworths*, in which Sophia Fairclough works as a cook and housekeeper for Mr Redhead, a gentleman farmer, and his family in Bedfordshire:

> The country was beautiful and peaceful, but I found myself longing for London. I would have given anything to walk down a typical London street made of rather dirty yellow bricks, the houses tall and semi-detached, with a flight of steps going up to the front door, and iron railings with rather straggly private hedges encased behind, and every now and then a cat asleep on a window-sill. I could imagine a man passing down the street disturbing the giant pigeons by shouting out the name of an evening paper, and a smell of toast in the air, and at the poorer end of the street, small boys would be making a frightful din on their roller skates. I longed to be queen of my own home with all my treasures around me. I would look out of the window at all the beauty, but it wasn't what I wanted.[20]

Barbara was desperate to return to London, but she recognized that at least she was now financially independent and her children were happy and safe at Weston. In a letter written in March 1941 she told Diana that

> The children love it here and have plenty of good food and fresh air ... Julian goes to a very good school and rides ... [Caroline] is very beautiful, and rather tall, curly golden hair and a lovely complexion, she is very loving and gentle, quite intelligent but not so quick as Julian.

She bemoaned the fact that John had not seen the children for several years, but revealed that she had finally managed to convince the Royal Artillery that he should pay her a weekly allowance for them of £1.1s (about £70 today). She also told Diana, with some pride, that she was now a very competent cook:

> When I first came here I had to cook so many things I had never attempted before, after I had the orders for the day I used to spend a quarter of an hour in the lav. with a cookery book but now I can cook anything. I don't turn a hair at a dinner party for ten and the cupboards are stiff with my bottled fruit, jams, jellies, mincemeat, plum puddings and my cakes are just like advertisements for flour, so I have got something I can always do to earn a living now.[21]

But in her heart of hearts, Barbara was becoming restless; although she liked the Turnbulls, she disliked being a servant and also badly wanted a home of her own. She was now 33 years old and her life seemed to be slipping away in a rural backwater. Her unhappiness with her status was later to inspire a melancholy passage in *Our Spoons Came from Woolworths*, which describes how Sophia Fairclough is excluded from the wedding celebrations held for Mr Redhead's daughter, Rose:

> Everybody went into the dining-room; I wasn't sure if I was meant to attend the wedding-breakfast or just wash it up in the scullery – nobody had said anything about it – so I sat on the kitchen table and waited for someone to come out looking for me; but only the girls who waited at table came out and a lot of laughter and noise [...] It made me sad and awkward, so I went up to my bedroom and sat looking out of the window and felt hollow and depressed. After a time there were voices and goodbyes and cars starting and I knew it was time to go downstairs and clear up.[22]

The experience of working as a servant – albeit as a cook/housekeeper rather than a scullery maid – was a salutary one for Barbara. The young upper-middle-class woman who had complained about her maids to Diana now understood what it was like to be at someone else's beck and call and to be entirely reliant on them for a living. While she retained a strong sense of herself as better than most and regarded domestic work as only a temporary phase in her life, Barbara began to develop a sympathetic understanding of the difficulties facing working-class women, although she could never tolerate laziness. Unlucky women, stuck in menial jobs, were to pepper her novels: Marcella Murphy, the servant who has only one nostril and no close relatives, is passed around the Green family after Mrs Green's death in *A Touch of Mistletoe*. Terrified by the bombing during the Blitz, she is comforted by Victoria, who sits up all night with her and who misses her badly when she dies: 'We had been through so much together. She left me her life's savings, which amounted to nearly three hundred pounds, and I arranged for her to be buried in the village graveyard, beside my mother and grandfather.'[23] Mrs Churchill, who comes to nurse Alice Rowland's sick mother and do the housework in *The Vet's Daughter*, and who is 'old and square under her man's cloth cap, her legs very far apart and her stockings wrinkled', has a 'hoarse voice that was full of warm feeling'. She brings much comfort into a home dominated by a cruel father. After Mrs Rowlands dies and Mrs Churchill is told to leave, she gives Alice her address in case she ever needs help: 'because, my poor dear, you don't seem to 'ave a friend in the world'.[24] There is compassion in Barbara's Dickensian portraits of these women servants, and also respect for their loyalty, their generosity and their ability to see through tyrannical or inadequate men.

* * *

In the autumn of 1941 the usual routine of Weston Manor House was disturbed when two policemen from outside the village knocked on the door. They wished to talk to Barbara about her husband, John Pemberton, who had deserted from the Royal Artillery in mid-September.[25] They wanted to interview him but he was nowhere to be found. Did Mrs Pemberton know of his whereabouts? Barbara made it clear that she and her husband had separated in 1935 and that she had no idea where he was. Privately, she was not surprised he had deserted, given how unsuited to army life he would have been. She later discovered that he had been desperately unhappy in the Royal Artillery and had one day decided that he could take no more. A relative had sent him £5 as a birthday present with which he bought a train ticket from Edinburgh to London. Soon after arriving at Euston, he rented a flat in Soho and quickly disappeared into its underground bohemian world. He managed to earn enough money by theatre scene painting and freelance commissions to keep body and soul together, and made sure he kept away from any figure of authority who might ask awkward questions. He was not the only one: by the end of 1941 over 20,000 men had deserted from the armed forces.[26] Those with artistic sensibilities headed for London and gravitated towards Fitzrovia, an area still popular with artists. They looked out for each other and rubbed shoulders with writers and painters who had managed to avoid being called up. In 1941 Dylan Thomas moved permanently to London, having been temporarily excused conscription because of a lung condition, and made films for the Ministry of Information 'rather than give his "one and only body" to the war'. George Orwell, who had been declared unfit for military service, was also based in central London and joined the Home Guard before working for the BBC's Eastern Service.[27] There were many other writers drinking in Fitzrovia, including Louis MacNeice, also employed by the BBC, and Roy Campbell, the South African poet, who was working as an Air Raid Precautions warden in 1941. John would have had good company at the bar.

When the police visited Weston, Barbara did not know where John was, but she soon found out through her London contacts and visited him occasionally. She kept her husband's address to herself, however; she knew that the punishment for desertion – anything from a few months' to ten years' incarceration in a military prison – could be severe and she did not wish that on him. She also realized that her plan to restart divorce proceedings would now have to be postponed, for that would mean revealing his whereabouts. The Pemberton family was deeply shocked by John's desertion. The contrast with his brother David – who had been so kind to Julian when he stayed with the Alldays as a child – was stark. David had died a hero's death in November 1940 at the age of 28. A squadron leader in the Royal Air Force, his Spitfire had been shot down during a German bombing raid. His plane fell to the ground and although he survived the initial impact, he quickly bled to death, both his legs having been completely severed in the crash. He was posthumously awarded the Distinguished Flying Cross and buried in Broadway in the Cotswolds, where his father now lived. Within the Pemberton family, John lived under a cloud after his desertion. His parents might have shown some sympathy despite their embarrassment, but John's future brother-in-law, who served in the Australian Navy, called him a coward and later refused to speak to Julian because he was the son of a deserter.

*   *   *

While John Pemberton was in hiding from the authorities after his desertion in 1941, Barbara and the children were safe and comfortable at The Manor House in Weston. Although she felt she was marking time working as a housekeeper there, it was a very fruitful period for Barbara in more ways than one. Not only had she become an excellent cook but, more importantly, she had started writing. In the evenings she would amuse the children with stories of her childhood in Warwickshire. There was an old typewriter in a small box room in the cottage and she began recording her memories of growing up in Bidford-on-Avon so that Julian and Caroline would have a record of their mother's early life. Perhaps the similarities between The Manor House and Bell Court and between Weston and Bidford had triggered her imagination. Writing also filled lonely evenings when the children were in bed: 'it was just something to do – to go back to your magical childhood', she told Ursula Holden many years later.[28] The fragmentary nature of the memoir and its short chapters might owe something to the fact that Barbara was always tired by the time she settled down to write; what was to become *Sisters by a River* reads as a series of tableaux rather than a coherent narrative. Nevertheless, she found the experience exhilarating and discovered that creating cameos in words gave her as much pleasure as sculpting or painting a picture. Like many gifted women before her, she soon realized that writing was also cheaper and more flexible than other art forms: she did not need to buy canvases or clay and she could write when it suited her.

Although Barbara was sometimes rather cavalier with the facts of family history for dramatic effect (her mother was 20 when she married, not 18, and her grandmother miscarried twins rather than having seven stillborn sons, for example), *Sisters by a River* vividly conveys the nature of her childhood and life in an English village in the early twentieth century. The memoir, peppered with misspellings suggesting a child-like mentality, combines humour with a sharp, unflinching insight into human nature. Despite the assumed naivety of the narrator, the memoir is many-layered and more complicated than it might seem on a first reading. The range of humour is wide, varying from minor amusing incidents such as the father finding that the matches in his matchbox had been replaced by ancient toe bones that the children have stolen from the local dig, to the comic macabre of death and decay, as when the children thwack the swollen corpses of pigs and goats in order to watch fountains of vile smelling body fluids spurt up into the air. Horrible incidents appear all the more grotesquely comic for being understated in the plain language of childhood:

> He bought her a goat and a white kitten to remember him by, but the goat burst and the kitten was run over by a train, all the same she did marry him just before she was eighteen, she also learnt how to cook.[29]

There is humour, too, in the inverse comic logic apparent in the narrator's child-like understanding of her mother's deafness: 'She was taken to several specialists but they could do nothing, one good thing being deaf stopped her having any more babies.'[30]

But alongside the comic run dark shadows: some of the most disturbing episodes in the memoir result from memories of an angry father. One day he beats his daughter savagely after she has made a mess with her breakfast egg, but it was 'nothing compared to the mess I was in when he had finished with me. I kept having a frightful nightmare that Daddy was a bellowing bull chaising me round the ash tree for nights after.'[31] There are several other such incidents when her father's rage results in physical violence. The child narrator's ambivalent feelings about her father – love mixed with fear – are brilliantly caught in a surreal vision of God the Father appearing to her as a large floating parchment bag, which glides up to her in the billiard room, inducing a terror that makes her faint to the floor. It is a hallucination that betrays both a vivid imagination and a deep-seated anxiety. But sometimes surreal visions are more comforting. The child and her sister Beatrix (based on Barbara's sister Nan), unable to sleep one night, see many beautiful different-coloured hats floating in the sky, a sight that soothes them to sleep. One of Barbara Comyns' admirers was to describe the episode as 'Chagallian'; another observed that it owed much to Magritte.[32] Barbara's first attempt at serious writing clearly indicates that her view of the world had been influenced by surrealism .

Country living and children are not romanticized in *Sisters by a River*. The grimmer side of rural life is ever present (one day the father's boat bumps against the floating corpse of a village boy) and the children's cruelty to pets and wildlife (operating on worms and riding rabbits until they 'squashed') is vividly described. The result is a picture of growing up in rural England that completely eschews sentimentality and nostalgia. It also seems to be a book in which everything is seen through the eyes of a child: the home and family relationships loom large, and important external events, such as the First World War, are entirely omitted.[33] But intimations of impending adulthood complicate the picture. The burden of menstruation and unhappy sexual outcomes are hinted at: the narrator observes that the menarches of Mary and Beatrix – described by the euphemism 'It' – are marked by mystery, blood and pain; a young maid is sent to the workhouse to have her illegitimate twins; and although we are never told what happened to beautiful little Jenny, a village girl, the way she changes following 'a wicked man jump[ing] out of a hedge' suggests rape.[34]

The narrative strategy is also more complex than it first appears, the language and naïve perspective of the child being offset by comments that betray the adult author. Examples include the sweep being liable for 'affaliation' orders (a child would hardly know about affiliation orders, although Barbara certainly did) and a memory of her mother walking down the path 'looking very like Hamlets father' after hiding herself away because of the bruises and black eye her husband had given her.[35] The narrator also sometimes refers to the adult self who is writing the memoir: 'when I'm applying for a job, or getting married'; 'Now I can cook anything'; 'Now I am grown up myself'.[36] The effect is complex: the child's voice gives a powerful sense of immediacy, whereas the adult voice suggests another, perhaps a more responsible and duller life waiting in the wings. The memoir ends with a letter dated 1 December 1941, in which Beatrix laments how 'Shellford' (Bell Court) has changed: the garden has run riot; bits of the house have fallen down; 'the coach house is a shop and there is also a hairdressers in the apple room, the engine room is called Shellford court café' and there is 'an evacuee mother and child living in the cottage the governesses used to sleep in'.[37] These closing words lend the memoir an elegiac air despite its dark undertones.

Sisters by a River is not a book for children, although its author's use of a naïve worldview was to become a hallmark of her later novels, even when her narrators are adults. Although Barbara was often shy and awkward with strangers, she was always able to communicate easily with children. She understood them and managed to inhabit the imaginative landscape of childhood throughout her life. She saw in children a clarity of mind and simplicity of expression which, in her view, many dismissed all too quickly. Some years later she was to write, 'I like to write about children because to me they often appear to be more alive and feeling than adults.'[38]

In January 1941 Barbara wrote to Diana thanking her for the fudge she had sent for Christmas and mentioned that she had started writing a book. She described it as not 'a child's one, but the way I write is so childish people may mistake it for one. I don't know who to send it to when it's finished, I don't expect it will ever be published but it keeps me amused in the evenings.' She had ideas for other books too: 'I have a children's book in my mind about eels, they are very romantic fish and go to the bottom of the Atlantic to lay their eggs, they are really more exciting than salmon.' The children's book was never written and the memoir was put away in a suitcase with some family photographs where it stayed for several years. Nevertheless, Barbara's writing career had begun.

8

Becoming Comyns

In 1942 Barbara decided it was time to move back to London. It seemed the right moment: the Blitz had ended in May 1941 and although London was still being bombed, it was not at the same intensity. Hitler was now turning his attention to Britain's other historic cities in what became known as 'the Baedeker Raids' (named after the famous German guidebook). Exeter, Bath, Norwich and York were all heavily bombed in April and Canterbury was attacked in late May. The Americans had entered the war in December 1941 and by early 1942 thousands of American soldiers were stationed in the UK, waiting to be involved in the planned invasion of Europe; there was suddenly a growing sense of optimism that the Allies could win the war. There were also pressing personal reasons why Barbara wanted to return to London. She was at heart an urban creature and was becoming bored with the countryside. She was finding company at The Manor rather dull now that the sparky Lucinda had joined the WAAF (Women's Auxiliary Air Force) and no longer enlivened the house with her energy and her laughter. Nor did she wish to remain a cook/housekeeper for the rest of her life and, most important of all, she desperately wanted a home of her own again.

Price offered her just that. One of his houses in London, 153 Abbey Road, had been bombed during the Blitz and, as a builder, he was able to reclaim the cost of repairs from the War Damage Commission.[1] With that money, or what remained of it, he decided to buy a lease on another house; as people were still fleeing the capital, property prices had reached rock bottom. He planned to convert the building into flats, keeping one for his own use. Would Barbara join him in the venture? This time, she decided she would. She had managed to save some money while working as a housekeeper and was willing to invest this in their joint purchase of a lease. She and Price were back in business together. Barbara's eldest sister Molly, who earned her living as a housekeeper, moved into The Manor with her twin boys (the result of a Hillmorton groom's successful seduction of her some years before) and took Barbara's place. Although Julian and Caroline were sad to leave The Manor, they were pleased to hear that they would be living with Price again.

On a warm day in the early summer of 1942, Price drove to Weston to collect Barbara, her children and a white giant poodle puppy (a parting gift from the Turnbulls) and take them to the newly acquired property in London. The journey into town, as described in *Mr Fox*, was somewhat surreal: 'we passed a number of bombed houses and in their gardens the trees had gone a whitish-grey from plaster, and some had curtains twisted among their branches, and on the roof of one house was a broken old piano'.[2] Barbara's new home, 103 King Henry's Road, was a big semi-detached house in Primrose Hill, an elegant part of north-west London. It was a handsome building of four storeys comprising a basement flat, a large ground floor area with three arched bay windows, and two storeys above. The house needed a lot of work but Price had made every effort to make the basement flat feel like home. He loved Barbara and wanted her to stay. If Barbara's account in *Mr Fox* is accurate, he had furnished the flat tastefully and equipped the kitchen with solid copper pans and a beautiful tea set (which was, however, stamped with the name of a well-known hotel, so presumably not an entirely honest acquisition). The kitchen cupboards were stacked with food that was tightly rationed and not easy to come by, such as tins of fruit and chocolate biscuits. The only sadness was that the Great Dane was no longer part of their household – he had been killed during a bombing raid – but at least they had the poodle puppy to replace him. Price's plan was to join Barbara and the children in the flat at weekends but to continue living in Hayes during the week while he worked at the Fairey Aircraft factory. Once the other flats had been converted and tenants started paying rent, Barbara and Price would share the profit after payment on the lease had been deducted. It seemed a good plan and Barbara was very happy to be queen in her own home again.

Meanwhile, Price's workmen – a small motley crew made up of deserters and petty criminals who had managed to avoid conscription – were working hard on the other flats in the building. Price's business acumen enabled him to take full advantage of the racketeering opportunities thrown up by the war. He paid his workmen reasonably well, but less than the going rate for registered builders and plumbers; as deserters and conscription evaders they had little choice but to accept what he offered. Price often sailed close to the wind as far as the law was concerned, ignoring for instance the many new building regulations brought in during the war, and bribing inspectors if necessary. 'With all these new laws it was awfully difficult not to be a criminal', thinks Caroline Seymour in *Mr Fox*, suggesting that perhaps Barbara was complicit with much of Price's racketeering.[3] He also encouraged his workmen to take whatever was needed – whether it was baths, furniture, table linen, lead piping or dustbins – from bomb-damaged houses that had been left empty by their owners.[4] Price had no qualms about plundering bombed houses for his own purposes. The owners would be able to claim compensation for damaged or missing articles on their return, while he could make good use of them and provide much-needed accommodation for people who had been made homeless by the bombing raids. He was not the only insouciant looter in town: stealing from bombed-out houses under cover of blackout hours was a common activity during the war, despite the likelihood of a prison sentence if you were caught. Residents of London who returned home in 1942, after the Blitz was over, found that 'whole streets of bombed houses had been systematically stripped of everything: carpets, beds, suites of furniture, cookers – even heavy iron mangles'.[5] Nor did Price allow petrol rationing to curtail his activities. The small petrol allowance for the private motorist made available in 1939 was abolished in 1942; petrol was to be used for official war business only from then on until 1945.[6] But there were always petrol coupons to be had illegally. Forged petrol coupons could be bought through underground contacts and occasionally legitimate petrol coupons that had been stolen in bulk from government departments found their way onto the black market. It was a dangerous game – black marketeering carried a maximum penalty of fourteen years in prison – but Price was a skilful negotiator and had no intention of letting war restrictions cramp his style.

While Barbara was anxious about the risks Price took, she appreciated the 'extras' he brought home and admired his resourcefulness. She had little time for writing or painting during 1942; she was left in charge of the tenants at 103 King Henry's Road during the week and there were invariably problems to be sorted out as well as the children to look after. She no longer had a typewriter and anyway Price was keener for her to earn money than to write – so she channelled her creativity into making small things that she could sell. 'I've been very busy lately painting things for shops, flowers on trays and all kind of junk. The flat looks like a warehouse, I get very bored with flowers because I paint animals much better', she wrote to Diana.[7] Air raids, of which there were several during the autumn of 1942, were also time-consuming. At the first sound of a siren, the tenants would rush down the stairs and congregate in the hall in Barbara's basement flat, which she did not mind apart from the fact that they wanted to chat and expected her to make them tea once the raid was over. The house suffered no major damage but windows frequently shattered during the raids and she had to oversee their repair.

Barbara also became caught up in Price's next venture. Once the conversion of 103 King Henry's Road was complete, he cast his eye on the adjoining house. Number 105 King Henry's Road was in a very poor state and Price bought it cheaply. Barbara and he spent most weekends planning what they would do with it. Her involvement in the renovation of the house next door later fed into Barbara's description of Caroline Seymour's experience in *Mr Fox*:

> All the deserters came back and started work on the empty house. I had to make them tea every afternoon, and they expected to have buns as well. Although they hadn't any ration-books they seemed to have masses of food and often brought pots of jam and butter to sell to Mr. Fox, and sometimes whole packing cases of tinned food. Perhaps one of their families kept a grocer's shop.
>
> Mr. Fox came almost every day to make sure the men were working properly. He was doing night duty at this factory now, and at first I wondered how he could manage with so little sleep, but he told me there were lots of rubber boats and he used to sleep in one most of the night and pay a man ten shillings a week to call him before the inspector came round.[8]

The work on 105 King Henry's Road proceeded apace – Price was an efficient foreman – and soon he and Barbara were drawing rents from seven flats.

*   *   *

Now that she was back in London, Barbara occasionally saw Diana and Rupert, both of whom wanted to stay in close contact with Caroline. After Christmas 1942, Barbara wrote to thank Diana for the toy she had sent Caroline, and it is clear from her letter that no rationing privations affected the festive celebrations at 103 King Henry's Road that year: 'I hope you had a good Christmas, we did, I managed to get a turkey and pheasant at about six o'clock on Christmas Eve when I'd quite made my mind up to a tin of MOR or something frightful. It was nice to be in our own home and have people here and let the children make a noise.'[9] In the same letter she told Diana that she and Price would soon be moving to a smaller house nearby, which 'would be cheaper as it's almost at the end of the lease and we would have six rooms for ourselves'.

That house was 15 Harben Road in Hampstead, near Swiss Cottage Underground station. Dating from the 1830s, it was a solid three-storey building, much more light and airy than the basement flat in King Henry's Road, although it needed some building work and redecorating. It also had a large back garden where Barbara decided she would keep chickens. Eggs were rationed so keeping poultry became popular during the war, even though official egg rations had to be forfeited in order to do so. In *Mr Fox*, Caroline becomes very fond of her hens, reflecting Barbara's affection for her poultry:

24 Julian and Caroline playing, c. 1941

They made up for the destruction they caused by laying heaps of eggs, and they had very nice natures. Eventually I had three cocks and six hens, and when I called 'Come on, all my fine cocks', the cocks came rushing to the kitchen window; and if I called 'Come, my fine hens', the hens would come tripping to me. Which shows how intelligent they were.[10]

Barbara carefully preserved surplus eggs by submerging them in water mixed with waterglass powder in a large earthenware crock. There they would keep for up to a year and would either be eaten by the family or exchanged for other rationed foodstuffs.

Soon after they moved into the Harben Road house, one of Price's builders arrived to do some work on the top floor, but before he climbed the staircase he presented Price with something he had 'found' on a bus. He had been sitting on the top deck, near an American officer who had placed a neat small case on the floor by his side. The workman – seeing that the American was deeply engrossed in reading a newspaper – picked it up and leapt smartly off the bus when it reached Swiss Cottage. On closer inspection, the case turned out to contain a brand-new Olivetti portable typewriter. Price bought it from the builder and immediately gave it to Barbara. Delighted to have it, she began writing seriously again. Price was away during the week; the children were at school during the day; and there was a lull in the bombing raids. For the first time for some while she had time to think and write. She began drafting ideas for the book based on Price that was to become *Mr Fox*. She also started typing up memories of her life in bohemian London during her twenties and her marriage to John Pemberton. It was the beginning of *Our Spoons Came from Woolworths*, which would eventually be published in 1950.

About this time, Barbara converted briefly to Catholicism. She certainly believed in wonders and the supernatural, but she was not a practising Christian. She was perhaps – like many suffering the horrors and deprivations of war – suddenly drawn to a religion that was rich in colour and ritual and that seemed to offer comfort in the form of a benign and all-powerful God. Her sister Nan had been a Catholic for many years, so Barbara had witnessed at first hand its impact on a member of her family. And Catholicism had also become not only acceptable but fashionable in literary circles after the conversions of Graham Greene (1926), Evelyn Waugh (1930), Roy Campbell (1935) and Antonia White (who, having lapsed as a Catholic, reconverted in 1940). Barbara also took great delight in provoking the Pemberton family and the Alldays, with whom she now had little contact, but who were staunchly anti-Catholic and who were horrified by her conversion and by her insistence that Julian should become a Catholic too.

From the children's point of view, it all seemed very odd. Julian, who was now 11 years old, was taken away from The Hall, a prep school he had been attending in Swiss Cottage, and sent to St Aloysius, a Catholic college near Archway in Islington, a bus ride away from Harben Road. The military had taken over the main Victorian Gothic building and the children were taught in temporary huts in the grounds. Julian had not much cared for The Hall, where he had been frequently caned, but he fared better at St Aloysius. Although he was small for his age and left-handed, with a headful of striking auburn hair, he was never bullied because Price had taught him how to stand up to anyone who tried to intimidate him. He made some good friends at St Aloysius and entered with spirit into their many mischievous pranks. One of these involved sitting behind a man wearing a trilby when on the bus and carefully inserting used bus tickets into his hat band. When the boys were successful, the passenger left the bus with the rear of his hat adorned with a row of upright tickets, wearing what looked to them like a miniature Native American headdress. Despite being happy at St Aloysius, Julian disliked intensely its religious ethos and frequently challenged it; his time at the college only confirmed his deep suspicion of religion in general and of Catholicism in particular. Nor did Barbara herself show complete commitment to the faith: not having a prayer book to take to Mass, she took instead her copy of *Alice in Wonderland* – which was bound in red leather with gilt-edged pages – rather than buy one. After a few months, she gradually lost interest in Catholicism, much to the relief of Julian, who had been forced to visit Catholic priests who made him recite the Catechism. To add insult to injury, they had declared that the names 'Julian' and 'Gustav' were pagan and insisted on calling him 'Joseph'.

The fact that Price knew many petty criminals and black marketeers meant that Barbara became a part of that world too. On pleasant evenings they would walk up the hill from Harben Road to the pub at Swiss Cottage and drink with the locals. There were a couple of petty criminals they regularly chatted to who specialized in robbing post offices and had it down to a fine art. They would send a 'spotter' to a post office who would memorize details of the interior and the position of the safe. Another man, called the 'fitter', would break into the building at night to take a wax impression of the lock on the post office door so that a duplicate key could be made.[11] When the air raid siren sounded and everyone ran for cover, the criminals would immediately leap into their small van and make a beeline for the post office. There, rather than prising open the safe on the premises, they used special equipment to sever it from its moorings; they then took it away in order to open it at their leisure. These two rogues frequently boasted of their exploits while drinking in the pub, and Price found it all highly amusing. There is no record of what Barbara thought but, while she was with Price, she must have learned a great deal about the underworld.

*   *   *

During 1943 Barbara decided that she would buy her own house. She thought – probably with good reason – that her application for divorce from John and for maintenance costs for the children would be looked on more favourably if she were living on her own. From her half of the income from the flats in 103 and 105 King Henry's Road and from the top floor flat in Harben Road (rented to a young woman who went under the stage name of 'Helen Burns') she had saved some money, but not enough to buy a house. She discussed her plan with Price who, hoping she might marry him once her divorce was finalized, thought it was a good idea and said he would help finance the purchase. They sold what was left on the lease of Harben Road but continued to take rents from 103 and 105 King Henry's Road. Late in 1943 Price bought a house in Adelaide Road and Barbara bought a large semi-detached house, 15 Greville Place in St John's Wood, a very fashionable and select part of north London. It was one of a sweep of splendid three-storey houses with large basements built in the early nineteenth century. It was much bigger than 103 King Henry's Road and had an imposing elegant staircase, French windows and a veranda at the back.

Barbara set herself up there as a dog breeder and her three breeding bitches produced four or five litters a year in the basement. Depending on how they grew, she would sell the poodle puppies as miniature, normal or giant. This activity brought in a very good income, for by 1943 Londoners had decided to ignore the government's previous advice not to keep domestic animals in cities during the war, and poodles had suddenly become very fashionable pets. Barbara also began dabbling in antiques, going to auction rooms to pick up items which she would then sell on for a profit to galleries and local antique shops. The children loved the house; there was space enough for Caroline to set up her various toy theatres and leave them out for days (since meeting Helen Burns she had become stage-struck) and for Julian to have a whole room for his latest enthusiasm, making model aeroplanes. That room also became the home of a fox cub which he named 'Foxy'. Intrigued by his school friends' report that a pet shop in Camden was selling 'baby wolves', Julian decided to spend his savings on one. Barbara's love of animals overcame her initial resistance, and Foxy was allowed to sleep at the bottom of Julian's bed at night and given free run of the house and garden with the dogs during the day. He was an affectionate creature who would bark 'yik yik' excitedly when Julian returned from school. Julian was devoted to him, despite his many fleas.

Always on the lookout for the next money-making scheme, Price suggested they should set up a piano 'restoration' business at Greville Place, as Barbara's new home became known. The three large reception rooms downstairs could each take a grand piano, so the house was perfect for such a venture. Barbara ran advertisements in various papers along the lines of 'Have inherited grand piano, can't play, must sell'. Encouraged by Price, she bought old pianos at auctions and had them retuned, cleaned and, if they needed a face-lift, repolished. Julian and Caroline were in on the scheme: they were told to keep the three reception room doors shut in case a potential customer should happen to see all three pianos at the same time and suddenly become suspicious. They were also briefed about who was meant to see which one. 'The worse scenario was when people played a piano and then heard another one answering from across the hall, Barbara rushing from room to room looking a bit flustered', Julian later recorded in his memoir.

This particular enterprise was to provide Barbara with some lively episodes for her novel. Mr Fox and Caroline Seymour, Barbara's fictional counterpart, spend a weekend cleaning an old piano and superficially repairing it with some ivories that Mr Fox has stolen from the piano in his factory canteen. To their delight, there is an immediate response to their advertisement:

> There was a ring at the bell and it was a sad-looking man with long hair and a sallow face. He was the kind of man who used to play in cinemas in the silent-film days. He sat down at the piano and did kind of limbering movements with his fingers to show how musical he was; then he attacked the instrument and great chords sounded and other things, too. The newly-stuck ivories

came flying off like playing cards, and the sad little man stopped playing and wiped his fingers on the inside of his trouser pockets, then ran them through his hair and gave me a reproachful glance and left the house without saying anything.[12]

Mr Fox carefully coaches Caroline in the art of evasive answers; she is to lie about the ages of the pianos, and if anyone asks for a piano's serial number, she is to tell them it has been sold because only dealers asked such questions. Like Caroline and Mr Fox, Barbara and Price made a huge profit from their piano business during 1943. The demand for musical instruments rose during the war, perhaps because people were looking for ways to entertain themselves at home, and Barbara – who had gained valuable experience in auction bidding when buying cars for Price – became skilful at bidding for pianos they could sell on for a profit. She and Price learned the ropes of the business quickly; they soon realized that for many customers, the shape of a piano's legs and its general appearance were more important than its tone. In truth, their piano business was more of a racket than a restoration project.

Although Barbara and Price now lived apart, they saw a lot of each other, partly because of the piano business and partly because Price enjoyed seeing Julian and Caroline, of whom he was very fond. Julian, who still regarded Price as a father-figure, would often cycle over to Price's home in Adelaide Road and spent hours reading his huge collection of *Autocar* magazines. When Price was busy or away from home, Julian would make the food for his dogs, a job that involved boiling fish or horse meat and mixing it with the remains of a stale National loaf, grey and unappetising bread introduced by the government in 1942.

In the summer of 1943, petrol rationing notwithstanding, Price took Barbara and her children and her sister Kathleen on holiday. They set off in Price's glamorous French Delage motor car, which guzzled petrol, and made their way down to Chapel Porth, a beautiful beach about halfway between Newquay and St Ives on the north coast of Cornwall. Price knew exactly where to stop for black market petrol and where to buy food. Finding Chapel Porth, however, was a challenge as signposts had been taken down (to hamper any German spies) and locals refused to give directions because the Delage was not a British car and was therefore deeply suspicious. At the end of a very long journey, Price and his entourage managed to find their accommodation – two rented caravans in a field at the top of a cliff. Barbara and Price slept in one caravan and Kathleen and the two children slept in the other. The views were magnificent but the beach was cordoned off by barbed wire; there were signs warning of landmines in the area and advising pedestrians to stick to designated paths. It was worth the uncomfortable scramble under the wire, however; the beach was deserted and the weather perfect. The final treat was having cream teas with the Holbeach family who owned a farm nearby and whom Price knew well. He seemed to have useful contacts across the whole of England.

Barbara was still very fond of Price but she began gradually to detach herself emotionally from him. Now she had her own home, she wanted to mingle once again with artists and intellectuals – and perhaps she had had enough of the criminal fraternity in which Price moved so comfortably. Francis Codd, still devoted to Barbara, often came for tea at Greville Place, but she also invited artist friends and became close to several other men at this time, although she kept these relationships secret from Price. One admirer was a 60-year-old podgy and balding man called William Ohly, the inspiration for Leon, a character in *A Touch of Mistletoe* who owns an art gallery off Bond Street. Ohly was an English sculptor and art collector who had moved between England and Germany, fleeing the latter in 1934 when Hitler became Führer. When Barbara met him in 1943, he owned a large house in Barnet and the Berkeley Gallery in Davies Street, Mayfair. Ohly called frequently at Greville Place to see Lötchen, a beautiful German woman who rented a bed-sitting room in the house, but after a while he began to turn his attention to Barbara. Sometimes, when Barbara visited him at the Berkeley Gallery, Julian would tag along. When his mother disappeared into the office with her new friend, Julian was left alone in the gallery. He did not like Ohly or his art collection, which comprised mainly Oriental and Renaissance art. He considered it 'dead' and much preferred contemporary painting and private views where you could see living artists talking to friends with drinks in their hands. Whether it was his prejudice against traditional art or whether it was resentment that his mother seemed to be slowly abandoning Price, something inspired Julian to express himself physically. This took the form of eating tiny fragments of paint taken from pictures and icons in Ohly's precious collection. Many years later he was to record in his memoir, 'I am very likely to have eaten some Giotto or Fra Angelico.' Fortunately for the world of fine art, Barbara's relationship with William Ohly lasted only a year or so.

Another admirer of Barbara's during 1943 was the composer Christopher à Becket Williams, who also wrote novels under the name Sinjon Wood and who was in his early fifties when Barbara met him. Although she thought his music was dreadful, Barbara liked him and he often came to tea at Greville Place. There he entertained her and the children with witty anecdotes. Some of these focused on the experience of his father, a clergyman who used to give the last rites to murderers before their execution. 'Becket Williams', as he was more usually known, would vividly relay macabre tales about executions that had gone wrong, including those of criminals who obstinately refused to die despite being robustly hanged. Inspired by these stories, Julian and Caroline enacted a mass execution of all their dolls and teddy bears by hanging them from pipes in the bathroom. Becket Williams, who was very good at hangman's knots, helped the children set it up. Barbara made her disapproval of this particular play activity very clear.

*   *   *

1944 brought several dramatic changes to Barbara's life. Her husband John, who had deserted in 1941 and who had been making a living as a theatre screen painter in London since then, was arrested in early 1944. He had been betrayed by a woman with whom he worked in the theatre world whose fiancé had also deserted and been sent to prison. Resentful that John seemed to have got away scot free, she had informed the authorities. John was court martialled in 1944 and sentenced to hard labour in Colchester Military Prison in Essex. There he suffered a nervous breakdown, shouting uncontrollably from his cell. He was duly hospitalized and when he had recovered enough to be released, was dishonourably discharged from the army. Despite her impatience with John's irresponsible behaviour as a father, Barbara showed sympathy for her husband at this time, and her fiction reveals compassion for those plagued by mental suffering. Her portrayal of Eugene Reeve's manic behaviour in *A Touch of Mistletoe* – when he shouts uncontrollably at work one day and tears off his clothes – is presented as the culmination of living every day with fears and strange fantasies; of having had 'mistletoe on his mind' for many years.[13] But John's arrest and imprisonment meant that Barbara no longer needed to keep her husband's whereabouts secret and that she was free to begin to divorce proceedings. There was now no reason for them to remain tied to each other by a marriage that had, to all intents and purposes, ended in 1935. She decided that she would see a solicitor in the near future.

Once they knew that Barbara and Price were now living apart, Diana and Rupert Brinton Lee welcomed her back into their circle and asked her if she would like to join them on a trip to the theatre. On Tuesday, 6 June 1944, Barbara went with them to the Arts Theatre in Great Newport Street. There she met a friend of the Brinton Lees, a shy and rather gaunt man called Richard Comyns Carr. On the following Thursday, he wrote to Barbara, having obtained her address from Diana, inviting her to lunch the following Wednesday at the famous Escargot restaurant in Greek Street.[14] Although she described Richard Comyns Carr to her daughter Caroline as 'Mr Grey' and as a 'grave and disapproving' man,[15] Barbara decided to accept his invitation. It was a decision that would change the course of her life.

25 Richard Comyns Carr

Richard Strettel Comyns Carr came from an illustrious, high-achieving family. His paternal grandfather, Joseph William Comyns Carr (1849–1916), had practised as a barrister before switching tracks to journalism, becoming a well-known art critic who enthusiastically championed the work of the Pre-Raphaelites. In 1877 he was appointed as a director of the Grosvenor Gallery and ten years later founded the New Gallery in Regent Street, which became an important venue for the Pre-Raphaelites and Aesthetic movement artists. He also wrote many successful plays; his *King Arthur* was produced by Henry Irving at the Lyceum Theatre starring Ellen Terry, with the sets and costumes designed by Edward Burne-Jones. Richard's paternal grandmother, Alice Laura Vansittart (née Strettel) (1850–1927), who was an artist and novelist, had designed the famous beetle-wing costume that Ellen Terry wore in 1888 when she played Lady Macbeth to Henry Irving's Macbeth. Both she and the costume were immortalized the following year in John Singer Sargent's painting *Ellen Terry as Lady Macbeth* (now in the Tate

Gallery, London). Following his many theatrical triumphs, Joseph Comyns Carr became passionate about opera and was responsible for the first performance of Wagner's *Parsifal* in 1914 at Covent Garden. Richard's father, Arthur Comyns Carr (1882–1965), was also a highly successful man. Called to the Bar at Grays Inn in 1908, he went on to have a brilliant career in the law. In 1907 he married Cicely Raikes Bromage, the daughter of a clergyman, and they had three sons, of whom Richard was the eldest. In 1946 Richard's father took part in the Tokyo War Crimes Tribunal, acting as prosecutor of Japanese and German war criminals, for which work he was knighted in 1949. A committed Liberal Party activist, he was elected to serve on the Liberal Party Council in 1936 and was president of the Liberal Party during 1958–59. Richard's father was a hard act to follow.

Richard Comyns Carr was born on 24 October 1908 at York Mansions, Battersea. He was a sickly child who suffered from a tubercular gland in his stomach during his early years and adolescence. His education was often interrupted by spells of illness, when he would be taught by tutors at home. He attended Clifton College in Bristol and spent a year in Paris before going up to Oxford University. After graduating in 1930 from Balliol College with a degree in Classics, he completed a Diploma in Economics and Political Science. In 1931 he returned home to live with his parents in Hampstead and tried his hand as a freelance writer, editing a curious collection of essays entitled *Red Rags: Essays of Hate from Oxford*, which was published in 1933, when he was 25 years old.[16] In 1936 he joined the BBC and shared a flat in St John's Wood, north London, with two Oxford friends, Anthony Gishford (a music journalist, who would eventually become director of the English Opera Group), and Simon Harcourt Nowell-Smith (an editor with *The Times* who was later to become a librarian and well-known book collector). Richard worked as a sub-editor, External News, for the BBC, which meant that he frequently travelled overseas.[17] In 1939, for example, he was sent to South America, returning in May from Buenos Aires to Southampton via Lisbon on the *Asturias*; he was recorded on the ship's passenger list as a 'BBC official'. Argentina had many German immigrants and possibly he had been sent out to explore its sympathy for the Nazi cause.

Aware that war would soon be declared, Richard joined the Royal Fusiliers Territorial Army division in July 1939 and in September became a full-time soldier. In 1940 he was promoted to sergeant and sent to Devizes in Wiltshire for training, but he collapsed on a route march and was hospitalized. There he was visited by someone – possibly Roger Hollis, a contemporary at Clifton College who was then working for MI5 and was to become its Director General in 1956 – who suggested that Richard should contact the Foreign Office when he recovered. This would not have been unusual. At the beginning of the war the Foreign Office was seeking to increase its staff and urgently needed more linguists. The Classics graduates were in particular demand: 'Latinists were invaluable in finding and making sense of the key words embedded in the evasive rigmarole of diplomatic exchanges: trained too in detecting fallacies, making distinctions between major and minor propositions, and giving clarifications in eloquent, impartial prose.'[18] Recruitment into the Foreign Office, especially its Secret Intelligence Service branch, more commonly known as MI6 (responsible for gathering intelligence overseas), was invariably by personal recommendation.

An Oxford Classics graduate who was fluent in French, Spanish and Italian, Richard Comyns Carr would have been just the sort of man the Foreign Office wished to recruit. In April 1940 he was duly appointed to the War Office; from there he went to MI5 (responsible for domestic and internal UK security issues) and was placed in its Spanish Section.[19] In 1942 he was transferred to MI6, where deputy chief Colonel Valentine Vivian was keen to recruit young academics and intellectuals as 'new blood'. There Richard joined Section V (which was responsible for counter-espionage operations and intelligence outside British territory), then led by Felix Cowgill. The main task of Section V was to obtain detailed information about enemy intelligence operations abroad, and this included liaising with and tracking a network of undercover agents in Madrid, Lisbon, Gibraltar and Tangier. Richard worked in sub-section Vd which covered Spain and Portugal; this was led by Kim Philby, who 'worked harder than anyone and [...] was always relaxed, completely unflappable'.[20] Unbeknown to his colleagues, however, Philby had been acting as a double agent since 1934, when he was recruited by the Soviet spy Arnold Deutsch.

Having recently returned from a Foreign Office mission in Sierra Leone, Graham Greene – described by George Orwell as 'a Catholic [...] but in outlook he is just a mild Left with faint C[ommunist] P[arty] leanings'[21] – was put in charge of the Portuguese desk in 1943. His first job was to produce a Purple Primer,

> a handbook containing a list of all persons in Portugal known to have been employed by Axis [German, Italian and Japanese] intelligence services, with a description of the role they had played [...] It was a monumental task, for there were on file almost 2,000 confirmed enemy agents [...] and 200 Germans living in Portugal with known Intelligence connections.[22]

Richard was given the same task in relation to Spain, a supposedly neutral country but one with a fascist government where the head of the Spanish police was on the German Intelligence payroll and where, it was rumoured, 12,000 Nazi secret agents were working.[23] Graham Greene and Richard

Comyns Carr were, then, colleagues before they became friends, which they remained after Greene's resignation from Section V in June 1944. Richard's Foreign Office colleagues also included Guy Burgess and Malcolm Muggeridge.[24] Philby was made deputy head of Section V in 1943. In 1944 he outmanoeuvred the strongly anti-communist Felix Cowgill and became head of the section, which was still 'a tight-knit little community, just a dozen officers and their deputies, and a similar number of support staff'.[25] In 1944, when Richard met Barbara, he had just been transferred to the newly created Section IX (Soviet Affairs), which was designed to handle 'any cases coming to our notice involving Communists or people concerned in Soviet espionage'.[26] Richard's research focus within that brief was Poland, Hungary and the Baltic States.[27] He worked closely with Philby, who became head of Section IX in November 1944, and whom he now regarded as a friend as well as a colleague. Having been temporarily released by the BBC so that he could work for MI6 during the war, Richard resigned from the corporation in August 1944.[28] He enjoyed the secret intelligence work and was confident that his future was secure in the Foreign Office.

Arthur Price and Richard Comyns Carr were chalk and cheese: one a flamboyant and attractive rogue who lived by his wits on the edge of the criminal world; the other a courteous, softly spoken and highly educated member of the upper class whose health was delicate. Despite finding him 'grey' at their first meeting, Barbara soon warmed to Richard's kindness, intelligence and dry sense of humour. His high forehead and aquiline nose lent him a scholarly appearance; his carefully combed hair, immaculate clothes and the fact that he smoked Balkan Sobranie luxury cigarettes suggested sophistication and a reasonable income. (Appearances can be deceptive, however; although Richard still had an allowance from his father, his Foreign Office salary was relatively low – as were most salaries in MI6, although they were paid free of income tax in order to preserve the anonymity of staff.)[29] He also listened attentively when she talked about her painting and her writing; she was deeply flattered. For his part, Richard quickly became infatuated by Barbara. Her quirky sense of humour, the amusing way she told anecdotes, her imagination and her beauty all captivated him. He also found her a fascinating blend of contradictions: on the one hand she was gentle, hesitant and punctilious – almost Victorian in her manners sometimes. On the other hand, she was open-minded and curious, holding firm and often unconventional views that she was not afraid to air. The fact that the first V1 bomb – or 'doodle-bug' – hit London the day before their first lunch date somehow seemed strangely apt. This quiet and clever man suddenly found his world turned upside down by a woman he had met by chance, just as London itself now faced fresh upheavals.

Within less than a month after meeting Barbara, Richard knew he was hopelessly in love. In a letter sent from the Reform Club in Pall Mall on 2 July 1944, he wrote:

I adore you and whenever I have left you there is a horrid gap, which I fill by thinking of how you looked and things you have said, and thinking of brilliant and fascinating things which I might have said but didn't [...] I believe you are a witch, really.

Writing again from the Reform Club a few days later he described their last meeting as 'sheer heaven' and Barbara herself as

unreal, as you say, and your house too, unusual as heaven ... Somewhere in this letter, where it is not too conspicuous, I should like to tell you that I love you more than I can possibly say in a letter and that I can still hardly believe I have met you and that you care for me.

In yet another letter he ventured that her bare feet were 'like pebbles washed up on the sand and your hair like the flight of a bird through a wood'. Just over two weeks later, he wrote:

My head is full of things I want to say to you [...] Perhaps in time I shall say them all to you, but it will take time, because I love everything you do and everything about you and it is difficult to know where to begin [...] Someday, if I turn to writing, I will have an anonymous portrait of which you can boast to yourself – a character in a novel with another name – or the unknown, unseen inspiration of a poem. It will say some of the things I feel most about you in a few words and will be perfect. But I doubt if I shall ever write and long therefore that you will be a famous authoress and I shall be trying to find the right restaurants to take you to so as to get photographed with you for the *Tatler*.

Despite his doubts about his literary abilities, Richard sent Barbara a brief poem in August:

Pearl of twilight, diamonds of silence, amethyst of shadows.
Your mouth against mine, your hair against my eyes.
Dawn will be sometime this week.

Not since her affair with Rupert Lee had Barbara been courted by such a cultured and sophisticated man – and no one had ever taken her writing seriously. She responded to Richard's letters with affection, but took pains to remind him of her chequered past; it was important to her that he saw her clearly and did not idealize her:

Richard dear this is just a letter to say you are the nicest man in the world and you have lovely eyes, they almost squint sometimes and it is fascinating, also you are very clever because the boiler is working now [...] I am getting to depend on you so, I can't imagine how I have managed all these years without you, please don't think of all the dreadful things I have done, I suppose a more discreet woman would not have mentioned them.

Richard decided that Diana, who was a close friend, should be told about his relationship with Barbara. In mid-August he wrote to her, thanking her for having introduced them and asking if he might bring Barbara with him when he next visited. He added:

> If you see us together I shall not have an opportunity to tell you what I think of Barbara, and in a way perhaps I should do so in this letter; but if I did I should only write a lot of rather obvious things and as you have known her much longer than I have you could probably supply a more objective character-sketch yourself. I will only say you could not have done me a better turn than in introducing us and I don't know how to thank you enough.

Diana replied by return, warmly including Barbara in the invitation to the farmhouse in Hedgerley, Middlesex, which she and Rupert were renting following the bombing of their house in St Quintin Avenue.[30] But she wrote with care and circumspection concerning Barbara's character:

> subsequent events had rather driven the Arts Theatre evening from my mind, so that your letter gave me quite a shock. I don't know that I should have taken the responsibility of bringing you together if I had known anything was to come of it, but as it has, of course I am very glad and wish you both all the best. I have known Barbara so long that I probably find it difficult to be very objective about her, but she is a fascinating person with a unique quality about her, very much herself. She always reminds me of one of those wide-eyed wiry little sea-daisies, sort of innocent and fragile and yet tough. Incidentally, I very much admire the way she has stood up to things.[31]

Diana was acknowledging Barbara's courage and resourcefulness while, at the same time, sounding a slight note of caution, should Richard wish to hear it. He did not.

During the summer of 1944 hundreds of V1 incendiary bombs rained down on London, a revenge measure prompted by D-Day, 6 June, when the Allies had landed successfully in Normandy. Pilotless and emitting a loud engine noise that stopped just before they dropped to the ground, the V1s were filled with high explosive and burst with a blinding flash; they were dreaded by the city's population, who viewed them as sinister as well as deadly. Barbara began to worry about the children's safety and sent them to stay with her sister Molly in Weston for the summer holidays. On 29 June Greville Place was damaged when a V1 bomb crashed down early one morning into Mortimer Crescent, an adjoining street. Barbara had just walked to the end of the garden to feed the hens when the bomb dropped. In a letter to Diana written later in August, Richard wrote: 'I happened to ring her up just afterwards and got the story red hot. As told by her it was one of the funniest first-hand narrations I have heard for a long time.'[32] Although she relayed the incident to Richard in comic vein, Barbara was lucky to escape serious injury; her bed had been cut to shreds by glass shards when the large sash window in her bedroom completely shattered. The bombing is described more somberly through the eyes of Caroline Seymour in *Mr Fox*, although the moment of levitation lends the passage a slightly surreal air:

> I heard a beastly flying bomb coming … Then I saw it making straight for me, and it came so low over the house slates fell off as it passed. I imagined it had a dreadful wicked face, but I couldn't move and then a great draught came. I went up in the air with the hens; we went in a kind of whirlwind; the dogs seemed to be sucked right away. Suddenly I found myself on the ground and my elbows hurt rather. The hens were all coming down, too, and there was a great noise of falling glass and slates and pieces of twisted metal like swords were flying around. I got to my feet and pulled my housecoat round me, but the seams had mostly come undone. Where the garden wall had been there was a heap of broken stones and twisted metal … I turned towards the house and as I did so an All Clear went, and I heard myself muttering, 'You damn fools, it isn't clear here.'[33]

In the novel, Caroline returns to the house to find Mr Fox 'lying rather twisted'; 'His eyes were open and he looked kind of jaunty, as he often did; but I knew he was dead.'[34] Price, the inspiration for Mr Fox, did not die in 1944 – but perhaps the episode symbolically marked for Barbara the moment when Price became dead to her as a lover.

*   *   *

Julian and Caroline stayed with their aunt Molly and her husband John Davidson, a farmer in Weston, for several weeks in the summer of 1944. They did not like it there; the only book Julian could find to read was Victor Hugo's *The Hunchback of Notre Dame* and the food was dreadful. His worst experience was when he had cold mutton for lunch one day and found a very vigorous maggot in it. Julian was told not to fuss and to eat it all, but left a tiny fragment of meat with the maggot still clutching tenaciously to it on the side of his plate. But at least they were safer there than in London, although Weston had its own dramas. That summer two American Boeing B-17 'Flying Fortress' heavy bombers collided near the village. Nineteen people were killed immediately and a villager had his head blown off by a machine gun he was trying to shift from the wreckage. Julian and his friend John Lawman scavenged the area and found a rubber dinghy which they inflated and enjoyed sailing on the lake until it was reclaimed by American Air Force personnel. A more macabre find was a pilot's boot with half a foot in it.

Barbara visited Julian and Caroline in Weston occasionally, and the children returned to Greville Place once school started again in September. They found that several large houses nearby had been destroyed by the bombs. It was not uncommon for people to pick flowers from the abandoned and overgrown gardens and even explore the derelict buildings, more out of curiosity than with the intention of looting. It was a dangerous pastime but an enticing one, which sometimes offered a peek into someone else's private world. As well as working on *Our Spoons Came from Woolworths*, Barbara wrote several short stories at this time. One of them, based on her exploration of a bombed-out house with Julian, conveys vividly the morbid fascination of such an activity. In the unpublished story 'Sunday Afternoon in St. John's Wood' – a title which seems to promise a peaceful interlude in an elegant part of London – a mother and child find some strange detritus in a 'bombed and blind-looking' large Victorian house. The building emanates an evil atmosphere, and among the ruins they come across 'some queer metal balls with spikes on them', an old helmet, a mouse carved from a cork, a stuffed rat, boxes of fossils and a 'frightful Japanese doll about three feet tall' whose face falls off when the boy touches it. The woman moves some broken glass on a bedroom window sill and uncovers a severed hand: 'It was an elegant slender hand, but had gone rather yellow and dried like a hen's claw and the skin thick and leatherish and in places it had peeled away and bones gleamed all white'. Horrified but laughing despite herself, the woman places the hand in an empty cigar box intending to report it to the police but – suddenly overcome with revulsion – she leaves the box in a gutter on the way home. Safely indoors, both mother and child wash themselves thoroughly but cannot seem to get rid of the smell of death and destruction. The woman accidentally spills a packet of salt and throws some over her shoulder for good luck, but it is some time before she feels calm again. The short story vividly conveys the proximity of death during the war, an everyday encounter that could evoke mixed reactions of fear, horror and hysteria.[35]

*　*　*

In her Introduction to the 1981 Virago edition of *The Vet's Daughter*, written many years later, Barbara mentioned that 'an old friend found the MS of *Sisters by a River* when he was looking through the family photographs and thought it should be published'.[36] With this encouragement, Barbara sent the manuscript off to several publishers, who all rejected it. But by

some means, in the autumn of 1944 the manuscript landed on the desk of
Tom Hopkinson, who had been an assistant editor of the magazine *Lilliput*
in the 1930s and was now the editor of *Picture Post*. Someone called 'Lotte'
– possibly Lötchen, William Ohly's close friend who was a lodger in Barbara's
house – had sent it to Hopkinson. Once he had read it, Hopkinson wrote
to Lotte in November 1944 suggesting how the book could be improved.
It had, he wrote, 'an admirable dryness, delicacy and wit' but it needed to
be made more coherent. Lotte showed Barbara the letter and she wrote to
Hopkinson to tell him that she would revise the book, adding some more
material. He replied:

Dear Mrs Pemberton,

I am glad you thought what I wrote about your book can be some use to you.
What I suggest you should do now, would be to write the six chapters you
have in mind, and then go carefully through the whole thing, if possible with
someone else, and see whether there are any places where you can re-arrange
chapters or sections of chapters, to make the flow a little bit smoother. Then
I should try it out in the ordinary way on at least one more publisher. Supposing
that's no good, I think we might publish two or three lengths of the Spider's
Web in *Lilliput*, with a heading something like 'The Novel Nobody will Publish'.
I think that might easily result in applications from publishers who might not
take the book if it came in the ordinary way.[37]

Hopkinson also advised against correcting the misspellings (which Richard
would almost certainly have advocated), saying 'the book was like cobwebs
and could easily disintegrate'.[38] It was all good advice. Barbara was buoyed
by his praise and began revising *Sisters by a River*.

She was also thrilled that Richard encouraged her writing. By the end of
1944 he had made it clear that he was very much in love with her – and
she could see that he would provide her with the security and respectability she was beginning to crave. In December Richard gave up his flat in
Lowndes Street in Knightsbridge and moved into the top flat in Barbara's
house. Whenever they were separated, he would write to her, in one letter
confessing that he was 'thinking of your face as it is in the morning, the
round face, the one from Tahiti, and the flowers you sometimes put in
your hair'. Writing to Diana, Barbara reported that 'Richard is very well
and fits into the household as if he had always been here', adding that she
was still waiting for her decree nisi. John Pemberton was now living at 89
Charlotte Street in Soho. He was well enough to take up scene painting
again, but when Julian visited his father in his London studio to watch
him paint a series of Susanna and the Elders, he noticed that his face
sometimes twitched uncontrollably, an indication of the mental suffering he
had experienced during the war. John was now in a new relationship, this

time with a woman ten years his junior, Antonia Hall, who was beginning to establish an acting career. He finally agreed to a divorce from Barbara on the grounds of his previous adultery with an artist's model. In the spring of 1945 Barbara attended the decree nisi hearing. Afterwards she wrote to Diana: 'The court was quite small and the judge was like a sleepy white cat wearing a wig, I remembered what you said about wearing black so I wore bright red.' She added, almost as an afterthought, '*Lilliput* is going to publish some of my junk next month and every alternate month for a time. I don't know what they pay.' In fact, she was paid quite well. When Richard wrote to Barbara during her holiday in Cornwall the following year, he told her she would be paid eight guineas (about £443 today) for 'Black Monday', which was to be published in the August 1946 issue of *Lilliput*.

Five chapters from what was to be published in 1947 as *Sisters by a River* were featured in *Lilliput*, 'The pocket magazine for everyone', between May 1945 and August 1946. They appeared under the name 'Barbara Pemberton' and the first instalment was duly introduced as 'The first extract from a novel nobody will publish'. *Lilliput* published writing by both established and new authors; the issues in which extracts from Barbara's memoir appeared included work by Baudelaire, Maxim Gorki, Robert Graves, Max Beerbohm, Wyndham Lewis and Antonia White. For the May 1945 issue, she was asked to write a short profile of herself, in which she noted that she was 'Married to John Pemberton, artist, and has two children of whom the younger, Caroline, writes dolls plays. Has two French poodles and five deaf cats, and a collection of antique furniture, all of which is kept in a large, rather bombed house in St. John's Wood.'[39] By omitting any mention of the divorce proceedings, Barbara managed to preserve a veneer of respectability, although she was clearly happy to indicate her eccentricity. Life seemed to be taking a turn for the better in May 1945. She was in love and now she was a published author – and the Allies had forced the Germans to surrender. On 8 May, Victory Day in Europe was a bank holiday during which people all over the country celebrated the end of the war.

In early July 1945 Barbara took the children on holiday to Eastbourne for a week. Their favourite poodle, Fallada, went with them, but Richard was left in charge of Greville Place and the remaining animal residents, including the other pet poodle which was called Vinegar Tom, and Foxy: 'I have fed the fox regularly. He is still set against making friends with me but is still very glad of the milk and egg. He won't touch it while I am looking at him but starts moving out of his basket to eat it before I have shut the door.' In the same letter, Richard complained that he was overwhelmed by work, signing off, 'Darling I shall miss you very much this week ... now that we are being parted for a whole week for the first time I know I shall feel as if we had lived together for years and my life were being most unfairly uprooted!'

Barbara and Richard had decided they would marry as soon as her divorce was finalized and that they would have a holiday on their own in September, whether or not she had received her decree absolute by then. While Barbara was away with the children in early July, Richard was busy writing letters to hotels in Cornwall. Finding it difficult to book a week that suited them, he remembered that Kim Philby's mother owned a cottage in Wales. He decided to ask him if they could rent it for a week, writing to Barbara that he had left 'a sealed letter for [Kim] mentioning our intended marriage and he has promised to ring his mother tonight about the cottage and let me know in the morning'. He ended the letter by asking how she was getting on with *Our Spoons Came from Woolworths*. Barbara replied from a rainy Eastbourne, 'I don't get very much time alone to write but have written three more chapters. I would so like to get it finished before I return.' The next day Philby confirmed that they could have his mother's cottage for a week in September.

Richard told his father about Barbara over lunch at the Café Royal in mid-July and asked him to dinner at Greville Place the following week so that he could meet his prospective daughter-in-law. She clearly made a good impression on Arthur Comyns Carr, who wrote to her soon after:

> I always felt about Richard that he has been handicapped, and that he is capable of a good deal more than he has so far achieved. I look forward to your being able to spur him on to great things. Life isn't going to be too easy for anybody during the coming years, but I hope there are some good times in store for you two and your children.

She was particularly touched by his comment, 'I think you both deserve more happiness than you have had in the past.'[40] It was a good month; not only was Richard's father, an eminent barrister, prepared to welcome her into his family, but Labour won the General Election on 26 July with a landslide victory. Although Winston Churchill had been a good leader in wartime, the British population did not trust him to deliver the social and welfare changes laid out in the Beveridge Report of 1942 that the country now so badly needed. Barbara and Richard were delighted by the socialist victory. Many houses were soon decorated with bunting and flags and a few even sported hammer and sickle banners – the Russians were regarded as heroes because they had defeated Hitler on the Eastern Front in May 1945.

On Monday, 20 August 1945, Barbara received her decree absolute by first post. By lunchtime she had received three proposals of marriage by telephone from the three men who loved her: Price, Francis Codd and Richard Comyns Carr. She accepted Richard. They were married on Wednesday 29 August in the Registry Office at Hampstead. Their two witnesses were Desmond Pakenham (one of Richard's colleagues in MI6, 'a calm, cautious man')[41] and Richard's sister-in-law, Margaret Comyns Carr. Barbara was about to begin a new life.

9

Spies, lies and fictions

While on honeymoon in Snowdonia, Barbara jotted down some ideas for another novel that she provisionally entitled *The Long White Dress*. She put these aside on her return to London, however, and turned her attention instead to writing a short biography of Leigh Hunt, the Romantic poet and essayist who counted Keats among his friends and who sailed to Italy in 1822 to join Shelley and Byron in their attempt to set up a new journal, *The Liberal*. It is hard to know why she suddenly decided to try her hand at non-fiction. Possibly she came across Hunt's poetry and partially identified with this cheerful but shy man of many talents who was constantly in debt. She might also have felt the need to prove that she could write something serious and well-informed; her husband was, after all, a highly educated man. Richard certainly encouraged the project and paid for her to become a member of the London Library, a prestigious private library in St James's Square, where she became a regular borrower.

Barbara enjoyed writing *Leigh Hunt in Italy* – 'I did a lot of research, which I loved – it seemed to make up for all the study I'd missed as a girl'[1] – and worked on it in bursts for six years. Her habit from this time on of painting at least one ceiling blue with white stars wherever she lived was inspired by the fact that Hunt had painted the ceiling of his prison cell in the Surrey County Gaol (where he spent two years as punishment for libelling the Prince Regent) with sky and clouds. Many years later Barbara's daughter Caroline wrote to her mother's agent, asking if he would look for the manuscript of *Leigh Hunt in Italy*, which the agency had mislaid. 'I remember so well her talking about his life and how he decorated his prison room ceiling blue with stars', she wrote.[2] The manuscript was never found.

At the same time as writing *Leigh Hunt in Italy*, Barbara was working on *Our Spoons Came from Woolworths*, which concludes sketchily with Sophia's marriage to a distinguished-looking, handsome artist called Rollo. Kind and thoughtful with 'a delightful voice', but also 'rather grave and quiet', Rollo is a thinly disguised portrait of Richard.[3] It was Barbara's tribute to her second husband. But while Richard encouraged Barbara's writing and painting, he was less keen on her various business projects, including the piano 'restoration' scheme and the dog breeding. He no doubt thought they were inappropriate activities for the wife of a government official.

Richard was an odd combination of the conventional and the unorthodox; of the worldly and the unworldly. On the one hand, he appeared to be a very traditional English gentleman; his boots and shoes were handmade, and he dressed expensively. He liked to take breakfast on his own in peace and quiet, so Barbara presided over two meals at the start of the day: Richard was served a good breakfast with numerous cups of tea in the dining room while the children noisily ate their puffed wheats in the kitchen. After breakfast he would set off, dressed immaculately, for his office in the Broadway Buildings in Westminster, where the newly created Section IX of MI6 was based. His return to Greville Place in the evening was always marked by a glass of sherry at 6 o'clock. Polite and punctilious, he liked order and routine. If he worked at home, he made it quite clear that he was not to be disturbed. A man of quiet dignity, he refused to run for trains, which meant that Barbara – who always flew down the street at the last minute – had to be ready for any journey far earlier than she thought necessary.

On the other hand, Richard was not quite what he seemed. He greatly valued independent thought and, to a certain extent, non-conformism. He enjoyed associating with London's artistic and bohemian communities and admired Barbara's eccentric creativity. He was also politically left-wing and subscribed to an anarchist magazine. He shared his thoughts on socialism with Barbara who, although she was not politically minded, gradually became influenced by his ideas. But while he was intellectually interested in economic systems and their impact on the destiny of nations, he paid little attention to the day-to-day business of getting and spending money, having been cocooned from financial concerns by his privileged upbringing. He was not a mean man but, after their marriage, a considerable time passed before Barbara realized that he had mistakenly assumed that, like him, she had a private income. When she made it clear that he would have to provide some extra housekeeping money, he seemed surprised, although immediately agreed to make her a more generous allowance.

Richard Comyns Carr found his work absorbing. His job included the recruitment and running of agents; handling the intelligence received from overseas; and dealing with other government departments in order to liaise with the intelligence services of friendly countries.[4] He was a conscientious and efficient intelligence officer, although not a leader, being content to observe the internal politics of MI6 rather than jockey for a higher position. When he moved into Greville Place he brought with him a large number of books – many of them on the Balkans – in preparation for his research into Poland, Hungary and the Baltic States for MI6. But it was not all hard work. Senior officers of MI5 and MI6 were strongly encouraged to become members of certain exclusive London clubs where the atmosphere of conviviality and trust, enhanced by plenty of alcohol, made it easy to pick up useful information. Richard belonged to two clubs: the Reform Club in Pall Mall – the traditional home of those with progressive political ideas, where Kim Philby, Guy Burgess and Anthony Blunt were members – and the Authors' Club in Whitehall Court to which Graham Greene and Malcolm Muggeridge belonged.

Club membership cost several hundred pounds a year and the price of drinks was high; Richard paid for this out of his own pocket, as did all MI6 staff. Heavy drinking and even alcoholism were tolerated so long as they did not interfere too much with work. In preparation for impromptu celebrations, Richard always carried a metal 'swizzle stick' in his top pocket with which he could evacuate the bubbles in champagne that gave him indigestion. He was not an alcoholic, but he could drink heavily without getting drunk – a useful asset within 'the Firm', as MI6 was known informally.

Barbara never visited Richard's clubs because they were not open to women, but she did enjoy the social life that came with being married to a senior government officer. Dining at the homes of Richard's work colleagues inevitably resulted in return dinners at Greville Place. One such dinner was to change the course of Julian's life. Although she had agreed to run down her dog-breeding and piano businesses, Barbara still bought and sold antiques, storing them in one of the bedrooms. Julian and Caroline loved sifting through Barbara's purchases looking for 'treasure' that they could purloin. One of Julian's trophies was an Indian tiger rug – its fierce glass eyes stared out balefully above a large open mouth full of yellowing curved teeth; the tiger was much envied by friends invited up to his bedroom. Another treasure was a dress naval cutlass which sported engraved allegorical figures, picked out in gold, on the blade. On the evening of Barbara and Richard's first formal dinner party, bored with being confined to the first floor, Julian decided to put it to good use and liven up the dull proceedings below. He made his way to the room above the dinner party and carefully levered up some loose floorboards. Having exposed the plaster of the dining-room ceiling, he plunged the cutlass straight through the ceiling rose below, an act which showered the dinner table with dust and fragments of plaster. He expected to hear a great burst of laughter, but instead there was an ominous silence. Barbara appeared, stony-faced, and said, 'You have done something very stupid.' For Richard it was the last straw. Not being used to children, he found living with a 13-year-old boy and a 10-year-old girl something of a challenge. Caroline, who was often reading or absorbed in her toy theatres, he did not mind. But Julian irritated him. The boy was noisy, always up to something and had a memory like a sieve. He had carefully explained how the name 'd'Artagnan' in *The Three Musketeers* should be pronounced only to have Julian pestering him about it again the next day. In his turn, Julian, who was used to Price's openly affectionate behaviour and frank expressions of anger when annoyed, was mystified by Richard's silent disapproval and taut facial expression when he appeared in the room. He sensed that Richard thought he was tiresome and he was right. Barbara and Richard agreed that the best solution would be to send him away to boarding school.

Julian was devastated when they told him. Not only had his beloved pet Foxy been turned out of the house and set free on Kenwood Common after the new cleaner had announced that she refused to do housework 'with that wolf running around', but now he was to be sent away again. His world seemed to be crashing down around him. But being sent to boarding school turned out to be the best thing to happen to Julian for some time – because Barbara bravely chose Long Dene School, a co-educational and very progressive small school of 120 pupils run along the lines of A. S. Neill's Summerhill. By 1945 the school had moved from Buckinghamshire to Chiddingstone in Kent, where it was run by Karis and John Guinness, members of the wealthy brewing family. Long Dene was housed in a Georgian Gothic-revival 'castle' encasing an earlier manor house and was surrounded by 45 acres of land; the school also rented an adjoining 300-acre farm.[5] As Richard did not drive, in the autumn of 1945 Price took Julian down to Long Dene in his 3-litre Bentley, accompanied by Barbara and Caroline and the two pet poodles. Although they were so different, Price and Richard did not mind each other; Richard accepted Price as part of Barbara's history and he appreciated the way her former lover was always ready to offer practical help. For his part, Price had come to terms with the fact that Barbara had moved up a tier socially through her marriage.

Long Dene was very different from the previous schools Julian had attended. Pupils were encouraged to address staff by their first names and were allowed a great deal of freedom; classes were small – between 12 and 15 children; a wide range of subjects was offered; the pupils made the rules at weekly school meetings where staff and students had equal votes; the delicious meals were made from farm produce and vegetarianism was encouraged. There was no uniform and during the summer the school became a land of bare feet and unsupervised adventure. The philosophy at Long Dene was that children achieved their best when they were happy and working to their strengths. Pupils had to do a reasonable amount of housework, washing up after each meal for example, but this was presented as part of living in a large family. Julian's first term was not easy but he soon grew to love Long Dene, where the expressive arts were encouraged and where his inventiveness and his gift for drawing and painting were quickly recognized.

The 'practical science' class – in which pupils took the engines of cars and motorbikes to bits in a large shed and then reassembled them – gave Julian enormous pleasure. He flourished at the school. Caroline would also later benefit from living in this unusual community where both she and Julian made lifelong friends.

The artist and illustrator Angela Landels, who was a pupil at Long Dene and a particular friend of theirs (and who later became art direc- tor at *Harper's Bazaar* and *Queen*), once described Barbara as emerging from her car on parent visiting days wearing striking clothes and unusual jewellery, like a 'beautiful immaculate gypsy', in stark contrast to the other mothers with their grey hair and tweed skirts.[6] Barbara was pleased that she had finally found a school where Julian was really happy. But in order to keep her son out of Richard's hair, she also made sure that he was not at home for too much of the long summer vacations; either she or Price took him on holiday to their favourite place near St Agnes in Cornwall each year, and he would stay on a few extra weeks with Price's friends, the Holbeach family, doing jobs on their farm. Sometimes Barbara and Price travelled down together with the children and Richard would join them later. She always loved Cornwall, remembered as a wild and magical place in *Mr Fox*:

> Often we discovered corks from fishermen's nets and sometimes glass balls, which we loved. One evening when I was alone on the beach a wave washed up three glass balls, and there they were, all wet and shining, at my feet. It seemed like a beautiful dream. Sometimes in the evening a seal would swim across the bay.[7]

Shortly after Julian started at Long Dene, Richard was told he would soon be posted to Portugal. Barbara decided that she would sell Greville Place; it was expensive to run and even if the whole house were to be let out as flats to bring in an income, overseeing the rentals from abroad would be difficult. In the event the posting fell through, but by this time the sale of Greville Place was almost complete. Barbara immediately bought a large Victorian house in South Kensington. Number 3 Milborne Grove was a terraced house of three floors and a basement; its six front steps led up to a fine stone portico. The house badly needed renovation so they decided to rent somewhere to live while the work took place. Richard's colleague Desmond Pakenham was about to be posted to Jakarta in Java for a spell, and suggested that while he was away they could rent his flat at 52 Roland Gardens. It was an ideal solution: Roland Gardens was only a few minutes' walk from Milborne Grove and only half a mile from where Barbara's sister Chloe lived in Old Church Street, Chelsea. By February 1946 they had moved into the flat, and Barbara was soon overseeing the Milborne Grove works. Richard was very happy to leave all such practical projects in her hands. Most days the only time she could find to write was between 5 a.m. and 7 a.m., and this eventually became her preferred routine.

*   *   *

Early in 1946 Barbara was contacted by Katherine Clutton of the literary agency Hughes Massie & Co. which was based in Fleet Street. Having read the extracts from *Sisters by a River* in *Lilliput*, she wrote to ask whether Barbara had succeeded in finding a publisher for the book, and if not, would she allow Hughes Massie to represent her? Barbara agreed; Clutton contacted several publishers, including Eyre & Spottiswoode, and in the spring of 1946 Barbara received some good news. After his resignation in 1944 from Section V in MI6, Graham Greene worked for the Political Intelligence Department, the propaganda arm of the Foreign Office. There he ran a section with the novelist Antonia White, producing a kind of *Reader's Digest* called *Choix*, to be dropped over France.[8] But Greene had also been acting as a part-time company director for the publisher Eyre & Spottiswoode since 1940, and in 1946 was working full-time for them, having been given the express task of expanding their fiction list.[9] On reading the revised version of *Sisters by a River* sent him by Katherine Clutton, Greene recommended that Eyre & Spottiswoode publish it. Clutton dealt with the contract in July and gently dissuaded Barbara from adopting the pen name 'Clover Weston', which she and her colleagues thought 'not the kind of name that gets itself taken seriously'; 'What about "Barbara Weston"? Or Barbara something else?' she added.[10] Barbara settled on 'Barbara Comyns'. In August 1946, when she was on holiday with the children in Cornwall, Richard wrote to her saying that he had received 'a phone call from Graham about your book. He wasn't sure whether or not to correct the spelling and decided to wait and see the proofs.' In the event, the book was published complete with its original misspellings.

In the same letter Richard referred to the kindness of Kim Philby and his wife Aileen during Barbara's absence:

> I dined with them last night and today we all went to the 'drinking-club' at the Markham Arms and they asked me back to lunch afterwards. It was a family Sunday lunch like we went to with Caroline. Josephine was very lively and pert and showed off as one would expect; the rather nice little boy was still as nice as ever and ate his lunch very slowly and exchanged jokes with Josephine which both of them thought extremely funny. The youngest is still noisy. He has grown a lot and developed a ferocious pair of eye-brows like a Chinese war-lord. One funny thing happened. Aileen produced stewed fruit after the Sunday roast. I knew Kim had no use for fruit himself, but apparently

he disapproves of it so strongly that he won't allow it on the table or have it served to his children. Aileen apologized for the wretched fruit but he walked upstairs in a huff and when I left they were still quarrelling about it.

Like many people, Richard and Barbara regarded Philby's slight eccentricities as amusing (he was averse to horses as well as stewed fruit) and found him generous, witty and charming. He was excellent at his job: highly efficient, he always mastered the relevant files and correspondence before meetings, and his judgement on intelligence matters was respected. He was also popular with his colleagues and generally regarded as a man of outstanding ability. It was obvious to many in MI6 that Philby would be a strong contender for the post of Chief in the not too distant future. How many of them suspected that he was also a double agent, working for the Soviet Union at the same time as MI6, is not at all clear; probably very few – although it has been suggested that Graham Greene's ostensible reason for resigning from MI6 in June 1944 (because he did not want the promotion Philby had just offered him) was not the real one. His official biographer has suggested that Greene 'resigned because he suspected that Philby was a Russian penetration agent'.[11] Whatever the reasons for Greene's departure from MI6, in the 1940s no one could have realized the impact that Philby was to have on British politics and security during the next two decades. Despite his resignation, Greene's love of travel seems to have been supported by MI6 for many years after he left the Foreign Office. Richard Greene, author of *Russian Roulette: The Life and Times of Graham Greene*, speculates that Greene's visits to Havana in 1956 and to Moscow in 1960 – to mention just two trips – might well have been funded by MI6 for its own purposes.[12] And, notwithstanding any reservations about Philby that he might have held during the 1940s, Greene's admiration for his colleague endured. Despite the later exposure of Philby as a spy and a traitor, Greene agreed to write the introduction to Philby's book *My Silent War*, published in 1968.

Although Barbara and Richard often mixed socially with his Section IX colleagues, her life was not entirely dominated by her husband's friends, especially as some of them disappeared for spells when posted abroad. Desmond Pakenham had left for Java and Kim Philby and his family left London for a posting in Turkey late in 1946. Barbara still saw her own friends, including Francis Codd, Becket Williams (who had kindly provided the transport for Foxy's liberation) and Price, who was by now pursuing his love life elsewhere and becoming very fond of a woman called Wendy Probert. Diana kept in regular touch and sometimes treated Barbara and Caroline to tickets for the ballet or the theatre. One such trip was to the Royal Opera House in February to see Margot Fonteyn as Princess Aurora in the Sadler's Wells Ballet performance of *The Sleeping Beauty*. Such treats were soon to come to an end, however; by the spring of 1946 Diana and Rupert had decided they would move to Spain, letting their London home and exchanging their busy urban life for a house in the Cadiz province of Andalusia. The English winters did not suit Diana, who suffered from asthma, and her condition worsened each year. Her aunt and uncle owned a beautiful house of Moorish design called El Almendral in the village of San Roque on the Bay of Gibraltar, not far from Algeciras. They suggested she try living there for a while to see if the climate in southern Spain during the winter suited her better than that of London. Barbara was a little jealous; she and Richard had considered moving abroad somewhere warmer soon after they were married but had been unable to decide where would be best.[13] She knew she would miss Diana but she still had her sisters Nan, Kathleen and Chloe nearby. She saw them frequently, especially Chloe, who had given birth to a baby boy by Caesarean section in the autumn of 1945. He had been named Simon Swyfte Faraday and his parents doted on him. They hired a nanny to look after him; no expense was to be spared in bringing up this much-wanted son. Holding Simon in her arms, Barbara began to think how much she would like to have a child with Richard. By

26 Simon Faraday's christening. Left to right: Chloe Faraday (née Bayley), Simon Faraday with his nanny, John Faraday

the early autumn of 1946 she knew she was pregnant; the baby was due the following April.

Barbara now became impatient to move into their new home, but the work on Milborne Grove took time – there were serious damp problems because a stream had been diverted under the house. Building work was delayed further when it was discovered that the lead sheeting on the roof had been stolen and would need to be replaced. By the beginning of March 1947 Barbara and Richard were finally able to move in, and Barbara's first priority was decorating the nursery. She had kept well throughout her pregnancy and, having had normal births with both Julian and Caroline, anticipated no problems with the delivery of her third child. A baby girl was born at home on 20 April, with a doctor and nurse in attendance – but she survived for only two days. Julian, who was boarding at Long Dene, was told over the telephone that the birth had been very difficult and, because of the doctor's incompetence, the baby's back had been broken during delivery and it had died. In fact, the baby had been born with congenital hydrocephalus (excess water on the brain) and spina bifida. It is likely that had the child survived, she would have been severely brain-damaged. Richard registered both the birth and the death on 22 April; the baby was given no name. Writing at the end of May to Diana, who was now living in Spain, Barbara first mentioned how happy she was living in Milborne Grove: 'we have been living here for nearly three months and it is so wonderful to have a home and garden again ... although it's just off the Fulham Road it has a country atmosphere and heaps of birds come and sing in the garden'. But she then added, 'I believe you have heard the sad thing that happened to our baby. I had a dreadful time having it but have quite recovered now but feel rather like a cat who has lost its kittens.'[14] Despite the casual stoicism of this letter, Barbara felt deep grief at the loss of her child and many years later told Caroline that never a day went by when she did not think about the death of her baby.[15] And in 1985, when she was 78, she wrote to a relative whose young son had recently died, offering comfort and recalling her grief at losing her daughter: 'We lost a baby and I could never bring myself to part with her clothes which she had never worn – I felt she might come back sometime and need them.'[16] It was more than thirteen years before Barbara felt able to tackle her loss in fiction. Flora, the main character of *Birds in Tiny Cages*, written in the early 1960s, also loses her baby. Flora enjoys painting the nursery walls and is showered with gifts for the child: 'She sometimes felt the only decent thing she could do was to produce triplets.' After a difficult labour lasting 36 hours, she is rushed to hospital for a Caesarean section. She survives but the baby dies: 'Her arms seemed to ache with emptiness' and she becomes desperate to move, 'to get away from the scene of her bitter disappointment'.[17]

Sensing Barbara's sorrow, Diana invited her and Richard for a holiday in San Roque. They accepted immediately; Richard began brushing up his Spanish and they spent the evenings reading about Spain. They decided to travel in late September, glad to escape temporarily the mood of grey austerity now enveloping Britain. There were rumours during the summer that the government would announce yet further harsh measures. Food and petrol were still being rationed and there had been electricity cuts and shortages earlier in the year during one of the coldest winters on record. The post-war American Loan granted to the UK suddenly provoked a 'convertibility crisis', with the result that dollars drained from the country and there was a run on the pound. On 6 August the prime minister, Clement Attlee, duly announced a range of cuts targeted at food, petrol and films, in order to help solve the financial crisis.[18] Barbara, who was approaching 40 in 1947, wrote to Diana, 'I don't think I shall try having another baby until things get better, but perhaps I shall be too old by then.'

In the same month Milborne Grove was burgled twice. Two men suddenly turned up with a handcart in broad daylight and told the cleaner that they had come to 'collect the refrigerator' (a luxury household item in those days), which they had presumably recently seen delivered to the house. When Barbara came home and saw it had vanished she was torn between anger and admiration at such bare-faced audacity. Then, soon after, thieves took most of Barbara's jewellery, including a pearl necklace that Diana had given her, and some valuable pieces that had belonged to Richard's mother. Barbara was exasperated by the police, who were 'awfully stupid and said they would question the men who were working in the next door house. I told them there were no workmen there and they said "Oh, yes there are, we have just seen three come out" and of course it was the burglars who must have got in there over the garden wall.'[19] Life in England felt bleak; Barbara could not wait to leave it for some sunshine in Spain. The prospect of the holiday had been, Richard wrote to Diana in July, 'a vision of hope to her for some weeks'.

Barbara and Richard flew to Gibraltar from Northolt aerodrome (used for civil aviation while Heathrow Airport was being built nearby) on 23 September and did not return to England until 18 October. The holiday was a success in that it distracted Barbara from thinking about her lost child and offered a break from the bleakness of austerity England. They were both charmed by El Almendral, with its Moorish patio courtyard and its beautiful views across a rolling landscape of olive, almond, juniper and carob trees. Its garden was a network of baked stone, orange and lemon trees, and blue-leaved cacti. Rupert, now 59, was focusing on his new surroundings and painting landscapes, which he occasionally exhibited in Gibraltar and London. Diana was collecting cats and dogs, even adopting strays that found their way into the garden; she was also developing a serious interest in botany. A keen gardener, Barbara brought back some prickly pear buds which she planted in seed boxes in the kitchen: 'The char woman is rather afraid of them', she wrote to Diana, 'I believe she thinks they are a kind of animal'. It was the beginning of several years of plants and seeds travelling between London and San Roque. Soon after her return, Barbara wrote to thank Rupert and Diana for their hospitality:

> It seems very sad not to be able to say 'When we go to Spain' any more and now it is all over and there is another of these dreadful winters to face. I can't tell you how much we enjoyed ourselves and to someone like me who had been abroad so little it seemed even more strange and beautiful than I expected. I so miss those bells ringing all the time on the cattle and the turkeys making that queer laughing noise in the distance and the beautiful sky and of course the sun.

By late October rations for butter, milk and bacon had been cut, Richard was in bed with flu and the English skies were darkening. Barbara might quickly have become gloomy were it not for the fact that *Sisters by a River* had just been published by Eyre & Spottiswoode. She did not like the photograph of her on the book's cover, nor the publisher's blurb – a 'lot of waddy writing on the back which is nothing to do with me', she wrote to Diana – but she was very pleased it had attracted considerable attention. A review in *Harper's Bazaar* compared her to Stevie Smith and to Daisy Ashford, whose novella, *The Young Visiters*, had been published in 1919 complete with spelling errors when she was nine years old. Barbara did not much care for the comparisons – but she liked being reviewed alongside John Lehmann, John Mortimer and Henry Miller. Barbara's favourite review appeared in the *Tatler*, in which Elizabeth Bowen described the novel as 'a curiosity' that came 'with its own engaging challenge', adding:

> All the same, this book puzzles me: its bat-witted artlessness seems to be almost too thorough – the high points are, as against this, very funny indeed. Well is it called a blend of gruesome and comic – I should go further and call it a non-indigenous, somewhat trans-Atlantic in manner, poor-white view of English family life [...] Pray form your own opinion of this unique work.[20]

The anonymous reviewer in the *Times Literary Supplement* was altogether more critical, arguing that the author's use of a 'mature irony' did not sit well with a memoir written from a child's point of view, but concluded encouragingly, if somewhat condescendingly, with the judgement that 'Miss Comyns ... is a highly imaginative writer who should become a welcome accession to the domestic tragedy school'. A few critics found the misspelling irritating, including Francis King in *The Listener*. After praising the book's 'comic incongruities', he complained that 'a hundred and fifty pages of spelling mistakes, lunatic grammar and classroom improprieties' had finally driven him to distraction.[21]

But these negative comments were offset by Barbara's first fan letters. One was from the novelist Julian MacLaren-Ross, who lived in London and frequented Fitzrovia, and who described *Sisters by a River* as 'the only good first novel which has appeared this year'. The second was from the writer John Heygate, a friend of Graham Greene, who lived in Ireland but spent much time in London, and who confessed that 'I read little passages at odd places out of the book before sleeping and laugh myself silly'.[22] (Both men were later to be commemorated as characters in Anthony Powell's *Dance to the Music of Time*.)

Although the reviews of *Sisters by a River* had been mixed, they stimulated Barbara to return to her writing in earnest. She made some revisions to *Our Spoons Came from Woolworths* and, encouraged by Richard, continued working on *Leigh Hunt in Italy*. On 1 January 1948 Graham Greene – in his role as a director of Eyre & Spottiswoode – took Barbara out for lunch

27 Publicity photo taken when *Sisters by a River* was published in 1947; used in a review of the novel that appeared in *Harper's Bazaar*

28 Publicity photo taken in 1947; used on the back cover of the first edition of
Sisters by a River

to discuss the publication *of Our Spoons Came from Woolworths.*[23] Katherine
Clutton of Hughes Massie had sent Greene the manuscript version of the
book in late 1946, and he had suggested some changes which Barbara had
worked on during 1947. Greene thought there might need to be a few
further amendments, and he was right. In March 1948 Ruby Millar at Eyre
& Spottiswoode wrote to say that the company's editorial board had suggested
'two slight expurgations' in the description of the childbirth episode. 'I hope
you will agree to let them stand because it is a pity to invite adverse criticism
on a book which in the main says something about the horrors of confine-
ments amongst the poor which honestly needs saying', she added.[24] Barbara's
book was clearly too frank in places for some tastes. Nevertheless, she
agreed to the expurgations, pleased that her second book had been accepted
for publication.

1948 had its dark patches, however. Barbara was increasingly worried about Richard's health; he seemed very prone to chest problems and it had taken him a long time to recover from his bout of flu the previous November. More seriously, Price – who had married Wendy Probert in the spring of 1947 – suddenly became ill and grew pale and thin, quite unlike his former robust self. Wendy urged him to see a doctor because there was blood in his urine. He was diagnosed with cancer of the bladder; it had already spread to other areas of his body by the time he was hospitalized in March. Barbara visited him frequently at Granard House, the Royal Cancer Hospital in Chelsea (now part of the Royal Marsden Hospital). Julian, who still regarded Price as his second father, went with her when he was home from school. The visits were distressing; painkillers were limited and Price was often in agony. A long metal chain with a wooden handle on its end hung from the ceiling, and he would pull on this when the pain was intense and heave himself into a different position. Price died on 10 May and was buried five days later. His death marked the end of a relationship that had taught Barbara and her son many things. Julian owed Price his readiness to stand up to bullies as well as his lifelong love of stylish cars and his mechanical ability with engines; Barbara had learned from him the business skills that enabled her to stand on her own two feet. His death left an emotional void in Julian's life and Barbara felt numb at the time, but she had already commemorated his cheerful opportunism in a memoir of her life with Price in a book yet to be published:

> If he had managed to get to purgatory or somewhere like that he would soon make a short circuit to heaven, and once there he would obtain the biggest and best harp, simply stiff with real gold leaf. Maybe he would do a little business with second-hand harps. He would never be content to sit on a cloud, at least not for long. I could imagine deserter angels of darkness would come and spray his cloud a different colour every day, and he would let off part of it as a self-contained flat. I felt quite sure he had an interesting future in front of him wherever he was, and he would never for a moment waste time going mouldy in a grave.[25]

* * *

Diana wrote regularly to Barbara, her letters full of anecdotes about her many cats and her Spanish domestic staff who seemed to lurch from one personal crisis to another. She often sent photographs of El Almendral and the San Roque area which Richard carefully filed away so that he and Barbara could look at them and dream of Andalusia during cold grey English evenings. In return, Barbara sent bulletins about their London life, including the progress of the prickly pears and her attempt to grow mushrooms in a dark corner of the garden. Caroline had smuggled a small black and white kitten into the house; after an initial protest by Richard, she was allowed to keep it and called it Sir Fitzroy. Their large poodle, Vinegar Tom, was causing chaos because he had suddenly decided that the postman and anyone else riding a bicycle was fair game for attack, but otherwise life went on as usual, with the occasional party being thrown for friends and relatives and visits to art exhibitions and to the theatre – Barbara was particularly impressed by Terence Rattigan's *Harlequinade* and *The Browning Version* that opened at the Phoenix Theatre in September. A lodger had moved into Milborne Grove in April, a sure sign that Barbara and Richard needed to boost their income, but he proved himself useful, despite being a heavy drinker. He would play chess with Caroline, now 12, and look after her when they went out in the evening. Her son and daughter were growing up: 'I expect the children will be wanting to give dances soon and worse still they will drink all our drink. Richard doesn't know the life in store for him', Barbara wrote to Diana.

Rupert and Diana returned to England for a few weeks each summer, moving between London and Worcestershire, where they had relatives. Barbara always looked forward to their visits, eager for news of life in San Roque. Diana had flown back to England in September 1947 to negotiate the sale of 7 St Quintin Avenue; she had bought El Almendral from her aunt and uncle in February that year and was now certain that she wished to live in Spain permanently. During that visit, Barbara confessed that she and Richard were running short of money and had contemplated selling Milborne Grove, which she loved, and buying a houseboat to live on, which would be cheaper than running a large house in central London. The plan fell through, partly because she became anxious that living on the water might not be good for Richard's health. Any thoughts about selling their home were, however, put on hold when Richard was told in October 1948 that he would soon be sent to The Hague in the Netherlands, where MI6 had a station, for a few weeks. There were two main reasons for sending MI6 staff abroad after the end of the Second World War: the first was the 'denazification' of countries formerly occupied by the Germans; the second was to counter the growing threat posed by the Soviet Union spreading communism throughout Europe.[26] It is probable that, at the dawn of the Cold War, Richard was sent to the Netherlands to work in one of or both these areas. Barbara decided she would like to go with him: 'I think he will have to pretend that I know Dutch (I do know 20 words) and when I arrive I could say the bombing during the war has made me forget it', she wrote to Diana. No doubt remembering the horrors of working as a kennel maid in a freezing Amsterdam, she added, 'I don't like Holland much during the winter but it would be a change and there wouldn't be any washing up.' It was arranged that Caroline would stay with Desmond Pakenham and his wife Crystal, now back from Java, while they were away.

Barbara and Richard travelled overnight by boat to The Hague on 9 November and checked into the Terminus Grand Hotel the next day. Richard was based at the Ambassador's house for his working days; he had no doubt been sent out to the Netherlands as a 'Passport Control Officer' – the usual cover for MI6 staff working in British embassies and legations abroad.[27] He worked a long day but had two and a half hours for lunch, during which time he and Barbara explored the local museums and art galleries. At weekends they travelled further afield, to Delft and Amsterdam. To her surprise, Barbara liked The Hague, apart from 'the bicycles which bear down on us every time we try and cross a road, they never stop and as there are no traffic lights there is no reason why they should, and I've come to look on them as a sort of flying bomb', she wrote to Diana. While Richard was working, Barbara socialized with other MI6 wives. In the same letter to Diana she reported,

> One woman I went to tea with told me that when they were in Lisbon recently a man used to bring wonderful sausages to the Embassy just like English pre-war ones and everyone bought them and they became so famous the police got suspicious and dug up his garden and found it stiff with cat skins and bones.

Enjoying themselves in The Hague, Barbara and Richard began to fantasize about how they would like to be sent abroad permanently.

They were back in London again by 16 December, although Richard had to return to The Hague on Boxing Day for three weeks. In mid-January 1949 he wrote to Barbara telling her how much he longed to be home again and also mentioned that his father had transferred the money he had asked for; 'It is a great relief to know the money is there.' It was becoming clear that he and Barbara were living beyond their means. At this time Barbara was unable to talk about her financial worries face to face with her sister Chloe, in whom she usually confided. Chloe and her husband John Faraday had recently moved with their young son to Madrid, where John, who was fluent in Spanish and Arabic, had secured a very well-paid post as De La Rue's agent for Spain and the Middle East. Barbara knew that John, who always read her letters to Chloe, would have been irritated by what he saw as Richard's financial incompetence. So, instead, she poured out her worries in letters to Diana, telling her that their lodger had been dismissed

> because he didn't pay his rent and sat starving in front of his electric fire all day and looked all yellow. I did give him a big breakfast every day but couldn't manage all his meals. He never went out and was so melancholy like a character in a Gissing story.

He was soon replaced, however, by one of Richard's rich colleagues from the Foreign Office. Running short of money, they desperately needed to supplement their income further, so Barbara stepped up her buying and selling of antiques and rented a stall next to that run by her sister Nan in Earlham Street, off Cambridge Circus in central London. She did not earn enough, however, to solve their financial problems: 'I sell bits of china and glass and any Victorian junk I can find. I really enjoy it very much and people come and tell me their life stories which I love hearing, but I don't make very much money because it's so difficult to find enough cheap junk', she wrote to Diana.

The children, though, were thriving: Caroline joined Julian as a boarder at Long Dene and was very happy there. Julian, now 17, was growing 'quite dashing lately' and enjoyed serving drinks when they had visitors. In the spring of 1949 he left Long Dene and enrolled at the Camberwell College of Art. During that summer vacation he worked at Cullens, an upmarket grocery store on the Fulham Road. One day he was surprised to be addressed by a tall woman with white hair and a straight fringe who announced, 'You don't know me but I know who you are. I am your great-aunt Madge and I've been keeping my eye on you for years.' He was cordially invited to dinner where he met 'James', with whom Madge Pemberton lived in a close but celibate relationship in Beaufort Street in Chelsea. Julian enjoyed talking to James, who had been Alfred Hitchcock's right hand man when the famous director was making films in England. He told Barbara about having met great-aunt Madge, but she still had no time for any of the Pemberton family and simply replied, 'Oh – her!' When Julian went to see Madge he always went on his own.

*   *   *

By the end of 1949 Barbara and Richard had decided to move again, ostensibly because the London fogs were bad for Richard's chest and because Milborne Grove still had damp and settlement problems. As soon as they had an offer, they bought another large house, but this time they went further afield – cheaper than buying in Chelsea or Kensington. Neri House, in Darlaston Road, Wimbledon, built in 1885, had a wide view across Epsom Downs. A letter to Diana makes it clear that the motive for the move was financial:

> We have bought a dreadful house at Wimbledon called Neri House, it looks
> as if a retired printer who was perhaps a mayor had built it. It has about
> twenty one rooms and is converted into four flats. It is very well converted
> but all the rents are controlled at about £140 so we got the house for only

£4,500. We will be living rent free and taking enough profit to pay off the mortgage so perhaps we will be able to live within our income, but a flat will be a sad exchange for our lovely house. One nice thing about it is that the garden is about an acre and really beautiful with squirrels and woodpeckers in it and there is a garage and a potting shed.

Barbara and Richard moved into the garden flat of Neri House in early March 1950. Far from being poky, as garden flats sometimes are, it was very spacious and had a huge room with a lowered ceiling. On lifting the ceiling trapdoor, the vaulted ball room above came into view. This had once been a very grand house. Barbara – who oversaw all the practical and financial aspects of moving – threw herself yet again into making a new home, and even briefly considered a different sort of money-making scheme: 'Do you think it would be a good idea to have a mink farm? You can have 1,000 on three quarters of an acre and they only eat fish and odds and ends', she wrote to Diana.

By the summer Barbara was enjoying planting in the huge garden and Richard, who had been very ill with pneumonia in January, was stronger and healthier. Even the pets, she wrote to Diana, had undergone a transformation: 'Our cat has completely changed and has become a hunting cat and crawls about on his tummy trying to stalk birds and sometimes catching them and the dog has started to catch squirrels which I think is frightful.' While enjoying exploring villages in Surrey and Sussex, Barbara and Richard slaked their thirst for city life by joining 'The Pheasantry Club' in the King's Road, Chelsea – a bohemian restaurant and drinking club – where they could meet their London friends. But even during their first year in Wimbledon, Barbara was beginning to feel that they did not belong in suburbia. They missed central London and were always travelling into town to go to the theatre or visit art exhibitions. In May she wrote to Diana,

> The people *are* stodgy here, they talk about Modern Art (Augustus John and Laura Knight) and Bernard Shaw is the only writer of the present day. They go for tiny walks all dressed in tweeds and breathe the good air and belong to tennis clubs and nearly everyone has a television.

But the children loved living in Wimbledon: Julian had a garage to mess about in and Caroline, who still had her heart set on acting, went riding and had plans to own a horse. After a brief period at the Wimbledon School of Art, she won a place at RADA (the Royal Academy of Dramatic Art). By November she had a small part in *The Gay Invalid*, an adaptation of Molière's *Le Malade Imaginaire* that starred Peter Cushing, Tod Slaughter and Elisabeth Bergner. The play opened at the Royal Opera House in Manchester in early November 1950 and Barbara and Richard travelled north to be there for the first night. Barbara was very proud of her daughter, who moved easily about the stage and coped well when A. E. Matthews forgot his lines.

Our Spoons Came from Woolworths, Barbara Comyns' thinly disguised tale of her life as a young wife and mother in London's bohemia, was published by Eyre & Spottiswoode in the summer of 1950. Barbara insisted on the book being prefaced by a sentence that reads: 'The only things that are true in this story are the wedding and Chapters 10, 11 and 12 and the poverty.' This note was almost certainly included so as to protect Rupert Lee and, more importantly, her daughter Caroline (who would not know the identity of her biological father for some years).[28] Despite this disclaimer, the novel accurately portrays several episodes in Barbara's life at this time, including the deleterious effect of grinding poverty on a marriage and the trauma of childbirth. The grimness is often punctured by humour, however – as when the unworldly Sophia mistakes the other pregnant women's urine samples for lemonade during an antenatal appointment and asks where she can get some. Barbara's vivid description of the humiliating ways in which poor women were treated in hospitals in 1932 still makes the reader wince though, and it is meant to. Beneath the narrator's cheerful naivety simmers an author's indignation at society's treatment of young mothers.

That authorial candidness about the experience of childbirth also informs Barbara's description of Sophia Fairclough's relationship with her lover, Peregrine Narrow, described in the novel as 'a distinguished looking, middle-aged' art critic separated from his wife Mildred, a character clearly based on Rupert Lee.[29] Peregrine listens intently to everything Sophia says as if it were 'very precious', and Barbara portrays her fictional counterpart's gullibility with wry amusement:

> This had never happened to me before, and gave me great confidence in myself, but now I know from experience a lot of men listen like that, and it doesn't mean a thing; they are most likely thinking up a new way of getting out of paying their income-tax.[30]

These lines were written by an older Barbara who, in her forties, was reflecting on a more naïve and younger self with both compassion and humour. She also presents Sophia's disappointment in her lover Peregrine – similar to her own disenchantment with Rupert– with an understanding not available to her at the age of 28: 'Now, looking back, I realize he was very romantic and sentimental, but at forty-seven he hadn't the energy or initiative to take on new responsibilities.'[31]

That older woman is also prepared to write about the way in which her younger self was introduced to sexual pleasure. If the relationship between Sophia and the experienced Peregrine in *Our Spoons Came from Woolworths* reflects that between Barbara and Rupert, it seems likely that she experienced sexual fulfilment for the first time in her life not with her husband, but with her lover:

> Some time later, when I realized I had been unfaithful, I didn't feel guilty or sad; I just felt awfully happy I had had this experience, which if I had remained a 'good wife' I would have missed, although, of course, I wouldn't have known what I was missing. I felt quite bewildered. I had had one and a half children, but had been a kind of virgin all the time. I wondered if there were other women like this, but I knew so few women intimately it was difficult to tell.[32]

Although she deals with female orgasm elliptically here (reviewers seemed not to notice it), Barbara Comyns was one of the very few women novelists to address this topic in 1950. It is also one of the rare occasions when she wrote about sex, albeit obliquely. Many years later she confided to her friend the novelist Ursula Holden that she thought authors often found the subject difficult and that their unease showed in the writing. 'I once thought of hiring someone to do a few pages that I could insert here and there', she added – but she resisted the temptation.[33]

There are plenty of sudden shocks in *Our Spoons Came from Woolworths* (including the doctor's suicide and the tragic death of Sophia's little daughter from scarlet fever), but the strange and disturbing power of the novel derives not from its plot or its characters, or any gothic undertones, but from what Maggie O'Farrell has described as 'the disparity between tone and content'.[34] The disjunction between the potential tragedy facing Sophia Fairclough and the jaunty frankness with which it is related results in a stylistic incongruity that unsettles the reader. A less fanciful and a more realistic book than *Sisters by a River*, *Our Spoons Came from Woolworths* was an extraordinary achievement for a writer still finding her feet.

Reviews, however, were mixed. One of the first to appear, by Julian MacLaren-Ross in the *Times Literary Supplement*, was sharp and condescending. Having praised *Sisters by a River*, which MacLaren-Ross described as 'less like a novel than a piece of family history recorded by a precocious child conversant with the novels of Gertrude Stein', he went on to dismiss *Our Spoons Came from Woolworths* as a 'rather commonplace story' in which Sophia, the main character and narrator, is 'shallow, foolish and capable of the complete ruthlessness which is a sign of retarded emotional growth'. He ended the review by extending this criticism to the author:

> Like her heroine, Miss Comyns does not appear to have quite grown up yet; she is still at the age of confusing selfishness with honesty, but her growth to spiritual maturity should be awaited eagerly by all those genuinely interested in the future of the English novel.

More than one reviewer criticized the way Barbara finished the book, including Lionel Hale, who thought that 'the happy ending which Miss Comyns claps on her chronicle of poverty somewhat resembles a marshmallow stuck on a heavily salted almond' – a comment that, according to her son, cut Barbara to the quick. Other critics were kinder. The reviewer for the *Irish Times* noted that 'Her eye is sharp, her humour pretty well continuous. It is, in fact, a rather good account of the destruction of happiness by poverty', while Eric Young wrote in the *Sheffield Daily Telegraph*, 'If the naivety is calculated, she is an extremely skilful writer; if not, she is still a very good one.'[35] Barbara was beginning to discover that her novels would often divide readers and reviewers. She was cheered, though, by the American edition of *Our Spoons Came from Woolworths*, which arrived in December and which she described to Diana as 'all done up in gold and leather for Christmas, it looks just like a family bible or Wordsworth's poems'.

The next year started well. Barbara was delighted that *Our Spoons Came from Woolworths* was warmly received in the United States. The *Chicago Tribune* reviewer described it as 'a curiously attractive novel; its style and the story it tells are strangely reminiscent of *Moll Flanders*'. In a review that was widely syndicated, the *Buffalo Courier-Express* critic commented that the book's 'uncompromising realism will invoke laughter and tears in all but the most cynical reader', and *The New Yorker* reviewer noted that 'The author resembles an English Anita Loos.'[36]

At this time, *The Gay Invalid*, in which Caroline had a part, moved to the Garrick Theatre in London's West End, where it ran from 24 January to March 1951. Barbara and Richard began to hope that perhaps Caroline would eventually be able to realize her dream of acting for a living. Barbara finally finished her book *Leigh Hunt in Italy* in June and Richard corrected all the punctuation and grammatical errors. They had agreed that he should not bother with the numerous misspellings and leave those to be corrected by the typist but, as he wrote in his diary, 'it is difficult to pass over some of the words. When she is faced with a long or Latin-ish word, Barbara loses her head. The word is either telescoped or strangely elongated. I think "fortunately" came out as "fortunaterrily".'[37] (Such continual difficulties with spelling suggest that she might have been dyslexic.) But, whatever its shortcomings, Barbara was relieved that the Leigh Hunt book was finished. She wanted to embark on another novel soon – but she could only write when she felt secure and emotionally settled. By midsummer, she felt there was something wrong between her and Richard, and committed her thoughts to a diary that ran from early July through to early August. They reveal her response to Richard's diary-writing in the evenings, an activity which suddenly seemed to absorb him utterly and to exclude Barbara from his thoughts:

Every evening after dinner Richard sits at his desk writing. He is supposed to
be translating an old French book which is always open beside him but yesterday
evening when I went to kiss him goodnight I saw he was writing about the
things he does every day, a kind of diary. He covered it up with his arms
which made me rather sad because I know he is always frightened I might
pry into his secret life and I do try not to.[38]

She was soon beginning to feel 'flat and dull' and recorded her unhappiness
in the entry for 18 July:

I think the thing that is really depressing me is the way Richard shuts me
away [...] I feel so angry when he puts that beastly old French book by him
and pretends he is translating it because he is doing it to deceive me. I expect
there are dreadful things in it about me. I mustn't get morbid about it. I must
be dignified and try to shut myself away from Richard in the same way. I
should make a secret life of my own and not bother about him so much.

But Richard's absorption in his diary did bother her. Her depression was
compounded by the fact that *Our Spoons Came from Woolworths* had sold
poorly both in the UK and the United States. She began to lose faith in her
ability to write, confiding to her diary on 25 July, 'My books will never be
much good I know partly because I'm lazy and badly educated and I am
sure I have a thick skull ... Perhaps I will never be able to write another
book. I am reading one about Jane Austen and she often went years without
writing.' Julian and Caroline helped keep her spirits up. During July she
and her daughter went to see N. C. Hunter's *Waters of the Moon* at the
Theatre Royal in the Haymarket and heard Purcell's *Fairy-Queen* performed
at Covent Garden; they also often went for walks together on Wimbledon
Common and in Cannizaro Park. Julian amused her with his tales of trying
to get a holiday job. He had applied unsuccessfully for work as a mortician:
'I am very glad but he is sorry because he thinks it might have given him
a warped view on life and improved his painting', Barbara wrote to Diana.
Julian ended up working more mundanely as a table-clearer in the Skylon
restaurant on the South Bank where the Festival of Britain was taking place.
There were enjoyable days out at the Festival with both Nan and Richard,
but Barbara was still fretting about her husband's diary. Finally, driven to
despair by Richard's emotional distance from her, Barbara put a 'nasty note'
in his desk; he responded by explaining that he had been suffering from
very painful toothache and that he had intended showing her his diary when
it was finished. Barbara was at once contrite, writing in her own diary,
'How horrid I am. He is so good and gentle but sometimes he becomes all
remote and I feel lonely and hurt and think he is regretting marrying me.'
    It is most unlikely that the change in Richard's behaviour resulted simply
from toothache; it is more probable that his emotional remoteness was a

response to the defection of Guy Burgess and Donald Maclean in May 1951. Burgess had been appointed as Second Secretary to the British Embassy in Washington in 1950 and had been working closely with Kim Philby who, since 1949, had been acting officially as First Secretary to the British Embassy in Washington. Unofficially, Philby was the MI6 representative with special responsibility for liaison with the CIA and FBI. Burgess was renowned for his drunkenness and louche behaviour; in early 1951 a number of indiscretions, including three speeding tickets on one day and a row about the Korean War in public with Franklin D. Roosevelt Jr at a cocktail party, made his position untenable, and he was ordered to return to London, which he did in early May.[39] In the meantime the FBI, working with codebreakers, had found strong evidence that the spy named 'Homer', who had been passing information about the US atomic energy policy and NATO to Moscow, was Donald Maclean, who had served in Washington between 1944 and 1948. By 1950 Maclean was head of the Foreign Office's American desk in London. Barbara and Richard liked him and his wife Melinda, whom they frequently met at parties; the Macleans were good company, their wit increasing proportionately with their intake of alcohol. But in 1951, afraid that Maclean, mentally fragile and now suspected of being a double agent, would crack under interrogation, the Russians ordered him to defect, forestalling a Foreign Office interrogation planned for 28 May. Before he left the States, Burgess met Philby for a meal and they went over the plan to exfiltrate Maclean. On 25 May Burgess – who had also been urged by Moscow to defect and who had been briefed to warn Maclean that he was now under suspicion – turned up at Maclean's home in Kent, from where they drove to Southampton. The two men caught a ferry to St Malo in France and from there travelled overland to Moscow. On Tuesday 29 May, Guy Liddell, then Deputy Director General of MI5, wrote in his diary, 'In view of the past association between Burgess and Maclean observed by Watchers, it seems pretty clear that the pair of them have gone off' – although no one knew where.[40] During the first week of June the story appeared in the press and reporters raced off to Paris to try to track them down – to no avail. Later, in 1955, a Russian defector would reveal that the two men had been spying for the Soviet Union since 1934 and were now living there. But in 1951 the government simply described the two men as 'missing diplomats'. As far as the general public was concerned, Burgess and Maclean had simply vanished into thin air.

Philby was suddenly deeply compromised; he had met both men at Cambridge and had been instrumental in recruiting them as spies for the Soviet NKVD – later known as the KGB – in 1934.[41] He had also worked with them for many years and Burgess had stayed at Philby's family home in Nebraska Avenue in Washington. Like Burgess, Philby was recalled to

London and on 12 June was closely questioned by Dick White, soon to become Director General of MI5. Philby feigned complete ignorance of his colleagues' spying activities. Several members of MI5 and a few senior officers in MI6, including Maurice Oldfield (later to become director of MI6), already suspected Philby of espionage, but Philby's friends in MI6 staunchly defended him. Despite several more rigorous interrogations conducted by a King's Counsel barrister, Helenus 'Buster' Milmo, and Jim Skardon, a highly experienced interrogator, MI5 could produce no hard evidence of Philby's treachery. Nevertheless, Philby felt the net closing in on him and agreed 'to resign because of an imprudent association'.[42] He resigned in July 1951, ostensibly to preserve good relations with the CIA and FBI, which were now pressurizing MI5 to winkle out any other double agents in MI6.

In his turn, Richard Comyns Carr was suddenly compromised by years of close friendship with Philby and was anxious that he, too, would soon be closely questioned. His diary for 1951, which had upset Barbara so much in the summer, includes nothing about Burgess and Maclean except the observation that the Foreign Secretary made a statement about them on 11 June and that the story was all over the newspapers. Daily entries are short and would have taken only a few minutes to write; the diary certainly contains nothing about the finer points of French translation. It is possible that Richard was carrying on Philby's work of bringing MI6 documents home and deciding which should be copied for the Russians, but there is no way of proving this. It is certainly likely that he was preparing himself for what would be the inevitable interrogation of all MI6 staff following the defection of Burgess and Maclean. No doubt he was closely questioned, particularly as he knew Philby so well, but, if so, he managed to persuade his superiors that he was innocent of espionage. Nevertheless, he was moved out of Section IX in MI6 and transferred to the Information Research Department (IRD) created in 1948 at the dawn of the Cold War and secretly funded by the British government. This department was responsible for issuing information to journalists and for distributing anti-communist propaganda across Europe and the Third World. Although the IRD, based in Carlton House Terrace in Westminster, worked closely with MI6's anti-Soviet section, it fell within the remit of the Foreign Office, rather than MI6, and dealt with less sensitive information than Section IX. The transfer was a clear indication that Richard was under suspicion. Given his left-wing sympathies, he would have found the IRD – which was involved in some dubious intelligence operations and was responsible for spreading anti-Soviet rumours and disinformation[43] – an uncongenial place in which to work. However, he must have been deeply shaken by recent events and was probably relieved that he still had a job.

Barbara stopped writing her diary in early August; perhaps Richard had regained his usual equanimity by then and so she ceased worrying about him; or perhaps – once the story broke in the national press – he shared his anxiety about Burgess and Maclean with her and she was simply relieved to know that his emotional distance during the summer had nothing to do with her. Just over ten years later, on 21 October 1962, Richard was to write in his diary:

> The Burgess–Maclean case was not a law court case because they fled the country; but it was certainly a cause célèbre. All the circumstances – the fact they were spies, the bad moral record of both of them, their Communist sympathies – thoroughly discredited the sophisticated, erratic, bohemian type of dabblers in Marxism.

Perhaps that is how he regarded himself – as a sophisticated dabbler in Marxist thought.

*   *   *

Barbara soon found something else to distract her from her worries about Richard. The tense months of June and July in 1951 were overtaken in mid-August – at least in Barbara's mind – by a very different sort of disaster that took place elsewhere. Both national and regional newspapers carried the story of a tragedy that had hit the village of Pont-Saint-Esprit in the Languedoc-Roussillon region of France. It was reported that four people had died and about fifty were in hospitals or in asylums. Their condition was attributed to ergot poisoning, caused by eating bread made with rye contaminated by a parasitic fungus. The symptoms were alarming and included psychotic episodes as well as physical pain: 'Hallucinations brought on by the poison have sent victims screaming that wild beasts and snakes are attacking them', declared one English journalist.[44] The mayor of Pont-Saint-Esprit commented, 'I have seen healthy people suddenly become terror-stricken and furious, tearing off their clothing and shouting with a hoarse voice.'[45]

Barbara decided that she would base her next book on the tragedy; she was always interested in the extraordinary and the macabre. The novel would open with two unmitigated disasters: a flood followed by an outbreak of ergot poisoning. Key to the story would be the fact that both events are beyond the villagers' control; they are swept up in and become the victims of terrible events that they simply have to endure. Although Barbara would later declare that the book was not at all autobiographical, it may be that what happened in Pont-Saint-Esprit unconsciously provided her with a way of obliquely expressing and exorcising the anxiety she had felt earlier in the summer. Barbara had obviously been deeply affected by her husband's emotional remoteness, mainly because she did not understand its cause at the time. Also, she had survived crises and episodes of horror in her own life, including extreme poverty, abortion, depression and a suicide attempt. The idea for the novel excited her; how people behave in extreme circumstances had always intrigued her, but it perhaps now carried a particular personal resonance. She looked forward to making a start on what would become *Who was Changed and Who was Dead*.

August also brought the excitement of being invited to Elstree to meet a Mr Morrison and a Mr Rogers from the Associated British Picture Corporation. They had read *Our Spoons Came from Woolworths*, thought Barbara had a gift for dialogue and invited her to write a film scenario. She decided on a plot about some lost old silver plate for which a reward is offered and which, it turns out, has been sold on a market stall. She finished *Phantasy in Seven Dials* by mid-September.[46] Disappointment lay ahead, however: her scenario was rejected by the film company in October. There was more disappointment to come. Barbara's literary agent at Hughes Massie had sent *Leigh Hunt in Italy* out for publication but it was rejected in September by Nicolas Bentley, a director at André Deutsch, and was soon to be rejected by The Bodley Head, despite Graham Greene's recommendation that they should publish it.[47] Nor was Hughes Massie having much luck in placing *Mr Fox Eats his Grapes*, Barbara's novel based on her life with Price. Richard called in on their office in early November, but a Mr Cook admitted that the agency was struggling to find a publisher for both books. He was considering trying them with Longmans but thought it would be difficult to find a publisher for *Leigh Hunt in Italy*. 'Barbara was very cast down when I told her the news', Richard wrote in his diary on 8 November.

By December both Barbara and Richard were feeling depressed. On the last day of 1951 Richard wrote in his diary,

> Our position at the dawn of the year 1952 is as follows: we have a thumping overdraft at the bank, we are trying to sell the house, Barbara has had disappointments over the last three books she has written, and I am wondering whether I shall have to have a tooth out.

Soon after Christmas, Barbara set about looking for a new home somewhere in central London; a move always energized her and now she could not wait to leave Wimbledon where, Richard noted in his diary in October 1951, none of the women she knew 'wore a speck of make-up and [where] she felt like a peacock in a hen-pen'. Other changes were afoot: in the spring Barbara received a letter from John Johnson, who worked at the literary agency E. P. S. Lewin in Chelsea. He wrote:

I was lunching today with George Buchanan who is, I believe, an old friend of us both. He suggested to me that I write to you in case I could be of any assistance with your literary work. If this is not the case, please excuse my enquiry. There are, however, openings in various markets and I should be very glad to put some suggestions to you. All I know at the present is that you have published two novels with Eyre and Spottiswoode.[48]

It is probable that John Johnson knew more than this letter reveals; most likely George Buchanan had told him that Hughes Massie had failed to find a publisher for either *Leigh Hunt in Italy* or *Mr Fox Eats his Grapes*. Barbara decided to move to E. P. S. Lewin and from then on Johnson acted as her literary agent.

The purchase of 24 Drayton Gardens, South Kensington, was a much bigger move. It was yet another handsome Victorian house which had a splendid columned porch and an attic as well as a basement. The only drawback was that it was being sold on a short lease. Barbara decided they should keep Neri House as an investment; the tenants' rents covered the mortgage and she very astutely let the garden flat for fourteen years in advance. The lump sum produced by this canny move enabled her to pay for the lease to be extended on Drayton Gardens. In early 1952 Barbara and Richard moved into their new home; Dora Philby, Kim's mother, was a near neighbour. Barbara set to work on turning an empty house into a home: the ceiling in one room was soon painted midnight blue with stars; she repainted most of their furniture and bought some more; she chose beautiful new colourful fabrics for curtains and cushions. In June she wrote to Diana:

It is lovely being in London again away from our dreary tenants. We suddenly felt we couldn't bear them anymore and Richard was very bored with the journey every day. I found this house without any trouble, it was the only one I saw and it was just what we wanted but frightfully dirty. It had been shared by eight young men and two dogs and it hadn't been cleaned for two years. I have done most of the painting myself and it was wonderful to see the house changing and coming all light and clean and the garden is full of flowers although it was filled with old tins and rubbish when we came, not even a bit of grass. I think this is the grandest house we have had but to pay for it we have to let the top floor furnished and a room in the basement.

Having finally got Drayton Gardens, as the house became known, to her liking, Barbara wanted to resume her writing – but there were frequent interruptions and once again the only time she could concentrate on it was early in the morning. The house was a busy place; it was often full of students from the Camberwell College of Art and RADA. One art student in particular, John Alford, a friend of Julian's, was captivated by Caroline; now 17, she was becoming a beautiful young woman, and Barbara found herself frequently consoling the young admirers her daughter had rejected. There were many parties at Drayton Gardens: the Comyns Carrs were generous hosts and the drink flowed freely at such events; the gin and tonics were famously strong and Barbara had a monthly order with Cullins on the Fulham Road for a large bottle of whisky. Barbara's sisters and her literary and artistic friends were always invited; her ex-husband John even came once, accompanied by Antonia Hall, whom he had married in 1946. It would be the last time Barbara would see him; in 1953 he was to leave Antonia and move to Paris where he would resume his life as a bohemian artist. Richard's colleagues were also invited to the Drayton Gardens parties. His guests included David Footman, chief of the Political Section of MI6 who was an expert on Russian revolutionary history and who had recruited Guy Burgess into the service in 1938; an urbane and sophisticated man who associated with left-wing intellectuals, he was suspected by Stuart Menzies, Chief of MI6, of working for the Russians.[49] On 5 July 1951 Richard wrote in his diary, 'David Footman and Angus Wilson gave distinction to the party.' Graham Greene sometimes turned up, as did Kim Philby who, since his resignation from MI6, had moved his family out to Rickmansworth in Hertfordshire. As all official or semi-official jobs were now closed to him, Philby had been reduced to working in a small import and export business owned by a former colleague in MI6. He was being closely observed by MI5's Watchers and had been shunned by some of his former colleagues, but Barbara and Richard stayed loyal to him. Philby's job was in the City and he often chose to spend the night at his mother's flat in Drayton Gardens rather than travel home to Rickmansworth, so he frequently called on Barbara and Richard. Tom Hopkinson, the former editor of *Picture Post* who had advised Barbara to revise *Sisters by a River* and placed extracts from it in *Lilliput*, was always invited, as were Augustus John, now in his seventies, and Dylan Thomas. The Welsh poet, who was often in the United States giving readings, was happy to follow the liquor when back in London and is remembered for downing huge quantities of alcohol and for urinating in the bath at Drayton Gardens. The sculptor Barney Seale, who had been so kind to Barbara during her poverty-stricken bohemian days, was still part of the Comyns Carr circle, and asked if she would pose for him again. She agreed and a vague likeness of her head adorned the top of a 22-foot totem pole exhibited at the Building Exhibition in Olympia in November 1953. Its purpose was supposedly to display the effects of colour on wood and it no doubt provided an interesting distraction from the more functional displays that surrounded it. It certainly caught the attention of one journalist who wrote a short feature article about it for the *Evening News*.

During these years, Barbara saw a lot of her sister Chloe and her family, who had returned to England and now lived in Kenton Court on Kensington

High Street. They also had a holiday home on Hayling Island, where Barbara stayed with them during August 1952. Chloe and John always came to the Comyns Carr parties. An acknowledged London beauty, Chloe frequently sat for artists such as Frank Slater and the society portrait painter Anthony Devas, whose wife Nicolette was the sister of Dylan Thomas's wife, Caitlin. The scandals that had surrounded her first marriage and its breakdown were now in the past and she was a respectable wife and mother. Or at least, so it seemed. In fact, she and Barbara liked a flutter on the races and spent hours scrutinizing a horse's form before laying their bets. Chloe's butcher knew several people in the racehorse business and he would give the two women tips; his meat was poor but Chloe patronized him for the sake of his insider knowledge. At first, the two sisters were lucky but after a while they had a bad run, with the result that they suddenly found themselves in debt to their bookmaker to the tune of £650 (almost £24,300 today). Loath to confess this disaster to their husbands (especially as John Faraday was a reformed gambler), they decided to carry on betting. To their huge relief, a number of lucky wins took them into credit. No one knew of their close financial shaves except Julian, who was deputed to telephone the bookmaker and who was sworn to absolute secrecy. The sisters still shared a penchant for risk-taking, but their gambling careers came to an end when Julian was called up for National Service with the Royal Irish Fusiliers in January 1954 and posted to Armagh. Recognized as intelligent and resourceful, within six months he had been sent back to England for officer training in Canterbury. But, like his father, Julian found army life stifling and uncongenial; he soon made it clear that he had no intention of committing himself permanently to the military. He was immediately listed as a 'potential deserter' and transferred to the Royal Inniskilling Fusiliers, an Irish infantry regiment of the British Army, which at that time was being sent to various trouble spots, including Egypt, Kenya and Cyprus. By the summer, Julian had been posted to Cyprus, where he was to spend the next eighteen months running the Intelligence Section, overseeing aerial surveys and creating new maps of the island. It was certainly preferable to rainy Ireland.

Meanwhile, in between cooking meals, hosting parties, seeing her sisters and converting the basement at Drayton Gardens into a self-contained furnished flat, Barbara continued writing *Who was Changed and Who was Dead*, getting up early to work on the book. She took her title from Longfellow's poem 'The Fire of Drift-Wood', in which the leaping flames of a fire made from the wood of wrecked ships take the poet's thoughts back to times past:

> We spake of many a vanished scene,
>   Of what we once had thought and said,

29 Julian Pemberton aged 22 when he was in the army

> Of what had been, and might have been,
>   And who was changed, and who was dead.

But the poem's mood of elegiac melancholy is very different from the tone
of Barbara's third novel. Set in rural Warwickshire in 1911 in a village like
Bidford-on-Avon, it encompasses the brutish and the innocent and opens
on a surreal note:

> The ducks swam though the drawing-room window. The weight of the water
> had forced the windows open; so the ducks swam in. Round the room they
> sailed quacking their approval; then they sailed out again to explore the
> wonderful new world that had come in the night.[50]

The Willoweed family at the centre of the novel comprises the selfish and
bullying Grandmother Willoweed, 'a dreadful black old bird, enormous and
horrifying, all weighed down with jet and black plumes' who tyrannizes the
household;[51] her son, Ebin Willoweed, a self-absorbed and lazy ex-journalist;

and his three children – Emma, the gentle and caring eldest daughter, Dennis, her sensitive and bookish brother, and Hattie, a sweet-natured mixed-race child conceived when Emma's mother had an affair, and whose birth led to her mother's death. The flood, an act of nature, and the ergot poisoning, brought about by human error, result in disasters of biblical proportions. Whereas many animals and birds drown in the deluge, with the bodies of pigs, peacocks and chickens swirling around in the water, the ergot poisoning takes its toll on the village's human inhabitants. Horace Emblyn, the village baker, decides to experiment by making some rye bread in order to cheer himself up (his wife is having an affair with Ebin Willoweed), but his unwitting use of diseased rye is catastrophic. There are many scenes of stark horror in the novel when the terrible sickness descends on the village: the miller goes mad and drowns himself and the butcher slits 'his throat right across like a great smile'.[52] The baker's innocent assistant, an old man called Toby, whose facial deformities – caused by a past accident with quicklime – make him a figure of fear and fun, is burned to death. The villagers, looking for a scapegoat, light upon him as the cause of the tragedy and set fire to his cottage: 'The fierce changing light revealed old Toby's charred corpse more terrible than he had ever been in life, and, although the doctor bent over him in compassion, most of the onlookers staggered away half fainting and some uncontrollably vomiting.'[53] The broken-hearted baker cannot live with what he has done and kills himself by drinking carbolic acid; 'he fell choking to the ground, consumed by burning pains more terrible than any that had been suffered in that village'.[54]

Who was Changed and Who was Dead focuses on the macabre and presents gore and violence as inevitable aspects of a cruel and bleak world. But the novel is not just one horror after another: it also contains many moments of black humour and several lyrical scenes that evoke the beauty of the Warwickshire countryside. The effect is one of Grand Guignol modulated by some light grace notes. The ergot tragedy affects the villagers differently; while it brings out the best in some, others turn to murder and suicide as a way of dealing with horror, their facial expressions deformed by panic and fear. Death and the threat of death is everywhere and the novel raises many questions. How can one explain such a tragedy in a Christian country? Why do the innocent, including the gentle Dennis who dies in agony from the poisoning, have to suffer needlessly? Why do some survive and others not? The novel offers no answers and there is no sense of any divine purpose to what happens; instead it embraces a dark fatalism. Along with the occasional dismissive reference to Catholics as 'papists', its scenes of horror and its implicit amorality might be why the book was placed in the category of 'indecent or obscene' and banned in Ireland in 1955 under the Censorship of Publications Act.

Yet the novel also shows that catastrophe can be beneficial: some survivors are changed for the better. Old Ives the handyman converts to Catholicism and finds much comfort in it; Ebin Willoweed is able to resume his career as a journalist; Emma finally escapes the emotional tyranny of Willoweed House and marries a young doctor, who takes her off to London. Tragedy can be cathartic, it seems. Yet the fact that the young doctor sees Emma, when he first meets her, as an El Greco Madonna suggests that he might be idealizing her, rather than seeing her clearly.[55] And, when married, Emma becomes the perfect wife and hostess, indicating that she has perhaps exchanged one kind of constraining environment for another one, albeit a more comfortable one. The novel's happy ending might not be quite what it seems. Barbara was later to write:

> It is the only book I have allowed my family to see while I was working on it [...] *Who was Changed and Who was Dead* is entirely unbiographical and I really let my imagination go. This was a help when I came to write my next book *The Vet's Daughter*.[56]

At the end of 1953 Barbara sent *Who was Changed and Who was Dead* to John Johnson, and by the following February she had signed a contract for its publication with The Bodley Head in the autumn of 1954. By that time, to Barbara's intense disappointment, several more publishers had rejected *Leigh Hunt in Italy*, including Harraps, which described it as 'well written' and 'very thoroughly researched' but 'too short'.[57] After she had worked so hard on the book, its failure upset her deeply and she needed good reviews of her latest novel to restore her confidence. In fact they were very mixed: 'So far I've only had four reviews – two shockers and two wonderful ones', Barbara wrote to Diana in late November. The 'wonderful ones' included a review in *The Listener* that described the novel as 'a modern myth, set in a formalized rural borderland between the real and the surreal, and using the aesthetic of *Cold Comfort Farm* for purposes both burlesque and serious'; it ended with a description of Barbara as 'a neo-Mandarin of individual and growing talent'. The reviewer in the *Irish Times* also liked the novel, which he thought 'a curious concoction of the idioms of Grand Guignol and Daisy Ashford, spiced with ingredients far more horrid than eye of newt and toe of frog'. And in the *Evening News*, John Connell saw 'echoes of Blake and Coleridge' in *Who was Changed and Who was Dead*, describing it as a book which 'has tenderness and ferocity and queer, magical charm which I can neither escape nor deny'.[58] But then there were the 'shockers', one of which was by John Betjeman in the *Daily Telegraph*. The novel, he wrote, 'reads like the work of a schoolgirl who has been given up by her teachers because she is so undisciplined at all the set subjects [...] No detail is too horrible to avoid meticulous child-like recording.' He concluded by briskly dismissing the publisher's claim that the novel was a 'little masterpiece'. It was the first review to be published and because it was syndicated, appearing in a number of newspapers, it did a lot of damage to sales of the book. Another negative review appeared in the *Birmingham Post*, in which the novel was described as 'like a nightmare, a queer, twisted phantasmagoria peopled with eccentrics and near-lunatics, and morbidly obsessed by images of blood, madness and death in various but always violent forms'.[59] By now though, Barbara knew that her books divided readers; so long as there were some good reviews as well as bad ones, she was not too downcast. She dug out the notes she had made for *The Long White Dress* in Snowdonia when on honeymoon and continued work on the book – later to be entitled *The Vet's Daughter*.

The failure of *Leigh Hunt in Italy* and the mixed reviews of *Who was Changed and Who was Dead* were, however, as nothing compared to the disaster that overtook Barbara and Richard in 1955. In May Richard was called for interview by a senior colleague in the Information Research Department. He did not tell Barbara. On 27 May the colleague wrote to Richard from Carlton House Terrace, where the IRD was based; the letter was headed 'Personal and Confidential'. It read:

> Dear Comyns Carr,
>   With reference to our conversation of yesterday, this is to confirm, with regret, that I have to give you three months' notice of termination of your appointment with effect from the 1st of June next. Your last day of service for pay purposes will therefore be August 31, 1955, and any outstanding annual leave should be taken before that date.
>   Before leaving would you kindly call on Miss Southern in Room 178 to hand in your Foreign Office pass and to sign a copy of the Official Secrets Act.[60]

It would be several weeks before Richard found the courage to tell Barbara that he had lost his job at the Foreign Office.

10

Ibiza

Many years later, in an interview in 1992 with the writer Jane Gardam, Barbara said of Kim Philby:

> He was always drunk but so nice and such fun. He used to come to dinner in Wimbledon and we all laughed all the time. He used to stay very late and then say he had to go back to the office and work. Truly we didn't believe it when the story broke that he was a spy. We still can't. Burgess yes – an awful man – but not Philby. My husband was sacked. They said that having worked so close to them he must have known. You must have known, they said, or you're a bloody fool; either way you must go.[1]

In another article about Barbara Comyns, published some years after her death, Jane Gardam quoted her as saying:

> I expect you've heard that my husband was a spy? He worked in Whitehall with Kim Philby. Oh, Kim was a delightful man. So funny. Always here playing cards. Neither of us had a notion! When he disappeared – to Moscow, you know – they sacked my husband. They said that either he must have known and therefore was a traitor, or that he hadn't spotted it and therefore must have been a fool.[2]

Assuming Barbara's comments were accurately reported, it is difficult to know whether she was being disarmingly honest or, in the spirit of some of her female characters, was responding disingenuously. Certainly there are some glaring anomalies: Kim Philby did not defect to Moscow until 1963 and Richard was sacked in 1955; the hysterical flurry of interest in Philby as 'the third man' who in 1951 had helped Burgess and Maclean defect did not surface until the autumn of 1955, by which time Richard had served his notice and was out of work.

What could account for these discrepancies in Barbara's account of her life at this time? According to her family, she was often casual about dates and facts and she became increasingly vague as she grew older. Nevertheless, what comes through clearly is her belief that Richard's dismissal had resulted from his friendship with Philby. She was probably right. Richard was employed on rolling three-year contracts by the Foreign Office and never had a permanent position. His last contract, awarded in May 1952, would have expired in May 1955, but the brusque tone of his letter of dismissal after fifteen years of service as a civil servant suggests that there was something more to his sacking than natural wastage – as does the fact that, according to his family, he was followed by a Watcher from the day he left the Foreign Office. It is possible that Vladimir Petrov, a Russian spy who defected in 1954 and who acquired political asylum in Australia on the grounds that he could provide information about a Soviet spy ring, galvanized the Foreign Office into looking for 'moles' within its ranks the following year. Petrov certainly confirmed that Burgess and Maclean had defected to Russia in 1951. That news was splashed all over the papers in September 1955, and the British government, no longer able to fall back on the phrase 'missing diplomats', was forced to issue a White Paper. However, this document did not mention Philby and played down the Burgess/Maclean affair.

Meanwhile, external pressure on MI5 and MI6 was growing. J. Edgar Hoover, director of the FBI in the United States, had been convinced for some time that Philby was a spy and was demanding that MI5 and MI6 should look more energetically for proof of espionage within their ranks. Exasperated by the British government's subsequent lack of action and by MI5's soft questioning of MI6 suspects, Hoover leaked the possibility to the American press that Philby had been 'the third man'. In October 1955, during Prime Minister's Questions in Parliament, Marcus Lipton, the Labour member for Brixton, accused the British prime minister, Harold Macmillan, of whitewashing Philby in the recent White Paper and of stifling discussion of his possible 'third man' activities. The following month brought a government response in the form of a statement from Macmillan, in which he confirmed that Philby had been a communist as a student but claimed that there was no evidence of any espionage activity and, indeed, that he had 'carried out his duties ably and conscientiously' while working for the government.[3] The next day Philby gave a press conference in his mother's living room at Drayton Gardens and, with consummate skill, lied smoothly and convincingly about his past, denying any contacts with communists since 1934. Philby was off the hook again. At the invitation of W. E. D. Allen, the former press counsellor at the British embassy in Ankara, he spent six months in Ireland helping compile a history of his host's family business.[4] Returning to London in 1956 he was found work in MI6. Although he could not officially be re-employed (Macmillan had been promised that he would go), it suited MI6, which was taking an increasing interest in the Middle East, to make Philby an agent in Beirut. His cover was arranged by Nicholas Elliott and George Young – both former colleagues in MI6 – who found him work as a 'stringer' (a non-staff correspondent) with the *Observer* and the *Economist*, which 'had a very close relationship with MI6'.[5] The editors of both publications agreed to share his services and pay him £3,000 a year (almost £94,000 today) plus expenses.[6] It no doubt helped that Nicholas Elliott, whom Philby regarded as a close friend, knew David Astor, the editor of the *Observer*, from his days at Eton.[7] Not until 1963 would Philby be unmasked as one of the most successful spies in British history, at which point he fled to Moscow.

Although Philby had lost his post as a senior officer in MI6, his path was smoothed to a career as a journalist, covert re-entry into MI6 and a fresh beginning in Beirut. Richard Comyns Carr suffered harsher consequences, which suggests that MI5 certainly found something amiss. There are several possible explanations for his abrupt dismissal: perhaps he confessed in May 1955 to espionage (although not at the level that Philby was operating); or he was found to be subverting the anti-communist work of the Information Research Department in some way; or he admitted to being complicit with treason, knowing that Philby had been spying for the Russians for many years but telling no one. The Foreign and Commonwealth Office claims that it destroys personnel files of staff once an individual reaches 85 or dies, whichever comes first, so the reason for Richard's dismissal remains a mystery. It has been suggested that 'No one in [Graham] Greene's circle shared his sympathy with Kim Philby', but that is not quite true.[8] Richard quietly stood by Philby, who left a desk, a dining table and four early Victorian chairs with him and Barbara for safekeeping when he moved abroad. He never reclaimed them. Richard found, as Philby had, that leaving the Foreign Office under a cloud meant that all government posts were closed to him. He was also now being shadowed by a Watcher who lurked discreetly in Drayton Gardens, which suggests that MI5 continued to view him with deep suspicion. Unlike Philby, however, Richard did not have friends with useful contacts prepared to step forward and find him work elsewhere. During the summer of 1955 he tried desperately hard to find another job, writing letter after application letter. It was a while before he confessed to Barbara that he was working out his notice at the Foreign Office and explained the sudden increase in his correspondence. He gradually became disheartened by his search for work; many potential employers thought he was too old at the age of 48 to start a new job and the few interviews he attended came to nothing. When writing her novel *Out of the Red, Into the Blue*, published in 1960, Barbara drew heavily on their life between 1955 and 1958; many years later in a letter to her agent she confirmed that three-quarters of it was true.[9] In the book, Richard becomes 'Raymond' and the nameless narrator, Barbara's fictional alter ego, reflects:

He hardly ever talked about his interviews or disappointments, and the only way I knew what was happening was by arranging appointments over the telephone when he was out, and by the letters that arrived for him. I felt horribly inquisitive looking at the postmarks on my husband's correspondence; but when I saw letters coming from places like Carlisle or Birmingham, my heart sank at the thought that we might have to live somewhere like that and leave London.[10]

By the autumn of 1955 Richard was still out of work and their money was draining away. Barbara was terrified of sinking into 'the poverty' again and did not see how they could keep Drayton Gardens much longer without Richard's salary. She felt immensely sad; she had worked very hard on the house and now loved it. They had often been perilously close to falling into serious debt even when Richard was in work, having a knack for living beyond their means. His small private allowance and the rent from the lodgers would not be enough to meet their outgoings; and the income from the flats in Neri House only covered the mortgage repayments on it and the cost of maintaining the building. They began to think about selling up and living abroad, where a warm dry climate would be good for Richard's health (he was in bed with pneumonia for three weeks in November) and where the sun would lift Barbara's spirits. Fantasies of Spain began to dominate the winter evenings again. Julian had recently sent them a present from Cyprus, described in *Out of the Red, Into the Blue* as:

> a little man ... about sixteen inches high and the colour of beeswax, and one of his hands clutched his heart and the other his stomach. His face somehow reminded me of a bewildered tortoise – perhaps it was his beaky nose and little hollow nostrils.[11]

Julian (who becomes 'Nicholas' in the novel) had attached a note to the figure which read, 'I hope this brings you luck.' Being superstitious, Barbara, like the narrator of her novel, would clutch the little brown wax figure from Cyprus to her and will him to find work for her husband.

*   *   *

Fate, if not good luck, did indeed intervene in the form of one of Caroline's friends who came to stay with her for a while. After her part in *The Gay Invalid*, Caroline worked with the Salisbury Repertory Company for a while and had played the secretary in the crime drama *Meet Mr. Callaghan*. Since then, she had been offered a few bit parts in plays and films but no major roles. To earn some money, she was working in coffee bars and had made several new friends. One of them, a young woman who had recently returned from living on the island of Ibiza for a spell, was looking for somewhere to stay in London. At first she asked if she could just leave a few bags at Drayton Gardens, but she ended up staying several months. She talked with great enthusiasm about Ibiza: how remote and unspoiled it was; how beautiful the climate; how blue the sea; how friendly the people; how cheap it was to live there. Richard and Barbara had flirted with the idea of moving to mainland Spain, but now they started to consider Ibiza. In January they discussed the idea with Richard's father, affectionately known as 'Pa', who loved to see his adult children embark on new adventures and who encouraged them. They also talked to Caroline and Julian about their plan. Julian was now back from Cyprus, having finished his National Service, and had just secured a job as a scenic artist with Associated Rediffusion, a new commercial television station. They both reassured their mother they would be fine sharing a flat in London if she decided to leave the country. By January 1956 Barbara and Richard were thinking seriously about moving to Ibiza.

A complication arose when one of Richard's job applications succeeded. He had worked for three years in the BBC News Department before enlisting in the Royal Fusiliers in 1939 and thought he might stand a chance when he saw an advertisement for the post of news assistant at one of the BBC's regional stations. Despite his diffidence in the interview, he was offered the job, accepted, and began work on 1 February 1956. But by this time both he and Barbara were excited by the idea of starting a new life on Ibiza and were reading as much as they could about the island. By mid-February Richard was finding his early starts at the BBC exhausting and the work dreary; he was also earning less than he had at the Foreign Office. He later confessed that he was not really interested in news: 'my eye is drawn more to a booklet on edible fungi or an article in the *Lancet* than to the front page of the *Daily Mirror* [...] I have not much of an eye for a story. To me reading the papers is a daily duty, which I have always had to perform because of my various jobs.'[12] Meanwhile, Drayton Gardens had been sold and their furniture was in store. Barbara and Richard moved into Bailey's Hotel near Harrington Gardens in South Kensington and, while Richard was at work, Barbara looked around for a small house they could afford in London. There was nothing that was not thoroughly depressing. February was cold and grey and Richard was still weak from his recent bout of pneumonia. Everything seemed to be conspiring to persuade them to move to Spain. In mid-February Richard resigned from his post, giving a month's notice.[13] It is possible that he was forced to resign – it has recently been discovered that MI5 vetted BBC applicants from its early days until the 1990s.[14] If Richard had been dismissed from the Foreign Office for his connections with Philby, MI5 would have reported this to the BBC, which might well have put pressure on him to resign. Either way, he was glad to leave.

They decided that Barbara would travel ahead to Ibiza and find somewhere for them to live while Richard finished his time at the BBC. A friend recommended that she should write to Leslie Grimes – known to his friends and family as 'Grimey' – a former cartoonist for the *Daily Sketch*, who had recently retired to Ibiza to paint. He was a man of pithy observations who later advised Julian that while living in Spain was a joy, 'getting money out of a Spaniard was harder than getting shit out of a blanket'.[15] He responded to Barbara's letter with a full list and lots of advice.[16] By early March Barbara was arranging for books and a few belongings to be shipped out to the island and was packing for her journey. After a period of feeling depressed and in limbo, she was now both apprehensive and excited. In 1956 it was not possible to fly directly to Ibiza; the journey had to be made either by sea from Barcelona or, after a flight to Mallorca, by boat from there. Barbara flew to Palma in Mallorca and stayed overnight in a hotel where, she told Richard on a postcard, she slept in a 'huge black four-poster bed' and felt 'a bit lonely, no one speaks English so far'.[17] On 7 March 1956 she arrived in Ibiza town with two suitcases and her typewriter. She wrote Richard a long letter from the Hotel España, a rather scruffy little place where she had to rely on candles for light in the evening:

Darling Richard,

I have arrived after a wonderful boat journey [...] the hotel is fantastic. I was met at the boat with a wheelbarrow and I couldn't believe this was the place I was to stay in. The ground floor is kind of ruins [that] are not used and you go up some very rough steps and the hotel is on the first floor [...]

I saw Ibiza nearly three hours before we arrived, it looks enormous from the sea and very strange and empty and foreign, quite deserted and [with] strange shaped hills covered in pine trees [...] The streets are fairly quiet, I expect because of the darkness. The town is built up a hill with a huge and modern looking museum right on top, otherwise it looks very Spanish and pretty, but I do hope it won't be too primitive for us.

Mallorca was beautiful from the air and I had time to have a look at Palma this morning, very bright sun and everything is green and pink or white, a very nice place but I thought rather expensive. I went to the market with great piles of fruit and tomatoes sold on their stalks and I saw what I thought was a walking bunch of bananas but discovered a man's legs underneath, it looked rather sinister like a Stanley Spencer painting.

The view of the harbour is terrific, your father will love it ... it does look a fascinating place, the sun shining and mule carts keep passing my window all stacked up with bread. Americans would have a fit, a good thing, it will keep them away. The other guests are all Spanish. The food isn't too bad, not too oily, but the three meals I've had have all been the same, the same soup slightly fishy, then a couple of fried fishes, then two slices of very tender meat, it could be anything, and fried potatoes and a banana.

The man from the [travel] agency took me to the boat. He knew Robert Graves because he taught his youngest boy grammar. I told him I was going to be the Robert Graves of Ibiza [...]

I have seen quite a lot of the English colony and didn't think much of them. They are all very brown and arty and scornful and the men have beards, some of them sit in the same café over a cup of coffee for four hours. The old ones are a bit awful, scruffy tweeds and red faces and an eyeglass. One or two people look quite nice but so scornful and they read clever French books.

Don't forget me and come all distant and far away, I am so longing for you to come and to see your civilized face again. Richard I don't want to grow awful and sit in cafés all day, do stop me if I get like that, I will stop you if you get awful.

With love, come soon.

The next day Barbara was up early, ready to explore the island. Chapter 11 in *Out of the Red, Into the Blue* gives a strong sense of Ibiza in 1956, although in the novel it is disguised as 'Ciriaco', after the island's patron saint, St Cyriac of the Baths, an obscure Roman martyr. Two years later Barbara wrote explaining this decision to Graham Greene:

There is really more truth than fiction in it but I think it should be treated as fiction. The ending is imaginary, and the foreigners in Ibiza I have described are mixtures of different people and not portraits, and I do not want it to be thought they are portraits of real people, or that the island is definitely Ibiza.[18]

In the novel, Barbara's fictional counterpart spends her first morning exploring Ibiza town, where the 'shops were dark and mysterious and had strange things hanging from the ceiling – long candles in coloured papers, peculiar sausages, strange pots and pans and enormous, strong-smelling dried fish'.[19] One day she hires a bicycle and goes further afield. She is completely enchanted by what she finds:

I would stand in an olive grove surrounded by the huge split and twisted olive trees, hundreds of years old. Perhaps an old man wearing a black hat and shawl would be minding a herd of goats. The ground would be all shimmering with white daisies and below were the almond orchards in blossom, each tree standing out like a little white tent. I'd think how impossible it was that I was likely to spend years looking at so much beauty every day.[20]

But although she loved the island, Barbara was miserable living in the hotel in Ibiza town: she was cold at night, uncomfortable in bed and tired of the monotonous diet. She decided she must find somewhere for them to live as soon as possible and began house-hunting in earnest, urged on by Richard who tried to keep her spirits up. 'We have to go through all this before we can start our life out there', he wrote, adding 'It is unspeakably depressing without you ... Write again as soon as possible, darling ...'

Within a few days, Barbara had found them somewhere to rent. It was a brand new house in Figueretas, then a quiet coastal area outside Ibiza town. Painted white, it had a small balcony that looked out over an endless blue sea. Barbara thought it would be perfect. She wrote enthusiastically to Richard:

> it is wonderful inside, all very simple and white, no work in it at all, a nice clean easily run kitchen with a stove as well as rings, and a sink, the first I've seen in Ibiza, a proper lav, a wash basin and taps, a well for the drinking water, a shower (cold), electricity, which should be better here because they are building a luxury hotel and it's all new wiring. There are four rooms and a kitchen and shower room, but the best thing of all is the fire place, a beautiful open fire, the thing I've been longing for ever since we left our house ... I found a beautiful deserted beach today and hardly liked to look at it because it seems a waste without you. There are lots of lovely places to see, everywhere you look, plenty of walks for your father ... Goodbye my darling, this letter is a bit disjointed because I put things down as I think of them ...

Barbara was now counting the days until Richard would arrive in late March with their black and white Welsh sheepdog, Coco. She was beginning to find her way around Ibiza town and the surrounding area, but still felt a conspicuous stranger. 'I am reading *Gulliver* and feel just like him myself', she wrote to Richard a few days later, duly reporting the island's goings-on with something of Swift's detached curiosity and delight in the ridiculous:

> The thing people seem to be most afraid of is Communism here, pretty unlikely, they are very prosperous, well fed and contented, but even old women who love and collect cats sometimes think one is a Communist and put it in a bag and throw it in the sea. I hope Coco isn't one, he may well be coming from Walham Green, but perhaps his Welsh ancestors were liberals.[21]

She was busy buying pots, pans and enamel water jugs for their new home, but 'for myself, I haven't even looked at an earring'. 'Goodbye my darling, hurry up and come and be the best husband in Ibiza', she signed off.

In his last letters from England, Richard detailed his travel arrangements and described taking leave of friends and relations. Caroline, now working for the *Times* Book Club and still occasionally offered small film roles, had cooked a delicious three-course meal for him as a farewell gesture. Chloe ('Clare' in the novel) and John Faraday had invited him round to their flat in Kenton Court in Kensington for dinner and Nan had joined them. 'I miss you terribly', Richard's last letter concluded: 'The old Victorian saying about "my better half" is quite true – only I feel as if I had lost three-quarters. Life is simply nothing without you.' He confirmed that he would arrive in Ibiza early in the morning on Thursday 22 March, adding that Barbara was not to be shocked if he and Coco appeared bedraggled after their long journey; they would be travelling across France and Spain by train before catching a boat from Barcelona to the island and would probably arrive looking very scruffy.

Barbara moved into the house before Richard's arrival and was delighted with it, her optimism reflected in the narrator's enthusiasm for their new home in *Out of the Red, Into the Blue*, in which the view from the windows is described as very beautiful, the rocks dotted with wild irises and lavender and rosemary. The interior, too, was charming: 'A long refectory table ran down the centre of the room and there were rush-seated chairs, and flowers were arranged in a sort of Roman urn […] Both bedrooms were very similar and on each dressing-table there was a vase of violets.'[22] In the book, the narrator returns to Ibiza town to buy fifty flower pots of various sizes and brings them back in a taxi. Wherever she lived and whatever the constraints, Barbara – like her fictional counterpart – had to have flowers and animals around her in order to feel she had a proper home. The next day she was down at the port early in the morning ready to greet Richard. When he arrived, with Coco in tow, she was relieved to see him but worried that he looked ill and drawn; Richard admitted that he was still recovering from a recent bout of flu. As he was cold and tired, Barbara decided to burn some logs in the fireplace that had so caught her eye when she first saw the house. It was a disaster. After an hour or so of trying to get the fire going, smoke billowed into the room, making their eyes stream. Upon closer inspection the next day they discovered that the lovely fireplace, complete with a pretty mantelpiece, had no chimney. It was merely there as a decorative focal point.

Despite such practical problems and the occasional short bout of homesickness, Richard and Barbara gradually adjusted to their new way of life and to living together in a small house. As the weather turned warmer, Richard was persuaded to leave off his English overcoat, leather gloves and felt hat, which made him very conspicuous – even the 'foreign colony' never wore hats or coats – but he continued to dress formally. 'The climate here is marvellous for about eight months of the year', Barbara wrote to Graham Greene in 1958; 'Richard loves the intensely hot weather and walks about in his grey London suit looking very cool and remote. People who do not know him call him Mr Thin the Mystery-Man.'[23]

Richard and Barbara established a routine of walking into town every morning to buy provisions and would stop for a drink at a bar before getting a taxi back up the hill. The shops, usually family businesses, continued to fascinate them; there was often an old grandmother 'stirring a pot on a charcoal brazier near the door, and usually several little girls were doing their embroidery or making lace' on the threshold of the dark interior.[24] Days were taken up with shopping, going for long walks in the mountain ranges, reading and writing, and socializing. Richard had decided he would embark on a career as a freelance journalist, specializing in news from Spain, and Barbara was mulling over the plot of *The Long White Dress* and drafting parts of it. Her driving lessons in London had taken her round the back streets of Clapham and Battersea and this run-down district of London became the setting for Alice Rowlands' home. A few years later she wrote, 'I failed my driving test, but enjoyed writing this book more than anything I have written.'[25] (She failed the test because, when the instructor told her to turn right or left, she looked down at her hands momentarily. When he asked her why she did this, Barbara replied that she always checked which was left by looking at her wedding ring on her left hand. Following a strong reprimand from the instructor, Barbara leapt out of the car, abandoning both him and her ambition to drive.) Another location in the novel was to be Hayling Island in Hampshire, where Mrs Peebles lives; Barbara knew the area well because Chloe and her husband had bought a holiday home there on their return from Cairo and she had stayed there with them several times. While working on *The Long White Dress* (later retitled *The Vet's Daughter*), Barbara was also making notes for another book. This was originally entitled *The Way We Live Now* (perhaps with a nod to Trollope, one of her favourite authors) but would eventually become *Out of the Red, Into the Blue*.[26] By the early summer, Barbara's many pots and the tiny garden at the side of the house were bursting with irises, carnations, wild marigolds, geraniums and marguerites, and the small bamboo fence around it was covered with nasturtiums and morning glory. One of her great pleasures was to walk down to the beach late in the afternoon to read and then swim in the warm Mediterranean, where small striped fish would dart alongside her. Richard usually stayed at home in the shade, reading or planning another article. He did not care for sunbathing.

There were, however, other domestic problems besides the smoking fireplace. Their house had still not been connected to the main water supply so they were forced to draw water up out of the well, Barbara marvelling at how much water two people can use in one day. The nearby new houses were soon taken, mostly by Germans who enjoyed sunbathing and exercising on their roofs and who were inclined to throw their rubbish on to the rocks, which attracted the wild cats of the area. There was also the challenge of Coco's perpetual feud with the small yappy Pekinese dog belonging to their English neighbours. Richard's father visited for a week in May and, distracted by the arrival of the taxi for an outing with him, Barbara forgot to put Coco on the lead. A bloody battle between the two dogs ensued in which the little dog came off by far the worst. The dogs were quickly separated and the Spanish maid rushed out to fetch the Pekinese, one of whose eyes had been gouged out by Coco. Richard went round to apologize to the dog's owners who, fortunately, were philosophical about what had happened and seemed more interested in Richard and Barbara's move to Ibiza than in their pet's traumatic experience.

The drains were the other major worry; once the house was connected to the main water supply, their inadequacy soon became glaringly apparent. There was a strange smell in the bathroom; then a damp patch appeared on the stony ground outside the house and eventually turned into a foul-smelling stream. The problem was finally addressed when their landlord decided he was going to build a large house nearby; this necessitated enlarging the small cesspit so that it would be deep enough to reach the sea. Two burly men, one young and very good-looking and the other old and gnarled, got to work with their pickaxes. Then the blasting started. The younger man would disappear into the pit down a rope and light the fuse. After a few minutes, he would speedily clamber up, while the older man 'ran about the rocks shouting "Da fuego!"'[27] On emerging from the depths, the younger man would throw himself down on the ground before the explosion sent sewage, rock and household waste spewing into the air. All this threw Coco into a frenzy of barking and howling.

Ibiza did not have London's cultural distractions but it offered plenty of small daily dramas and at least one festival a month. There were also various religious events, including what seemed – at least to English eyes – the extraordinary ceremony of the 'Blessing of Cars'. Once a year all the drivers in Ibiza would take their vehicles to the large square in Ibiza town and would park them in lines. A priest would then walk up and down the rows shaking some holy water on each car and blessing it. Barbara told Julian that she thought it was dangerous to walk on the pavement during the next few days because, after the blessing ceremony, cars would career around at twice their normal speed, their drivers assuming that divine dispensation would prevent any accidents.

In June, Julian arrived with two friends for a fortnight's holiday, having driven across France and Spain in a 1925 Bayliss Thomas car. En route to Folkestone at the beginning of their trip, a half brick flew off a lorry at some speed and damaged the car's radiator. This meant that it needed refilling every fifty miles throughout the journey to Ibiza, and they were sometimes reduced to hanging perilously over bridges and ledges in order to fill a can with water. Although Julian's friends stayed elsewhere, Barbara and Richard's home was soon littered with swimming shorts, a guitar, Penguin books and espadrilles. Barbara was no doubt torn between feeling sorry when they went – she liked the company of young people – and relief that she and Richard had the house to themselves once again. Julian's place was, however, soon taken by Caroline, who arrived in July and stayed for almost a year. Now 20 years old, she was a striking young woman who

30 Caroline Pemberton as a young woman

had inherited Rupert Lee's fine facial features and her mother's thick dark hair. Soon the house in Figueretas was full of admiring young men who would turn up at the front door on the least excuse and would gaze at Caroline, lost for words, until Barbara shooed them away.

* * *

Barbara and Richard had been living in Ibiza for less than six months when Caroline arrived, but they were already beginning to worry about their finances again. They had brought some money with them from England but it was now dwindling and they had little coming in. Richard's father continued to pay him a small private allowance, but *Our Spoons Came from Woolworths* and *Who was Changed and Who was Dead* had not sold very well, so the royalties were smaller than Barbara had hoped. Richard had managed to place a few articles but the money was soon eaten up by

31 Richard and Barbara in a restaurant, Ibiza

the bills they ran up on the island. In Barbara's unpublished short story entitled 'Something to Celebrate', set in Ibiza, 'Guy' (a younger version of Richard) greets his wife when she returns from the harbour with the news that his English agent has placed two of his articles on Spain and has sent a cheque for £100 (about £3,000 today). Delighted, the two fictional characters celebrate with a meal and a bottle of wine and begin speculating:

> If we placed even one article a month we would be able to manage very well, life was so cheap on the island. Then there were the novels, one every two years perhaps which would more than pay for a visit to England. What about leaving the island and moving to Madrid or Barcelona and leading a more civilized life? We could buy a flat, start a family, pay someone to do the boring typing. If we were moving to the mainland we would need a car, a new one, not second-hand. And so we went on until the wine was finished and flies settled on the greasy plates and the little cat asked to be let out.

But in the story the next day the landlord calls demanding the two months' rent they owe; then the milkman turns up and asks for his bill to be settled; later the 'Charcoal Man' appears asking for the money owed him – 'We seemed to have got through an awful lot of charcoal although it was summer.'[28] The young couple's experience reflects that of Barbara and Richard,

Barbara Comyns

who were in dire straits financially by October 1956: the milkman refused to leave any more milk unless they paid his bill and payment was overdue for water and electricity. They were down to their last few pesetas when some money arrived from Richard's father. In *Out of the Red, Into the Blue* money troubles beleaguer the two main characters, 'cropping up again like horrible humps on our backs'.[29] Debts and final demands besieged Barbara and Richard, even though they were living relatively frugally in the blue of a Mediterranean island, partly because their Micawber-like optimism always tempted them to spend beyond their means. They had also underestimated their outgoings: a lot of their income was taken up by life insurance payments, the mortgage on Neri House, fees for furniture storage and income tax.

An obvious economy would be to move into Ibiza town where they could walk everywhere and would not need to pay for taxis. An additional bonus would be that the water and electricity supplies functioned more efficiently in the town. Also, the building work near their home in Figueretas had now started in earnest; huge piles of rubble appeared and the noise and the dust were getting them both down. And so in October 1956 Barbara and Richard moved. They left their brand new small house for a bigger but rather damp house in a noisy and run-down area in Ibiza town. One of its saving graces was that it had a garden on which the sun shone all day and which boasted a variety of small trees: an apricot, a pomegranate, a lemon and three orange trees. Caroline was keen on the plan, seeing the potential of the old house, and helped them move in. For her 21st birthday in early November Barbara made a cake, but there was no spare money for presents. Caroline was happy though: she had a new Spanish boyfriend, José Urbano del Castillo – 'Pepe' for short – who, having recently qualified as a banker in Spain, was taking some time out in Ibiza.

Pepe was a cheerful young man and an excellent cook who would occasionally spend hours making delicious fish dishes for them all. In *Out of the Red, Into the Blue*, he is described as 'handsome in a compact, sculptural way. He dressed like a tramp, and behaved rather like one, although he came from a good Madrid family and had had an excellent education.'[30] Caroline's other Spanish admirers and her previous Scottish playwright boyfriend were soon replaced in her affections by the delightful Pepe, a resourceful individual who decided to open a bar in order to make some money. However, it was soon being investigated by the authorities, who had been alerted by the local populace that a young French woman was dancing naked there in the evenings. An article in a Belgian travel magazine about her exploits finally sealed Pepe's fate and the police closed his bar down. With the profits from selling the bar he then set up a launderette. Few houses on the island had a washing machine so he was convinced it would be a great success. He even employed a local woman to work the two large Bendix industrial washing machines in which he had invested. This venture was, however, also doomed to failure. The electricity supply in Ibiza town was unreliable and was particularly weak during peak daytime hours (mainly because the local residents had worked out a way to siphon off the power illegally), so the woman Pepe employed found herself doing most of the launderette work late in the evening when the current was stronger. Her husband objected to such unsociable hours, so the woman left and Pepe was then in sole charge. Rather careless in practical matters, he often mixed people's laundry up and it became quite common for a resident of Ibiza town to be approached by someone commenting, 'I think you are wearing my shirt', or 'Isn't that my dress you've got on?' But Caroline continued to love him, despite his commercial failures; his warmth and charm had won her heart.

That winter was clear and bright but the old damp house was bitterly cold at night and first thing in the morning. Barbara's rheumatism was causing her pain and she longed for the summer. Like her fictional counterpart in *Out of the Red, Into the Blue*, she watched her carefully tended flowers come into bloom in the early spring with great pleasure and found that pottering in the garden lifted her worries about money and the challenges of living on Ibiza. Money did indeed seem to be getting tighter all the time. Richard and Barbara decided they could no longer afford to continue paying Caroline her small allowance, so she advertised herself as a teacher of English in the local paper in order to earn some money. Her students turned out to be mainly young men, keen to spend an hour or so in her company, even at the price of having to learn another language.

In May 1957 Julian arrived from London, having motorcycled across Europe. Caroline decided she wanted to go back with him after his holiday on the island; Pepe was soon to leave for Madrid but was planning to go to London to start an English-language course in September – so he and Caroline would be reunited there in the autumn. While Julian was in Ibiza, Barbara asked him to retrieve some buckets from the well in the garden from which they drew all their water. There was a knack to hooking on the bucket before you dropped it down and if this was not done securely, the bucket plunged into the water below. Julian fixed a hook to a long pole so that he could haul up the lost buckets and shone his torch down into the depths. The light revealed a two-foot band of gleaming cockroaches solidly encrusted above the water line. From then on Barbara and Richard boiled all their water. There was no hope of getting rid of the cockroaches, which were ubiquitous on the island. Barbara's fictional counterpart in *Out of the Red, Into the Blue* swears she can hear them marching into the house at night: 'They often came in under the front door as if there was a notice marked "Cockroaches' Entrance". I was terrified of them and it was Raymond's job to destroy them, which was rather sad because he liked them.'[31]

Barbara had been writing steadily throughout their time in Ibiza, and by the end of 1957 had two books ready to send to her agent, John Johnson, who had left E. P. S. Lewin in 1956 to set up his own literary agency in Henrietta Street, Mayfair. The books were very different in kind; just as the resolutely realist *Our Spoons Came from Woolworths* had been followed by the macabre *Who was Changed and Who was Dead*, so the gothic tale of *The Vet's Daughter* (which Barbara still thought of as *The Long White Dress*) was now complemented by the realist *Out of the Red, Into the Blue*, which was three parts memoir and one part imagination. Barbara probably worked on both books at the same time; certainly glimpses of her life in Ibiza creep into the Battersea world of *The Vet's Daughter*, in which the vet sews in a peke's eye and the daily help grows a vine from a grape pip and sunflowers twelve feet tall, just as Barbara did on her Mediterranean island. *Out of the Red, Into the Blue* – notwithstanding the recurring shadow of money problems and a few tiffs between the narrator and Raymond – is a light-hearted account of living on Ibiza in the mid-1950s and carries the dedication, 'For all the people who spend winter evenings planning to live on Mediterranean islands'.

On the other hand, *The Vet's Daughter* is a surreal, dark tale about human cruelty which features a man who abuses both his wife and his daughter. Set in the Edwardian era, the novel is the story of Alice Rowlands, the 17-year-old vulnerable daughter of a bullying veterinary surgeon and his ailing wife. (Alice's father's tendency to fly into a rage and his habit of biting at his black moustache suggest an exaggerated version of Barbara's own father.) Alice's only moments of joy are those snatched when her father is out and her mother can reminisce about her happy childhood in Wales. *The Vet's Daughter* is, however, laced with macabre humour, some of which is evoked by the plight of the vet's creatures (a parrot, for instance, that exhibits neurotic symptoms, having been confined to the lavatory because of its anti-social shrieking) and the weirdness of dislocated animal parts becoming household objects (a monkey skull on the mantelpiece and a horse's hoof used as a doorstop, for example). Yet the novel presents a world in which people are frequently treated worse than animals. The fate of Alice's mother, who is suffering from cancer, and who is casually 'put down' one evening by her husband, takes the novel into the chilling realm of domestic gothic. Her father subsequently installs his mistress, Rosa Fisher, as his housekeeper. Life for Alice then becomes even more difficult: 'Nothing could be worse than home', she thinks to herself'.[32] But life does get worse. To her horror, Rosa, who works behind the bar at a local pub, sets her up with a porter from the local hotel who then tries to rape her. Traumatized,

she takes refuge with the kind daily help Mrs Churchill, and finds herself
levitating from the sofa where she has been left to rest and recover:

> I was so ashamed – however many baths I had I'd never be really clean again
> […] In the night I was awake and floating. As I went up the blankets fell to
> the floor. I could feel nothing below me – and nothing above until I came near
> the ceiling and it was hard to breathe there […] quite soon, it seemed, I was
> gently coming down again. I folded my hands over my chest and kept very
> straight, and floated down to the couch where I'd been lying. I was not afraid,
> but very calm and peaceful. In the morning I knew it wasn't a dream because
> the blankets were still on the floor and I saw the gas mantle was broken and
> the chalky powder was still on my hands.[33]

Subsequent levitations occur after other traumatic episodes. Alice's uncanny
ability takes the reader into the world of the magical and the surreal, but
it also suggests metaphorically the mental state of psychological dissociation
often seen in abuse victims, for whom it is a coping mechanism. Alice literally
detaches herself from the real world and wills herself to float above pain
and fear. The only time she displays her strange talent in order to impress
– she has become infatuated with a handsome young man called Nicholas
– is a disaster. He is horrified by seeing her rise above the ground and
thereafter distances himself from her. Her father's plan to financially exploit
his daughter's strange gift brings the novel to a tragic conclusion that is
described sparely and lyrically, in which Alice goes to her death dressed as
a bride. The final transcendental episode fuses the bridal carriage with the
hearse to become the Blakean 'marriage hearse', suggesting that marriage
for many women leads to the death of the self. Read more broadly, the
novel also suggests that a young woman with a rare talent might well face
suspicion or exploitation in her life.

The Vet's Daughter is a book in which the transforming power of the
imagination features as a blessing and as a curse; it is also a book about
the banality of evil. The friendly and inoffensive poor man with a ginger
moustache – whom the reader and Alice meet in the first few lines of the
novel – appears again at its very end as an onlooker who is crushed to
death by the hysterical crowd. We know little about him, but his fate is
that of an innocent bystander killed by a cyclone of nefarious greed. With
its blend of realist detail, magical realism and the gothic, the novel was a
brave experiment in breaking down genre boundaries and anticipates the
work of Angela Carter, which did not appear until some years later. It was
unlike anything else written in English during the 1950s. Barbara posted
both typescripts off to John Johnson, optimistic that The Bodley Head – which
had brought out *Who was Changed and Who was Dead* – would agree to
publish them.

In January 1958 Barbara and Richard decided that they needed to rethink their future. They could not afford to move back to London, but neither could they afford to live comfortably on Ibiza without more money. The charm of the island was also beginning to wear rather thin; 'I hadn't expected to be exactly comfortable in Ciriaco, but the shortages were exasperating', thinks the narrator of *Out of the Red, Into the Blue*.[34] Charcoal for the oven and paraffin for heating were often scarce. The magazines and journals posted fortnightly from England, which included the *New Statesman* and the *Observer*, kept them in touch with culture and politics at home but also intensified their occasional bouts of homesickness. The narrator of the unpublished short story 'Something to Celebrate', set on Ibiza, laments to her husband, 'I'm so tired of being always abroad, always a foreigner on this tiny island. I want to go home'; yet she also thinks, 'We had beauty, the sea and the sun, wine too, so why complain about discomfort, loneliness and boredom?' Increasingly Barbara and Richard, like their fictional counterparts, realized that they were city people who were wearying of a simple lifestyle devoid of sophistication and culture.

They were also tired of being surveilled by MI6, which had planted a Watcher on the island soon after they arrived in the spring of 1956; like the Watcher in Drayton Gardens, he was discreet, but Barbara and Richard were well aware of his presence. They had also discovered that letters they sent to England via the post office in Ibiza town took several weeks to reach their destination and friends and relatives often complained that the envelopes had been opened and resealed. So instead of using *los correos*, the post office, Barbara began waiting for the Barcelona boat to arrive and, at the last minute, would run up the gangway and hand their letters directly to the person in charge of the mail sacks. Presumably MI6 thought that Richard and Barbara might flee to Russia via Morocco; the weekly boat from Barcelona sailed from Ibiza to North Africa before returning to mainland Spain, so it would have been relatively easy for them to 'disappear'. The British government certainly wanted to avoid another spy scandal, and its close scrutiny of Richard at this time suggests that it had some cause for suspecting him of espionage, or of having been complicit with it.

Barbara and Richard's money troubles and the strain of being under surveillance inevitably resulted in tensions and bickering. In an interview with Ursula Holden many years later, Barbara claimed that she and Richard never quarrelled except when they'd lived on the island of Ibiza. 'She advised couples not to go there if they wanted to avoid rows; that it could be something to do with the winds there.'[35] Whatever the causes of the strain between them, the time seemed right to leave the island. Barbara and Richard decided they would sell Neri House in Wimbledon, which would provide them with some capital, and move to mainland Spain. Although they had regarded the property as an investment asset for the future, Hawes, the estate agent handling the rentals, kept sending them bills and had just written to tell them that a chimney stack needed replacing – which would cost a great deal of money. At the beginning of March 1958, almost exactly two years after she had travelled from England to Ibiza, Barbara made the journey in reverse, leaving Richard alone on the island. She had several reasons for returning to London; Caroline was marrying Pepe in Kensington on 26 March; she had made an appointment to see a consultant about her rheumatism; John Johnson, her literary agent, wished to talk to her about her work; she needed to check on the state of Neri House and the garden before it went on the market; and she wanted to see her sisters, especially Chloe, whom she had missed very much and who had recently moved into 20 Drayton Gardens with her husband and son.

Barbara stayed with Julian in his rented flat in Queen's Gate Terrace in South Kensington during her six weeks in London and enjoyed city life once again. Meanwhile, Richard had applied to teach English as a foreign language at the British Institute in Barcelona, one of three such institutes in Spain run by the British Council (the others were in Madrid and Seville). Spain was facing many changes, not least its incorporation into the European Organization for Economic Co-operation the following year, yet its educational system was inadequate at all levels. Young people and professional workers were growing restless and were critical of what was available. They were thirsty for engagement with other languages and cultures and wanted to embrace a more modern outlook on the world than the Spanish government, still wedded to the Church and traditional family structures and led by the conservative General Franco, could provide. The British Council, sensing a new mood in the country, was keen to extend the teaching of English and access to British culture, so was actively recruiting more staff. Richard received a letter inviting him for interview. He was simultaneously liaising with the rental agent, an estate agent and their building society in England about the sale of Neri House and trying to organize their finances so that he and Barbara would arrive in Barcelona with some money. Once again Richard's father stepped in and made a contribution.

Barbara and Richard constantly exchanged letters during her time in London. Soon after she arrived in England, Richard wrote, 'I cannot tell you how empty the house seems without you – there were so many little ways in which you made it all come to life. Write soon.' The weather did not help; Ibiza was suffering a cold grey spring: 'Even the Iberians have been wrapping themselves up', Richard told her. 'There is a man who goes round with a donkey carrying panniers filled with charcoal or dung or something who wraps his head up so that he looks like a Bedouin.' But Barbara's trip to London was useful and enjoyable. The consultant suggested a course of treatment for her rheumatism and reassured her that her pain was simply the result of living in a damp house in winter; once she moved somewhere drier, she would be fine. Her sisters were delighted to see her, and Caroline's wedding was a low-key but happy event in Kensington. The only disappointment was a letter that Richard forwarded to Barbara at the end of March from John Johnson with news that The Bodley Head had rejected both *Out of the Red, Into the Blue* and *The Vet's Daughter* (still entitled *The Long White Dress*), despite the fact that Graham Greene, now a director of the firm, had previously recommended her as a promising novelist. (In the late spring of 1957 Greene had advised Max Reinhardt, managing director of The Bodley Head, that it would be 'worth keeping an eye' on Barbara Comyns, 'a crazy but interesting novelist whom I started when I was at Eyre & Spottiswoode'.)[36] But presumably The Bodley Head had decided that, after the mixed reviews and relatively poor sales of *Who Was Changed and Who Was Dead*, they did not want to risk publishing another macabre novel by Barbara Comyns. Deeply disappointed, and unaware that Greene, whose novels she much admired, had praised her work to Max Reinhardt, early in April 1958 Barbara asked Johnson to

32 Marriage of Caroline and Pepe in London in 1958

send him a copy of *The Long White Dress*. Greene read it and immediately wrote to Alexander Frere, the chairman of William Heinemann (his own publisher) and a good friend of almost thirty years standing, urging him to consider publishing it:

> I have just finished reading the novel I spoke to you about by Barbara Comyns and apart from a short rather romantic passage near the end I think it's an extraordinarily good book – wild and Gothic and vivid, the best she has done yet [...] I am sending it to you herewith. I don't like the title which means nothing, and I would suggest changing it to *The Vet's Daughter* as the whole crazy atmosphere is about life in a veterinary surgeon's home.[37]

Frere, a man of sardonic humour and 'genuinely literary instincts',[38] soon contacted Johnson with an offer to publish the book. He also agreed with Greene that *The Vet's Daughter* would be a much more appropriate title.

The date for Richard's interview in Barcelona was finalized for late April, and he wrote to say that, assuming it went well, he would enquire about renting somewhere temporarily while they looked for a more permanent home. The plan was that he would travel by boat to Barcelona, and that Barbara, having flown straight from London, would join him there so that they could look at properties together. Provided they could find somewhere to live, they would move to the city in the summer and Richard would start teaching in September. It would be a fresh beginning in a sophisticated Spanish city where they would be able to enjoy urban life once again and earn enough money to keep their heads above water. And, with luck, they might just find themselves free of the MI6 Watcher.

This is not, however, the ending of *Out of the Red, Into the Blue*, which in so many other ways is true to Barbara's life at this time. In the book, Raymond is suddenly offered a job back in London and they leave Ciriaco in late June, having sold all their furniture locally beforehand. It takes the narrator a while to adjust to living in a city again. Although she loves going to art galleries, the cinema and the theatre, she misses the beauty of the island:

> Sometimes I could almost see the great purple and red banana flowers growing amongst green split leaves, and the pine trees spreading down to a curved, almost silver beach with black nets drying on it, and clear, clear water in which I could see darting striped fish.[39]

After a spell in a hotel, Barbara's fictional counterpart and her husband move into a house that sounds remarkably like 24 Drayton Gardens, the house Barbara left behind when they moved to Ibiza. Or perhaps, as she finished the novel, Barbara was thinking, rather enviously, of Chloe's new home at 20 Drayton Gardens. In *Out of the Red, Into the Blue*, Raymond and the narrator are delighted with their London house; he happily unpacks his books which have been in store and she finds the little man from Cyprus wrapped in a quilt in a drawer. It is as if they had never left England, and that life on Ciriaco was a dream. Perhaps that is what Barbara really yearned for: a return to her previous home in Kensington. But it was not to be. She had married Richard for better or for worse and they would soon be bound for Barcelona.

11

Settling in Barcelona

After packing up their belongings in June 1958, Barbara and Richard treated themselves to a short holiday before setting off for Barcelona. They moved into the main hotel in Ibiza town for a few days' luxury, then spent 'a delicious week at a pension in pine-woods along the coast'. After flying from Ibiza to Barcelona (with Coco travelling in a box at the back of the plane), they spent a fortnight at Castelldefels, a small resort between Barcelona and Sitges, which was, Richard thought, 'on a miniature scale, something between Margate and Maidenhead'. During those two weeks they hunted for an apartment in the city. By mid-August 1958 Richard and Barbara were living in a small rented flat in the Calle de Balmes, 'in a neighbourhood that is slightly down-at-heel but very near the smart avenues – the Paseo de Grecia and the Diagonal, a fashionable part of Barcelona'.[1] Soon Richard was teaching at the British Institute nearby. Like Leo Elliot in Barbara's 1964 novel *Birds in Tiny Cages* (in which Barbara draws on her first year in the city), Richard's Spanish, 'although not completely fluent, was precise, and his appearance, with his high-bridged nose and long thin body dressed in beautifully cut English suits, was an asset to any school'.[2] Throughout the autumn they explored Barcelona and enjoyed the facilities offered by the British Institute, which included a good lending library, much to Barbara's delight. As part of its programme to introduce the Spanish to British culture, the Institute also arranged concerts, plays and occasional lectures by visiting speakers. Barbara and Richard began to socialize with other English expats through the British Institute and the British Club; life in Barcelona was a far cry from that on a Mediterranean island.

Thanks to Graham Greene's recent intervention, Heinemann decided to add Barbara to their list of authors and in June she signed a contract with them for the publication of *The Vet's Daughter* in February 1959. She also learned that she would become a grandmother soon; Caroline was pregnant and the baby was due in December. The future looked promising. But although Barbara was enjoying living in a city again, she sometimes felt lonely. She and Richard had spent most of their time together while living on Ibiza; now, he was out of the flat for eight or nine hours a day teaching and often came home exhausted. Barbara was a poor linguist and Catalan, rather than Castilian Spanish, was spoken in Barcelona, which added to her difficulties – so she did not find it easy to socialize with the local residents. Although the main characters of *Birds in Tiny Cages* are younger than their real-life counterparts – Flora Elliot is 31 whereas Barbara was 50 when she and Richard moved to Barcelona – much of Flora's experience mirrors aspects of Barbara's life at that time. Like Barbara, Flora lives in a flat on the Calle de Balmes; she used to sell antiques on the King's Road when living in London and badly misses her sisters. Without work and projects of her own, 'the capable Flora' who had managed her life so well in England begins to lose her self-confidence and independence, and 'became as she had been as a girl', reflecting Barbara's fear of losing her identity when she was not working or writing.[3] There are other parallels: when Leo is teaching private pupils in their flat, Flora troops off to the wonderfully warm and sunny reading room in the British Institute to look at the latest copies of the *Observer*, the *Sunday Times* and *Vogue*, just as Barbara did while Richard was working. But although she often spent time at the Institute, Barbara was still shy of strangers and rarely attended lectures on her own. Flora, similarly inhibited, engages more with the old black tom-cat that haunts the Institute garden than with its human visitors: 'She liked to think the cat was a great scholar who read the reference books when the Institute was deserted at night.'[4]

Barbara returned to England for a few weeks in early March 1959. She stayed with Julian in his flat at Queen's Gate Terrace, where Caroline, Pepe and baby Eduardo were lodging temporarily. Pepe was teaching at the Berlitz School of Languages but grumbled about the rate of pay, which he supplemented by taking private pupils. 'Caroline and Pepe seem very happy though in spite of being so poor', Barbara wrote to Richard.[5] She was pleased to see her sisters, especially Chloe, and was delighted with her three-month-old grandson, who had dark eyes and black curly hair.

After the mixed reviews of *Who was Changed and Who was Dead*, she was relieved to discover on arrival in London that her latest book was attracting a great deal of praise. John Johnson had sent her six copies of *The Vet's Daughter* in early February and she had been thrilled to see a tribute from Graham Greene on the back cover:

> The strange off-beat talent of Miss Comyns and that innocent eye which observes with childlike simplicity the most fantastic or the most ominous occurrence, these have never, I think, been more impressively exercised than in *The Vet's Daughter*.

She was also greatly amused to discover that Heinemann had placed an advertisement in the *Daily Telegraph* asking readers to write to them if they had experienced, or seen, an act of levitation. It was a ruse to draw attention to the imminent publication of *The Vet's Daughter*, which closes with the narrator levitating over Clapham Common. Heinemann got more than they bargained for: they received many earnest letters, including some from India, which documented first-hand experience of the phenomenon, and one from Margate (a spoof, signed 'A. Levitatas'), in which the author claimed that an aunt and a grandmother had been able to levitate but condemned it as a 'filthy habit'. Several readers claimed to have levitated as small children. All were politely answered by the Publicity Manager at Heinemann, who recommended Barbara's novel in his replies.[6]

33 Cover of the first edition of *The Vet's Daughter*, published by William Heinemann Ltd in 1959

With the exception of a lukewarm piece in the *Times Literary Supplement*, the many reviews were all excellent and appeared in a wide range of newspapers and journals. Kenneth Allsop wrote in the *Daily Mail*, 'This is a triumph, a walk-over win, a novel so original in its vision, and beautifully exact in its writing, that I am lost in admiration.'[7] High praise indeed, and so it went on. The *Manchester Guardian* reviewer described *The Vet's Daughter* as 'a curious, original book in a class of its own' and as 'a story that is macabre, sad and sardonically funny by turns'. Enid Bagnold in *The Times* praised it as 'pregnant with some kind of magic stuff that held one tighter than a handcuff'. The *Tatler* reviewer confessed that she found *The Vet's Daughter* 'The strangest, saddest, most haunting novel' she had read for a long time and thought it a 'flawless little book' with the 'looming sense of tragedy of a bizarre nightmare'. In *The Bookman*, Richard Church praised the novel but noted that 'the shrewd reader will wonder how it was engendered, for something more than a mere report in an Edwardian newspaper must have stimulated the imagination of the author'.[8] He was right. In the *Sunday Express*, Robert Pitman, who described the *The Vet's Daughter* as 'one of the strangest and most compelling novels that has been published for years', established that the newspaper report was a fiction:

> During the week I phoned Barbara Comyns who now lives in Spain. She told me 'My publishers have misunderstood me. There never was any such cutting. I've made it all up. You see, I first thought of the story when I was taking driving lessons round Clapham Common. I intended to end it happily. But then one night I dreamed about that crowd and the tragedy. I had to invent the cutting to explain it.'[9]

Other accolades came from the *Publisher's Circular* ('Written with a Gothic beauty and quite absorbing'); the *Evening News* ('an exquisite and pathetic parable [...] its sorrow lies too deep even for tears'); *Country Life* ('This way of writing – bare, economical, beautiful – grips you on the first page'); *The Spectator* ('Miss Comyns brings off her increasingly outrageous plot [...] by muting the girl's voice to a chilly, hypnotic, dryness. The result has all the tinted horror of wax fruit under a glass dome'); and *The Sphere*, in which Aldous Huxley admired the novel's 'melancholy magic'.[10] Among all the glowing tributes, there was one article that particularly pleased Barbara. She wrote to Richard: 'There was a staggeringly good review of my book in the *Listener*, the perfect review by Goronwy Rees [...] I am glad he doesn't know I'm Miss Comyns.' Rees, an influential critic, who had worked for the *Spectator* in the 1940s and for MI6 for several years, had known Guy Burgess well;[11] he would also have come across Richard, but presumably had not realized that the author of *The Vet's Daughter* was Richard's wife. The review opened:

It would be difficult to praise *The Vet's Daughter* sufficiently without being led into extravagance; perhaps it is enough to say that it is both beautiful and strange. Miss Comyns has told her fantastic and pathetic story so well that it is hard to separate the elements out of which it is made up, and indeed one cannot do so without destroying the beautiful unity of tone and atmosphere which pervades her book and gives it a kind of originality which is very rare indeed.[12]

Barbara's new publisher was delighted with the reception of *The Vet's Daughter*, and the Heinemann senior editor overseeing her work, James Michie, took her out for a splendid lunch in Mayfair. Michie – a poet and translator in his own right – was good at spotting talent and would soon be responsible for the launch of Sylvia Plath's *Colossus*. Among other things, they discussed the forthcoming publication of *Out of the Red, Into the Blue*; Michie was optimistic that the novel would sell well, given the success of *The Vet's Daughter*. Pleased that – with the help of Graham Greene – John Johnson had managed to place her two most recent books with Heinemann, Barbara treated her agent to lunch at the Casa Pepe restaurant in Soho. 'I reserved a table by phone and said I wanted a quiet one as I would be talking business', she wrote to Richard: 'This seemed to delight the manager who kept dancing attendance, really thinking we were lovers. We were put away in a corner by ourselves. I was the only woman in the place, otherwise nothing but greedy business men.' Like Michie, Johnson encouraged Barbara to get on with her next book, but reported that he had had no luck so far in placing a novel by Richard entitled *The Escapist*: 'the publishers like it but say it's a bit thin', she wrote to her husband. Richard's book was never published and he soon gave up trying his hand at fiction. Apart from that slight disappointment, everything went well and Barbara much enjoyed seeing *A Taste of Honey* at Wyndham's Theatre and *Irma la Douce* at the Lyric Theatre with Julian. 'Next time I come to England, I want to really enjoy it and have you here too and no work, lots of films, theatres and food', she wrote to Richard.

Barbara also managed to move Neri House matters on a little. One of the apartments had just fallen empty; Barbara was pleased because the Wimbledon house would be easier to sell with one flat vacant. In the meantime – having seen how cramped they all were at Julian's place – she suggested that Pepe, Caroline and Eduardo might live in the empty flat rent-free until Neri House was sold. A week after arriving in England, Barbara moved to Wimbledon and she and Pepe set about cleaning and decorating the empty flat; the first thing they did was transform the bathroom by painting its ceiling blue with white stars. It was a large, six-roomed apartment, so Caroline and Pepe advertised two rooms to let. Barbara showed a potential lodger – whose nose had been smashed to a pulp with a rowing oar during a marital dispute – around the flat, and he bored her with endlessly prosaic accounts of his subsequent operations. Barbara found Pepe in the kitchen sprinkling salt on a floor mop. 'He said they always do that in Spain to make visitors go who stay too long', she wrote to Richard.

It had been a good trip to London, but Barbara was pleased to return to her husband and their dog Coco – and to the warmth of Spain. The damp cold of England had provoked another attack of rheumatism: 'I don't think I will ever be able to live in England again unless I want to be completely stiff', she wrote to Richard. But her busy time in London had also made Barbara realize that, stuck in a poky city flat with no garden or balcony and with Richard absent most of the day, she was bored in Barcelona. The title of her novel *Birds in Tiny Cages* suggests as much. The image is used several times in the book; Flora frequently notices the cages of small singing birds that are sold on the Ramblas and that hang from windows and balconies everywhere. But the phrase also suggests the plight of a woman who is trapped in a small space with nothing to do. Because she is bored, Flora is easily seduced by Parker, an English sculptor and a roué in his early forties who dresses casually in a fisherman's jersey, jeans and canvas shoes. She later deeply regrets the affair and her own naivety, recognizing that she had only succeeded in trapping herself in a different way with Parker: 'The Spanish for cage is "jaula" or "prisíon". I suppose we all live in cages, sometimes we are forced into them, but usually we make our own.'[13] There is no evidence that Barbara had an affair while living in Barcelona but, like Flora, she certainly felt trapped in a small flat and might well have embarked on a relationship with another man. If so, she came to realize that this was no solution to her feelings of boredom and frustration. Energized by her trip to London, she returned to the Calle de Balmes determined that she and Richard would move. They could not afford the high rents charged in the city centre for large flats with balconies, so they started looking outside Barcelona.

They decided they wanted to live in San Cugat des Vallès, a pretty area between Barcelona's seaside plain and the Collserola mountain range; it was 12 miles north of the city and well connected to Barcelona by a fast and reliable train service. Barbara was charmed by the town of San Cugat and later recorded her impressions of it:

> Driving through San Cugat you would not notice many shops but there must be nearly two hundred. Some are private houses with a few baskets of fruit and vegetables arranged by the doorway; but more and more shops are being fitted with modern shopfronts. The grocers – 'colmados' – are almost used as clubs and the family who owns one's particular 'colmado' become intimate friends. They are usually run by women, the men having their own business or employment. [...] There are cool 'bodegas' smelling of wine, their windows

filled with an amazing array of bottles including Spanish whisky called DYC [...] There are a few butchers but meat and fish are usually bought in the market. On winter evenings I love to wander round the 'pueblo' [village] gazing into the shop windows and into the workshops where they make cart wheels or the blacksmiths' or the place by the dried-up river where they make barrels. The tradesmen of San Cugat are inclined to use the customers they trust as a sort of bank and often it is over a year before they present their accounts. They are not very fond of cheques and are surprised when they call with their bills that one does not keep large sums of money in the house. It is well over a year since we received our last account from 'lampista' – plumber-electrician, but I have heard he plans to take his wife to the Holy Land in the New Year so we can expect our bill about then.[14]

Having found an area they liked, Barbara began to focus on one place in particular, La Floresta, a large village surrounded by pinewoods that looked down on a walnut grove and a vineyard, its 'stunted vines black and twisted like Dali moustaches'.[15] On clear days there were good views of Montserrat, the mountain-top monastery that housed an ancient carving of the Virgin Mary known as 'the Black Madonna'. Barbara found a vacant flat above a shop in the Camino del Bosque that was close to the station, convenient for Richard's journey into Barcelona every day. They moved in during the early summer of 1959.

More space inevitably invited the prospect not only of many pots of flowers on the balcony but also more animals. In July Barbara acquired another pet and wrote to Diana, a great cat lover, with the news that she had just bought a Siamese kitten: 'It looks quite a good one, with a squint and kink in his tail. He has eaten most of the electric wiring and has to be watched all the time. He is worse than a monkey.' Barbara assured Diana that she liked living in La Floresta:

> Here is our rural address and we are very happy. We have miles and miles of green woods to look at and out of the corner of our left eye we see the village and station. The houses here resemble elaborate dog kennels painted pink or white. It is really beautiful here and quiet except on fiesta days, then it is quite unbelievable. People arrive all day carrying suitcases and bundles full of fireworks and food. They look like refugees. At about eight o'clock the dancing starts and they light bonfires, let off their fireworks and eat and drink all night. Every bar and shop has music screaming out of it. They even dance on the station roof.[16]

She also shared some good news with Diana: she had just heard that *The Vet's Daughter* would be serialized by the BBC Home Radio Service on *Woman's Hour* in the autumn, read by Celia Johnson. She was delighted: there would be a good fee and it would keep the book in the public eye. Richard had recently been told that he was entitled to a summer holiday with pay and that his salary would be increased from September. Life was looking up.

A month later, Barbara was writing to Diana in a very different vein. During a visit to England in the summer, driving Diana to visit relatives, Rupert was killed in a car crash in Chipping Norton, Oxfordshire. A burst tyre had caused him to swerve into an oncoming bus, and he died instantly. Diana suffered only minor injuries.[17] Barbara heard the news from Chloe by letter and immediately wrote to Diana, still in England recovering from the accident:

> It is the most terrible shock, which seems even worse after seeing you so recently under such happy circumstances. We left you completely dazzled by your happiness and sympathy towards each other.
>
> Poor, poor Rupert. The only consolation is that it was a wonderful way to die, but it seems such a waste when he was so alert and full of life. You both have a special enjoyment of the little things in life that most adults lose.
>
> I can't bear to think how lost and sad you must be feeling [...] Richard sends you his love and sympathy, but I'm unable to put what we feel into words. You have both been so mixed up in our lives and marriage and we certainly would have never been brave enough to come to Spain if it hadn't been for your example.

Whatever Barbara now felt about Rupert's abandonment of her twenty-four years before when she was pregnant with his child, his death came as a terrible shock. Caroline still did not know that Rupert was her real father and would not know for some time. Barbara invited Diana to stop over in Barcelona on her return journey to San Roque; from now on their lives would become more entwined and Barbara would travel down to Andalusia to stay with Diana at least once a year.

* * *

Out of the Red, Into the Blue, Barbara's novel about their two years on Ibiza, was published in January 1960. Although it was well received, it did not attract the same level of serious attention as *The Vet's Daughter* and was generally pigeonholed as local colour writing. Anne Piper in the *Sunday Times* decided that the book's aim was only 'light entertainment' and Ronald Bryden in *The Spectator* agreed, describing it as a 'witty, companionable and good-natured' piece of writing. Martin Moore in the *Daily Telegraph* saw it as a 'long letter home [...] a light-hearted, sometimes hilarious, story of improvident adventure', while the *Manchester Evening News* critic thought it 'a delightful piece of real-life escapism. Highly recommended reading after a bout of flu and fog.' The *Times Literary Supplement* reviewer, however, recognized that *Out of the Red, Into the Blue* transcended the usual run of travel books and thought its author triumphed 'over a mannered style and an overworked genre, sounding the deeper levels of humour, so that one is disturbed as well as amused'. In the *Observer*, Penelope Gilliat noted that Barbara Comyns 'writes with the eerie flatness of Stevie Smith', adding 'she has a style like a basilisk's eye, and she can be funny in a stony way'. But there was a sharp sting in the tail at the end of the review: '*Out of the Red* is the sort of anecdotal work that has made "feminine" an abusive term about the arts: a book by a woman writer, whereas *The Vet's Daughter* was by a writer who merely happens to be a woman.'[18] More than one reviewer noted that emigration to a Mediterranean island did not solve the characters' financial problems, despite their best hopes.

Nor did the move to mainland Spain deliver the financial security that Barbara and Richard had anticipated. Richard's teaching, which he found exhausting, was not well paid and the devaluation of the peseta in 1959 did not help. He decided to concentrate on freelance journalism and managed to obtain a post as a 'stringer' – a non-staff journalist – with the *Daily Telegraph*. Many ex-MI6 staff members, including Kim Philby, became journalists as cover for their espionage activities abroad; they would research a particular topic and submit an anodyne article to their newspaper while sending more detailed and classified information on the same topic directly to MI6. It is possible that Richard was retained by MI6 on this basis, although, unlike Philby, who was paid a good salary for writing for the *Observer* and the *Economist*, Richard was paid on a word count basis by the *Telegraph* – but the post gave him a good foothold in the world of journalism. Spain was in a very volatile state during the 1960s and newspaper editors were eager for news of an anticipated upheaval. There was growing unrest with Franco's agenda and impatience with his project of isolationism; students and liberal professionals were protesting at restrictions and censorship and demanding a better education system – particularly in the area of foreign-language teaching – and freer exchange with other countries. 'Spain is in a moment of evolution', the Counsellor to the British Embassy in Spain had written to the head of the British Council in 1957: 'If we wish to influence Spanish thinking, this is the time to redouble efforts in the cultural field.'[19]

Certainly, as an Oxford-educated teacher of English, Richard was useful in the 'cultural field' – and he would also have been useful as an MI6 agent who could keep an eye on political and social developments in Spain at this time. Julian and Caroline, when they visited Barbara and Richard in Barcelona, noticed that Richard was often in deep conversation with well-dressed men in dark bars – and he made it clear that such conversations were important and not to be interrupted.[20] Many years later Barbara mentioned in a letter to her son that 'People from the Foreign Office often came to see him when we were in Barcelona', suggesting that Richard certainly remained in contact with MI6 and possibly continued working for them.[21] Richard's early articles, written for the *Daily Telegraph*, focused mainly on tourism and local aspects of Barcelona: 'On Picasso's Trail in Barcelona' (28 October 1960); 'Shadowy Streets and Medieval Palaces' (3 June 1961); 'Transformation in the Ramblas' (29 November 1961), for example. But gradually the articles he wrote for the *Telegraph* and later the *Economist* and *The Times* became more political and wide-ranging, including pieces such as 'Anarchy Dies Hard in Spain' (15 October 1963 – a topic in which Richard, who subscribed to an anarchist magazine, was particularly interested); 'Soviet Boost for Spain' (20 March 1966); 'Spain's Cuban Trade' (21 May 1968); and 'Spain's Nuclear Energy Plans' (31 October 1968). Detailed information on these topics would have been of great interest to MI6 and, while it is impossible to prove that Richard worked as an undercover agent while living in Barcelona, it seems likely that he did. Certainly Barbara's family members believe that he liaised with MI6 while living in mainland Spain.

In January 1960 a short story Barbara had written, entitled 'Sardinas for the Cat', was published in *Harper's Bazaar* and soon afterwards she submitted the first draft of *The Bad Travellers* (later published with the title *Birds in Tiny Cages*) to her agent. Barbara was due to stay with Chloe and John at 20 Drayton Gardens in October and arranged to have lunch with John Johnson and James Michie while she was in London. She was dismayed to learn that *Out of the Red, Into the Blue*, which Michie had thought would do particularly well in the United States, had sold only about 2,000 copies and that Heinemann had lost heavily on it. Michie also told her, over lunch, that they would not publish *The Bad Travellers* in its current form. It needed a great deal of revision before they would even consider it: 'They say it would take someone five days working eight hours a day to put the spelling and punctuation right', she wrote gloomily to Richard. Michie also told her quite firmly that the best thing in the novel was the character of Parker and that when he disappeared two-thirds of the way through, it lost all momentum. Barbara was downcast and poured out her sorrows in a letter to her husband:

> I managed to be awfully cheerful through the lunch and eat the most expensive things – out of season strawberries and lobster. I thought at least I'd get that out of them and if I died after from indigestion, it wouldn't much matter. I haven't told anyone here about all this – too utterly shaming. Please don't tell anyone either. I had a terrible night wallowing in my shame. I would like to change my name and go somewhere where no one knows I write and they won't ask when my next book is coming out. I may try a few short stories or articles because if they get published it will keep people quiet a bit. But I shall never write another novel. I had no faith in that book from the start and wish

I'd never sent it. I know it's hard for you to understand me suddenly becoming such a failure. I won't go on about this. One thing, it wasn't a shock because I knew it was coming. I rather dread my lunch with Johnson tomorrow and hope he does not try to make things sound better than they are […] Goodbye my darling I shall be glad to see your intelligent face again and hear your nice voice. There is no one like you here. Very much love and I'm sorry about being such an oaf of a writer. B.

John Johnson did indeed try to soften the blow. He agreed with Michie's comments but thought that Barbara could greatly improve the book by rewriting the last few chapters and that she should not give up on it. But he also brought her up to date with what she had earned over the previous year, and she was disappointed to find that, after tax, it was less than she had expected. 'It is a dreadful waste of time writing books', she complained to Richard in the next letter home. While Richard was elated at having had a long article accepted by the *Economist*, Barbara suddenly found herself in the doldrums about her work.

On her return, Barbara tried to settle down to revising *The Bad Travellers*, but although she loved La Floresta, she found it difficult to concentrate fully on her writing during the day:

> First there is the sound of water running through the pipes in the bedroom ceiling. That's the first sound that wakes me in the morning, then the sound of someone hosing under the window, but the main sound of all which goes on almost continually, is the rattle of bottles, bottles being unloaded and put in the cellar, cases of empty bottles being stacked in the yard. A man and a boy spend all day moving cases of bottles about. The ones in the yard facing our window have come so high that they reach the top of the large wall, every sort of bottle, beer, milk, coca cola and fruit juices, champagne and wine bottles, but no one ever seems to take them away. Then there is the strange thumping sound that comes from under the floor, rather like builders hammering, but I think it is the girls bashing meat about in the shop. The strangest sound of all is the sighing, groaning sound that goes on all day and night, stronger in the kitchen than anywhere else, a little like a ship's engine. I think there must be a huge machine somewhere in the cellars. Then there is the sound of humans, mothers calling their children mostly and little boys playing football in the yard, the builders next door shouting to each other, steps crunching the cobbles in the yard, but more than anything else, the rattle of bottles.[22]

They had also discovered that the winter brought problems in La Floresta. While the summer was blissful – 'cuckoos sing all day and nightingales all night and swallow tail butterflies as large as bats fly in through our windows' – during the winter the rain was very heavy, 'and as our house is perched on a large rock [it] is inclined to get flooded, always during the early hours of the morning and I have to bail it out like a leaking boat'.[23]

34 Barbara in Spain with her grandson Eduardo and her daughter Caroline,
c. 1961

Barbara persuaded Richard that they needed to live somewhere quieter
and drier in the winter, and she soon found a house for rent in San Francisco
Xavier Street, next to the San Cugat golf course. Formerly a small summer
resort for the Barcelona bourgeoisie, the district was rapidly expanding,
but the tree-lined street was in a quiet residential area which was surrounded
by almond groves, fields of corn and vineyards. Their new home, 'the first
real home we have had since we left England' Barbara wrote to Julian, had
been built in traditional style and had roses climbing up a timber archway
over the front door. It also had enough space for Barbara to have a dedicated
writing room. She was delighted to have a garden again and soon after she
arrived she planted a willow, a cherry tree and some cypresses. Richard
could still get into Barcelona easily by train and the house was also better
for the pets, which now numbered three: Coco and the Siamese cat had
been joined by a cross-spaniel dog called Annabel. There was a large terrace,
where Barbara loved to sit in the afternoons, soaking up the sun and reading,
with the animals around her. The Siamese cat, as mischievous as ever, was
quick to pounce on any invading lizard and, when successful, would sit
with the lizard's tail 'waving from her mouth like a giant tongue', much to

Barbara's consternation.[24] As the nearest shops were half a mile away, Barbara bought a moped on which she could get around: 'I fly about on it and it gives me the most marvellous sense of freedom. Much better than driving a car and rather how I hoped skating would be, but it wasn't.'[25] Once they had settled into the house, she set to work revising somewhat listlessly *The Bad Travellers* and, with more enthusiasm, started drafting ideas for a new book to be called *The Skin Chairs*.

During 1961 Barbara wrote a poignant short story called 'The Birds', about a small boy who has been deeply disturbed by his mother's death and whose behaviour puzzles the adults around him, much to his distress. The tale shows a remarkable ability to enter into a child's mind and was published in the autumn issue of Sainsbury's *Family* magazine. By the end of the year she had finished *The Skin Chairs* and sent it to John Johnson, who wrote to say that he liked it. So did the reader for Heinemann, who remarked that one of the more eccentric characters 'is as good a grotesque as any of the grown-ups in *David Copperfield*'.[26] The novel might seem rather haphazardly put together on first reading, but it is a powerful story structured by themes found in her previous work: relations between mothers and daughters; the emotional abuse and neglect of children; the censorious attitude to eccentricity or difference adopted by those who choose to conform; the casual cruelty and atrocities that people inflict on each other. Everything is seen through the eyes of Frances, a ten-year-old girl living in a Leicestershire village with her five siblings and widowed mother, who is continually criticized by her nearby wealthy relations, the Lawrences. Although Barbara told Ursula Holden many years later that 'Only the skin chairs are true. I saw them',[27] in writing the novel she drew strongly on her own life during the late 1920s when she was living with her mother and two sisters in Stratford-upon-Avon. Frances's mother, vague, tractable and hopeless with money, resembles Barbara's own mother in several ways, although she is kinder and more interested in her children. The Lawrences are a horse-riding family and are acutely conscious of their social status. They continually chide Frances's mother for living beyond her means and are clearly based on the Darby family of Hillmorton, who were always quick to criticize Barbara's widowed mother.

Physical deformities are common in the village: Frances's sister Clare was born with a hand missing, a baby in the village has water on the brain, and a local eccentric, a widow, Mrs Alexander, has huge scabs on her head. Emotional dysfunctionality is also rife. On seeing her sister's pet mice scurrying close to the skirting board, Frances recalls that 'There used be a girl in our village who was continually beaten by her parents and I remembered she used to walk like that, close against the walls.'[28] (In *The Vet's Daughter*, Alice's mother, terrified of her husband, also keeps close to the wall.) Frances becomes involved in two relationships that give her nightmares. The first is with Vanda Martin, a young widow, who starves and neglects her baby so that it nearly dies and has to be hospitalized twice. Frances and her cousin Ruby try to care for this child and are mercilessly exploited by Vanda who, obsessed with her lover, a wealthy major, takes advantage of their good nature. The second friendship is with Mrs Alexander, who wears a turban (to cover the scabs) and gold-painted shoes. She is driven about in a bright yellow car by her chauffeur and keeps a menagerie of monkeys and tree frogs in her home. She insists that Frances keep her company because she is lonely – her own daughter died at the age of three – but her emotional dependency soon becomes an embarrassment and a source of acute anxiety for Frances. This dark side of life is weightily represented by the six skin chairs, owned by a general in the village, that give the book its title and that haunt Frances's imagination:

> The General's wife looked at them ruefully and admitted that the chairs were covered in human skin.
>
> 'He brought them back with him after the Boer War, isn't it horrible? Five of them are black men's skins and one white. I believe if you look at them carefully you can see the difference. He used to adore them, silly old man.'
> [...]
> With a feeling of awe I gazed at the chairs thinking of the poor skinless bodies buried somewhere in Africa. Did their souls ever come to see what had happened to their skins or had they forgotten all about them? And did the workmen who covered the chairs know what gruesome work they were doing?[29]

As the novel develops, the skin chairs come to stand for acts of inhumanity on a spectrum of cruelty that ranges from emotional bullying (readily found in the pretty shires of middle England) to the atrocities of war in South Africa.

But, as in all Barbara Comyns' work, a wry sense of the absurd lightens the darkness and the novel ends happily, with baby Jane being adopted by the doctor who treated her in hospital and Frances's mother being rescued from poverty and her bullying relatives through marriage to the kind Mr Blackwell, a wealthy retired brass founder from Birmingham who buys the general's house. Frances and her siblings move into their new home with their mother after the wedding, but Frances is full of trepidation. Terrified of the skin chairs, which she thinks she can hear groaning at night, she eventually resolves her fear of them by holding a ceremony in which she baptizes and 'buries' them. In a bizarrely surreal episode, she gives the chairs the names of six poets: Percy Shelley, George Byron, Edgar Allan Poe, Alfred Tennyson, William Yeats and 'Anon. Circa'. The last sentence of the novel sees her at peace, having read aloud the Baptism service and most of the Burial Service, 'leaning forward in Percy Shelley with my head on the table'.[30] Even while it lends the book a final note of macabre humour and incongruity, the ending offers a blessing for the dead victims of the Boer War and for all victims of cruelty and exploitation. Barbara was pleased with the novel; it had been far easier to write than *The Bad Travellers*.

* * *

Life in Barcelona gradually developed a yearly rhythm: Barbara would stay with Julian in London for a few weeks early in the year, when she would see her sisters and talk to her agent and publisher, leaving Richard behind to care for the animals and get on with his work. During the summer she and Richard would rent a flat for a week or two by the sea, often in Castelldefels, a coastal resort with a beautiful beach about 12 miles south-west of Barcelona – or sometimes in Sitges, a little further south. Then, alone, Barbara would visit Diana in San Roque in August. That would be followed by another visit to London in the early autumn, when she would stay either with Julian again or with Chloe and her husband at 20 Drayton Gardens. During the London trips, she would shop at Peter Jones and Harrods for clothes to take back to Spain, buying good-quality underwear and jumpers for Richard and dresses and coats for herself. However short of money they were, they both liked to dress well; Richard in particular was unwilling to drop his sartorial standards. Barbara was in London in March 1961 for Julian's marriage to Patricia Selby, a divorcee with two children. Pat was an intelligent woman with a successful career as a newscaster and a businesswoman behind her, but she saw herself as a failed mother and had been traumatized by the event that prompted her divorce – she had found her husband making love to her sister. Despite her achievements, she seemed mentally fragile and Barbara felt slightly anxious about her.

With plenty of space in the house on San Francisco Xavier Street, Barbara began painting again, and her work shows the continued influences of naïve art and surrealism, a mode that still suited her view of life as bizarre, often macabre and full of odd conjunctions. The British Institute in Barcelona held an exhibition of paintings by its members every year, and Barbara always entered a few pictures. Richard recorded in his diary in January 1962 that Barbara had

> started another painting – of a bull chewing a disproportionately large lily, with a trumpet floating in the air above him. She has done four others – of a cock stamping on straw, of a seagull looking up at a descending balloon, and one called 'Boots and Ladders' and another called 'Mole's Castle in the air'.[31]

'After all', Barbara wrote to her friend George Brendon in England, an aspiring writer whom she had met through John Johnson, 'John Bratby has

35 Painting by Barbara entitled *Mole's Castle in the Air*, c. 1962

turned to selling mad novels so why shouldn't I sell mad paintings?'[32] Barbara's writing consequently gave way to painting during 1962, although she had started a new novel, provisionally entitled *The Green Girls*, set during and after the war.[33] This later became *A Touch of Mistletoe*. She was also anxious to finish her revision of *The Bad Travellers*, but the Urbano family – Pepe, Caroline and their children – were keen to come and stay, which would mean little time for writing.

Having abandoned language teaching, Pepe had worked as a stoker at Battersea Power Station and then as a statistician in an animal food factory before landing a post as a lecturer in Spanish literature at Baghdad University in Iraq. Although he had a degree in economics and literature from the University of Madrid, he was not an academic and only managed to secure the job through brilliant references provided by the Spanish ambassador to Iraq (the father of a friend) and an Eton housemaster (who used to drink in Pepe's bar on Ibiza). Caroline and Pepe had recently added a daughter to their family; a baby girl called Mariquita. She had been born in 1961 in Barcelona because Caroline wanted to be near her mother when giving birth to her second child. When they visited Barbara and Richard, the Urbano family liked to stay for several weeks. In May 1962 they drove from England,

36 Painting by Barbara entitled *Thrush Singing to Hanging Fish*, c. 1962

where they had been holidaying, to Barcelona. Having only recently returned from her spring visit to London, Barbara was faced with looking after house guests. Richard had a rented office in the Calle de Mallorca in the centre of Barcelona, to which he could retreat to write his articles; Barbara had a 'writing room' in the house but that was no protection against interruptions from visitors. She loved her daughter's family and enjoyed playing with the children, buying beach toys before they arrived and embarking on small adventures with them, such as mystery walks in the woods and placing coins on the railway track that would be squashed flat when a train thundered by. But the combination of typing up Richard's articles and shopping and cooking for four adults and two children left her exhausted and with no energy or time for her own work. She began to worry about falling behind with *The Bad Travellers*, and also about how *The Skin Chairs* would be reviewed when it came out in August. John Johnson and James Michie liked it and were confident it would do well, but the mixed reviews for *Who was Changed and Who was Dead* had shown her that not everyone had a taste for the comic macabre.

Barbara need not have worried. *The Skin Chairs* was published on 7 August 1962, and although some reviewers thought it less original than

The Vet's Daughter, it was generally well received. The *Illustrated London News* critic admired the author's 'consistently sure touch' in writing a novel about a young girl reacting 'to an atmosphere of odd happenings and eccentric grown-ups'. Richard Church liked its 'economy of phrase' and found the novel 'marked by the same macabre detachment of spirit' to be found in the work of Richard Hughes, while Laurence Meynell praised 'the remarkable luminosity which this unusual writer achieves in her vision of the world we all live in and of the people who inhabit it'. For Anthony Burgess, writing in the *Observer*, Barbara Comyns was

> one of our most original talents. The qualities that made *The Vet's Daughter* so remarkable are all here: beauty, pity and terror conveyed without strains or protestation, as coherent a vision as any book about childhood yet presented. 'Weirdly mysterious' is how Frances describes the skin chairs to her great-aunt: that will do for the book too.

Olivia Manning in the *Sunday Times* thought the novel 'conveys exactly the dreamlike, often sinister, world of the imaginative young'; the only flaw, she added, was that the end was 'too cosy'. Susan Chitty in the *Sunday Telegraph* praised the author's ability to conjure up a child's fear and thought *The Skin Chairs* 'A strange, beautiful and very engaging book', while Siriol Hugh-Jones in the *Tatler* admired her 'simple style, a sort of Douanier Rousseau quality in prose'.[34] There were some minor grumbles – Dudley Carew in the *Times Literary Supplement* found the self-imposed viewpoint of a child a limitation, and the anonymous reviewer in *The Times* thought the book rather shapeless – but they were outnumbered by the many positive reviews. Barbara was pleased and relieved. When 'Pa', Richard's father, who took a keen interest in her writing, came to stay for his 80th birthday in September, they had a double celebration.

However, early December was darkened by news of death: Julian wrote to say that his father, Barbara's first husband, had recently been found dead in his flat in the Rue Saint-Sulpice in Paris. John Pemberton died at the age of 54, probably of a heart attack, and his body was not discovered for several days. He had abandoned his second wife, Antonia, in order to pursue the life he loved, that of a bohemian artist, and had later married (possibly bigamously) a very successful French Canadian dancer. She left him in 1961 and John had been devastated by the collapse of the relationship. His landlady in Paris had contacted Julian with news of his father's death, and told him that John had recently had trouble climbing the stairs and seemed to be suffering from heart problems. John's estranged third wife organized the funeral and told Julian he need not attend. Although they had lost contact with each other over the years, Barbara was still affected by her first husband's death and could not sleep the night she read Julian's letter, writing to her friend George Brendon soon after:

The thing that makes me so sad is the thought of him dying alone like that and struggling up the stairs. Ill and perhaps with no money. He was always dreadfully poor and borrowed money from anyone who let him have it including me. He led the maddest life and was the family black sheep, but had a lot of charm and the one thing he was serious about was painting. We were both so young when we married and were so happy at first, but everything went wrong pretty quickly. I can't bear to think what his last days may have been like.[35]

Richard was rather more censorious, writing in his diary on 11 December 1962:

Perhaps it was a good thing he died at the age he did, still able to marry and go about, and painting in Paris. It is difficult to imagine how he would have managed when he was old. He had always lived the same sort of life – short marriages or mistresses, pub-crawling, party-going, and painting for his own pleasure.

As she grew older, the winter and the loss of light depressed Barbara. This sad mood, combined with the melancholy news of John's death, made her miserable as the year turned. The house in San Cugat, although spacious and beautiful, was not easy to heat: 'The winter here is a bit of a struggle and I waste a considerable amount of time trying to warm the house, running backwards with damp logs trimmed with woodlice.'[36] And whereas they had lots of visitors during the summer (sometimes too many), she saw few people during the dark months of the year. Richard's status as 'our man in Barcelona' for the *Telegraph* and other papers earned him respect in the city and resulted in many invitations to official functions and banquets held for eminent people from politics and business. Occasionally Barbara went too, but more often than not Richard went alone, which left him free to spend time gleaning 'insider' information from senior civil servants: 'This is the hand that shook Franco's hand', he would say to Barbara on his return home. Richard's growing social and professional commitments meant that Barbara was left on her own a lot, which she did not mind during the summer but disliked in the winter. If they moved to central Barcelona, she would see more people throughout the year and Richard would be able to walk to his office. The charm of bourgeois country living – their next door neighbour was a retired English bank manager – was also beginning to wear rather thin and Barbara began to fantasize about a flat in Barcelona. They decided they would think seriously about moving back to the city but agreed they could not afford it at that time.

* * *

The following April saw Barbara in London again, staying first with Julian and Pat – who were expecting a baby in September and were now living in

Grange Park in Ealing – and then with Chloe and John Faraday in Drayton Gardens. Barbara was disappointed to be told by her agent that once again a book that had been well reviewed had sold poorly: *The Skin Chairs*, like *Out of the Red, Into the Blue*, had sold only about 2,000 copies. Barbara wrote in despair again to Richard and begged him not to mention the low sales to his father: 'No invitations to lunch or arrangements for Publisher's lunch. I'm right out of fashion in fact "not with it" any more. I can hardly bear to go to Johnson's office to collect the money.' Richard did his best to console her:

> The news about *The Skin Chairs* certainly is a nasty surprise. After the good reviews and the paragraphs about it being in demand at bookshops and libraries I thought it must have sold well. I won't reveal it to anyone – luckily people here are not so inquisitive about that sort of thing as they are in England and, as for my father, I have been for some time taking advantage of the fact that we are at two ends of the postal service to ignore his questions. If I had written such a good book and had reviews that showed it was appreciated, I should not care about publishers or agents; but I know you feel differently. It gives me a great contempt for the publishing world. In the old days, although they refused good books, publishers seem to have backed their judgement; nowadays they knuckle under as soon as the sales disappoint them. I should not bother now about producing books to satisfy Johnson or Heinemann's; but sooner or later you will feel inspired and write something they will clamour for. You must keep up your writing, because it has become better and better.

Soon after returning to San Cugat, Barbara's spirits were lifted by a letter from Roderick Cook, an English man who now lived in New York and who was to have great success as an actor and director on Broadway. A keen reader, he wrote to say how much he enjoyed her books, adding, 'It is extraordinary that after reading you, even one's favourite authors like Muriel Spark and William Golding sound affected and "literary". It is like hearing a singer whose voice is small, but always absolutely true and clear.'[37] He was dismayed that Barbara's work was not published in the States and wanted to remedy the situation. He had enlisted the help of an editor at *Harper's* magazine and of Jean Stafford, the short story writer and novelist, both of whom promised to bring Barbara's work to the attention of readers and secure an American publisher for her books. Although nothing came of his plan, his letter was enough to encourage Barbara to return to her writing at a moment when she was losing faith in it.

Unusually, in June 1963 Richard travelled alone to England. He needed to liaise with the *Daily Telegraph* and the *Economist* about his work and to record two talks for the BBC Spanish Service. There were also personal reasons for his trip: he wanted to visit his father, who was convalescing in Bath, having recently had his left leg amputated below the knee to prevent the risk of gangrene associated with the poor blood flow caused by clogged arteries. Barbara wrote to Richard from San Cugat:

> I am managing quite well on my own really. I get up at seven and have a shower and breakfast, then work on *The Bad Travellers* for about two hours. I find it much easier to work really early, before I have been fretted by living ... The evenings are the worst but I have the B.B.C. on if there isn't a thunderstorm and I have it by my bed. I read and listen to hot Jazz until twelve so that I sleep deeply and don't hear robbers and ghosts prowling round ...

On his return to Spain, Barbara told Richard that she had heard from Caroline that the Urbano family – now numbering five, as a little girl called Nuria had been born four months previously in Baghdad – would be arriving soon. In early July the Urbanos left Iraq – where a military coup in February had destabilized the country, making it unsafe for foreigners – and drove through Jordan, Syria, Turkey and Greece. From there they crossed by boat to Brindisi and drove the length of Italy and along the French Riviera. They arrived in Barcelona on 1 August, tired and dusty but very proud of their exploits, which had included almost getting lost in the desert after leaving Baghdad. Although Richard, like Barbara, was relieved to see them arrive safely in Barcelona, he confided his worries to his diary:

> This visit comes at rather an unfortunate time. We are very short of money. Last year we ran through the remains of our reserve – the money we had got from selling our Wimbledon house. I had to ask my father for £200 at the beginning of the year and since then he has been impressing on me that he cannot let me have any more. I am running an overdraft at the bank here and before Caroline wrote I was wondering how we would get through the coming months. All this comes when Barbara is struggling revising the novel she has just sold to Heinemann's.

It did not get any easier financially: Richard had anticipated that they could survive on the money he earned through his journalism, but that had proved to be a vain hope. By the summer of 1963 he was reduced to borrowing from friends and taking a loan from their grocer in Barcelona. In order to bring in a little more money, Barbara had started giving English lessons at home, but she did not enjoy them and soon gave it up.

The Urbano family was closely followed by Simon Faraday, Chloe's 17-year-old son, who had previously arranged to stay with Barbara and Richard during the summer. He was a witty and charming young man, but spoilt and rather lazy. He had been enrolled for officer training but had not liked army life, so was learning to be a forestry contractor. He knew he would be very wealthy when his parents died so he approached work casually, all ambition annihilated by his inheritance expectations. He could also be devious and untruthful. His parents had given him money to take with him

to Spain but, on arrival, he told Barbara and Richard that he had brought
none with him – so they gave him money when they could ill afford to. He
then wrote to his parents complaining that Barbara and Richard were mean
and made him pay for his own food, which was untrue; Barbara was an
excellent cook and she and Richard were generous hosts. Chloe and John
sent their son more money. When Barbara realized what was happening
she wrote to Chloe, who refused to believe that her son could behave so
badly. The two sisters, usually very close, quarrelled fiercely about Simon,
and their argument was followed by a rift that was to last for many months.
With Caroline and Pepe and their three children in residence, as well as
Simon, the house in San Cugat was packed, and Richard documented the
chaos with some disgruntlement in his diary:

> The children are running round the house all day [...] Caroline strides from
> one end of the house to the other, hanging up laundry and, wherever you are
> Pepe appears with a cigarette as a bland spectator. Add to all this life the
> animals – with the cat screeching for food in her Siamese way and Annabel's
> two puppies emerging from their places in the cupboard and yelplng for the
> teat. Barbara tries to find time to finish her book between perpetual laundry,
> perpetually preparing meals for five grown-ups, three children and three animals
> – and perpetual washing up.

The last straw was a plague of carpet beetles in the house: Caroline and
Pepe had brought with them some rugs from Iraq, and the bugs in them
had bred. Richard noticed that the linen cupboard had become infested and
'so was Barbara's writing room, where they had put some of the rugs: the
creatures had crawled up the walls and settled behind pictures'. Barbara
shot out early the next morning to buy some insecticide, afraid that Simon
would return to London with tales of a dirty, bug-ridden house. Meanwhile,
Pepe and Caroline had decided to move to Madrid rather than return to
Iraq, where the political situation had worsened.

By the time all the visitors left in September Barbara was exhausted and
worried about completing *The Bad Travellers*, for which she had signed a
contract with Heinemann in late July. She and Richard could not afford a
holiday together, so they decided that Barbara should spend four days by
herself in a hotel in Castelldefels. She returned refreshed and to the good
news that she had another grandson – Pat, Julian's wife, had been safely
delivered of a little boy named Nicholas. Barbara threw herself back into
revising her novel, which she decided to rename *Birds in Tiny Cages*. After
a hectic summer, the autumn was consumed by work. She concentrated on
her writing and Richard took on evening teaching to raise some ready cash.
He researched topics for articles and wrote them up during the day, but
every weekday evening saw him teaching Spanish to office staff in an American

factory near the port. Barbara's description of Leo in *Birds in Tiny Cages* as looking 'utterly worn out' and 'so exhausted that his voice became flat and hoarse' no doubt owed something to her observation of her husband at this time.[38]

1963 had not been an easy year, and it ended with both Barbara and Richard feeling tired and dispirited. Moreover the winter was bitterly cold and their water pipes froze: there were three heavy snowfalls and they were reduced to washing in snow and drinking melted ice: 'Icicles with brandy are quite a good drink', she wrote to her friend George Brendon, adding:

> The cold seemed to get into Richard and he was ill on and off for six months and began to look like D.H. Lawrence in his last days, also we had the most sinister money worries that went on and on. When the money situation had cleared a little, I let this house to friends and took a tiny flat by the sea for two months and Richard stopped coughing and recovered as if by magic. It was exactly like those Japanese flowers that swell up in water.[39]

Birds in Tiny Cages, previously entitled *The Bad Travellers*, was published in June 1964, but most reviewers damned it with faint praise, noting that the novel did not have the power and originality of either *The Vet's Daughter* or *The Skin Chairs*. In a benign but anodyne review in the *Daily Telegraph*, Iain Hamilton described the book as 'like a letter dashed off to an old friend', although he praised the author's 'carefully casual style' The *Illustrated London News* reviewer thought it 'a curious little novel', but noted that the author 'writes with great delicacy and has the true observer's eye', while the *Punch* reviewer dismissed it as 'readable enough' with 'Dufy-like flashes of toy-bright visualisation'. The most perceptive review appeared in the *Sunday Times*, in which Jeremy Rundall noted that 'if there is something of the sadness of Françoise Sagan, it is a more mature melancholy, given to compassion rather than self-pity'.[40] Barbara was disappointed that the reviews were lukewarm, but she was now concentrating on finishing *A Touch of Mistletoe* and, by December, had started a new novel 'about Mrs Quale's brothel for elderly gentlepeople'.[41]

1965 brought more death. In early January Barbara learned that her nephew Simon had died in a tragic accident at the age of 19. Chloe and John had recently bought their son a Mini Traveller, in which he took great pride. Coming home from a party in Surrey in the early hours of the morning, he decided that he was too tired and too drunk to drive any further, so he pulled into a layby. As the night was cold, he lit a heater he happened to have in the back of the car. The fumes it produced sent him into a coma, and he was pronounced dead on arrival at hospital. His death certificate simply recorded that 'Simon Swyfte Faraday' died an 'Accidental death' from 'carbon monoxide poisoning (fumes from oil heater)'. The loss of their only child hit Chloe and John very hard; Chloe was hysterical with grief. Although Barbara wrote immediately to her sister, she did not fly to London to be with her; Simon's devious behaviour in Spain had caused a rift between them that was yet to heal. And money was still short at this time: there was simply not enough spare to pay for a return air fare to London. Soon after Simon's funeral, Chloe and her husband moved out of Drayton Gardens into a large house in Fernshaw Road in Chelsea; Chloe could no longer bear to stay in the home where she had brought up her son.

In April Richard's father died and Richard flew to England to help his two brothers, the official executors of their father's estate, with the funeral and probate matters. Barbara and Richard were very sad; they were fond of 'Pa', who had always encouraged them in their various ventures and who had frequently come to their financial rescue just as the bank was threatening to close Richard's account. But his death meant that Richard was left a good sum of money. In his final will, made in December 1964, Sir Arthur Comyns Carr had appointed Richard's brothers, John and Cecil (known as Robin), as his trustees. They, and only they, would inherit the trust fund and have control over it. Richard – perhaps because he had already been given a great deal of money over the previous twenty years – was left £1,000 instead. But the rest of the estate, worth approximately £27,000, was to be divided between the three brothers, who would each inherit £9,000. With £10,000 in the bank (about £241,240 today), Barbara and Richard decided to realize their dream of buying a flat in Barcelona.

12

The San Roque venture

During 1965 Barbara's writing had been constantly interrupted – by deaths in the family, by a stream of visitors and by having to type up Richard's work: 'Very long, dull grey articles for papers like *World Today*, *The F.B.I. Review* and Banking papers, but they pay very well and are worth writing for.'[1] But by February 1966 she had finished *A Touch of Mistletoe*, a rather melancholy novel, and sent it off to her agent, John Johnson. Her first husband's death in 1962 seems to have triggered a desire to revisit that period of her life when she was married to a penniless artist and living in London. A few years later, Barbara wrote to Graham Greene explaining the title: 'The mistletoe – a tree-killer, man-killer – is an omen. I got the idea driving through France in the winter when the bare trees were so covered with it, I was afraid of catching it myself.'[2]

Eugene Reeve, who marries Victoria Green, the book's narrator, bears some resemblance to John Pemberton – but his character offers a kinder portrait of John than that of Charles Fairclough in *Our Spoons Came from Woolworths*. Eugene is a gentler, more sensitive man than Charles and dotes on their small son, Paul. Eugene's fear of mistletoe echoes that of Barbara: we learn that as a child in France he saw many dying trees covered with it, and thought he could hear them crying out, 'I've got the mistletoes'.[3] In the novel the parasite comes to stand for any malignant force or suffering that taints a life. Eugene's death from insulin treatment for schizophrenia introduces a note of tragedy and leaves Victoria having to work hard to provide for herself and their child. After a period of deep grief, she marries Tony Ferris, an entertaining, louche crime writer who binge drinks and who gradually begins to feel trapped by domesticity. Eight years into their marriage he takes up with an ex-girlfriend and abandons Victoria. Finding she is pregnant with Tony's child soon after he has left, Victoria decides to have an abortion, after which she feels she has been irrevocably tainted with mistletoe. They divorce amicably in 1945, by which time Victoria has found a job in an advertising studio, but she also works three evenings a week as a waitress in a nearby restaurant.

After various short-term affairs, she drifts into a relationship with an older man called 'Monty' Dadds, who lives in an ugly flat in Putney and whose main interests are golf, tennis and squash. Now 41 and frightened of living alone on the poverty line for the rest of her life, Victoria agrees to marry him. Although she remains grateful to 'Dadds', as Victoria calls him, for having rescued her from penury, she feels dead inside and recites lines in French from La Fontaine's fable 'The Crow and the Fox' to keep her mind occupied when he makes love to her. Dadds becomes obsessed with waste and grows ever more small-minded, going through the contents of the dustbin and pointing out how slices of lemon recently served with a fish dinner – now nestling among the ashes and tea-leaves – could have been used again in soup. Meanwhile, Victoria's art work becomes flat and dull, indicating the cost of the compromise she has made for the sake of security.

After four years Dadds falls ill, and within a short while dies of cancer, leaving most of his estate to his sister. In an episode oddly prophetic of what was to happen ten years later in Barbara's own life, Victoria's adult son comes to the rescue and offers his mother a flat above a shop on which he has just taken a lease. Determined to avoid the accusation of another 'cosy ending', Barbara closed *A Touch of Mistletoe* with Victoria and her sister visiting the graveyard in the village where they grew up, laughing and crying together as they talk about their lives and past loves. John Johnson, Barbara's agent, liked the book, which he thought 'a picaresque kind of novel' that brilliantly captured the atmosphere of the 1930s.[4] In May 1966 she signed a contract with Heinemann for its publication the following year.

Later that month, Barbara and Richard moved into a flat in Fernando Puig Street in the fashionable residential district of Sarrià-Sant Gervasi in Barcelona. The Putget neighbourhood, in which they lived, was at the top of a steep hill. Nearby was open land which would soon be turned into a public park. From their small balcony, they looked out over wooded slopes down across the city to the sea beyond and could see ships coming into Barcelona harbour. It was ideal. Barbara used her moped to zoom up the 'puig', or hill, with her shopping, and she started to colonize the balcony with pots of freesias, marigolds, wallflowers and morning glory, all grown from seed sent from England. She also managed to squeeze in a stone urn with water lilies and three goldfish. 'As you can imagine', she wrote to her friend George Brendon a year later, 'there isn't much room to move on my balcony and the poor dogs have to keep their tails between their legs and there is only just room for me to sit with a glass of beer and a book. Once the bottle of beer shot through the bars and poured down a man's neck and I had to give him 25 pesetas.'[5] The flat was not as big as the house

37 Barbara in San Cugat during the 1960s

near the San Cugat golf course, which meant that sometimes visitors had to stay in a nearby small art deco hotel, but that was no bad thing as far as Barbara was concerned. When Julian and Nicholas came to visit, Julian booked a room in the hotel while Nicholas stayed with his grandparents. The pattern was repeated with Caroline and Pepe who, when visiting, would take a room in the hotel while Eduardo, Mariquita and Nuria would stay in the flat with Barbara and Richard. Now that they were based in Spain, Caroline and her family also spent at least one holiday a year in Diana's house, El Almendral, in San Roque, sometimes overlapping with Barbara's August visit there. The children loved the place; the house and the land around offered endless opportunities for exploration and adventure and they spent hours in the cool swimming pool.

While she enjoyed being a grandmother, it reminded Barbara that she was no longer young, and fear of old age and dependency was gradually creeping into her books. In *Birds in Tiny Cages*, Flora is appalled to see 'a shabby old woman' who has slipped on dog mess lying on the ground, revealing 'her poor old head [that] was almost bald'.[6] In *The Skin Chairs*, Frances meets her sister at the train station and is horrified to see

a bent old woman being helped along the platform by her two daughters. So
slow she was and bent forward so that her chin almost touched her stomach
[...] She could not control the spit that was dribbling from her mouth, and
every now and then one of the daughters would wipe her lips with a man's
handkerchief [...] As I watched the old woman, I realized for the first time
that one day I would turn into an old woman and crumble away like a dead
leaf.[7]

And in *A Touch of Mistletoe* Victoria Green is depressed by signs that her
beauty is fading:

One morning, as I was arranging my hair, I saw three thick white hairs running
through the black like frozen rivers. Then I examined my face carefully for
other signs of age and noticed a very slight blurredness and odd lines that
looked as if they had been drawn there, and I saw that my eyes seemed to
have shrunk a little and the whites did not look so fresh.[8]

Barbara had started having her hair tinted when she was in her mid-fifties
to hide her grey streaks, and by 1966 she was aware that she was ageing,
writing wryly to Richard from San Roque in August that year, 'I went to
the pool and swam without any bad results except two gardeners who went
away after they saw me close to – one of the compensations of being a
grandmother.'[9] But she was oddly vague about exactly how old she was: a
diary entry for 27 December 1964 reads, 'My birthday – I can't remember
which', and in 1969 she was to write, 'My birthday. I don't know which
but I'm getting pretty antique' (she was 62 that year). She did not like
getting old and assumed an insouciant amnesia about her age as a form
of denial.

Another way of dealing with the fear of getting old and falling into
poverty, though, was to laugh about it. The nightmare cameos of old age
in Barbara's recent fiction would soon be offset by the humour of her next
book, which was to be a comic celebration of the older woman. Having
begun life in late 1964 as a book called *Mrs Quale's Brothel*, it was now
provisionally entitled *Amy Doll's House*. But the summer of 1966, during
which she had planned to get their flat straight and work on the novel, was
interrupted by a bout of appendicitis. After several medical consultations
in June, Barbara had her appendix removed in Barcelona on 5 July. She
soon realized that Spanish hospital conventions and procedures were very
different from those of English hospitals: relatives were expected to play
a large part in washing, supporting and entertaining the patient. During
her week's stay in the hospital, Richard visited her in the evenings and
Caroline came once from Madrid. The staff thought this very odd, and a
cleaner told her in no uncertain terms, 'It is all wrong being here by yourself
and writing and writing all the time'. She was unaware that Barbara was

documenting the noisy involvement of Spanish families in their relatives' welfare:

> Sometimes in the evening there is an operation and the family are allowed to watch through the glass doors. Thirty came for the next appendix after mine. One afternoon I thought a christening party was in progress, there was so much laughter and talking and I imagined I could hear glasses of champagne clinking, but it turned out to be twenty people of the same family watching a Caesarean take place. The patients are always surrounded by their families who help look after them, at least they are washed, but I wouldn't like to have all those people chattering in my room, sometimes they quarrel about the treatment. Two women were having an argument about the angle an unconscious patient should be lying, one wanted him propped up and the other flat on his back. They both became so excited, one turning the handle on the bed one way and the other, the other – until eventually the poor patient was shot out of bed and had to be returned to the operating theatre.[10]

In early August Barbara packed her bags for her annual holiday at El Almendral. This time her visit was to double as convalescence, so she took plenty to read, including books by Balzac and Christopher Isherwood. While there she worked in detail on the plot of her next novel. It would feature four middle-class women in their late fifties and early sixties living in Kensington, who supplement their meagre incomes by casual prostitution. Their landlady, the timid Amy Doll, who tries to shield her 14-year-old daughter from the goings-on in her house, is a reluctant 'madam' who would prefer her tenants to earn their extra cash by other means. Barbara decided there would be nothing gothic or really dark about the book; if readers were no longer responding to her particular brand of the comic macabre, she would try plain comic instead. By the late autumn, she had rewritten the first chapter and was working hard on the novel, now entitled *The House of Dolls*. December brought the proofs of *A Touch of Mistletoe*. Correcting them, she worried that parts of it seemed 'sentimental and gushing' and became anxious about its reception.[11]

A Touch of Mistletoe was published on 24 April 1967 and was reviewed mainly in regional newspapers and magazines. 'I must say I share your disappointment in the lack of reviews *A Touch of Mistletoe* has received in the national papers', wrote John Johnson to Barbara, adding 'I don't think Heinemann's have advertised it very well and I have told them so.'[12] Jeremy Rundall in *The Scotsman* praised the novel as 'Moving, intelligent and painfully observant' and admired the 'excellent vignettes of pre-war Fitzrovia', while the *Punch* reviewer remarked that 'the prose, whether one calls it disciplined-naïve or Defoe-like, covers subtleties of construction'. Laurence Meynell in the *Express & Star* thought the novel 'utterly convincing [...] the whole book is written so as to hover between tears and laughter in a manner which is irresistibly touching and funny'. The only review in a national newspaper, the *Observer*, was spiteful, dismissing the novel's first-person narrative as 'indiscriminate prattle', while the *Times Literary Supplement* reviewer damned the book with faint praise:

> The confrontation of stultifying comfort and impoverished creativity is not an original subject, and Miss Comyns, firmly on the side of the romantics, has no new discrimination to make. Basically sentimental, her book is rescued from triteness by the precision and variety of its detail, the occasional hits of an honest, if sometimes irritatingly simple style, and a determined optimism which is not entirely naïve. Miss Comyns covers a good deal of O'Brien country without becoming maudlin.[13]

As this comment suggests, Barbara's novels were now being compared with those of other women writers whose work was being widely reviewed during the late 1960s. The decade saw the rise of the Women's Liberation Movement and with it greater interest in publishing women's fiction. Authors being praised included Edna O'Brien, Margaret Drabble, Muriel Spark, Sylvia Plath, Jean Rhys and Angela Carter. Maire Lynd, the in-house fiction reader for Heinemann, noted in her report on Carter's *The Magic Toyshop* that she 'did not like the beginning of this novel, which is written by a younger, more knowing, Barbara Comyns; but once the heroine has moved to London, the book does take on a certain fascination'.[14] The comment presaged a slide in Barbara's reputation, and she was indeed to watch Angela Carter's literary star rise as her own waned during the 1970s. All these novelists and many more placed women at the centre of their books and were candidly exploring their characters' feelings and their often vexed relationships with men. Barbara's fiction was being measured against theirs and often found wanting. In a decade that saw the rise of Second Wave feminism, women's consciousness-raising groups, the introduction of the contraceptive pill and the fight for equal pay and opportunities, the faux-naïve narrator was perhaps no longer quite so appealing. Barbara wrote to the publicity agent at Heinemann's asking why there had been only one review of *A Touch of Mistletoe* in the national newspapers: 'My books have been published for over seventeen years and none of them have received this stoney [*sic*] silence before, even the ones that were more or less failures', she complained.[15] She received a soothing reply and copies of some regional reviews, but the lack of reviews in the main press confirmed Barbara's sense that her work was now 'out of fashion'. Olive Shapley's warm recommendation of the book on the BBC radio programme 'Talking About Books', aired in mid-June, offered little consolation.

Barbara was cheered, however, by news from Johnson in May that the film producer Terence Baker was interested in making a film of *The Vet's*

Daughter. The plan was that Bridget Boland, a well-established screenwriter whose films included the celebrated *Gaslight* (1940), would write the script and that Barbara Ferris would play the part of Alice Rowlands. R. H. Enterprises, a film production company, was offering £100 (about £2,220 today) for the purchase of a six months' option on the film rights, renewable for a further six months for another £100, with a final payment of £3,000 (about £66,600 today). In a letter to Johnson dated 29 May 1967, Barbara replied enthusiastically, 'I'm sure it would make a fascinating [film] and after the Fellini film and *Blow-up*, it wouldn't seem at all strange.' (Fellini's *Juliet of the Spirits* had been released in 1965 and Michelangelo Antonioni's *Blow-up* in 1966.) It was the first of many such requests for the film rights for her work, none of which came to fruition due to lack of funding.

*   *   *

In late July 1967 Barbara received an extraordinary letter from Diana, who was in London, outlining a proposition that took her entirely by surprise. Even Diana called it a 'dotty sort of letter to write'. In it she invited Barbara and Richard to consider 'ending their days' at El Almendral in San Roque. She wanted Caroline, Rupert's daughter, to inherit the house when she died and eventually for it to pass to Caroline and Pepe's children. In the meantime, she was inviting Barbara and Richard to give up their flat in Barcelona and move in with her rent-free. Diana, now 70, was coming under pressure from her nephews and nieces to put her affairs in order. They had suggested that she should set up a company, with El Almendral listed as one of its assets; this would help to alleviate death duties and the house could be used as a holiday home by the family. But Diana wanted to leave El Almendral to someone who would live in it and love it as she did. She was also deeply concerned about her menagerie (she wanted all her animals to die natural deaths at home) and her garden, which she wished to be preserved in its current state and not 'dug up and replanted with pink geraniums'.[16] Barbara, who had always thoroughly enjoyed her August holidays in San Roque, replied the next day:

> Your letter was such a surprise it took me over three hours before I could mention it to Richard. I think I should write immediately without going into details (there are so many) to say it would be marvellous to end our days at El Almendral if it could be worked out, but not if it was going to upset all your nephews and nieces. Richard was terrified of the idea at first, but now he has got over the shock is coming round to it. The quietness and all that appeals to him. Of course the main inducement is the thought of Caroline, Pepe and the children living there one day, but I won't mention it to him while it's just a wild idea. There is nowhere I'd rather be. Where else would you

find badgers, kingfishers, turtles and exotic birds flying over the garden, Burmese cats climbing up the creepers and two dear donkeys? It was all looking so beautiful when I last saw it.

On receiving Barbara's reply, Diana began to set things in motion. In September she wrote to Barbara with the news that during the summer she had seen her lawyers and accountants to try to work out the fate of El Almendral and to change her will, which was very complicated owing to Spanish inheritance laws:

> It sounds all right to say you would leave someone a house, but Spanish death duties for anyone except next of kin are so enormous that there would be nothing left. We are trying to get round this. I have a financial adviser who is so wily that I sometimes think he must be mad; however, my nephews and nieces have great faith in him, so maybe he will swing it. He is now taking it up with some Madrid lawyers.

It was the beginning of what was to become a long and protracted legal discussion, in both England and Spain, about whether it would indeed be possible for Diana to leave her beautiful house to Caroline. Over the next eighteen months Barbara and Richard were constantly sent draft proposals outlining possible financial arrangements and alterations to Diana's will, as well as suggestions about which rooms they might live in at El Almendral. It was finally agreed that after Diana's death, Barbara and Richard would live in the house and look after the cats, the donkeys and the badgers. In return, they would receive income from an investment of £10,000 (almost £220,000 today) as soon as they moved in; all repairs, the financial upkeep of the house and the salary of the chauffeur/handyman would be paid for by the trustees. There would also be an administrator for the Estate who would oversee matters and arbitrate if there were to be any family disputes. According to a letter written by Diana to Barbara on 2 January 1968, Caroline would eventually inherit the house and, on the death of Richard and Barbara, she would also inherit the £10,000 investment. Barbara replied in January 1968 agreeing to the proposals: 'The thought of living in your house makes old age something to look forward to.'

* * *

Meanwhile, Barbara got on with her life. In October she flew to London and stayed with Julian, his wife Pat and their son Nicholas (now nearly four) in their flat in Kew Gardens Road. Barbara wrote to Richard enthusing about Kew with its 'beautiful village green and dear little houses by the river', and said she was enjoying spending time with Nicholas, who had an immense toy car collection. The rift with Chloe had still not healed so they did not meet, although Barbara did see her other sister, Nan. The visit included, as

38 Exterior of El Almendral

39 Sitting room of El Almendral

always, a shopping spree in Harrods and Peter Jones. 'I hope the bills were not too awful!!! I threw all the invoices away without looking. Couldn't face them', she wrote to Richard. Neither she nor Richard could bear the thought of economizing on clothes, however precarious their financial situation. She also managed to find someone to type up *The House of Dolls* and sent it off to John Johnson shortly after she returned to Barcelona. He replied encouragingly: 'I think it is a delightful book and your particular deadpan kind of style suits it admirably.'[17] But in December Johnson told her that Heinemann had rejected it: 'They have lost money on both *Birds in Tiny Cages* and on *A Touch of Mistletoe*', he wrote, adding that they were not willing to take a risk on *The House of Dolls*, which was much shorter than her other novels. 'The publication of short novels is a very real problem', Johnson added.[18] Barbara replied, 'What horrible shocks I'm having lately. Being a writer is enough to give one ulcers. Lovely things happening, then in a matter of weeks being right at the bottom of the ladder again without even a publisher.'[19] Johnson sent the novel out over the next few months to The Bodley Head, Eyre & Spottiswoode, Cape, Macmillan, André Deutsch, Weidenfeld & Nicolson and Secker & Warburg, all of whom rejected it. Barbara agreed to rewrite *The House of Dolls* and make it longer, but she was losing confidence in her work, and in September 1968 she asked Johnson to put it aside:

> I think that one day my books may have a come-back, at least I hope so. I could start again with a different style and under a different name, but I feel a bit old for that. As it is, I paint and do a lot of typing for Richard so I'm not wasting my time.[20]

No longer writing, Barbara now spent many hours painting and socializing with the coterie of English artists living and working in Barcelona. She also enjoyed going to art exhibitions with Richard; a friend wrote some years later that she loved 'all the great Spanish painters from Velazquez to Miró' and that she much admired the work of the Barcelona-born artist Antoni Tàpies.[21] She often bought classical music records but was also a great Beatles fan and was very amused when her canary went wild with delight when she played their latest record.[22] Always a keen reader, she now read even more voraciously and helped in the library at the British Club in Barcelona. Brief comments in her diaries and letters about authors and books give a good sense of the eclectic range of her reading and her strong reactions to other writers' work. She thought Stendhal 'a marvellous writer'; she enjoyed Charlotte Brontë's *The Professor* but considered her 'spiteful' about Catholicism; she 'hated' Scott Fitzgerald's *This Side of Paradise* (although *Tender is the Night* was one of her favourite books); she thought John Fowles's *The Collector* 'excellent'; she found Tolstoy's *Death of Ivan Ilyich* 'very real and moving'; she greatly admired Michael Holroyd's biography of Lytton Strachey; she thought Waugh's *Brideshead Revisited* 'a very sad book'; she found that *Dr. Zhivago* left 'strange pictures in my mind'; she judged Solzhenitsyn's *Cancer Ward* 'the best book I've read for years'; but she was appalled by an American biography of Byron, in which 'Leigh Hunt picks his nose and eats the bogies, his wife farts all the time, particularly when she eats Gorganzola cheese, Mary Shelley has a moustache, and so on'.[23] She also read and re-read Trollope, a perennial favourite.

Now that Caroline and Pepe were living in Alcalá, a town about 20 miles north-east of Madrid, Barbara saw them more frequently and often went on holiday with them to seaside resorts such as Tarragona. The family camped and Barbara stayed in a nearby hotel with their dog Annabel. She was very happy to spend days on the beach with her grandchildren but drew the line at sleeping under canvas. Life was full and busy but she had periods of mild depression and occasional anxiety dreams about old age and poverty, one of which she recorded in her diary in December 1969. In the dream she was back in Bidford, the village in which she had grown up:

> I spent most of my life trying to preserve the historic old Norman bridge that crossed the Avon near my old home, eventually they pulled it down and built a fantastic silver bridge that looked as if had been made of silver Meccano in its place. By this time I'd grown into an old white haired woman and I made my living selling models of the new bridge from a stall nearby.

In the late summer of 1969, Richard had given her a folder containing descriptions of her dreams during the previous year. He had written them down each day after she recounted them over breakfast. 'It was so interesting reading them', she wrote in her diary on 30 August, 'some are quite sinister'. One dream clearly conveys Barbara's anxiety about the spectre of poverty that continued to haunt her:

> I had to work in a brothel in a red lamp district I had become so poor. We were made to parade up and down in cages, some of us naked to the waist and the others naked below the waist – luckily I was among the former ones. We only earnt 15/- at a time and I thought 'I shall have to do it at least twice a day merely to live'. There was a notice up next door saying 'Perversions aquí'.[24]

Barbara's dreams remained important to her; she was later to tell her friend Ursula Holden that, when writing a book, the dreams she had about it at night would often result in altering whole chapters the following day.[25]

In September Barbara was surprised to receive a letter from Paris from Graham Greene, now based in Antibes on the Côte d'Azur where he had moved to be close to his partner Yvonne Cloetta:

> I have been out of touch with you and Richard for so long that I know nowhere to write except c/o Heinmanns and I hope they will forward the letter. Where are you and what are you doing? It is with horror that I notice that *The Skin Chairs* was published seven years ago. I hope you haven't stopped writing (perhaps I have been out of England and failed to get your latest books) and

please remember anything you write will be of interest to your old friend. I am connected with The Bodley Head and if anything has gone wrong with your relations with Heinemann please let me know. Anyway, my love and best wishes to you and Richard – Graham.[26]

Barbara replied, documenting her dissatisfaction with Heinemann and her woes over *The House of Dolls*. She took some time writing the letter, worried that it might be too long and gushing: 'I'd rather not know famous people – I never know how to treat them', she wrote in her diary in October. Greene responded quickly:

Thank you so much for your long and interesting letter. I don't know how I missed your two novels after *The Skin Chairs* – *Birds in Tiny Cages* and *A Touch of Mistletoe*, but I shall try to get them now. Some of the change at Heinemann may have been due to the departure of Frere who was the managing director. As a result of that I left Heinemann myself.[27] It was Frere who on my advice took you on and he was really interested. I would very much like to have seen *The House of Dolls* and perhaps if it has been turned down by The Bodley Head I could interest someone else in it.

Do give my love to Richard. I'm glad he's so well and working so hard.

Yours affectionately,

Graham

Plucking up courage, Barbara decided to send Greene *The House of Dolls*, now revised and longer. In the final version of the book, set after the Second World War, two of the four lodgers are impoverished divorcees, one is a shy widow and the fourth a splendidly resourceful Spanish woman, Señora Augustina Puig, who suggests to her fellow lodgers that they might go on the game. Her backstory explains why women sometimes make such a choice. As a girl, the Señora worked as an assistant in her parents' butcher's shop in Barcelona, but was suddenly sent away to be the servant of a rich customer. There the señor tried to rape her; her screams resulted in his walking away 'as if it had nothing to do with him'. She was instantly dismissed and sent home; her family never forgave her. After becoming the mistress of a retired British major who owns a villa in Sitges, a coastal town south of Barcelona, she eventually moved to England with him. After his death, she worked as a waitress in Brighton and London and then, returning to what she knew, found a job in a Walham Green horsemeat shop. (Horsemeat and donkey meat were sold and eaten in England, especially in Yorkshire, until the 1930s; they resurfaced occasionally when other meats were in short supply – as in wartime.) When Señora Augustina moves into Amy Doll's house as a lodger, she is the mistress of a chocolate salesman. From there it is 'only a step' to what she calls 'my casual gentlemen'.[28] She tells the other three women where to meet likely customers and how much to charge them.

Unlike Victoria Green in *A Touch of Mistletoe*, who decides on marriage to a dull and small-minded man rather than face poverty in her old age, the characters in this book choose the oldest profession in the world as their solution and care not a fig for convention (although their landlady does). The comedy in the novel derives from the rivalry between the women, the poor health of their clients and the exigencies of the English class system. There are no virile lovers here: the male customers are more often looking for comfort than lustful encounters. The novel offers a comic and poignant picture of the older man as emotionally needy, sometimes demanding and occasionally pompous. The only redeeming male character is a kind police-man who eventually marries Amy Doll. It is not a book that flatters the male sex.

Barbara posted the book to Greene on 8 December and nervously awaited the latter's reply. 'Oh I do hope he likes it and it will be published after all the disappointment', she wrote in her diary that day. Soon after Christmas, she received a letter from Greene in which he wrote:

> I am sorry. I don't care for *The House of Dolls*. It doesn't seem to me up to the standard of your other novels. To my mind something has gone wrong with the distancing – and it doesn't seem quite as cool. Of course this doesn't mean that a publisher could not be found because it's a great deal better than most novels which are published. Would you like me to forward the typescript to an agent?
>
> A happy New Year and don't curse me too hard for causing you all this trouble.
>
> Yours, Graham

On 10 January 1970, the day she received Greene's letter, Barbara wrote in her diary, 'Feel very sad. I was sure he would like it. He must wish he had left well alone and hadn't got in touch with me. Nothing to look forward to now.' The next day she wrote to John Johnson enclosing a copy of Greene's letter and alerting him to the fact that Greene would be posting the longer version of the novel to the agency – but that she wanted it shelved for the time being, having completely lost faith in it.

Apart from his criticism of Barbara's technique, Greene might not have liked the book's subject matter – older women of modest means who turn to prostitution to make ends meet; it perhaps appeared trivial or distasteful to him. Or he might have mistaken comic writing by a woman for frivolity. But beneath the wry comedy, Barbara was exposing the financial insecurity that faced many older women in the mid-twentieth century, especially those who had no pension and no husband to provide for them. John Johnson wrote in late January 1970: 'I think you have certainly improved it but if we didn't sell the earlier version I rather doubt if we shall sell this so I am putting it aside as you ask.'[29] Barbara was devastated by the rejection and saw it as the end of her writing career. Explaining this to her friend George Brendon in England, she wrote:

> When an author has had eight novels published and their publisher suddenly drops them it does make a bad impression on other publishers [...] Anyway, I've written all I have to say. I couldn't bare [*sic*] to spend every spare moment for at least two years typing, writing and revising a novel which would be unlikely to be published.[30]

The failure of what she now thought of as her last novel might well have been a factor in Barbara's growing enthusiasm to move down to Andalusia to live with Diana in San Roque. Why not embark on a new venture if there was no longer writing to shape her life and absorb her energy? And she loved El Almendral, 'The Almond Grove', a beautiful large house with a field of bee orchids behind it, surrounded by hundreds of almond trees. When Diana was away in the summer on her six-week travelling adventures, either cruising around Europe or on safari in India or Africa, Barbara would join Caroline and her family in San Roque, where they all stayed in the house and looked after Diana's many animals. Richard's work kept him in Barcelona but he would come for a week or so. Before they arrived in the summer of 1970 Barbara wrote to Diana, 'For the maid's information, I think the children's ages are – Eduardo 10 (huge eyes and lots of questions), Mariquita (tall and rather shy), Nuria 7 (small and frail-looking but very lively and intelligent). They all speak English as well as Spanish' (Eduardo was actually 12 and Mariquita 10). Although the children were not aware that their mother might inherit El Almendral, all the adults (with the exception of Richard, who still had some reservations about the move) were excited by the prospect of Diana's house becoming their family home.

Meanwhile, Diana was endlessly negotiating with lawyers, bank managers and her financial advisers about her plan to leave the house to Caroline. But she was also working to her own timetable. She currently employed a young Australian woman as a live-in companion. 'Jim', as she was known, was an excellent cook, a good driver and, most important of all, a cat-lover. Diana knew that Jim would be leaving in the near future and seems to have thought of Barbara as an unpaid replacement: 'About your coming here, I think the answer is when Jim goes, and that will depend on the progress of her love affair with the married Spaniard, or when her mother dies', she wrote in December 1970. She promised to give Barbara four months' notice of the date when she and Richard could move in and gave fair warning of her staff's idiosyncrasies, particularly those of her chauffeur and handyman, who was called Pepe, like Caroline's husband. But the same name was all they had in common. Diana's Pepe had a curling black moustache, which inspired the children to call him 'Pepe Bigotes' ('Pepe Moustache') – the nickname was a useful way of distinguishing him from their father in conversation. Small, dark, thin and excitable, this Pepe acted as overseer of the estate and, Diana wrote, was 'definitely too big for his boots, very ambitious and a fearful liar and mischief maker'. He could also, however, be 'quite charming and very useful'. Diana confessed, 'I do owe him something and cannot exactly throw him away.'[31] Such letters prompted Barbara to write to her friend George Brendon in England, 'I expect when we move down to our decaying mansion in Andalusia, we will look back on our peaceful and rather uneventful days in Fernando Puig with nostalgia. I feel we are due for some shocks down there.' She was right.

Notwithstanding this premonition, Barbara was keen to get on with the next stage of her life. She wanted to let their flat in Barcelona when they moved; it would give them an income and they could always move back if things didn't work out with Diana. But Richard thought they should sell it; he reasoned that they would need the capital to supplement his pension (he was now 62), especially if his career as a journalist proved hard to sustain once they were living in Andalusia. Caroline's husband, Pepe, now a banker in Madrid, thought that the value of the flat in such a desirable area would rise sharply over the next few years and urged him to reconsider, even flying to Barcelona to talk to him in person about it. But Richard was adamant that they should sell it. Like most of the financial decisions he had taken during his life, it was not a good one.

* * *

After renting a flat in Sitges for several weeks during the summer, Barbara and Richard returned to Barcelona in the early autumn to put their flat on the market and start making preparations for their new life in the south of Spain. 'We are going by boat with all our animals and the furniture by road and [it] will take several days', she wrote to John Johnson.[32] They sailed from Barcelona on 17 November 1972 and arrived in Algeciras the following day, to be met by Caroline and Pepe, who had offered to help them move into El Almendral. (Jim, Diana's companion, having had a terrible row with Pepe the handyman, had left in October and had reverted to her former profession as a journalist.) The arrangement was that Barbara and Richard would live rent-free with Diana, but would contribute towards the cost of food and electricity.

The house, which had fourteen rooms, was built in Moorish style around a large patio which had a central fountain and cloisters on each side. Originally a large farmhouse, it had been bought in the late nineteenth century by a Cuban general who had turned it into a gentleman's residence. It was sold

to the Brinton family in the early twentieth century, by which time it had
become a British enclave in Spain: 'The old gardener painted a Union Jack
and nailed it on one of the gates during the Civil War and wouldn't let
anyone pass', Barbara wrote to her friend George Brendon. Downstairs
there was a large formal dining room as well as three bedrooms; the upstairs
comprised a beautiful salon and several smaller rooms, one of which was
full of Rupert's musical instruments. In addition to the main kitchen, there
was a specially designated small kitchen with a 'cat fridge' that was always
jammed full with fresh (or not so fresh) fish and chicken. Diana's seven cats
probably ate better than some local children. Behind the house there was
an extension comprising a garage and harness room/donkey stable, over
which there was a large studio where Rupert used to work, as well as two
more small bedrooms. There were also some outbuildings, one of which,
the *casita* (a cottage) was rented out, as well as a large outdoor pool that
one of Diana's nephews had installed. Richard was to have a small bedroom
as his office and Diana suggested that Barbara should have Rupert's studio,
which had been doubling as a granary and storeroom, as her writing and
painting space. In her letter to George Brendon, Barbara related the challenge
that faced them as they cleared these and the rooms they were to live in:

> Kicking fifty or sixty years of junk out of the rooms we have taken over,
> broken polo sticks, photographs of Queen Mary and her ladies all in court
> dress at a meeting of some old hunt, broken lav seats and chairs, masses of
> old iron, hundreds of jam jars, old ladies' water colours and painting sets and
> lots of iron things that look like giants' chastity belts. The furniture took five
> days to get here from Barcelona, then the men arrived drunk ... We had paid
> for six men to unload, but only two came, one with bent knees and only one
> tooth – a wobbling gold fang ...

In the same letter she described the loveliness of the surrounding area:

> The scenery is beautiful and extraordinarily green at the moment with wild
> narcissi growing in the fields and the rivers and streams full and rushing. The
> garden is wild and like a Rousseau painting with cats (eight) instead of wild
> animals. In spite of the cold and bad weather it is filled with flowering trees
> and bushes, mimosa, oranges and lemons, the usual Spanish flowers, plumbago,
> bougainvillea and even orchids. Diana travels about the world collecting rare
> plants. There are masses of interesting birds flying around, while I have been
> writing a huge speckled vulture has flown past the window and a hawk has
> been circling around all day. The storks are just arriving. There are kingfishers
> and yellow wagtails along the stream. Now flocks of long-necked egrets are
> flying past.[33]

All was well to begin with. Since moving to Spain, Diana had become an
expert botanist and was good friends with Betty Allen, a world authority

on ferns, who lived nearby. Diana let much of the 43 acres of land around the house run wild so that she could study the plants that grew there and she had a large collection of specimens in her 'botany room', which were to be gifted to Seville University on her death. She enjoyed painting watercolours of plants and was preparing a book on the local flora of Algeciras. An ardent traveller and a voracious reader, she and Barbara enjoyed long conversations about plants, books and places. Diana occasionally took Barbara out in her car, with Pepe driving, to local beauty spots where they peered at birds through their binoculars and searched for rare wildflowers, trips which Barbara much enjoyed. Soon after her arrival, Diana made it clear that Barbara was to be responsible for meals, shopping and overseeing the servants. She also presented Barbara with a long list of instructions on how to look after her cats when she was away. Each cat had distinct personality traits and food dislikes, and they were to be pandered to accordingly. She clearly anticipated travelling more now that she had Richard and Barbara to look after the house and the animals. It was a sign of things to come.

Diana had many British ex-pat friends, most of whom lived near the port city of Algeciras, about 7 miles away on the Bay of Gibraltar. Once the worst of the winter had passed, there were endless long lunch parties held on the patio, sometimes for as many as 50 people. As she was a good cook, Barbara was often involved in the preparation of the numerous dishes, and initially she enjoyed socializing with Diana's friends and was always interested to see their homes when the return invitations arrived: 'Tomorrow we are driving along the coast to a great Wild Life party with famous naturalists and Prince Bernard of Holland and people like that', she wrote to Julian early in 1973.[34] Richard was still busy writing and returned occasionally to Barcelona to research commissioned articles. Barbara spent many hours typing them up and would reward herself with a swim in the pool afterwards. In January Richard was interviewing older residents for an article on how people from abroad who had settled in Spain were managing on their pensions (not very well, it turned out). This was soon to become a topic of burning personal interest for Barbara and Richard; the pound had recently been devalued and they quickly experienced problems with claiming Richard's full pension. Payment for his articles was irregular and seemed to result in disproportionate deductions to his state pension: 'It really means we are much poorer if Richard continues to write, but he can't do nothing. He only earns about £400 a year in odd sums and taxis cost him at least a hundred', Barbara wrote to Julian. This was an exaggeration; Richard was occasionally paid up to £200 for a week's work (about £3,150 today), as when the *Times Supplement* commissioned him to write an article on Barcelona's trade and the Spanish economy in early 1973. Nevertheless, they began to dip into their capital and to feel anxious about their financial future.

During 1973 Julian, who had by now left his wife Pat and had taken their son Nicholas with him, decided to visit Barbara, keen to see how his mother was adapting to her new life. After his separation from Pat, he had taken a commercial lease on an old bakery, part of which he converted into a large workshop. He advertised in the *Telegraph* for a housekeeper 'for a scruffy house in Twickenham. Own room with television and central heating. Masses of spare time'; in *The Times* the advertisement read 'Scruffy father and son need organizing. Opportunity to earn extra cash in studio workshop.' Jeanette, a young woman with a daughter called Mary aged 10, like Nicholas, answered.[35] Less than two weeks after she started working for Julian, he came home, exhausted after a long day's work, to be greeted by Jeanette offering him a gin and tonic. After supper, they made love; from then on, Jeanette became Julian's partner as well as housekeeper.

In April Julian suggested that they visit El Almendral, taking Nicholas with them (Mary would stay in England with her grandparents). Barbara encouraged the plan and reassured Julian that he would like both Diana – 'She is a bit like Edith Sitwell' – and Pepe, the chauffeur gardener: 'He has been very useful to us and he is good at mending and getting things done with care', she wrote. On their arrival, Julian and Jeanette were warmly greeted by Richard and Barbara, whom Jeanette remembers as 'quite petite, slender and very tanned, with a high, broad forehead and flashing eyes'.[36] Although Barbara was taken aback when Jeanette hugged her on arrival (Barbara always behaved rather formally when meeting someone for the first time), she soon warmed to her son's new partner, who was quick-witted and attractive with a pale complexion and long dark hair. The visit was a great success. Nicholas loved the house, writing in the Visitors' Book that he especially liked its 'wonderful ants' which marched up and down a wall in great numbers. It rapidly became clear, however, that Julian had reservations about Barbara and Richard's decision to end their days at El Almendral: 'He thinks life is rather full of problems for us here', she wrote in her diary on 22 April, adding that her son 'wants us to live in a cottage he has in Wiltshire, very pretty with central heating etc.' Julian's observation was astute, but Barbara was still optimistic about her future in Andalusia and enjoyed playing hostess to her family in Diana's large house. Caroline and her children came for a holiday in the early summer: 'Eduardo has two hours guitar lessons every day and has to do some homework but they manage to spend a lot of time in the pool. Pepe has made Nuria a little house which she loves and Mariquita draws and plays the piano which hasn't been touched for twenty years', Barbara wrote to Jeanette.[37]

Barbara, who always rose energetically to the challenge of making a new home, was overseeing the installation of a separate bathroom for herself and Richard (who loved to soak for hours in the bath) and had established some unusual plants and a banana tree in a small courtyard which Diana had given over to her. In early 1973 she was still much amused by the high tenor of emotional life in southern Spain and by the many small dramas that seemed to afflict the household. By this time, Diana had given her the responsibility of overseeing the cook and the maid. The latter had taken 12 days off over Christmas and was very unreliable; when she did appear, she never stopped eating, so Barbara was bracing herself to sack her. The food produced by the old cook, who could hardly see, was so dreadful that Barbara began to prepare separate meals for herself and Richard. 'The poor old cook', she wrote to Jeanette in the early summer of 1973,

> has the place full of ants and fries them with the food, sprinkles ant powder in all the dishes then serves the food all mixed with it. One night we couldn't eat our dinner, it tasted and smelt so dreadful and later we found she had used cement and glue, mixed with sawdust that Pepe had been working with in the kitchen. She thought it was breadcrumbs!

In the same letter Barbara described how fire had almost engulfed El Almendral. She had noticed late one afternoon that the hedge was alight and ran immediately for Pepe, who fortunately was at home, entertaining some friends. The fire spread rapidly:

> By this time there was a horrible roar and explosions and people had come running from the village. The little cottage in the garden was surrounded by flames and about twenty trees blazing away. Fortunately the worst part was by the swimming pool and we have all those tanks filled with water. I organized a chain of people with buckets and Diana was right in the front with a huge shovel banging out the flames. Pepe was almost fainting and his moustache went white with the shock. After about three hours we got it under control, still smouldering and glowing but not flaming [...] All through the fire there was a strange little old woman with her own hose, Wellington boots and a huge straw hat. She worked away as if she was a professional fire-fighter and Diana said 'Perhaps she is the Virgin Mary in disguise.' When things had calmed down a bit we thanked her and she said 'But it was me who started the fire.' She had lit a tiny fire in her back yard and a wind had suddenly sprung up and the fire had leapt over the road and roared up the hill.

Barbara took such trials and dramas in her stride and was trying to feel positive about the future, reassuring Julian in the same letter:

> We can't afford to move back to Barcelona and we both feel much more confident we can make a go of it and are a bit old for another upheaval [...] Don't worry about us. We are managing better every day [...] and at least we

can't complain that we are bored because there is always some drama going on, fire, hippies, cook going off her head or people thinking they have been poisoned and servants fighting.

However, by the end of 1973 Barbara was feeling less optimistic, and a note of regret began to creep into her letters to Julian. Neither she nor Richard could drive, so if they wanted to go to anywhere on their own, they either had to rely on Pepe to give them a lift or pay for a taxi. They were beginning to feel trapped. There had also been several rows over trivial matters. One of them had erupted over the fact that Barbara had transplanted some sweet peas into pots on the patio. Diana made some spiteful comments about her using the patio as a nursery, which prompted Barbara into immediate action: 'Although they were pretty heavy I marched out with them and started throwing them away, then couldn't face killing them after all my loving care and hid the rest in one of the orchards', she wrote to Julian.

Diana had always worried about her health even as a young woman; now she was a hypochondriac and was constantly arranging appointments with the doctor or optician, which she expected Barbara to attend with her. There were other tensions: when Caroline and her family arrived for a holiday, Diana vied with Barbara for Nuria's affection. She was particularly fond of Caroline's youngest daughter who, like her, was very interested in wild animals and plants, and would spend hours showing her pictures of them in books. She also occasionally gave Nuria small pieces of jewellery and generally behaved like an indulgent grandmother.[38] This irritated Barbara intensely; although Caroline was Rupert's daughter, *she* was her mother, not Diana; there was no blood tie between Diana and Nuria. There was also the ongoing problem of theft. Soon after her arrival, Barbara had 6,300 pesetas stolen from her cupboard, and whenever Caroline and her family came to stay, some of the children's clothes went missing. One day Caroline saw Pepe's daughter Dianita wearing Mariquita's best top in San Roque. 'All very nasty', wrote Barbara in her diary in July 1973. When she bought some towels for their new bathroom, they disappeared within a day. And in late October Barbara and Diana discovered from the household accounts that Pepe was fiddling the books. Barbara made a note in her diary that he was

> over charging in a most sinister manner, over double for everything he bought – 56 pesetas for 2 litros of milk, 40 pesetas for a kilo of apples instead of 15. Diana spoke about it and he was furious, then his fury turned to me. I always end up as the villain – 'Dona Barbara says ...' etc.

And although Diana had many friends and interests, she had become attention-seeking and somewhat cantankerous in her old age, as Barbara complained to Julian in a letter written in 1974:

She has rather a horror of domestic things and never speaks to the servants if she can avoid it. She has been very difficult about her food lately, worse than usual. The last time I was cook she said she felt sick all night afterwards as if I'd been trying to poison her. I'd taken so much trouble.

Barbara found that she often felt tired. As well as cooking some of the evening meals, she was now expected to oversee and organize the frequent large lunch parties at El Almendral and to help entertain Diana's house guests, who sometimes stayed for a week or two, not an easy task when Diana took a three-hour siesta in the afternoon and went to bed soon after 7 p.m. And when Diana left on her long trips abroad, she assumed that Barbara would run the household, which involved keeping the servants in check, looking after all the plants and animals and organizing meals and provisions. Barbara began to feel she was not much more than an unpaid housekeeper. She realized that she was growing nostalgic about their Barcelona flat with its central heating (El Almendral was a difficult house to heat in the winter) and confessed to Julian in a letter that she was becoming resentful of the small humiliations Diana inflicted on her. Richard was also growing miserable; he badly missed the buzz of Barcelona, particularly all the social and political contacts he had made there. As a respected foreign correspondent, he had often been invited to dinners and banquets where he had been able to glean useful information for his articles. That side of his life had now vanished, to be replaced by long liquid lunches with expats at which he had to make small talk and be polite to people he didn't much care for. He had also built up a reputation as a good translator in Barcelona, but that work dried up as soon as he left the city. Richard grew morose and tensions rose between him and Barbara and between Diana and Barbara. At the end of 1973 Barbara wrote in her diary, 'The years go so quickly now. I did not enjoy the last one at all. So many upsets, fires, servant problems, people dying …'

In early 1974, after several acid exchanges, Diana suddenly changed her will so that Barbara would inherit £5,000 worth of shares when she died (about £72,000 today). It was her way of apologizing to Barbara for her unreasonable behaviour and making it clear that she wanted Barbara and Richard to stay. But the promise of £5,000 when Diana died did not allay Barbara's concern about money. They had spent £400 (about £5,755 today) on the new bathroom and some bedroom cupboards, and living in San Roque was proving more expensive than living in Barcelona. It cost them £5 for a return taxi trip to Algeciras if they wanted to go shopping or have lunch out on their own; another expense they hadn't thought about was a monthly bill of £12 for Richard's newspapers and journals, posted from England. They were getting through their capital 'at an alarming rate',

Barbara wrote to Julian, adding, 'I do feel we should leave here and do something about earning some money before we are too old.' She went on:

> Richard will never return to England but he could manage on his own in Barcelona and there will be money coming for another three and a half years from the sale of the flat. It should be enough to keep him in a small hotel. I'd like to return to England where they would have to give me my full pension and buy and sell antiques. It means I'd have to start off from the beginning, just like I did when you were children, but there would only be myself to keep and if Nan can manage it, I can [...] At the moment I'm a non-person, just a reflection of Diana doing everything at her time, no friends of my own and no life. I can't even put on the radio or television because of Richard's work. I do so long for a kitchen of my own where I can cook when and what I like. I feel all my last years are being frustrated and wasted and although Richard is a dear person, he is a broken reed to depend on. I am sorry to say all this and please don't mention it to Chloe or Nan. I hate people knowing what a mess we have made of things. Don't worry either but just let me know if it is possible to return to England, but only if I can have my own little home in Kew or near you somewhere, but not on top of you. If it is impossible we may move to Sitges and rent a flat there but Richard will never earn enough to pay the rent etc. and I can't earn anything here [...] I hate telling you our troubles but feel I should write while we still have some money left.

As this letter suggests, the loss of her autonomy, her longstanding anxiety about falling into poverty, and the strain of living with Diana were all taking their toll on Barbara's marriage. Despite Richard's impractical nature and his hopelessness with money, the relationship had worked well in the past, especially when they had 'Pa' on hand to solve their financial crises. Barbara's ability to box and cox with London properties had also worked greatly to their advantage. But now she and Richard were not communicating well and their marriage was breaking down. Barbara recorded this painful state of affairs in her diary, writing on 24 May 1974 that 'We had a sort of quarrel, R looking all horrible and almost brutal, saying spiteful things. When we have got away from here perhaps we should part, we have so little in common anymore and don't feel the same about each other.' Feeling powerless, she was beginning to project her frustrations and resentments onto her husband, writing to Julian:

> We are just being miserable and cut off from life for nothing. Just a terrifying future in a rotting house surrounded by thieves. Richard and I would still see each other from time to time, but he costs so much to keep warm, sometimes surrounded by three gas fires all burning at once and the windows never opened and needs masses of taxis and new clothes all the time. I could never live simply with him. He is a dear gentle man, but far too expensive and unreliable to live with and never tells me anything until all the money has

gone. I haven't told him that I'm thinking of starting on my own in England, but if he can get back to his beloved Barcelona and we don't have a real break, he will be quite happy …

The last straw, so far as Barbara was concerned, was Diana suddenly announcing over a Sunday lunch in May that when her tenants moved out of the *casita* nearby, she was going to let Pepe the handyman and his family live there indefinitely. Barbara was horrified at the thought of Pepe and his noisy family turning the grounds into 'a real shanty town'; 'We want a peaceful old age', she added.[39]

Once the idea of returning to England took hold in Barbara's mind, it was not easily dislodged. By the early summer of 1974 she was determined that they would leave El Almendral and was asking Julian to help them. By this time Richard had agreed that it would be the best solution to their problems: 'To my surprise Richard now says he wants to come to England and might be able to get part-time work teaching Spanish, perhaps in London County Council evening schools or private classes', she wrote to Julian. Richard certainly did not want a separation and was happy to let Barbara hatch plans with Julian for their departure, despite his reservations about returning to cold damp winters in England. Once it became clear that Julian would indeed step in and do everything he could to help them, even buying them a house, Barbara began to look forward to what the return to England would offer: a house and garden, however small, that would be their own; freedom to earn some money; the ability to claim their full pensions, which had proved impossible in Spain; a free health service ('Doctors cost the earth here', she wrote to Julian) and free travel during the day. 'I might start writing again if I was happy and stimulated', she added. Apart from letters to family and friends, she had written very little while living in El Almendral, although, as is clear from her diary at this time, she had vague thoughts of writing a book called *The Return* or *Going Back*.

Barbara did not want to jeopardize the prospect of Caroline and Pepe inheriting El Almendral, but did want to make it clear to Diana, who would be setting off on a gorilla safari in Uganda in July and not returning until late August, that they intended to leave during the summer. She assumed that, as long as she handled their departure carefully, Diana would still want Caroline to inherit her home. Barbara was already anticipating the conversation she would have with Diana, and rehearsed it in her letter to her son:

I shall tell Diana that we can't stay because our capital won't last much longer and we need our full pension to help us out and that we must work. I shan't say anything to cause bad feeling so that Caroline and Pepe don't suffer. She will offer me a salary to stay on, but I'd rather be dead than have money from her. She would rub it in every day.

Barbara braced herself for a long conversation with Diana, who 'got in an awful state and said she knew she should have paid me a salary for all I do here', Barbara informed Julian by letter. But the conversation ended amicably, with Diana saying that she would advertise for a housekeeper/ companion during the summer. Barbara then wrote Diana a long letter, explaining in detail why they were leaving. It ended:

> Don't forget we love you and are very sad about all this but the future here would be unbearable and very frightening. If you were in our position I think you'd be off like a shot.

Diana replied immediately, opening her brief letter with, 'You have been getting worked up about nothing darling. Of course I want you to stay here', adding that she would happily reimburse Barbara for the cupboards and the new bathroom. She signed off,

> Anyhow, please don't talk about going – it makes me miserable. And don't do too much and then feel you are being used. I don't want you to do anything you don't want to do, and I can talk to the servants. As I said, I am lazy and let people do things for me, but I don't expect it.

But Diana's letter and all her reassurances were not enough to change Barbara's mind now that she knew she had somewhere to live in England. Julian had put in an offer on a Victorian cottage in Albion Road in Twick-enham, a pleasant suburban area in south-west London, but, on reflection, he decided it would be too expensive to renovate, so withdrew the offer. There was not enough time left to buy another house, so he and Jeanette moved out of 64 The Green in Twickenham, the large property which Julian was leasing commercially and had renovated. This comprised a shop within a large house (originally a bakery) and a stable block that Julian had converted into a big workshop for his scene painting and props business. He and Jeanette moved into a house on the Petersham Road in Richmond which belonged to the parents of one of Nicholas's school friends. The relocation of the father's job to Scotland had resulted in the whole family suddenly having to move north. The father invited Julian and Jeanette to live in their home rent free for a year; the quid pro quo was that they would look after the house and that Julian would loan him his Citroen Safari car for the journey to Scotland. During that year, Julian suggested, Richard and Barbara could live at 64 The Green.

They bought night flight tickets for 17 August, and it was arranged that Julian would drive down a few days earlier in a large van, and that he would transport their furniture, books and china back to England. Diana would be returning from her travels on 19 August, after their departure, so there would be no last-minute confrontations or recriminations. But despite such well-laid plans, Barbara was still in a highly anxious and nervous state in early August. 'I so hate being exposed to all Diana's whims and being a kind of slave ... If only I was dead and safe and resting', she wrote in her diary. She added a few days later, 'Don't know why I was so miserable, we shall be away and facing our new life soon and really our money worries are not so bad as usual.' She would indeed soon be back in England and everything went ahead as planned, although Julian was rather put out to find that his mother expected him to transport several heavy concrete troughs and urns for the garden as well as furniture and books. By the time they had finished packing the Commer van, which was designed to seat 12 people, it was heavily overloaded and swayed perilously from side to side as Julian drove through Spain and France. Leaving El Almendral with Richard on 17 August, Barbara took with her many plant cuttings, secreted in her clothes, and a poem she had recently written:

Sometimes I'm tired of being always abroad,
With the dusty palm trees swaying,
And the hot dry winds or the cold one,
With icy fingers savagely pinching.
The big brown eyes, and harsh foreign voices,
The sly smile or indifferent shrug.
The brilliant, burning sky and the dark, damp
Houses with the checked tiled floors
Of all colours.
The oil, garlic and flies, cockroaches, drains
And mosquitoes combined with tough meat.
The waiting for letters that never come.
The dark, dirty bars where the waiters sniff
And spit when not busy. The one-eyed cats.
I'm tired of all these things and being abroad
Where the birds don't sing the same.[40]

The long romance with Spain was finally over.

13

The return to England

Number 64 The Green in Twickenham, otherwise known as 'The Old Bakery', was a large corner building that, from the front, looked out on to a pleasant green with chestnut trees. In the summer months the gentle sounds of a cricket match sometimes floated through the windows, and each morning and evening saw dog owners exercising their pets. Formerly part of a large bakery complex dating from 1812, number 64 was now a self-contained house, in which a downstairs area served as a glass-fronted shop that Julian let to a local antique dealer. The house itself had three bedrooms, a living room, a kitchen, a bathroom and a small walled garden as well as a back yard with a gate to the side street. Julian's large workshop adjoined the house at the rear. Soon after their arrival in August 1974, Richard went off to stay with his old school friend Michael Norton for a few days and Barbara set to work with a paint brush, noting in her diary, 'I have nearly painted the whole house. I went mad and painted the passage and kitchen floors violet, deep purple – and it looks lovely.' Energized by home-making once again, she went on a spending spree and in September bought some material with a William Morris design for the living areas and some with sunflowers 'whorling round' for the bathroom. She also quickly stepped back into her former role as an antique dealer, buying small items from the shop downstairs and asking her sister Nan, who was still trading in central London, to sell them on: 'Nan has sold the brooch I paid £1 for £9 – eight pounds profit!', she wrote in her diary in late November. She also occasionally helped out in the studio when Julian was under pressure to meet a deadline for a commission or an exhibition and liked chatting to the artists he employed. And reclaiming the neglected small walled garden at 64 The Green was a challenge she enjoyed; ten months after their arrival Richard wrote in his diary:

> Barbara has done wonders with the garden [...] Now [it is] full of flowers and the carved stone urns we brought back from Spain are a blaze of colour. There is a grass-covered mound on one side and in this Barbara has now sunk a miniature pond of plastic material. It is to have fish when it has collected enough rain water and green to make it habitable for them.

But although they were relieved to have escaped El Almendral, Barbara and Richard had mixed feelings about their return to England, which had changed dramatically since they left in 1956. It was, Barbara wrote to Diana, 'more like Spain every day – shops opening and shutting when they feel like it, people being more cheerful and friendly than they used to be, everyone drinking wine, hardly anything delivered and a jolly sort of inefficiency'.[1] But they had changed too. They had left England as a party-going couple in their forties, but returned feeling rather frail and much older. Some of their former friends had died and some had moved abroad. Barbara even found herself thinking nostalgically about their flat in Barcelona. However, she gradually adjusted to living in England again, telling John Johnson, her agent, a few months after their arrival that 'Although we hate the climate we don't regret leaving Spain'[2] – and she particularly enjoyed walking in Richmond Park and exploring nearby Richmond, which was full of narrow streets, interesting small shops and elegant houses. There was no sign of any MI6 Watchers keeping an eye on Richard, presumably because his defection to Russia from Spain via North Africa seemed less likely now he had returned to England. And Barbara began to write again. In early December she sent an article entitled 'Sun isn't Everything' to Johnson, who responded enthusiastically with a plan to send it out to the Sunday newspapers. He had some good news too:

> I have also approached the BBC who earlier this year had formal plans to broadcast an adaptation of *The Vet's Daughter*, which is still on the cards. I have suggested to them that in the present circumstances you would be an ideal person to interview on *Woman's Hour* or something like that, and have asked them to get in touch with me.[3]

By Christmas Barbara had begun to relax and was feeling optimistic about the future. She had lost weight while living at El Almendral, presumably through anxiety, but in January 1975 she discovered she had put on a stone. She also found her mind was suddenly buzzing with ideas for stories and articles.

Meanwhile, Richard was looking for work. He was still writing articles about Spain for *The Times* and occasionally the *Economist*, but it was much harder to research them from England. He had applied unsuccessfully for a teaching post in nearby Kingston and had also failed to secure a job in journalism, specializing in English economics. Money was becoming tight and they agreed a new arrangement for housekeeping: Barbara would pay all the domestic bills and buy food from their combined pensions. Other expenses would be covered by money they earned through Barbara's writing income (although her royalties had been dwindling of late) and fees for any articles Richard managed to place. Having failed to find a job, Richard placed an advertisement in the *Richmond and Twickenham Times*, offering lessons in Spanish. By October he was teaching a married couple one evening a week at 64 The Green, and the following year he took on several more students. Anxious to keep in contact with all things Spanish, he sometimes travelled up to the Spanish Institute in London for lectures and the occasional cocktail party. He missed Spain, particularly Barcelona, more than Barbara, and he later returned there occasionally for news and information when researching an article. In the summer of 1977 he stayed in a hotel in the city for a few weeks while Spain held its first General Election since 1936. Barbara wrote to him, passing on Caroline's irreverent view of Spanish politics: 'She was very amusing about the election. The Communists sold such becoming red scarfs that even the Fascists were wearing them. She says you must get in touch with the Falange Autentico who are followers of Primo de Rivera with anarchist ideas!'[4] Despite the jokey tone of this remark, it seems likely that it contained a kernel of truth. Like Graham Greene, who described himself at the age of 53 as 'an anarchist',[5] Richard remained intellectually a radical, although both he and Barbara voted Liberal once they returned to England.

Barbara kept in touch with Spain through her correspondence with Diana, who reported regularly on the small dramas of life at El Almendral, which included the recent birth of a child to Pepe's daughter Dianita when no one (including Dianita herself apparently) had known she was pregnant. Diana called at 64 The Green in September 1975 en route to Australia, and had lunch with Barbara and Richard; 'it all went very well', Barbara wrote in her diary. If Diana was puzzled by their decision to leave the beautiful El Almendral to return to much more modest accommodation in England, she did not say so. She also saw Barbara and Richard in the summers of 1976 and 1977, but then there was a three-year break before she visited England again. In August 1980 Barbara and Richard went to Chelsea to meet Diana and her friend Gertrude. 'Diana friendly but very fragile (she's about 83) and far away and tiny – about 4 foot 10 inches ... It was quite a shock meeting [her] after three years. Our lives have been so close at times ...', Barbara wrote in her diary that month.

Early in 1975 Barbara and Richard decided to add a dog to their household (they already had a canary). It was a doomed project. At different times they adopted two small elderly poodles with rotten teeth from the RSPCA dogs' home, but both had to be put down within the year: one proved to be aggressive and the other developed cancer. That failed project aside, Barbara was enjoying life; she was feeling more energetic than she had for some time. She took up oil painting again and resurrected some of her old canvases in order to varnish them. Their social life picked up when she and

Richard began to make contact with some of Richard's former Foreign Office colleagues, including Desmond Pakenham. Lunch guests from other circles included Brian Haughton, the ceramics specialist, and Giles Playfair, the author, and his wife Ann. It was stimulating to be mixing with such company again. And, to her delight, Barbara was now able to get about on her own: Julian gave her some money to buy a bike so that she could cycle the two miles or so between 64 The Green and Petersham Road, where he was living with Jeanette. They agreed that she would repay him by maintaining the Petersham garden and decorating the house. The bike gave her a measure of independence that she treasured after being reliant on other people for lifts at El Almendral. She cycled frequently to the local library, piling books into the basket on the front of her bike. She decided she would start collecting first editions of Mrs Henry Wood, the prolific and popular Victorian author, and asked Nan to look out for them. She also scoured the local shops for books, much to Richard's amusement, as he noted in his diary in May 1975:

> This afternoon she went off to a shop in the high street that has furniture displayed on the pavement along with brass pots and pans, china, statuettes and other oddments. Within three-quarters of an hour she staggered back carrying two shopping bags loaded with solidly bound, Victorian looking books – well over a dozen of them. She had found a set of one of her favourite novelists – Mrs Henry Wood – including 'East Lynne'. Some of the pages were still uncut, and they were contemporary editions; they may not be first editions, but they will keep her happy for some time.

A conservative and Catholic writer, Mrs Henry Wood might seem a strange choice for Barbara, but as authors they had some things in common, including an interest in the supernatural – and Barbara admired the Victorian novelist's ability to produce page-turners, writing in her diary a few years later, 'What fun they are and so satisfying.' During 1975, her taste as eclectic as ever, she was also reading books by Muriel Spark, Agatha Christie, Anthony Hope ('an extraordinary book about India'), Blackmore's *Lorna Doone* ('I loved it once but it seems very tedious now'), Flaubert, Joyce Cary, Nancy Mitford and Solzhenitsyn, among others.[6]

Barbara was now keen to establish a writing routine; she was producing short stories but also thinking that she might try writing another novel. There were regular interruptions however; typing up Richard's articles for commercial journals such as *The Banker* often took up three or four days at a time. Family matters also claimed much of her attention: she frequently saw Julian, Jeanette and Nicholas, and Jeanette's daughter Mary. The two children sometimes came to stay for a few days at 64 The Green – although

Barbara refused to accommodate their pet, a black goat called Carbonella, which had been smuggled in from Spain under Jeanette's long skirt after a holiday there one year. Caroline and Pepe, who were still living in Madrid, came to England in the summer and stayed in a friend's Victorian mansion flat in Hampstead Heath for several weeks. They brought with them presents of brandy, olive oil and perfume. Their children were growing up: Eduardo, now 17, had taken up smoking and was – like many adolescents – silent in the company of older relatives. Mariquita, aged 15, 'looked beautiful in a long green dress', and Nuria, 12 years old, was still young enough to enjoy dancing about in front of her aunt and uncle, competing for attention, as Barbara wrote in her diary on 2 July 1975.

And then there were Barbara's sisters. Kathleen and her husband Teddy Catford now lived in Maidenhead in Berkshire and Barbara saw them only occasionally, having to rely either on Julian or on visitors such as her son-in-law Pepe to give her a lift there. But Nan often came over for lunch and they went to art exhibitions in London together; in October they saw the Sydney Nolan exhibition at the Marlborough Fine Art Gallery – 'strange and amusing but a bit flashy' – and some Russian paintings at the Royal Academy: 'On the way home I kept thinking I could see domes and snow and ordinary buildings looked Russian', Barbara wrote in her diary. Both she and Nan were deeply worried about their youngest sister, Chloe, who had fallen ill early in 1975. It transpired that she had a brain tumour; she had undergone a mastectomy some years previously and the cancer had now reappeared. The prognosis was not good. When Barbara returned to England in 1974, Chloe was not very mobile but she was enjoying having painting lessons at home. Her decline thereafter was rapid: by the following spring she had become an invalid who could hardly talk. When Barbara visited Chloe in Chelsea, she could see that she needed a nurse, but her husband John would not contemplate having one in the house. The old affectionate rivalry between the sisters had evaporated completely and any rifts had been forgotten; Barbara felt only compassion for Chloe, writing in her diary in April, 'They have everything and a beautiful house and garden, and money, good looks, but nothing but misfortune ... was so sad to see Chloe. She knows she will never get better.'

October brought more sadness: Pat, Julian's wife, killed herself by taking a massive overdose of drugs with alcohol and putting her head in a plastic bag, then tying a cord round her neck. She had choked on her own vomit. 'How could she do such a thing, poor woman, she must have had a horrible death', Barbara wrote in her diary. Julian was asked to identify the body in the mortuary and, at the inquest, to give evidence on Pat's state of mind at the time of her suicide. Barbara and Richard temporarily took Nicholas under their wing. The whole family was badly shaken by Pat's suicide. To take their mind off the tragedy, a few weeks later Barbara and Richard adopted a mild-natured greyhound from the RSPCA dogs' home. 'She is beautiful', Richard wrote in his diary, 'with a silky light-brown coat and very gentle, and we have named her Petra. Her gentleness compensates for the fact that she is really rather large.' Barbara enjoyed walking Petra along the towpath, 'which, I like to think, must be very much the same as it was when Virginia Woolf walked there with her dog sixty years ago'.[7] Petra settled into her new home happily and was to give them pleasure for seven years; she was later immortalized as the 'aged and gentle greyhound' belonging to Bernard and Gertrude Forbes in *The Juniper Tree*.[8]

On the first day of 1976, Barbara wrote in her new diary,

> Now another year has come. The last one wasn't too bad. The worst things are Chloe being so ill, money worries and disappointments with my writing, dogs dying, the goat breaking its neck, Pat committing suicide. The good things were the lovely summer and all the flowers in the garden, Caroline and the children coming, having English books and television, not being foreigners.

*   *   *

The following year brought the same mixture of light and shade. Barbara had grown fond of Nicholas, her grandson, who often came to stay at 64 The Green for a few nights. One of their treats was trips to the cinema; in February the Disney comedy *The Absent Minded Professor* reduced them to tears of laughter, and in May they cowered in their seats when watching *Jaws*. They had fun together: both loved board games and 12-year-old Nicholas invariably beat his grandmother at Scrabble, despite Barbara's facility with language. But there were also sorrows. Chloe was rapidly deteriorating and Barbara was shocked by her sister's appearance when she visited in February, writing in her diary, 'She is so fearfully ill it is dreadful to see her.' The once beautiful Chloe now looked 'about 80 and chokes and cries … I can hardly believe anyone can live in such a state.' By mid-March she and Nan were alarmed not only by their sister's physical state but also by her husband's behaviour. Barbara usually wrote only a few lines each day in her diary, but a fuller entry in mid-March suggests how anxious she had become:

> For a long time we have thought John was not always kind to her, perhaps even cruel, but he never, never leaves us alone with her. She seems so unhappy and afraid, but can't communicate, speak and hardly write. Margery [John Faraday's sister] suddenly phoned Nan although they are not good friends and, crying all the time, said John is terribly cruel to Chloe and says fearful things about her, that she is an animal etc. She said she was so ashamed and frightened of her brother. She couldn't tell us how dreadful John was. Nan

phoned Chloe's doctor about ten times before she found him and feeling very nervous told him we were not happy about Chloe and what Margery said. The doctor said he was very worried himself and had heard dreadful things from the woman who rents the basement flat below. He is planning to get Chloe out of the house even if it means a court order. He thinks she is at risk of John killing her. [John] was so considerate and loving the last time I went but has said some rather cruel things on the phone since.

It is difficult to know now what could have prompted John to behave in such a way; there is no evidence of abuse in the marriage before Chloe fell ill. Indeed, family members were confident that John adored his wife. Perhaps she had become incontinent and he was finding it difficult to cope both practically and emotionally with her decline. Possibly he had entered into a state of denial about the imminence of her death, offloading his sense of impotence and anger in rages against his wife. Or perhaps he was not the ideal husband he appeared to be to outsiders and was a verbal abuser behind closed doors. Whatever the cause, and whatever the truth of the matter, both Barbara and Nan were much relieved when John finally agreed to have a live-in nurse to look after Chloe, who was now confined to her bed and unable to communicate. She no longer wrote on her notepad or even listened to the radio, and when Barbara visited her sister in late May, she recorded in her diary how horrified she had been to see her reduced to making 'terrible groans and noises all the time'.

Although she felt miserable about her sister's illness, at the same time Barbara was cheered by a promising revival of interest in her books. In late March *The Vet's Daughter*, adapted by the playwright Shirley Gee and directed by David Spenser, was broadcast in four episodes on BBC Radio 3, with Julie Hallam playing Alice. With a few reservations, Barbara thought well of it: 'It was very good on the whole, quite chilled my blood', she wrote in her diary, adding, 'A little too much horror at the beginning. The young man was rather poor. The father played by Nigel Stokes was particularly good. Alice talked in the sad child-like voice I expected her to. Gwen Ffrangcon-Davies wailed too much I thought.' Barbara wrote to Shirley Gee to thank her for adapting the novel for radio, and the playwright replied, 'I was so happy to hear from you, and that you enjoyed the play. I loved *The Vet's Daughter* and felt angry that such a book should just disappear.'[9] The play was repeated in June on Radio 4 in the Monday Night Theatre slot, having been flagged up by Jeremy Rundall in his 'Radio Choice' column in the *Sunday Times* as 'funny' and 'slightly surreal'. Barbara received a cheque for £122 (almost £1,220 today) from her agent as fee for the Radio 3 broadcast of her novel and £176 (£1,758 today) for the Radio 4 transmission. She was delighted, writing in her diary, 'I am so pleased – I would so like to build up a little money in the bank. Now all I want is for

The Vet's Daughter to be made into a film.' John Johnson had more good news: although he had not been able to place Barbara's article 'Sun isn't Everything', the BBC had decided to serialize *A Touch of Mistletoe* on Radio 4's 'Woman's Hour' in October and were offering a fee of £289 (almost £3,000 today). 'The money will come in very useful because my old Spanish washing machine has died and after a fortnight of washing clothes in the bath I've ordered a new one', she wrote in April 1976.[10]

Early in the summer of that year, Julian suggested that Barbara and Richard might like to move into a modern Wates house that he was buying in Ashburnham Road in Ham, a pretty area near the river Thames and close to Richmond. He assured them that it would be more comfortable and peaceful than 64 The Green and easier to look after. Barbara balked at the idea; she had always preferred to live in old houses (and indeed, feeling nostalgic, had recently walked past her former home in Milborne Grove, pleased to see that the willow tree she had planted there years ago was thriving). But she promised Julian she would go and look at it. She was pleasantly surprised. It was a neat modern house, close to the green space of Ham Riverside Lands on the Thames and not far from Richmond Park and Ham House, a beautiful seventeenth-century building owned by the National Trust. It also had a pretty enclosed garden, ideal for their greyhound Petra and their recently acquired cat, George.

Julian, for his part, was keen to move back into 64 The Green because his love life had suddenly become complicated. Jeanette was not sure if she wanted to continue living with him and she certainly did not want to marry again. The relationship was becoming sour and Julian turned his attention elsewhere. He had only recently finished working on props for the *Star Wars* film, helping design and produce the storm trooper helmets, and was now approached to provide the props and scenery for a puppet show series to be made by Tyne Tees Television. A young, dark-haired puppeteer called Nicola asked him for a lift north in exchange for helping to unload the van on arrival. The hotel was old and dingy, the weather was hot and Julian's window refused to open. He ended up in Nicola's room, where the window opened easily. The next morning the manager complained about Nicola's cries of delight during the night and they were asked to leave. It was the beginning of an intense but short-lived relationship in which both partners were on the rebound from recently failed affairs.

Barbara and Richard travelled to Barcelona for three weeks on 11 June, mainly so that Richard could meet old contacts and collect information on Spain's political and business worlds for future articles, one of which, 'Catalonia a Magnet for Spanish Workers', appeared in *The Times* in August. While there, they received a letter from Nan saying that Chloe had died in St Thomas's Hospital in Lambeth on 23 June.

Returning from Spain in early July for Chloe's funeral, they found Jeanette sleeping in the workshop. She wanted to resume her relationship with Julian, she said, and was threatening to kill herself if he married Nicola. She promised that she was now 'a reformed character', but Barbara was not convinced. She wrote to John Johnson that there was

> a lot of drama going on between two girls who both want to marry my son and he can't make up his mind which one he wants. They both work in the studio, one like an overblown gypsy and the other a General's daughter who drives a powerful motor-bike almost undressed, otherwise she is a gentle, clever girl. We like her very much but think the gypsy will win.

On 9 July Barbara and Richard flew out to Spain again for another three weeks, for a holiday this time, not quite knowing whether they would be living at 64 The Green when they returned or whether they would be moving into the Wates house in Ham. Once back in Twickenham, they found that Julian had moved out of the Petersham Road house and that he and Nicola were now living in the office room above the shop at 64 The Green. Barbara felt awkward in Julian's house now that he had resumed living there – especially as he announced that he wanted to marry Nicola. In early August Barbara and Richard moved out of 64 The Green and into the house in Ham: it seemed the best solution all round. Despite her initial reservations, Barbara came to love the house in Ashburnham Road, writing in her diary in August that the area was 'very quiet, like the country, lovely walks and wild flowers'.

Late summer brought news that, having holidayed in Tenerife, Caroline and Pepe had just bought a house on the island and had decided to live there permanently. Barbara was sad that she would see less of her daughter and her three grandchildren, although she did manage to travel out to visit them twice over the next few years, each time leaving Richard an elaborate list of instructions about how to care for Petra the dog, George the cat and their two budgerigars. She and Richard celebrated their 31st wedding anniversary on 29 August by buying a wisteria to plant in their new garden. She also made Richard a special cake to mark the day, as she did every year for his birthday in October and for their anniversary in August. She was a good baker and made a cake at least once a week, holding a gin and tonic in one hand and a wooden spoon in the other. In the early autumn she and her sisters visited John Faraday fairly frequently, concerned about his mental state following Chloe's death. Barbara noted in her diary in September that, while she and Kathleen sorted out their dead sister's clothes, John – a man who had lived through many violent events in the Middle East – just 'sat on Chloe's bed and cried'.

*   *   *

Further good news about Barbara's work followed in 1977, when Sandy Wilson – best known for his musical *The Boyfriend* – approached Barbara's agent with a proposal to adapt *The Vet's Daughter* for the stage. Barbara was thrilled and John Johnson arranged that she would collaborate as an adviser on the script for a reasonable fee. In November she eagerly read Wilson's stage version of *The Vet's Daughter*, which now carried the title *The Clapham Wonder*, writing to Johnson in December that she thought it was 'a very clever adaptation indeed'. The prospect of the income it might raise kept her cheerful during yet another period of anxiety about money. In March she received the agreement for the production of *The Clapham Wonder*: 'I must sign it then I get £100. Very useful at the moment for the electricity bill', she wrote in her diary. She took Nicholas to see a production of Sandy Wilson's musical *The Boyfriend*, which was coincidentally playing at the Richmond Theatre, and looked forward to a trip to Canterbury to meet the cast of *The Clapham Wonder* and have lunch with Wilson. Barbara hoped that the musical, directed by David Carson, would bring her fame and fortune.

The Clapham Wonder was also a useful distraction from her worries about Julian's love life, which was soon to become even more complicated. Faced with a contract from the Ideal Home and the National Trust to produce a model village featuring about thirty of their properties, complete with river and a cricket match, Julian needed more staff quickly and employed several artists on short-term contracts. Jeanette – who had spent some time in the Seychelles trying to set up a drama school there – returned to England in August 1977, the project having failed, and suggested to two sisters who were looking for studio work that they might contact Julian. One of these sisters was Sally Fletcher, a talented scene painter. She was so good that Julian kept her on and they soon became lovers. Julian had married Nicola in Richmond in July, but by the end of the summer it was clear that the marriage was threatened by Julian's affair with Sally. Nicola became pregnant in September but she realized that her marriage was disintegrating. She and Julian separated in November, much to the dismay of Nicola's parents, who were worried about their daughter's future as a single parent. Nicola put down a deposit on a three-bedroomed end-of-terrace Victorian house at the other end of The Green and Julian made her a director of his company with a very generous salary so that she would be able to pay off the mortgage relatively quickly.[11]

Barbara was deeply troubled by these developments and became very anxious. She assumed that Julian would need to sell the house in Ashburnham

Road, where she and Richard had settled happily, in order to honour his financial commitment to Nicola. On 8 April 1978 she wrote in her diary, 'Cold, felt depressed and worried'. Relations with Julian, with whom she usually got on very well, became strained. Although she tried to understand why Julian had found his relationship with Nicola suffocating, her son's behaviour reminded her painfully of her first husband's attitude to marriage and children, and she wrote to Julian trying to explain why she was so distressed: 'The reason I'm particularly upset is that John wasn't at all kind to me when I was having you and I felt so lonely and defenceless. Now history is repeating itself …'[12] Having convinced herself that Julian would soon be selling 221 Ashburnham Road, Barbara wrote to his secretary in mid-April in order to clarify who would pay some outstanding bills on their home, ending her letter plaintively:

> We may sell all our things and return to Spain or go into an old people's home in Kent – a kind of charity for distressed gentle-people started in Victoria's time where they have a croquet lawn but no dogs allowed and church on Sunday. I was so happy about my play and now all these horrors have come.[13]

But Barbara's worries about her future were needless: Julian's business had become highly successful, with a turnover of about £1,000 a day (about £8,570 now) before deductions. In the spirit of Price, he also enjoyed restoring and selling vintage cars and had recently made a healthy profit on a Ford Thunderbird. He did not need to sell 221 Ashburnham Road and reassured Barbara that she would not have to move.

About this time Barbara began to draft a new novel, to be based on her return to England, writing in her diary,

> I've an idea for a book – 'Waiting'. Elderly people retiring to a new little house on a garden estate waiting to die but things keep happening. They feel even more intensely than when they were young. Some good things happen, some exciting and some almost horrifying.

John Johnson wrote to tell her that Michael Joseph would like to see what she had written so far and might be interested in publishing it – and anything else she had written previously that remained unpublished. Barbara replied in April:

> I'd rather Michael Joseph saw a rough draft of the whole book than a sizeable chunk. This will take some time because I'm usually rather a slow writer because I like to live in my books. It would be marvellous if Michael Joseph took three books at once. Do you think it a good idea to change the title of *Mr Fox eats his Grapes* to just *Mr Fox*? Not so clumsy. I am so looking forward to going to Canterbury to see a rehearsal of *The Clapham Wonder* on 18th, also to meeting Sandy Wilson.

The play opened at the Marlow Theatre in Kent on 26 April 1978 and Barbara and Richard travelled by train to Canterbury for the first night. The weather was atrocious: thick fog made their journey difficult and they were worried about getting home afterwards. 'I do feel nervous: I so hope it is a success and comes to London', she wrote in her diary before they set off. After she had seen the performance she added,

> I was fairly pleased with the musical although it guyed my book in a way. The acting [was] rather poor – Lucy and Alice were good; Rowlands overdone, Mrs Rowlands inaudible. We had to leave before the curtain came down. I'd so longed to go in front of everyone calling 'Author'. I don't think the play will come to the West End though.

She was right. The reviews in the papers over the next few days were not good. Although critics praised the acting talents of Jan Todd (who played Alice) and Anita Dobson (who played Rosa Fisher), they gave the musical a pasting. In the *Guardian*, Nicholas de Jongh dismissed the production as 'sheer risible melodrama', and Irving Wardle in *The Times* noted acerbically that it was 'the first musical I have seen containing a duet with a deaf mute'. Eric Shorter in the *Daily Telegraph*, while praising the production as well acted and well sung, declared that, unlike its main character, it never got off the ground, and wondered whether the aim was 'a literal melodrama'.[14] 'I rather I wish I could vanish', Barbara wrote in her diary. The production closed after a three-week run on 20 May: 'Last night of *The Clapham Wonder*. Have heard nothing about it since the first night. Feel depressed about it. My last chance to earn any money', she wrote in her diary. She did her best to put the experience behind her but it came back to haunt her in a spiteful piece in *The Times* in October:

> We have, however, decided to awarded the PHS Challenge Silver Earplug for stultifying boredom to Barbara Comyns Carr of Richmond for a last line which suggests to us a play of unparalleled dreadfulness, of an audience snoring soundly in the stalls and fighting for the fire exits in the balcony, of a performance so wooden that bits of scenery could be used in place of actors, of a script so leaden that the rule book of the Associated Society of Locomotive Engineers and Firemen would read like Oscar Wilde in comparison.[15]

*   *   *

During the summer other developments claimed much of Barbara's attention: Nicola and Julian's baby, George Gustav, was born on 22 June 1978, and the following day Barbara went to see her new grandson: 'He really is beautiful, so compact and well made', she wrote in her diary. A few days later, Nicola went to stay with her parents in Hartley Wintney in Hampshire,

taking George with her. She lived with them for three months, Julian visiting
her there occasionally; on her return to Twickenham, George went to a
nursery so that Nicola could return to working full-time in Julian's studio.
Over the next few years Barbara would help out occasionally, stepping in
at short notice to look after him if Nicola had to produce some artwork to
a deadline. Barbara met Sally Fletcher, Julian's new girlfriend, for the first
time in January 1979. Julian had driven to London from South Wales with
her in an open-top car and on arrival Sally was very cold; Barbara jokingly
referred to her for a while as 'that woman of ice', but soon found that she
could not help liking her son's new partner, despite disapproving of his
behaviour. Intelligent, creative and candid, Sally soon won Barbara over.

About the same time, Richard was taken on as a house manager at the
Richmond Theatre, a beautiful turn-of-the-century building on Richmond
Green. The work was way below his capabilities, but by 1978 any hope of
obtaining a post as a lecturer or translator had evaporated. Richard was
now 70 and not in good health; his doctor had diagnosed hardening of the
arteries as the cause of occasional pains in his chest. Barbara was aware of
his growing frailty but reassured herself that being a theatre house manager
was not a physically demanding job – and the money usefully supplemented
their small income. Richard found the work tiring though, especially when
he went in for a matinee and then had to stay for the evening performance,
which meant a 12-hour day. His job also affected Barbara's routine: they
now had their main meal at lunchtime because Richard had to get to the
theatre well before the evening performance started. But she was pleased
that Richard liked the work; he enjoyed watching the productions and his
courteous and gentlemanly manner made him popular with theatregoers.
And one of the perks of the job was free tickets, so Barbara often took
Nicholas or Nan to see plays that caught her eye.

Despite such continuing claims on her time, Barbara managed to finish
the first draft of *Waiting* by early March 1979 and, after some revisions,
submitted it to her agent at the end of April. She was also working on a
'musical play' entitled *Orphan Island*, the 'whole thing to be like a gentle
pantomime', with music dating from 1855 to 1920, but 'not music hall
music', she wrote in her diary. Perhaps the failure of *The Clapham Wonder*
had made her think she could do better herself. John Johnson, now retired
but still keeping contact with some of his authors, had recently sent Barbara
a letter informing her that Virago might reprint one of her books: 'the terms
are rather modest but I think it would be good to have the book back in
print [...] What do you think?'[16] Barbara thought it was a very good idea
indeed. Andrew Hewson, Johnson's former assistant who had taken over
the literary agency in 1977, sent *The Vet's Daughter* and *Out of the Red,
Into the Blue* to Carmen Callil in the hope that she might include them in

the Virago Modern Classics series. She liked *The Vet's Daughter* very much. On 1 June 1979 Barbara and Carmen Callil signed an agreement stipulating that the novel would be published within two years. Virago would offer an advance of £250 (about £1,700 today), £100 of which was payable on signature of contract, the balance on publication. The agreement also contained a royalty clause which offered 7½ per cent on both hardbacks and paperbacks.[17] Soon after it had been signed, Callil asked Barbara to write an introduction to the Virago edition of the novel, giving an outline of her life. Barbara stalled, explaining that she found that sort of task difficult, but Callil was persuasive and Barbara eventually settled down to writing the introduction in November.

Carmen Callil had founded Virago Press in 1973 as a feminist publishing company that published books only by women. The idea behind the Virago Modern Classics series with its distinctive green covers, launched by Callil in 1978, was to rediscover and celebrate women writers and to challenge the conventional idea of a classic novel. Within a year, Virago had brought several women writers back into print. The first book in the series was Antonia White's *Frost in May*, originally published in 1933; novels by Sylvia Townsend Warner and Christina Stead soon followed. Graham Greene knew Antonia White through working with her during the Second World War in the Foreign Office Political Intelligence Department and, as a director of Eyre & Spottiswoode, had persuaded the company to reprint *Frost in May* in 1948.[18] He was therefore very pleased to see that Virago had just reissued it and wrote to Callil in September 1980 from his home in Antibes on the Côte d'Azur. He suggested that she might consider publishing Barbara Comyns' books, although he discreetly left out any mention of their correspondence during 1969–70 about *The House of Dolls*. Unaware that Callil had already decided to include *The Vet's Daughter* in the Modern Classics list, he warmly recommended Barbara's work:

Dear Carmen Callil,

I read your article on the Virago Press in the *Times Literary Supplement* with great interest. Can I persuade you to investigate the novels of Barbara Comyns? When I was a publisher just after the war I published her first two books, *Sisters by a River* (a very funny book described by Elizabeth Bowen as 'a curiosity of literature, a blend of the gruesome and the comic') and *Our Spoons Came from Woolworths*. This was at Eyre and Spottiswoode in 1947 and 1950. When I ceased to be a publisher I got Heinemann's to take on her books and they published an excellent one, *The Vet's Daughter*, in 1959 and *The Skin Chairs* in 1962.

Perhaps of all these books, *The Vet's Daughter* is the best. I notice that I contributed a quotation to the jacket which may of course put you off reading the book, but here it is: 'The strange off-beat talent of Miss Comyns and that innocent eye which observes with childlike simplicity the most fantastic or the most ominous occurrence, these have never, I think, been more impressively exercised than in *The Vet's Daughter*'. I am ashamed to say that I know nothing of what happened to her after this time. Her husband was a colleague of mine in MI6, Richard Comyns Carr, and I believe he went to live in Spain. I do urge you to take a look at these books perhaps beginning with *The Vet's Daughter* and going backwards.

> Yours sincerely,
> Graham Greene.

PS If you have difficulty in obtaining the books either from Heinemann or Eyre & Spottiswoode I will bring them to London on one of my visits.[19]

Callil replied warmly with the news that Virago would be releasing its edition of *The Vet's Daughter* in January 1981, adding:

> It is of course due to you that we are – her agent sent it to me with a strong recommendation from you some time ago; this meant it went immediately on the top of my reading pile. I read it and loved it [...] I know your interest in her work will give her a great deal of pleasure. And I'm enclosing the cover. Walter Crane may seem an odd choice but I thought it summed up her ending on the common rather well.
>
> If you have any other suggestions, I hope you'll write again; anything you suggest would get instant attention – the seven of us who work here have admired – and read – you from afar for many years.[20]

Meanwhile, Richard had managed to place an article on the Spanish economy with *The Banker* for a fee of £180 (about £920 today). With that, and with Barbara's advance from Virago for *The Vet's Daughter*, they were in the clear financially again, at least for the time being. Barbara was hopeful that the publication of *Waiting*, which her agency had sent to Virago, would bring in more money. But in August she heard from Andrew Hewson that Virago had refused it and had also rejected *Out of the Red, Into the Blue* for inclusion in the Modern Classics list. Hewson enclosed the rejection letter from Callil and Barbara replied:

> I agree with Carmen Callil. 'Out of the Red' isn't a very interesting book. This is partly due to three-quarters of the book being true and my fear of libel; also it is dated because Ibiza is completely different now and very commercialised. The novel I would love to have re-published is 'Who was Changed and who was Dead'. Unfortunately the day it came out John Betjeman gave it a really vicious review, calling it a 'horror comic' amongst other things. He was really upset about it and, as the review was syndicated and he was very popular at the time, it did a lot of harm. There were about four or five good reviews later, but they didn't help much. I'd like 'The Skin Chairs' to be re-published too. It had marvellous reviews and I thought my fortune was made; but it didn't sell well. It might now. Fashions in books seem to change so quickly. I

hope 'The House of Dolls' will eventually be published because I so enjoyed writing it.[21]

Another month brought another rejection: Hewson had sent *Waiting* to Michael Joseph, but John Johnson wrote in September to say that although he liked the book, he thought it would be difficult to promote, and had finally turned it down. James Michie, now at The Bodley Head, also rejected it in October, explaining why in a letter to Johnson:

> I was glad you sent me Barbara Comyns's new book because I have always liked her writing. *Waiting* was no exception: I found it very pleasant reading and was moved both by the gaiety and the lack of self-pity. It is therefore with much more than conventional regret that I have to say I do not feel we can offer to publish it. Hers is a frail, highly individual talent which could just flourish in publishing conditions ten years ago, but which, I fear, would have a small sale and some respectful reviews in hardback nowadays, and no paperback sale. These are brutal words, and I am sure you have heard them before: I am only sorry that it has to be me saying them to you – and to her.[22]

Having read Michie's letter, Barbara wrote to Johnson in October, asking him to put her novel away for the time being, adding:

> There may be a revival of interest in my books in the not so distant future. Remember Barbara Pym! All the same, I shan't be writing any more books. It is time I retired now I'm seventy. I couldn't face starting on Chapter One again.

Having decided to abandon fiction, Barbara returned to her musical play, on which she had made little progress. She was also finding it hard to write the introduction for the Virago edition of *The Vet's Daughter*, but Carmen Callil gently cajoled and encouraged her to finish it. Callil had a gift for handling recalcitrant women authors: she listened intently to them and took a genuine interest in their lives and problems, even doing practical chores for Antonia White, who was almost 80 when *Frost in May* was reissued by Virago in 1978.[23] Although Barbara did not need that sort of help, she was cheered by Callil's faith in her writing and managed to submit the introduction in January 1980. She was relieved to hear that Callil liked it, writing in her diary later that month: 'Had a letter from Miss Callil saying she is delighted with my foreword. Also enclosing a cheque for £25. Very pleased about this.'

Perhaps Callil was aware that Barbara was despondent and had lost confidence in her work because, when in early October she sent her the mock-up for the Virago cover of *The Vet's Daughter*, she enclosed the two letters she had received from Graham Greene and suggested that Barbara might want to write to thank him for his support. She also suggested a meeting – they had signed the contract for *The Vet's Daughter* separately and had not yet met each other: 'Quite soon we move from our attic office in Wardour Street to Dover Street W.1. I was wondering if you'd like to come in to tea one afternoon as there we'll have more space?' Barbara was immensely pleased to receive Greene's letters; she had always greatly admired him, both as a writer and as a man, but had assumed, after his cool response to *The House of Dolls*, that he was no longer interested in her work. Here, though, was proof that he thought she was a writer of the first order. 'Thank you so much for sending the copies of Graham Greene's letters. I was so surprised and pleased', she wrote to Callil. 'I thought he must have forgotten about my books by now. Actually, he did write to me once or twice while we were living in Spain, but the last letter must have been at least nine years ago.'[24] The next day she wrote to Greene to thank him for recommending her books to Virago and to explain why she and Richard had decided to return to England (inflation and the sinking pound). Perhaps wounded by James Michie's remark that hers was a talent which no longer suited the fast-changing world of modern publishing, she also explained why there would be no more novels by Barbara Comyns: 'I write very little now partly because I feel I don't fit in with the eighties. I find most of the novels published very unsatisfying and very imitative: they appear to be written with an eye on what will please the critics.'[25] Greene replied a week later:

Dear Barbara,

I am delighted to hear from Virago that as I wished they are republishing THE VET'S DAUGHTER. I have written again to urge them to follow it with some of the other novels all of which as you know I have admired. I don't see why you have stopped writing because you don't fit in with the eighties. Nor do I. But you have never fitted in to any particular period and that has been one of the spells in your books.

Do give my love to Richard.
Affectionately,
Graham[26]

Greene's letter gave Barbara the encouragement she needed to at least start thinking about writing another novel. The contract with Virago also resulted in invitations to publishing events. 'Tea at Virago at 4 o'clock', Barbara wrote in her diary on 13 November 1980, adding, 'Virago has a fascinating office in Ely House which once belonged to the Bishop. They are in the attics, such pretty rooms and imaginative decorations and a busy girl in each room. I enjoyed myself and hope I didn't stay too long.' She took with her a copy of *The Skin Chairs* which Carmen Callil had asked to see. In December she went to a Virago Christmas celebration: 'Charming,

40 Barbara with Lennie Goodings at a Virago party in the 1980s

friendly party – about 40 women and only one man hiding away in a little room', she wrote in her diary. It was at one of these events that she met the novelist Ursula Holden, who reminded her that she had sent Barbara a fan letter in 1967 when she was living in Spain. In that letter, written thirteen years earlier, Ursula (writing under her married name Ursula Dixon) had expressed her admiration for Barbara's work – 'I so like your sad surprised kind of humour'. After meeting at the Virago event, the two women went on to become good friends.

The following year, in January 1981, Virago Press released its edition of *The Vet's Daughter*; its green cover featuring Walter Crane's painting *Lilies*, a study of a young woman with long, crinkly, blonde hair wearing a Grecian dress painted in profile against a background of white lilies – perhaps chosen to suggest Alice Rowlands' innocence as well as her death on Clapham Common. The novel was promoted in Virago catalogues and the book's release prompted an article by Caroline Moorehead in *The Times*. Moorehead, who travelled to Ham to interview Barbara, wrote perceptively about her life and work and described her as a writer who

> mixes invention with reality, giving to each the same weight, and drawing generously and without coyness on her own life for character and occasion. When she discusses her books it is to place them in her own past [...] The mildly mystical approach to her subject, with its overtones of inescapable gloom, is expressed in final form in language so precise and economical – a way of writing acquired through much reading of Defoe – so pared down of

all unnecessary words that it conveys a sensation of truth, 'of realness almost exaggerated' as she accurately puts it [...] The house in Richmond is neat and full of Dresden statues and half naïf, half surrealist pictures of her own, a curious visual complement to her writing.[27]

The article was good publicity for both Barbara and her book. The reviews of the novel that followed were generally admiring, describing *The Vet's Daughter* as 'a vivid and unforgettable reading experience' (*Manchester Evening News*), 'weird and compelling' (*Morning Star*), 'beautiful and haunting' (*Irish Times*). Alan Hollinghurst, then a lecturer at University College, London and yet to produce the novels that would make him famous, wrote in the *New Statesman* that the 'vividness and innocence' of *The Vet's Daughter* 'have the revelatory intensity of the narrations of Pip or young David Copperfield. It projects its fantastic story with a tangible realness and manages to make public and inevitable a realm of private sensation close to nightmare.' The *Times Literary Supplement*, however, damned with faint praise, noting that although the novel had 'a special kind of tainted charm', it was 'limited in achievement but valuable as a curiosity', while the *Spectator* reviewer remarked caustically, 'Since the narrator dies at the end of the book, it is a mystery how the book came to be written. Occult powers are all very well, but posthumous autobiography is a hard trick to bring off.'[28] Dyed-in-the-wool realists never quite understood Barbara's fiction.

But many readers did. The Virago edition of the novel attracted a lot of attention and sold reasonably well. In February Barbara heard from Carmen Callil that *The Vet's Daughter* would be published by Dial Press in the United States in association with Virago. In March the book was featured in 'Pick of the Paperbacks' on Radio 4, and Barbara was interviewed for 'Woman's Hour' ('to my surprise the interview went very well', she noted in her diary). The only shadow in her life at this time was caused by an announcement from Julian in April that he had now decided, after all, to sell 221 Ashburnham Road in order to raise money to buy a house where he could live with Sally and their baby daughter, Lucy, born in October 1980. Lucy, now aged 18 months, had recently hurt herself badly when playing in the workshop, and he and Sally had decided that 64 The Green was not a suitable place in which to bring up a child. He suggested that Barbara and Richard might move back there once the Ashburnham house was sold. The news threw Barbara into a state of panic and depression, despite Julian's promise that he would make several improvements to 64 The Green before they returned to it. Her diary entry for 8 April 1981 is full of despair:

The future looks worse and worse all the time. I don't want to take an overdose of Valium or something in case they bring me round again and I hate blood.

I'd like to take something that makes me vanish completely, no funeral expenses or inquest.

But later in the month her mood lifted when Andrew Hewson contacted her to tell her that Dial Press would be paying her an advance of $5,000: 'I can hardly believe it. I was expecting 500 at the very most', she wrote in her diary. She was keen to save money so that Richard could give up his theatre job when it became too much for him, especially now that the theatre manager had taken to bullying him. She was also cheered by the number of readers who contacted her saying that they had enjoyed reading *The Vet's Daughter*; one of these was the author Jane Gardam, whose novel *God on the Rocks* had been nominated for the Booker Prize in 1978. Other readers wrote to say that *Our Spoons Came from Woolworths* had been their favourite book many years ago, and that they were delighted to see the Virago paperback edition of *The Vet's Daughter* as they had assumed the author was dead by now. Barbara did indeed feel in a strange way that she was coming back from the grave, having not published anything for fourteen years. And in July *The Vet's Daughter* was featured in the Radio 4 programme 'A Good Read' with extracts read by Michael Holroyd and Bel Mooney. Barbara was delighted: 'It was marvellous and should send up the book sales. I almost ran off to Richmond to buy a copy myself', she wrote in her diary in July.

Despite nagging worries about having to move yet again, 1981 ended well. At a large party at the Virago office on 1 December, Barbara met someone she described in her diary as 'an American book spotter' who told her that her 'American publisher walks about with my book under his arm saying "I've got a little gem here"'. Carmen Callil had just sold *The Vet's Daughter* to the Canadian publishing company Lester and Orpen Dennys and, by the end of the year, Barbara had signed an agreement with Virago to publish *Sisters by a River*, *Our Spoons Came from Woolworths* and *The Skin Chairs*, all within two to three years. This time the advance was £400 per title, instead of the £250 offered for *The Vet's Daughter*. Barbara felt that at last her work was being properly recognized – and she was delighted that she was now making good money out of her books without having to write another word.

14

Hauntings

Barbara enjoyed the renewed interest in her work but she still suffered from periods of anxiety: about money, about family, and about where she and Richard would end up spending their old age. In 1982 she was 74 years old. Fifteen years had passed since the publication of *A Touch of Mistletoe*, her last novel, and she was no longer sure that she could rise to the challenge of writing another book, especially after the failure of *Waiting*. Although Virago seemed very successful and had revived her reputation, she was worried about that too. In late February Carmen Callil wrote to say that Virago was joining three other publishers (Chatto, The Bodley Head and Cape). 'Rather sad', wrote Barbara in her diary in February. 'They were such a dear little publisher and no men.' It was the beginning of many such amalgamations in the publishing world during the 1980s that would see small firms being swallowed by multinational companies.

Barbara was also saddened by Diana Brinton Lee's death in Spain in February. Although Barbara had not seen Diana for two years, the friendship between the two women had been long and complicated, and her death seemed to mark the end of an era. The idea of Caroline inheriting El Almendral had been abandoned some years ago, the family having decided that it would simply be too expensive to run. So what, Barbara wondered, would happen to Diana's home now? She and Caroline soon discovered that, true to form, Diana had decreed that it should not be sold until the last of her pets had died. She had made provisions for Pepe, the handyman, to care for the 24 cats, two dogs and one donkey as long as was necessary. Diana's plan meant that the property could not be sold for some while, despite the interest shown by several local purchasers, including the mayor of San Roque, who had hoped to turn El Almendral into a centre for student summer courses. In the end, El Almendral stayed in the Brinton family, Diana's ten nephews and nieces installing a Welsh couple to manage the property, which they then used as a holiday home.[1]

Much of Barbara's time during the early 1980s was taken up by family duties and problems: Caroline needed advice and support because both her daughters were being difficult. The eldest, Mariquita, now 22, had lived with Barbara and Richard in Ashburnham Road during the autumn term of 1979, while she was studying art in London, but it had not worked out well. Barbara worried about her granddaughter staying out late and thought her boyfriends unsuitable, while Richard disliked Mariquita's casual attitude to mealtimes, about which he was punctilious. Barbara confessed to Caroline that they found it a strain being responsible for Mariquita, and her granddaughter had been immediately recalled to Tenerife, returning a few months later to a flat in Bayswater to continue her art studies. Barbara kept a quiet eye on Mariquita and met her fairly regularly, even taking her in February 1982 to see *Aladdin* at the Richmond Theatre where, she recorded in her diary, she squirmed at Les Dawson's jokes. By March, Mariquita had acquired a boyfriend who was fourteen years her senior and who worked in a casino by night. Mariquita's announcement that she might marry him threw Barbara into a state of alarm. Even though Mariquita was no longer living with her, Barbara still felt some responsibility for her granddaughter and it weighed heavily on her. To her great relief, Pepe and Caroline recalled Mariquita to Tenerife again in May.

Caroline was also anxious about Nuria, now 18, who did not want to go to university but who was bored in Tenerife and, according to her parents, spent too much time partying. Her father had recently had a heart attack and decided that, if he was going to die, he wanted to die in Madrid, where he had grown up. In August 1982 Pepe and Caroline moved back to Spain, taking Mariquita with them. Eduardo, now 24, announced that he wanted to live permanently in Tenerife and Nuria remained on the island for another year before leaving in 1983 for Madrid, where she embarked on a course in business studies and interpreting/translating. Barbara was pleased; travelling to Madrid was easier and cheaper than flying to Tenerife and her two granddaughters would now be closely supervised by their parents.

Julian and Sally's two-year-old daughter, Lucy, also made occasional claims on Barbara's time when the childminder, Karen, was ill or on holiday. She was anxious too about her grandson Nicholas, now 19. Although he worked as a travel agent and was living in a flat in London, she still saw him fairly regularly for games of Scrabble and walks in Richmond Park. She worried about his bouts of heavy drinking and, like the rest of the family, did not much care for his newly acquired Spanish girlfriend. The upheavals in Nicholas's life and his mother's suicide were now taking their toll on his mental health and he was beginning to use alcohol as an analgesic.

Gardening at home and tending her recently acquired allotment took Barbara's mind off family problems, as did spending time with new friends. Reading remained a great solace; she enjoyed Willa Cather's *A Lost Lady* and Scott Fitzgerald's short stories, and was re-reading Quentin Bell's *Virginia*

Woolf: A Biography – 'how good it is', she wrote in her diary in March 1982. Literary matters still took up some of her time even though she was no longer writing. She wondered whether she should correct the misspellings in *Sisters by a River* for the Virago edition, but Carmen Callil persuaded her not to:

> I can imagine that some people would find it an irritating affectation, but the novel does work like that, and Alexandra noticed how very cleverly the spelling and punctuation gets better as your heroine grows older. No, don't change a word [...] I like the book as it is, cobwebs and all.[2]

Callil invited Beryl Bainbridge to write a fresh introduction for the Virago edition of *Our Spoons Came from Woolworths* – she thought the two writers shared a similar sense of humour – but Bainbridge refused, wanting to concentrate on her own work. Callil then approached Ursula Holden, whom John Johnson had arranged for Barbara to meet the previous year, thinking they would enjoy each other's company. Initially Ursula rather intimidated Barbara: 'She is very serious and no sense of humour, a dedicated writer though and good on dialogue', Barbara wrote in her diary in March 1982. As the two women came to know each other better, their evenings together were leavened by alcohol and, gradually, much laughter. By the summer they were good friends: 'Enjoyed Ursula's visit. She was looking so slim and young. We drank a lot of German wine, talked about our books and ate a not very nice dinner', Barbara recorded in her diary in July. In April Barbara had enjoyed afternoon tea at the Savoy with one of her American editors, the author Joyce Johnson. Still shy with strangers even in her seventies, Barbara had dreaded the occasion, noting in her diary:

> Very frightening. I'll have to talk about my books in a very serious intense way. Actually I hardly ever think of them now I've stopped writing – I'm only interested in the money they bring in, all the difference to our old age having these royalties coming in from time to time – so unexpected.

During the meeting Andrew Hewson flagged up the possibility that Barbara might write another novel, but she demurred, saying that she was preoccupied with moving house and had no time to write at the moment. She was unsettled by the viewings at 221 Ashburnham Road and anxious about the future.

By the early summer Julian's offer on a riverside house on the Thames in Shepperton had been accepted, and 221 Ashburnham Road had a buyer. Contracts were exchanged and in June 1982 Barbara and Richard moved back to 64 The Green. To her surprise, Barbara found that she was pleased to be living there again, despite the minor irritation of having to answer the workshop telephone when there was no one there to take the calls. It was a quirky house and somehow seemed a more appropriate residence for a writer than the Wates house. It was also cheaper to live there than in Ham because Julian paid all the utility bills and the rates. After the business of settling in was over, Barbara had a sudden burst of energy and decided she wanted to write again after all. By the autumn she was sitting at her desk, facing a blank sheet of paper: 'Tried to start a new novel. Typewriter wouldn't work, my brain the same. Wrote three quarters of a page', she wrote in her diary on 27 October. Two days later she noted: 'Tried to re-write first page. I only get about half an hour to write in. Get up extra early and write when house is quiet and telephone too.' But by early November she had finished the first chapter and wrote to Andrew Hewson, 'Although writing conditions in this house are very difficult I have at last started on a new novel – perhaps just because it is difficult.'[3] The inspiration for the book was the Grimm Brothers' tale 'The Juniper Tree'. It had haunted Barbara's imagination for many years, but in her new novel the story was to be set in modern times in Richmond and Twickenham. Barbara was beginning to feel excited about it, although unsure whether she had the stamina to see it through. Meeting the prolific author Naomi Mitchison at a Virago Christmas party encouraged her; Mitchison was 85 years old, still writing and was looking forward to the publication of her next novel, *Not by Bread Alone*. Barbara went home determined to get on with her book.

And get on with it she did, despite family calls on her time and necessary visits to her agent's office in Clerkenwell Green. On 16 November 1982 she received an urgent phone message from Andrew Hewson about a meeting with two women who had set up an independent film company, Moonlighter Productions, based in north London. They wished to discuss with her their plan to make a film of *The Vet's Daughter*: 'I feel a bit frightened', Barbara wrote in her diary that day. Just over a week later she travelled into London to talk about the project with the company's co-producers, Genista McIntosh, who was planning controller for the Royal Shakespeare Company, and Jane Jacob-Hood, a stockbroker who was also sponsorship director for the RSC. Hewson calmed Barbara's nerves: 'He is charming, like a dancing bird', Barbara wrote in her diary that evening. Moonlighter Productions had bought the film rights for a two-year period in January 1982 and since then had put together an impressive team which was ready to start work immediately once the funding had been raised. Deborah Moggach was to write the screenplay; Adrian Noble, then associate director of the RSC, would direct the film; Michael Gambon had agreed to play Euan Rowlands and Sheila Hancock was to play Rosa Fisher. George Fenton, well-known for his scores for both theatre productions and television programmes, had agreed to write the music.[4] Barbara had high hopes, once again, that her work might reach the big screen. But the early 1980s were a lean time for

British film-making. Major film companies such as EMI and Rank were pulling out of British production and, with competition from television and video sales, cinema audiences were shrinking and investors were cautious. Even though at £500,000 (over £2 million today) the Moonlighter Productions budget was a modest one, and despite the fact that the film option on the novel was renewed in February 1984, McIntosh and Jacob-Hood failed to raise enough funding to make the film.

In early April 1983 Barbara travelled with her brother-in-law, John Faraday, to Spain to spend a week with Caroline and Pepe in their new home in Madrid. Richard wrote to her from Twickenham, sending her 'much, much love', and with news that Julian had just put a life-size figure of a pig in a window of the shop (now no longer rented out) at 64 The Green. Barbara's son had made the fibreglass animal for a televised fairy story in which a wicked witch changes a child into a pig. It was an eye-catching, if eccentric, addition to the building and made a perfect landmark for interviewers and visitors. By the time a reporter from the *Richmond and Twickenham Times* visited Barbara in March 1985, the pig had been joined by a dragon: 'Sure enough there they were: an extremely dusty green dragon lurking murkily and menacingly in one window, with a rather despondent pink porker in the one alongside.'[5]

Soon after Barbara returned from her holiday, Virago released its edition of *Our Spoons Came from Woolworths*, its cover illustrated by Stanley Spencer's *Marriage at Cana, Bride and Bridegroom* (1953). She was pleased to see the novel in print again and liked the cover illustration. The painting, inspired by the Bible story in which Jesus turns water into wine at a wedding celebration, harks back to the artist's own doomed marriage, showing Hilda Carline in the act of awkwardly sitting down at her wedding to Spencer in 1925. Despite their both being artists, Spencer saw his wife as muse and soul-mate while expecting her to take full responsibility for running the house and bringing up their two children. Hilda's own artistic talent, not surprisingly, withered during her marriage years. Spencer's vision of the world, an arresting combination of domestic realism and the surreal, complemented Barbara's fiction perfectly, as did the painting's implicit narrative about a failed marriage between artists. As a reissue of a book first published in 1950, the Virago edition *of Our Spoons Came from Woolworths* did not attract many reviews, but it did catch the attention of those who had not previously come across novels by Barbara Comyns. Patricia Craig, for example, admired her 'distinctive manner [...] you could call it faux-naif with a touch of fatalism [...] Small-scale, homely and odd though it is, there is nevertheless something sharp and engaging about this book.'[6] A year later, Barbara confirmed in conversation with Hermione Lee during an interview for Channel Four that much of the novel was true, especially the section about giving birth – 'I wrote that part when I was in hospital after I'd had my son who is 50 now!'[7]

At the end of May, Barbara heard from Andrew Hewson that their French agents had sold *The Vet's Daughter* to Éditions Flammarion for an advance of 10,000 francs (worth about £900 then, about £3,800 today). Buoyed by that news and by Virago's publication of *Our Spoons Came from Woolworths*, Barbara set herself a deadline: she would finish her new novel by the end of the year. She even abandoned her 1983 diary in May, saving her creative energy for the book: 'I was so busy last year, writing *The Juniper Tree*, I had little time for a diary and put it away unfinished, a thing I seldom do', she wrote in her diary on 1 January 1984. On the same day she added, 'I do hope it gets published. I'm quite pleased with it but it may have faults I never noticed. At least it's an original book.' Hewson liked *The Juniper Tree* and sent it to Virago as soon as he had read it. Within a week or so, Virago responded:

> As you know, we are very committed to Barbara, and because of this have thought very seriously and carefully about this new novel. I'm afraid, however, that as it stands we don't feel we can publish it. Despite its real strengths, it is, overall, much weaker than any of her other novels (all of which I've read and am devoted to) […] this novel seems to me overlong in places, less assured, and more ordinary.[8]

Hewson was disappointed and Barbara was devastated; she was convinced it was one of her best books. Hewson sent the novel out again, this time to Chatto & Windus, which speedily rejected it: 'Feel shocked and sad. I don't like this year so far', Barbara wrote in her diary on 28 January. The next day she received a letter from Hewson:

> Virago think the book needs more work and I am enclosing a letter from Alexandra Pringle in which she says we should feel free to go elsewhere if the prospect of revision fills you with alarm and despondency. When you have had a chance to digest her comments please give me a ring and we can discuss how best to proceed.[9]

The list of revisions did indeed fill Barbara with alarm, and she scrawled 'No major alterations, easier to write a new book – rather be shot' – at the end of Hewson's letter. Hewson continued to send the book out but with no success. Pavane/Pan held on to it for a long time but finally rejected it in May, at which point Hewson decided he would send it to Methuen, 'who now have a first rate fiction list', as he assured Barbara in a letter.

Sad though she was at what looked like the failure of her novel, Barbara had other matters on her mind during the first half of 1984. Her grand-daughter Nuria arrived in January with her Spanish boyfriend, Juan Pablo Gray (his mother was Spanish but he took his surname from his English father), and announced that she was four months pregnant. They had been unable to marry in Spain because, having been born in Baghdad, Nuria had no birth certificate and the Catholic Church would not marry her without one. In England all that was needed was some form of identification, so she and Juan Pablo married on 1 February in a registry office in Twickenham. Julian and Sally took Nuria into their home and Barbara took charge of practical matters, taking her granddaughter for a pregnancy examination, registering her with the West Middlesex Hospital for the birth, and arranging appointments with various housing associations and the local council. While remaining calm on the surface, Barbara was deeply anxious about Nuria's future. She was also worried about her sister Nan, who had become ill and lost a lot of weight. And John Faraday had suddenly become rude and aggressive, accusing her of selling the houses she and Richard had owned for less than their market value and of having left for Ibiza without telling him and Chloe. The latter charge was certainly not true; Barbara had dined with them the night before she travelled and Richard saw them several times before he left England to join her on the island. It was all very wearing emotionally.

However, Lucy, her three-year-old granddaughter, an intelligent and inquisitive child, lifted her spirits. She often spent time with Barbara at 64 The Green and grew close to her grandmother, who kept a special Mr Men mug for her use only. She remembers Barbara as being patient, kind and very different from other grannies – 'she did not have her hair permed or colour-rinsed and she always wore trousers rather than skirts or dresses'. They had pet names for each other: 'Supergran' (after a television programme they watched together) and 'Lucy Bossy Bottom'.[10] Barbara enjoyed reading to her granddaughter, as she had to her own children when they were small, and they spent hours transforming mundane objects through the art of découpage – cutting out pictures, gluing them on to things and then varnishing the finished products. Lucy did not much care for Richard though, who seemed to her an austere and remote figure. Lunch was always eaten in silence and the child found him an oppressive presence. After his death, Lucy suggested to Barbara that they should cut the buttons off his suits; she knew he liked to dress well and reasoned that he would not come back if his clothes had been spoiled.

In April the family arranged a 21st birthday party for Nuria which everyone enjoyed. Just over a month later Nuria gave birth to a healthy baby boy and called him William. May ended well too: Andrew Hewson rang Barbara to say that Methuen wanted to publish *The Juniper Tree* and were offering an advance of £2,000 (over £8,000 today). Throughout the rest of 1984 Barbara worked with Elsbeth Lindner at Methuen on the novel; 'So young but very capable', Barbara noted in her diary in July. In turn,

Lindner was struck by Barbara's presence – 'an elfin, slightly elusive personality. She looked like a child, small and seemingly innocent, but – like her writing – there was wit and worldliness below the simple surface; also tantalizing glimpses of an earlier, perhaps colourful existence.'[11] In October Lindner sent her a mock-up of the book cover, a stark black and white design featuring a magpie perched at the top of a juniper tree between two bigger black gnarled trees. Barbara liked it: 'It has just the Gothic and menacing look I hoped for and it is also very decorative.'[12] Lindner suggested only minor alterations to the novel, including changing the stone lion in the Forbes's garden into a bear, in order to avoid being sued by the owners of a house in Sheen Road in Richmond whose stone lion was locally famous and had been the inspiration for the lion in the novel.

The Juniper Tree is an unsettling and brilliant book: the Chagallian surrealism that permeates much of Barbara's work here lifts the mundane and domestic into the realm of the magical and the sometimes terrifying, but the novel never fails to convince. Set in the pleasant areas of Richmond and Twickenham between 1979 and the early 1980s, the book is haunted by the ghastly violence of the Grimm Brothers' tale 'The Juniper Tree', in which a stepmother, favouring her own daughter over her husband's son by his first marriage, murders her stepson and cooks him in a stew to feed to her spouse. Barbara took several elements from the tale, including its opening in which a beautiful woman cuts her finger peeling an apple, her blood dropping on to the white snow; she also has the woman die in childbirth and her son killed by the heavy lid of a chest falling on his neck. Motifs from the original – such as the woman's craving for juniper berries and the bird's extraordinary role in the story – haunt the suburban and carefully realized world of *The Juniper Tree*. In the interview with Hermione Lee early in 1984, when asked whether she was writing another novel, Barbara admitted that she had just finished a rather 'strange' book and that she had forgotten just how 'gruesome' the Grimm tale was, despite having read it to her children many years ago.[13]

The novel's first-person narrator, Bella Winter, is a 27-year-old single mother whose two-year-old biracial daughter, Marline (nicknamed 'Tommy', but whose birth name echoes that of 'Marlinchen', the name of the daughter in the Grimm tale) is the result of a one-night stand with someone she met at a party. Bella's beautiful face is disfigured by a scar on her left cheek, a reminder of a car accident that happened when her former boyfriend was driving carelessly; she thinks of it as 'a fearful centipede running up my face'.[14] The scar also suggests inner suffering; her father left home when she was small and her mother is emotionally remote and verbally cruel. Bella is the product of a dysfunctional family and is therefore potentially vulnerable to further abuse. Hard up and lonely, she feels separated from the world and from others. The only people who befriend her when she lives in a dingy flat in Bayswater are illegal immigrants who fix her meter so that she pays less for her gas and who give her food: 'A girl from the Canaries unbuttoned her blouse and gave me one of the steaks that were plastered there and I couldn't refuse to take it when they were so kind to me.'[15] When we meet Bella, she is alone and miserable. That is, until she meets the Forbes, a rich and sophisticated couple who live in Richmond in a large Georgian house and who befriend her soon after she starts a job selling antiques in a small shop in Twickenham.

Bernard Forbes, an art dealer who owns a gallery, and his beautiful wife Gertrude gradually adopt Bella, and she is encouraged to visit them and stay at their grand home with its carved stone bear in the front garden. Tragically, Gertrude dies in childbirth and the grief-stricken Bernard turns to Bella for emotional support and practical help in looking after his small son Johnny. They spend time together and he teaches her about art and arranges for her to learn French – but then he begins to pressurize her to marry him and to leave her job in the antique shop, which she loves. Slowly succumbing to his neediness and to promises of a better future for her daughter, Bella gives up her work and the flat that goes with it, and agrees to marry Bernard, despite her inner misgivings. She realizes that he does not love her as she loves him and senses that he is being condescending when, referring to her 'chatter', he calls her 'Bel-Gazou', a Provençal phrase suggesting the soft warbling sounds of birds. Bella begins to feel that Bernard treats her more like a child than an adult and it becomes clear to the reader that he needs to subsume her identity to his own. Bella chooses submission in order to make him happy but is aware that her choice comes at the cost of her independence and freedom: 'Bernard, how Women's Lib would hate me if they knew how I felt about you', she says just before they marry.[16] The novel's dénouement is swift and ghastly. Bernard grows tired of Bella and finds another vulnerable young woman to seduce; Johnny dies in the same way as the small boy in the Grimm Brothers' tale, albeit accidentally; Bella buries him beneath the juniper tree in the garden and soon after attempts suicide. In the psychiatric ward where she gradually recovers from her breakdown, Bernard tells her that their marriage is over and that he is moving to Brussels. The novel ends with Bella reconciled with her mother and their purchase of a large house in Chiswick where they live with Marline. Bella works as an art buyer and Peter, a gentle and talented man previously employed by Bernard, rents their basement where he sets himself up as a freelance picture restorer. After her divorce, Bella marries Peter, who is devoted to her and fond of Marline. The novel closes with Bella pregnant and making a last visit to the house in Richmond, now owned by an Arab family. 'The carved bear still guarded the house. It seemed as if he recognised me with his cold stone eyes.'[17]

In *The Juniper Tree*, Barbara Comyns uses colour and pared-down language to create extraordinarily vivid scenes. She also skilfully and subtly combines the atavistic fears and desires that inform the Grimm Brothers' tale with the everyday world of south-west London in the twentieth century. Although this is not an autobiographical novel like *Our Spoons Came from Woolworths*, it draws on several aspects of Barbara's life for its emotional dynamic. These include having been brought up by an emotionally remote and cold mother; her relationship with the sophisticated Brinton Lees, in particular Rupert, whose love for her was short-lived; and her fear of poverty and her struggle to provide for Julian and Caroline when they were children. In creating Bella's daughter Marline, she drew on her two granddaughters, Lucy (for the child's personality) and Mariquita (for her looks). *The Juniper Tree* also reflects the material reality of Barbara's own life. She based Bella's flat above an antique shop on 64 The Green, and Bella sells a 'little chair made of elm, with a heart cut out of the back' just like the chair Barbara inherited from her grandmother.[18] Bella collects Staffordshire china, as did Barbara; Bella's 'Spanish virgin with her delicately carved hands and gold-embroidered robes'[19] resembles Barbara's much-cherished virgin in a glass case that she bought in Barcelona and which is now owned by her granddaughter – and so on. Above all, Bella, like Barbara, is a survivor. The book is haunted not only by the Grimm Brothers' tale but also by aspects of Barbara's own life.

It would be a mistake, though, to read it simply through the lens of autobiography. *The Juniper Tree*, like *Our Spoons Came from Woolworths*, explores the fate of many young mothers whose choices are constrained by poverty and isolation; it is also a novel about surviving domestic abuse and trauma. The racist attitudes expressed by some characters towards Marline – Bella's ex-boyfriend refers to her as a 'little blackamoor' and the Forbes's nanny thinks their baby boy will be 'contaminated' by her – also suggest the abuse a child such as Bella's daughter would face growing up in late twentieth-century England.[20] The book is, as Margaret Drabble was later to observe, 'one of her most successful, confident and curious productions', having 'the clear pure narrative quality of a fable, but also [showing] a humanity and maturity not always evident in her earlier stories'.[21]

* * *

Although Barbara was delighted that *The Juniper Tree* had found a publisher, her pleasure was overshadowed again by worries about her family. Nuria's husband seemed unable to hold down a job; Barbara's sister Nan, of whom she was very fond, had a stroke and died in early June; Nicholas married his Spanish girlfriend in August, much to everyone's dismay, and was out of work by November. And Richard was becoming frailer and falling more often. In September he gave up his work at the Richmond Theatre and by the autumn was in and out of hospital for tests. Always thin, he now began to look gaunt as his weight dropped dramatically. The fainting fits lasted longer each time until Barbara began to describe them as 'comas':

> Even when he was safe in bed there was the danger that he had been overtaken by a coma. I'd hold the torch near his face and sometimes he'd wake, his vivid blue eyes all unfocused would look into mine, then he'd return to sleep [...] The [fainting fits] happened about twice a year, nearly always in the early morning and usually in the bathroom. I'd be downstairs and suddenly there would be this forboding [*sic*] crash as if it were a much heavier man than my thin husband falling. Sometimes he'd be unconscious for quite a long time and I'd bring him round by sponging his stark white face and it was wonderful when life flowed back and his eyelids fluttered. He'd say 'It was nothing, just a little dizziness.'

In this unpublished document of three chapters headed 'Rough Ideas', Richard becomes 'Paul' but Barbara was clearly writing about her husband's last few months and her emotions as she watched his decline.[22]

After a particularly bad fall one evening in late November when Richard collapsed and fell onto an electric fire, Barbara called for an ambulance and he was admitted to the West Middlesex Hospital for treatment. In 'Rough Ideas' she describes the drama and the pathos of that night:

> At first Paul refused to go with the men and cried out in his distorted voice 'No. No. Not necessary' and I felt so sorry for him; it was like a poor old dog being taken to the vet for the last time. They couldn't take him against his will, but one of the men said 'You must have hospital treatment. Think of your poor wife.' Then he gave in but there was a little more trouble over the stretcher until he gave way again and was carried down the narrow twisting stairs and out of the house in a minute. It was a little stretcher, rather like a child's sledge. It was all so quick, almost as if smash and grab people had snatched Paul away. I couldn't believe this was happening to us. Neither of us had been taken to hospital during the forty years we had been married. I returned to the house and collected a few things Paul might need, pyjamas and a dressing-gown and toilet things, but would he ever need them? Could he be dying?

Julian's wife Sally drove Barbara to the hospital and took her home after she had filled in all the necessary forms and made sure Richard was comfortable. Then Barbara sat by the phone all night until 6 a.m., when she was allowed to contact the hospital. The news was good: Richard had regained consciousness and seemed much better. A friend drove her to see him in the morning; she found her husband 'smiling in his gentle way and talking in his usual soft voice', seemingly oblivious to all the coughing and shouting going on around him in the ward. He told Barbara he had slept deeply during the night and had a beautiful dream during which he had heard the most wonderful music. 'He said it went on for hours and he had felt so wonderfully relaxed and happy.' Since they had not been to a concert for many years, Barbara thought the experience strange, and wondered, despite her scepticism about an afterlife, whether Richard could 'have been on the edge of Heaven' – but then quickly dismissed the idea. Instead, she started making plans about moving; the bathroom at 64 The Green was in the loft and reached by a narrow staircase – not really suitable for an invalid. Later, in February the following year, she realized that she and Richard must have been the only two people who did not know he was dying, and wrote in her diary, 'I knew he was very frail but he was so cheerful, death seemed a long way away.'

From November onwards, the ritual of hospital visiting took over most afternoons, Barbara catching the bus after lunch unless Sally or Julian gave her a lift. She would find Richard, now free from his drip, sitting at a table reading or writing, with his papers strewn across an empty bed.

> I think he was pleased to see me, yes, I'm sure he was because he used to write down the little things that had happened in the ward that he thought would amuse me. I'd come clumping through the ward with a plastic chair from the hall and a carrier bag with *The Times* sticking out, orange juice, books and toilet things and letters, of course. We'd have quite a lot to say to each other but when I said I was going he never tried to detain me, but he did kiss me with feeling. He always reminded me to return the chair to the hall, so as not to give the nurses extra work.

Richard kept himself mobile, practising walking up and down the stairs, so that he would be able to manage when he came home to 64 The Green. 'My husband seems to be a little better and we hope he will be out of hospital before Christmas', Barbara wrote to Elsbeth Lindner at Methuen on 9 December. Meanwhile, her literary life provided occasional brief distractions from her worry about Richard. A Virago advance copy of *Sisters by a River* arrived on 11 December, its cover featuring John Singer Sargent's *Carnation, Lily, Lily, Rose*; 'Ursula Holden's introduction is very good, more than the book deserves', Barbara noted in her diary that night. And on 19 December she went to the Virago Christmas party, returning home to find that Caroline and her family had arrived for Christmas.

Richard's assumption that he would be home for the festivities proved false, however. His doctors were not happy about discharging him, even for a short period. Impatient with all the treatments and tests he was being put through, he refused to have a recommended two-day blood transfusion and discharged himself on 22 December, arriving at 64 The Green in a taxi. He now weighed just under seven stone. Glad though she was to have him home, Barbara was desperately worried about what would happen if he went into a coma over the holiday period. But Richard stayed well enough to enjoy Christmas Day, when Caroline and Pepe, Nuria, Juan Pablo, little William and Sally, Julian and Lucy all arrived at 64 The Green to exchange presents, returning later to Julian's home in Shepperton so that Barbara and Richard could enjoy a small turkey on their own. The day is described in 'Rough Ideas':

> On Christmas day Paul and I didn't have dinner with the family, but we had a great present-giving with drinks and mince-pies and brilliant wrapping paper scattered nearly knee-high. The children ran round with balloons and the baby, our great grandchild, crawled through paper tunnels. The smell of slowly roasting turkey floated upstairs and it was almost like a normal Christmas except for a vague sadness. I noticed that Paul's presents were suitable for an invalid – pyjamas and boxes of soap, bathroom scales and a large sponge, not the usual expensive books, Parker pens, silk ties, cigarettes and the small cigars he was so fond of. When they had all gone home, I went downstairs to inspect the little turkey nestling in its silver foil wrapping, then cast an eye on the dining table. I put away the silly red and gold crackers I'd arranged so carefully. How could the two of us sit there pulling twelve tough crackers? I doubt if Paul could have pulled even one.

In the New Year Richard gained a little weight but soon lost it again, and he was readmitted to hospital on 21 January. Barbara's relatives were quick to show their love and offer practical support, but she was very frightened: 'I didn't know how fortunate we were when Richard was well seven months ago', she wrote in her diary on 22 January. Richard died of pneumonia two days later, his lungs already weakened by chronic obstructive pulmonary disease, and his death was announced in *The Times* on 30 January. 'I can't believe it somehow. We will never be together again. He always promised I'd die first', Barbara wrote in her diary that evening. Caroline and a friend were with her during those first days of shock, and they and Sally helped arrange the funeral at the South-West Middlesex Crematorium on 1 February, which turned out to be a mild and drizzly day. Barbara was pleased that so many people, including friends and old colleagues, as well as family, were there. She thought her husband's coffin looked 'so light and lovely' but was upset by the clergyman's 'ugly shouting grating voice' – until she reflected that Richard would simply have been amused by the man. The mourners were invited back to 64 The Green after the funeral; Caroline cleared up during the evening and Barbara simply lay on her bed, 'wave after wave of tiredness' sweeping over her, as she wrote in her diary that evening.

It took her days to deal with the letters of condolence that arrived at 64 The Green, many of them attesting to Richard's intelligence and kindness. 'I admired R tremendously for many things, especially perhaps for his wisdom and honesty. He was one of my very best friends, someone quite out of the ordinary', wrote Desmond Pakenham.[23] A few weeks later Barbara discovered that Richard had left her £71,000 worth of shares: 'at least it will come in useful if I have to go into a nursing-home or become unable to live on my own', she wrote in her diary. Barbara knew that Richard had inherited about £80,000 from his widowed Aunt Lucie, his aunt by marriage to his uncle Philip Carr (who had dropped the 'Comyns' from his name). Barbara had been very fond of the beautiful, elegant and witty French aunt, who would often sport bright green nail varnish and who enjoyed raising controversial topics at polite dinner parties. She had visited Lucie frequently in the care home in which she spent her last years. She knew that Richard had speculated on the stock market with the money Lucie had left him and, given her husband's financial ineptitude, she was pleasantly surprised to find he had managed to hold on to most of it.

Barbara did not record her feelings of grief in her diary in any detail; instead they went into 'Rough Ideas', which vividly conveys the sense of loss and dislocation she felt on her husband's death:

> I can't get used to shopping for one. Little tins of baked beans and that kind of thing […] I buy too much fruit and it starts to wither in the bowl if my granddaughter Nuria does not call, pushing little William in his pram before her in the proud way she has. It took several weeks before I could speak to the milkman and reduce the milk. I'd been able to mention that my husband was in hospital, but to say he was dead seemed so final. A few days ago I returned his library cards, both paper and plastic. I handed them to the girl but didn't know what to say at first, then mumbled that he had gone abroad and would not return for a long time. She seemed to understand. Today I found our passports. I'd been searching for them for weeks, then found only mine in an unmarked envelope and I thought 'Of course, he has taken his with him' and ceased to look for it. I was surprised when it appeared a few days later.

According to Ursula Holden, Barbara repeated the journey to the West Middlesex Hospital for several days after her husband's death, even though it now had no purpose: 'The 267 bus driver would look for her as she crossed the Green, slowing until she reached the stop. After Richard's death he saw her and slowed down as usual. "I hurried and got on the bus, he didn't know about Richard and I couldn't say"', Barbara told her.[24] Barbara

also felt guilty that she was alive when her husband was dead, as she
recorded in 'Rough Ideas':

> Since his death I find that I have a guilty feeling. There is nothing he would
> mind me seeing but he would mind me touching his papers and even more
> throwing them away without his permission. At least I have got rid of all the
> shoes now except for a pair of galoshes which I thought might be needed in
> a shoe museum if there is such a place and then there are a pair of wooden
> shoe trees that look like carved feet, dainty pointed feet as if about to dance.
> I've put them on a high shelf with his tie press. I feel it might be all a mistake
> and he'll return and be upset when he finds so many of his things missing.
> Now I plan to sell some of his more expensive books that are too dry for
> ordinary people to read, *The Problem of Party Government*, *A Concise Diction-
> ary of Finance* and *Estructura Economica de España*. It is no good keeping
> books and such big ones, books I could never read even if I was on a desert
> island. This feeling of guilt, though. It isn't only that I'm casting out my
> husband's belongings, it is when I feel a bit happy or enjoy the sun and hearing
> the birds sing in a spring-like way. Then there is eating. At first I couldn't eat
> I felt so sick and shivery. Now I'm eating the marmalade I'd bought for his
> breakfast. He so enjoyed it and now I've started eating it although I hardly
> ever touched it before. I even feel guilty when I enjoy people's company and
> we are all laughing together and when I watch ordinary things that are beautiful
> like silvery rain running down twigs and new leaves pushing up through the
> earth and the days when I'm feeling really well ...

Barbara's diary entries after Richard's death, by contrast, record facts rather
than feelings – who she has seen and where she has been; notes about the
publication of her books, what she is reading: plenty of Trollope – 'I like to
read my old safe friends *not* Fay Weldon'; also Virginia Woolf's diaries and
To the Lighthouse, which she was re-reading alongside Sir Leslie Stephen's
The Mausoleum Book ('There is just a little of Richard in Stephen').[25] She was
reading Edith Wharton too, including the short stories and *The Children*.[26]
Although her grief does not enter her diary, she does mention 'seeing' her
husband. In March as she was sitting in the evening at his desk dealing
with documents about his death, she 'suddenly felt [his] presence and felt
quite stunned'. One night in early October she thought she saw 'Richard
standing by his bed and taking his dressing-gown off. He was all silver and
the palest gold and I thought I could hear him breathing. When I put the
light on he wasn't there anymore but I found a large insect buzzing away.'
During the day, however, Barbara had plenty of distractions from her
sadness. People looked in on her frequently and sometimes suggested an
outing – a friend took her to see Roger Rees playing Hamlet at the Barbican
in April and she saw the film *A Passage to India* with Sally in mid-May:
'The most beautiful film I have ever seen, quite perfect', she wrote in her

diary that night. The Virago reprints of *The Vet's Daughter* in 1981 and *Our Spoons Came from Woolworths* in 1983 had created a new audience for her work, and many readers contacted her out of the blue to say how much they enjoyed her novels. She usually replied, despite finding it an awkward chore. An American fan, Joanna Hansen, received a letter saying how nervous Barbara was about the imminent publication of *The Juniper Tree* and how Richard's death had left 'a great lonely hole' in her life – but 'I suppose I'll gradually become used to it. At least I have my children and grandchildren and one little great grandchild.'[27] Another fan, Adinah Thomas, an aspiring author then living in East Sheen, wrote enthusiastically to Barbara about her work and they became firm friends, staying in touch for some years. 'Growing old is a bore', Barbara wrote in her diary on 19 May, but she was beginning to enjoy life once more, despite the survivor guilt she described so poignantly in 'Rough Ideas'. She even started writing fiction again: 'I'm writing a book but it is unlikely it will be finished, it has become like a jig-saw puzzle, all little unconnected bits', she wrote in her diary in late March. She also made an effort to keep in touch with her remaining siblings – her eldest sister Molly, her youngest sister Kathleen and her brother Dennis. Occasionally she went to Chelsea to see her brother-in-law, John Faraday, now ill himself with heart disease.

*   *   *

The Virago reissue of *Sisters by a River* and the publication by Methuen of *The Juniper Tree* early in 1985 brought a flurry of reviews and interviews, one with Sheridan Morley for the BBC World Service which was broadcast on 17 April: 'I didn't sound so good, rather priggish and strained … it turned into a discussion of *The Juniper Tree*, they both seemed to think highly of the book', she wrote in her diary that night. The reprint of *Sisters by a River* was generally welcomed, albeit in brief notices. Katya Watter in the *Times Educational Supplement* thought that events in the memoir were described 'with crystalline macabre objectivity' and found it 'a strange, disturbing book, oddly poetic and well worth reading', while the *Irish Press* reviewer predicted that it would become 'a classic of childhood'. But what Patricia Craig called the book's 'artlessness' divided readers just as it had in 1947; David Holloway, for instance, was irritated by the 'constant misspellings'.[28]

By contrast, *The Juniper Tree* was widely and enthusiastically reviewed. Hinde Thomas, in the *Sunday Telegraph*, found the novel 'curiously moving', and Isabel Quigly in the *Financial Times* described it as a 'delicate, tough, quick-moving […] haunting book'. The *City Limits* reviewer thought it 'a magnetic fusion of sympathy and violence', and Selina Hastings in the *Daily*

Telegraph described Barbara as 'a novelist of exceptional gifts' whose style has 'the luminous clarity of a painting on glass'. For Miranda Seymour, the novel was a 'multi-faceted little jewel of a tale, rare in its visionary qualities, beautifully told'. In a long review in the *Times Literary Supplement*, Patricia Craig noted that Barbara had turned the Grimms' tale on its head by making the stepmother a central character and 'by not endowing her with blackness of heart'. She continued:

> like other Comyns heroines, Bella recounts her singular experiences with a childlike directness and impassivity, which are very striking [...] What is solicited is not so much pity for those ill equipped to cope with peculiar troubles [...] but rather approval for the way characters are not got down by atrocious circumstances. Comyns's heroines, and her novels, are plaintive, strange and robust all at once [...] The old, outlandish tale is an appropriate model for a novelist like Barbara Comyns, whose imagination is drawn to the odd, the macabre and the picturesque. As an exercise in reconstruction, using the old ingredients but producing a fable for a different age, *The Juniper Tree* could hardly be more satisfactorily accomplished.[29]

Barbara was pleased and relieved. There were no negative reviews; after eighteen years of silence, her novel was a triumph. Her work was now celebrated, helped perhaps by the fact that readers had been primed by Beryl Bainbridge's black humour and Angela Carter's magical realism.

But Richard was not there to share her success. By early September she had abandoned her new novel: 'Felt depressed. Have put away the book I am writing. It is all jerky. I don't feel like writing really. I've nothing to say and it gives me a kind of restriction on my chest', she wrote in her diary. Grief came in waves and September was a bad month. Having disposed of Richard's shoes and books soon after his death, she still had to deal with his clothes. In mid-September, she packed her husband's suits and overcoats into plastic bags, hoping that a friend would help her take them to a charity shop: 'He did love his clothes so much, always taking them to the cleaners or brushing them', she wrote in her diary. The task is vividly fictionalized in 'Rough Ideas':

> Early this morning I put my husband's hats into the street. I couldn't mix them with the rubbish, potato skins, cat food tins, and tea bags so they had a black plastic bag to themselves. Five hats and a Spanish beret he wore on windy days. He was devoted to his hats. Once he lost eight when we were travelling. Two of them [were] specially designed for him by a Catalan hat artist, Señor Prat,[30] who had studied art with Picasso and Miró. Beautiful hats they were, just suited to his lean profile. I worried in case the hats became scattered over the road to be run over by the heavy traffic but they stayed safe in their black bag until ten-thirty when the dustmen collected them and most likely churned them up with filthy things, but I didn't see it happen [...]

41 Photograph of Barbara in her late seventies taken in the garden of 64 The Green; it appeared on the back cover of *The Juniper Tree*, 1985

There was a drawer filled with ties, he'd been collecting them for some years. Some rather beautiful and others almost ugly like the mauve one he used to wear when he fenced many years ago. It is hard to find anyone who wants old ties – suits perhaps, but not ties. There were two wardrobes filled with suits and coats, three overcoats and at least nine suits and eight jackets with contrasting trousers waiting to be given to someone.

While respecting her need to grieve, family and friends made sure Barbara did not feel lonely. Nuria often popped round with William (whose favourite game was to hide onions from the vegetable rack in unlikely places such as the oven or china cupboard), and Sally and Julian took her to several exhibitions, including 'Homage to Barcelona: The City and its Art, 1888–1936' at the Hayward Gallery – 'I'm so glad we went', Barbara wrote in her diary in late November. And then there were the literary parties – one held by *Books and Bookmen* in Carlton House Terrace in October – 'Richard used to work there in the attics for the Foreign Office many years ago', she remembered – and the usual Christmas party at Virago, where she chatted to Naomi Mitchison again. There was also good news from her agent: an American publisher was offering a $3,000 advance for *The Juniper Tree*, and *Sisters by a River* would be published in the States before Christmas. 'I'll be covered in dollars', she told her diary.

But she missed Richard badly. On 3 November she wrote: 'Kept forgetting I was alone in the house. I imagined he was in his room and planned things to tell him.' And a diary entry for 20 November describes how she thought she saw her husband in the early hours of the morning:

> He was wearing yellow pyjamas and muttered something about investigating a noise he had heard. He hung onto the door handle for a moment making it spin. Then he vanished through the door and I touched the handle which was still moving but he had gone. He never had pyjamas that colour.

She spent Christmas Day at Shepperton with Julian and his family; it was a happy occasion, but Richard's absence was always with her. She woke up at 64 The Green the next morning on her own: 'I've never been alone at Christmas before', she wrote in her diary, adding, 'A sad year for me'.

15

Legacies

During the last years of her life Barbara Comyns' books aroused a lot of interest and she began to think of herself as a truly successful novelist. Cheques for royalties and advances arrived regularly and she suddenly found that she was relatively affluent. Her new-found income did not stop her worrying about money, however; fear of 'the poverty' continued to haunt her despite her bulging savings accounts. Nor could financial stability protect her against the ravages of old age, which included the pain of arthritis and increasing forgetfulness. The death of relatives was also an unwelcome reminder of mortality. In late February 1986 Chloe's husband John died: 'I wish I'd been with him. I think he was afraid of dying. I am too ...', she wrote in her diary on the day of his death. Caroline's husband Pepe was diagnosed with cancer in the early summer and given four months to live, although in fact he survived until February the following year. In early June 1986 Barbara drew up a will with her solicitor and confided to her diary, 'How sad it is that we have to die, much better if we just faded away or turned into birds.' But there was the consolation of new life: Julian and Sally's second child, a boy they named Rupert, was born on 8 October.

There was also new life for Barbara's books: the publication of *The Juniper Tree* the previous year had revived interest in her earlier work. In January 1986 Genista McIntosh, who, four years previously, had tried to raise money to make a film of *The Vet's Daughter*, talked enthusiastically about the novel on a BBC World Service programme. In the summer Virago reissued *The Skin Chairs*, using the same formula they had chosen for *Our Spoons Came from Woolworths*: a fresh introduction by Ursula Holden and a cover displaying a Stanley Spencer painting. The front of the Modern Classics edition of *The Skin Chairs* featured Spencer's *Gardens in the Pond* and Barbara liked it very much. But she did not care for the words on the back cover that described her as 'the author of eight charming, eccentric novels' and the book as 'quirky': 'I don't like the blurb but I never do. They are usually arch or silly and live up to the word "blurb"', she wrote in her diary on receiving her advance copies. As a reissue, *The Skin Chairs* was not widely reviewed, but it was warmly received by those who did review it. Kathy Page described it in *City Limits* as 'one of the most vivid accounts of childhood that I've read', and Patricia Craig noted in the *Times Literary Supplement* that, like all Barbara Comyns' work, the novel was 'very primitive and plaintive, and, as ever, curiously effective'.[1]

Eighteen months after Richard's death Barbara still thought about her husband a great deal and was to note the anniversary of his death in her diary every year. 'Richard died three years ago today', she wrote in January 1988: 'I think about him so much but don't see him late at night as I did for some time'; and, in October that year, 'Found one of Richard's diaries written in Barcelona 1961–2. Very moving – how kind and thoughtful Richard was.' In January 1989 she wrote, 'How quickly the time goes. Life hasn't been the same without him. No-one to tell anything to – good and bad things. Although he was so serious, we laughed a lot.' However, by the summer of 1986, although still grieving for her husband, Barbara had begun to feel less guilty about taking pleasure in life and was immersing herself in gardening and reading. At one point she was absorbed by Frances Spalding's biography of Vanessa Bell, a book that prompted a memory she recorded in her diary: 'I was introduced to her once at a London Group private view. I was with Rupert, I remember. I was impressed by her height. I think she wore a strange hat.' In between devouring twentieth-century biographies and modern fiction, she returned to the Victorian novels she loved – 'Reading Mrs. Gaskell's *Wives and Daughters* – so enjoying it. I read it many years ago, thirty at least. So modern in some ways', she noted in her diary in July. She also enjoyed being feted by her editors at Virago who were pleased that the reissue of her books in their Modern Classics series had been such a success. On 24 July they treated her to lunch in London, after which she went to the National Gallery, where she was transfixed by the painting *Tiger in a Tropical Storm (Surprised!)* by Henri Rousseau, enthralled by its dreamlike scenario of a tiger among lush foliage and exotic flowers. She had long recognized a kindred spirit in Rousseau, whose vision was simultaneously naïve and surrealist, amusing and alarming; she had always designed her abundant gardens with his paintings in mind.[2] 'I'd love a print if they have one', she wrote in her diary that night.

This relatively peaceful interlude in her life was soon interrupted, however, by a message from Elizabeth Fairbairn, a literary agent at John Johnson Ltd, who had just come across the typescript of *Mr Fox Eats His Grapes*. Along with much else, Johnson had taken this manuscript with him when he left E. P. S. Lewin in 1956 to set up his own literary agency. Having failed to find a publisher for the book, Johnson had shelved it and it had gathered dust in the agency's office for over thirty years. Barbara's agent Andrew Hewson immediately sent the typescript to Methuen, which responded in

August, offering an advance of £2,000 (about £7,214 today) prior to publication. A week later, Elsbeth Lindner, who had worked closely with Barbara preparing *The Juniper Tree* for publication, wrote to say that *Mr Fox Eats his Grapes* would need a few small alterations. Barbara was delighted that the book, written long ago, would now see the light of day, even though her recollection of its plot was vague: 'Actually I can't remember how it ended …', she confessed to her diary. Elsbeth sent her a list of suggested changes and by mid-September Barbara was working rather anxiously on them. Sensing that she needed support, Elsbeth drove to 64 The Green for lunch on 2 October, bringing with her a bottle of French wine and a calming influence. In her diary that night, Barbara wrote, 'Then we started on the book. We really worked together very well as we had both made a list of things that were repeats or inaccuracies and that kind of thing. Now there is the publicity to be dealt with. I'm not very good at it.' Elsbeth and Barbara agreed that changing the title to the more simple *Mr Fox* would be a good idea.

1986 also saw the publication of Barbara's work in the United States through St Martin's Press. *Sisters by a River* and *The Skin Chairs* received good, if sometimes puzzled, reviews and brought Barbara an advance of $1,500 and further royalties. *The Juniper Tree*, however, drew unqualified praise from American reviewers. In England, Virago was preparing *Who was Changed and Who was Dead* for reissue and in mid-November Barbara received her advance copies: 'I do hope all goes well. It has a special place in my heart although I had little success with it when it was published before. It shocked people and I thought I'd overdone the horrors', she wrote in her diary in mid-November. The novel was published in January 1987 and, in her introduction, Ursula Holden noted how well its author 'deftly balances savagery with innocence, depravity with lyric interludes'.[3] Once again the cover featured a Stanley Spencer painting, which pleased Barbara: 'It is strange how well his paintings suit my books. I had thought of a Breughel', she noted in her diary in June. Virago's choice this time was a detail from the unfinished *Christ Preaching at Cookham Regatta*, the picture's amalgam of the mystical and the mundane curiously apt for a novel about ghastly deaths and transformations in a pleasant Midlands village. Published to mixed reviews in 1954, some of which had been openly hostile, the novel was received more positively in 1987, much to Barbara's relief. 'The striking events of the plot are recounted in Barbara Comyns's customary manner – clear, uninvolved and ingenuous', wrote Patricia Craig in the *Times Literary Supplement*.[4]

Money was now flowing in from her work – and John Faraday's legacy brought her even more. A wealthy man at his death, he bequeathed money to 24 individuals and four institutions. Barbara was the second beneficiary on the long list: Faraday left her £3,000 (about £10,500 today) as well as 'my Irish Silver sugar basin tongs and bowl, all her grandmother's dessert plates; six pieces of Staffordshire China; one painting of Chloe's and four pieces of furniture'. In addition, the proceeds of sale from John's property were to be divided between five people: Barbara, her daughter Caroline, her sister Kathleen, her brother Dennis and a friend of John's. Barbara's other remaining sister, Molly, received nothing, although Barbara later sent her £500. Julian also received nothing, a mark of John's disapproval of his having left his second wife, Nicola, the daughter of a military man like John himself. In September 1987 the house in Fernshaw Road in Chelsea, where John and Chloe had lived for many years, was sold for £526,000 (almost £2 million today). Barbara knew she could expect to inherit a good sum of money as her share of the legacy and began to think seriously about buying a house of her own.

But there were always family worries. Early in 1987 Kathleen was diagnosed with lung cancer and was scheduled for an operation in July. In the same year Nuria and her husband Juan Pablo separated and he returned to Spain, leaving William without a father and Nuria with very little money. And John Johnson, Barbara's previous literary agent, who had become a good friend, died in June 1987. Now almost 80, Barbara was suffering from arthritic pain in her back and legs and began to feel her age; she had not expected to outlast Richard so long. But she enjoyed the company of younger members of the family and was always pleased to see Nuria and William, whose antics amused her. She was also very fond of her granddaughter Lucy, whose love of reading and writing short stories impressed her. Her great-nephew, Christopher Bayley (grandson of her brother Dennis), a photographer, had taken many images of her for publicity purposes and he and his fiancée Emma, who was secretary to the Archbishop of Canterbury, occasionally visited for afternoon tea. She liked them very much and attended their wedding at Lambeth Palace: 'It was such a change to go to a wedding not a funeral. I was expecting a coffin to appear at any moment', she wrote in her diary in May. In the face of old age and impending death, the young lifted her spirits.

Good news about her work also cheered her. In 1987 BBC Radio 4 decided to serialize *The Juniper Tree* on 'Woman's Hour' in November with Harriet Walter as the narrator – and in December her agent informed her that a publisher in Paris, Deux Temps Tierce, was interested in commissioning translations of *Who was Changed and Who was Dead*, *The Skin Chairs* and *The Vet's Daughter* for sale in France. Best of all, in the early summer *Mr Fox* was published and attracted many good reviews and only two damp squibs, both concerned about the dangers of using a faux-naïve style when dealing with wartime subject matter.⁵ Patricia Craig, in the *Times Literary Supplement*, admired the effectiveness of Barbara Comyns' 'muted comic manner' and thought the book 'an odd achievement', although less striking than *The Juniper Tree*. In the *Daily Telegraph* Nina Bawden confessed to enjoying the novel for 'its innocence, its straightforwardness, its charming lack of guile', and Shaun Usher in the *Daily Mail* urged his readers to 'Hunt down *Mr Fox* forthwith for its peerless evocation of an era.' Mary Wesley, in the *Daily London News*, also applauded the novel's evocation of life during the 1940s:

> Barbara Comyns wrote this book soon after the war and mislaid the manuscript. Whoever found it deserves a medal. I recommend it for its hilariously accurate descriptions of war, when the likes of Mr Fox flourished in a world in which new laws and red tape made it awfully difficult not to be a criminal. Whether she is describing the exhilaration engendered by wasting money; cold and discomfort; the terror and mess of air raids, or Mr Fox *en route* to purgatory – where he will make the shortest circuit to heaven and the biggest harp – Barbara Comyns had me by the throat in that chokey state between laughter and tears given us by all too few writers.⁶

Barbara's work had found its moment. Kate Saunders, then a 25-year-old journalist, was so impressed by *Mr Fox* – 'it comes up as fresh as a daisy' she wrote in her review⁷ – that she visited Barbara at 64 The Green, which she described as 'a sort of Gingerbread House'. The result was a lively overview of Barbara's life and work published in the 'People' section of the magazine *Books*. During the interview Barbara knocked three years off her age and confessed (without naming Price) that the death of her wartime lover had shaken her: 'The man he is based on knew I was writing the book and he was awfully pleased. I didn't like to tell him I'd killed him off because it made a better ending. He died about a year later – it rather frightened me.' Saunders described Barbara's novels as 'bizarre as Surrealist paintings', depicting a world in which characters 'seem to exist in a perpetual Mad Hatter's tea-party'. The article ended with an extravagant accolade: 'If this extraordinary lady decided to publish her shopping lists, I for one would read them.'⁸

Feeling more confident now, Barbara wrote to Andrew Hewson at John Johnson Ltd, asking whether they still had the typescript of *The House of Dolls* which, like *Mr Fox*, had failed to find a publisher; she had enjoyed writing it and was curious to know whether she would still like it. They found it and a few days later she was leafing through the novel she had finished eighteen years previously. She also began to wonder whether it might be worth digging out the many short stories she had written over the years. She mentioned the idea to Elsbeth Lindner, who was enthusiastic, so, during the rest of the summer and the early autumn, Barbara began the task of revising 'Sunday Afternoon in St John's Wood', 'Something to Celebrate', and 'The Pear'.

Barbara was now receiving many letters from admirers and requests for interviews. A very private person, she had mixed feelings about her sudden fame, and meetings with strangers still made her anxious. She initially welcomed enquiries in early January 1988 from a mature American postgraduate, who then flew from the States to interview her. At first they got on well, but Barbara later panicked when she discovered that the student wished to read all her papers and edit some of her work. She confided to her diary in February that she did not want her 'to go through all my manuscripts and letters and photograph them. It would take days and I hate her way of talking about my work, most embarrassing.' Within a fortnight she received a 2,000 word letter from the well-meaning student, begging her to reconsider, but Barbara, feeling a mixture of guilt and irritation, refused, having recorded in her diary that 'She did talk about writing a thesis about my work, but that was all. It has upset me a lot.' There was a limit to the amount of intrusion she would tolerate.

Other approaches were more welcome. During October 1987 Teresa Grimes, a film director, wrote to Barbara. She had been struck by how visual Barbara's writing was and wanted to make a film of *Who was Changed and Who was Dead*. She was also considering a documentary about Barbara as a writer and painter: 'I am currently making a series of films called "Five women Painters" (Laura Knight, Winifred Nicholson, Nina Hamnett, Dora Carrington and Eileen Agar) so that perhaps gives you an indication of my own interests', she wrote.[9] She lunched with Barbara at 64 The Green several times during the next few years and took out an option with John Johnson Ltd for the right to adapt *Who was Changed and Who was Dead* for the big screen. By a strange and happy coincidence, Teresa turned out to be the granddaughter of Leslie Grimes, the cartoonist who retired to Ibiza and who had advised Barbara many years previously about life on the island and what to take when moving there. Barbara dug out old photographs of her family and her childhood home in Bidford-on-Avon: 'I was particularly excited when she showed me a picture of the garden flooded by the river, just as it was in *Who was Changed and Who was Dead*', Teresa wrote later. Six years after first meeting Barbara, she remembered her as

> frail and slim; white hair, strong face; her voice was quite low and husky and she spoke quickly and abruptly. Conversations with [her] were occasionally disconcerting because she would appear not to reply to a question or comment – but then you would gradually realise that she was answering you, but in her own roundabout, unobvious way.

Teresa was confident that Barbara's work would translate successfully into film and thought that the mixture of savagery and innocence in *Who was Changed and Who was Dead* would sit well in the tradition of British films such as Alberto Cavalcanti's *Went the Day Well?* (1942), 'in which the tranquil surface of rural life in picture-postcard villages is disturbed by wilder, unrestrained and independent forces'.[10] She was a determined woman and even travelled to St Petersburg in 1991, where she managed to persuade a film company to make the film in Russia – but she still had to raise a third of the budget in Britain. 'We've just been very unlucky in that the last few years have seen the worst downturn in film production in Britain. There seems to be very little money about. So bear with me while I persevere', she wrote to Barbara.[11] Two more film options – on *The Vet's Daughter* and *The Juniper Tree* – were taken out in the late 1980s by other keen film-makers. 'How wonderful if they made three films of my books at the same time', Barbara wrote in her diary in early 1989.

The warm reception of her novels had caught the eye of musicians too, and Barbara received letters from several interested in adapting her work. Andrew Vores, a Welsh composer living in the United States, wrote in May 1988 asking for permission to set to music Barbara's précis of *Sisters by a River*, which appeared on the back cover of the Virago edition. Barbara replied, 'It is a lovely idea and I do hope I will be able to hear it.'[12] During the same month David Sulkin, then director at the English National Opera, invited Barbara to afternoon tea in early June to meet Alec Roth, an English composer with whom he planned to collaborate in adapting *The Vet's Daughter* for the opera stage. The gathering was to take place at a house in Oakley Square, where Barbara had lived in 1930. She was nervous about the journey and meeting new people, but Nuria drove her there, and to her surprise, Barbara thoroughly enjoyed the afternoon, recording in her diary that evening:

> Lovely party, wonderful food. Met lots of interesting people. David Sulkin talked about turning *The Vet's Daughter* into an opera. It was so strange going to Oakley Square after all these years. The Church where I was married has been pulled down and council flats built. The old houses that still remain are in beautiful condition. The same trees are still in the square, some of them lime. I used to love the smell.

This was only one of a number of uncanny repetitions in which people and places from Barbara's younger days reappeared in her last years, as if to remind her of her life's trajectory.

Sadly, none of these projects came to fruition, much to Barbara's disappointment. She was very pleased, though, with what she called the 'magic money' associated with them – the cheques that came her way when people bought the rights to her books in order to adapt them. Sums for advances, royalties, broadcast fees and film rights were all carefully noted in her diary. She never lost the habit of keeping a tally of her income and any money owed to her. 'Paid 1,000 pounds into the Halifax so there is six thousand rustling there' and 'Paid 3,060 pounds into my High Interest account so now there should be 10,000 pounds bringing me interest' are only two of many such diary entries made during her last few years.

* * *

Always coy about her age, Barbara kept the significance of her birthday in 1987 a secret: 'My eightieth birthday. No one knew, which pleased me', she wrote in her diary on 27 December. But growing older brought nervousness and a lack of confidence. She found looking for a house during 1988 exciting but also stressful; she was needlessly anxious about whether she could afford it and worried that she might make a bad decision. After viewing several houses in Twickenham with Julian and Sally, in April 1988 she settled on 65 Hamilton Road, a Victorian terraced two-bedroomed cottage that faced directly on to the pavement at the front but that had a pretty, well-kept garden at the back. It was not perfect, but Barbara could see its potential, writing in her diary: 'The decorations at no 65 are frightful but some white paint will make a great difference. The conservatory is most attractive, a bar to eat from and all this beautiful greenery.' With her legacy from John Faraday and her savings in the Post Office she was able to buy the house outright, although she was still worried about not having enough left for an emergency: 'It will leave me short of money, practically no income but there will be my book earnings and odds and ends [...] and the old Age Pension has been increased. Much better to be short of money than have a huge debt weighing on my mind', she confided to her diary. In fact, she had a great deal of money in various savings accounts and was advised by her solicitor to remake her will for that very reason the following year. Barbara found the process of buying the house exhausting, and by June 1988 she felt worn out: 'It is all too complicated for me. I have grown so old and tired – very afraid I have taken on too much.' But, helped by Caroline and Nuria, by the end of that month she had moved into her new home. She was soon training climbing plants up trellises in the conservatory and inviting friends such as Ursula Holden and Adinah Thomas round for lunch. 'Richard is very pleased with this house', she told Ursula, soon after moving in.[13] For Barbara, the world of the dead and that of the living were never very far apart.

During the same year, Caroline was also house-hunting, looking for somewhere as a base in England. Pepe had died over a year earlier and she now wanted to see more of her brother Julian and his family, and spend some time with Nuria and William. With her legacy from John Faraday, she planned to buy a house in Twickenham but, after visiting one of her old flames, John Alford, who was now Director of Art at Shrewsbury School, she decided to look in Shropshire. Within a few months, she had bought a cottage in Stanton upon Hine Heath, a quiet and small village surrounded by farmland. Caroline still had the house in Madrid where she had lived with Pepe, and she and Nuria, together with William, moved between England and Spain for weeks at a time during 1988 and 1989. 'They come rushing in and out like waves', Barbara wrote in her diary. In Madrid Nuria met a wealthy and sophisticated Italian called Egidio ('Edgy' to his English friends), with whom she fell in love. They spent time in both Madrid and Milan (his home city), returning to England late in October for a few weeks, when they visited Barbara, who wrote in her diary afterwards:

> To my surprise Nuria turned up at 65. She was accompanied by her Italian lover. He is very small but arresting. Rather like John Pemberton. He is about 40, I think, and has a bald patch in the middle of his head […] I like this new man friend she has but someone is going to get very hurt. Strangely enough they both resemble each other, small and lively.

Confident that this relationship would last, Nuria told Barbara she was giving up her flat in Twickenham and would be living mostly in Madrid with Edgy; she planned to stay in Caroline's cottage in Shropshire when she returned to England for occasional visits. But Barbara's intuitions were right: within a few years Nuria discovered that Edgy was two-timing her and had recently fathered a child with another woman. Heartbroken, she returned to England with William and made her home in her mother's cottage in Stanton upon Hine Heath, managing to make ends meet by working as a dental nurse and giving Spanish lessons in order to augment her welfare benefit payments. She would drive down to Twickenham with William occasionally to see Julian and Barbara, of whom she was very fond.

Throughout the summer of 1988 Barbara was painstakingly revising *The House of Dolls* for Methuen, which had offered £2,000 (about £6,700 today) in advance of publication. Elsbeth Lindner and her colleague Briar Silich from Methuen drove over to Twickenham occasionally to help and advise: 'Strawberries and wine and all kinds of good things they brought with them, also a lily in a pot', Barbara wrote in her diary in September. The corrections were finished that month and the book was scheduled to be published early the following year. In late December Barbara was recovering from a chest infection and spent time resting and reading a new book about Kim Philby that Julian and Sally had bought her. She recorded in her diary:

It went off the rails sometimes but I enjoyed it very much. I always wondered what happened to Aileen. They were so close when we knew them but she was very domineering although she looked so pale and gentle. She was mad on having babies because she thought Kim would be faithful to her if she had a large family but he wasn't.

On the first day of January 1989 she started her new diary with the entry:

Rather long since I spoke to anyone but I'm getting better. The year's over. I have bought a house (freehold), put some money into several banks, have a book published in France, two books are sold for films, at least the rights are. Don't feel very well, just old and weak. Need a lovely surprise.

Family concerns preoccupied her at this time and exacerbated her sense of weariness: Barbara's granddaughter Mariquita, Nuria's sister, had recently had an illegitimate child while living in The Hague; she was now a single mother, alone and impoverished, a state Barbara remembered from her own early life. And her grandson Nicholas, Julian's son, was drinking heavily and had recently been sent home in disgrace from Spain where he had been staying with Caroline and Nuria. But there were distractions that took her mind off such worries. In mid-January 1989 she travelled to the Groucho Club in London to join Alexandra Pringle and Lynn Knight for a Virago lunch. Her agent Andrew Hewson was also there, 'looking very dashing'. She enjoyed the meal but confessed to her diary that she 'found it difficult to hear what anyone was saying there was so much noise. It was very tiring. I felt bewildered with all the noise.' Barbara had always loved London but now she found travelling in cities increasingly stressful; by September she dreaded catching buses and trains and found the journey to Chiswick to have tea with Ursula Holden 'awful': 'it was difficult to know when to get off the bus, so many flashing lights. Left my spectacles behind and lost a ten pound note', she confided to her diary. She turned down several invitations as the year went on, including one from a French journalist who interviewed her at 65 Hamilton Road and who warmly invited her to Paris, and one from Teresa Grimes to a private view at the Tate Gallery. Barbara's increasing frailty and lack of confidence about travelling was beginning to shrink her world.

The 'lovely surprise' she had wished for at the beginning of the year came, however, in the form of great success for her work during 1989. In January *The Skin Chairs* was serialized in ten instalments on 'Woman's Hour' and in the same month Virago published its edition of *A Touch of Mistletoe*, its green cover featuring Stanley Spencer's *Hilda and I at Burghclere*, a domestic family scene suggesting stress and disenchantment rather than contentment – an apt reflection of the novel's contents. This time the introduction was by Patricia Craig, who warmly praised the author's use of a 'child's unclouded vision and candour'.[14] The *Daily Telegraph* reviewer found the novel 'episodic, funny and charming', and Brian Fallon in the *Irish Times* described Barbara Comyns as 'one of England's most underrated writers since the war' and the book as 'at times close to Jean Rhys territory [...] a minor classic'.[15] Reviews of *A Touch of Mistletoe* were eclipsed, however, by the praise showered on *The House of Dolls*, which was released on 2 March 1989. The novel that Graham Greene had not liked and for which John Johnson had not been able to find a publisher now attracted widespread acclaim.

Methuen had decided to keep quiet about the fact that *The House of Dolls* had been written over twenty years earlier, so reviewers assumed this was a brand new novel from Barbara Comyns and often drew attention to her age. 'Barbara Comyns – 80 this year – has a sharp understanding of the humiliations of increasing age and decreasing prospects', wrote the reviewer in the *Mail on Sunday*, while Nicholas Best in the *Financial Times* suggested that the novel was 'a delightful comedy in the Ealing tradition', adding, 'The author pokes gentle fun at the English passion for respectability, and writes with a clarity and sureness of touch remarkable for someone in her 80th year.'[16] (In fact, Barbara was in her 82nd year.) While several reviewers praised the book as hilarious and entertaining, more perceptive critics noticed that its dark humour conveyed a political message about class, age, gender and money. '*The House of Dolls*, by Barbara Comyns, is a satanic work worthy of the black minds of Beryl Bainbridge or Molly Keane [...] The position of single older women in this society, emotionally and financially, is vulnerable', wrote Alice Thompson. In the *Independent*, Kate Saunders drew attention to the novel's 1960s setting, when class barriers were breaking down, and described the book as 'a magical novel' and its author as a 'vastly underrated' writer. Justin Lovell, in the *Literary Review*, was of the same mind and compared Barbara's work to that of 'other fine writers – Mary Wesley, E. F. Benson, Muriel Spark, even, in a memorable party scene, Evelyn Waugh'; he noted the originality of her work: 'once between the covers one feels oneself to have stepped off a prosaic street, into a house of possibilities and everyday strangeness'.[17]

Among the increasing flow of fan mail, Barbara received a letter in 1989 that really pleased her. It was from the great-granddaughter of Charles Dickens, the author Monica Dickens, who had recently returned to England after the death of her American husband in the States, where she had lived for thirty-five years. 'Thanks to Virago, I have just read *The Vet's Daughter* and *A Touch of Mistletoe*, and am hastening to thank you for hours of pure pleasure and total fascination', she wrote to Barbara.[18] A few weeks later she wrote again, this time to congratulate Barbara on *The House of Dolls*: 'it's you at the height of your powers, and that's putting it very high

[...] I love your idea about having the old girls find their entertainment in going to funerals.'[19] The two women began a warm correspondence, although while she praised Monica's novels in her letters, Barbara was more honest in her diary: 'I don't like them at all – a bit morbid and the characters seem too small.' But she was impressed by Monica who, now 75, was about to travel to America and Scotland to research material for her next book. Monica's energy prompted Barbara to consider writing again, albeit with a somewhat bizarre shift of focus: 'I sometimes think I might write about bees. There is a bee club about five minutes away and Caroline and Sally belong to it', she wrote in her diary in November. This idea was soon abandoned because another project became more pressing. Elizabeth Fairbairn of John Johnson Ltd had found the typescript of *Waiting* – the novel rejected by publishers in 1979 – and had returned it to Barbara some months previously, suggesting she revise it, presumably in the hope that it might now find its moment, just as *Mr Fox* and *The House of Dolls* had done. Barbara made a resolution to tackle it in the New Year.

Other letters brought sadder news: her eldest sister, Molly, who had a difficult relationship with her son, and who had recently moved from her Hertfordshire farmhouse home of many years into a council bungalow, was unhappy. Barbara had never been close to Molly and visited her rarely, but she did write to her, sometimes enclosing money. Aged 86, Molly was becoming increasingly forgetful, writing to Barbara, 'I don't do much cooking. I can't remember what I am doing. Is your brain alright? I suppose it must be if you are still writing books! I've heard several of your plays on the radio.' Age and unhappiness made Molly nostalgic for the past; in another rambling letter from Weston she wrote,

> Do you remember the three lavender bushes at Bell Court, almost trees? I often think of Big Meadow with its seven donkeys and all the lovely wild flowers that grew there. We used to see how much pollen we could get on our shoes. One of the gardeners used to let me lead a horse at haymaking. I was so proud.[20]

Barbara's other surviving sister, Kathleen, suffering from cancer, was growing weak and frail. Having visited her in March 1989, Barbara wrote in her diary, 'Poor little Kay she is so thin and ill – her lungs are affected now. She weighs less than five stone. She looked strangely beautiful with a kind of orange glowing light around her. Her legs are almost as thin as pencils.' Kathleen died a few months later, and Barbara was deeply upset to discover that she had been buried before her husband Teddy informed the family of her death; she was also upset by his claims that Kathleen had always hated Chloe, writing in her diary in late June: 'I was very shocked and cried a lot when Teddy stopped talking [...] He has a great girlfriend and thinks of nothing but her and she made all the funeral arrangements and we were not asked. This is a muddle but I feel so sad.' When Sally took Barbara to visit Teddy in July, he was calmer and reassured Barbara that he was fine: he had three kind women friends who cleaned and cooked for him. Given the celibate nature of his marriage to Kathleen, who thought sexual intercourse was a horrible business, the women were probably more than 'friends'. According to Julian, Barbara's son, at least two women were to challenge Teddy's will after his death three years later.

*   *   *

These sad family matters were offset in 1990, however, by more good news about Barbara's books. Methuen had been taken over in 1987 by Octopus, which later created a paperback imprint called Mandarin Books, and *The House of Dolls* was published as a Mandarin paperback in 1990. The novel's back cover was festooned with quotations from the best reviews, and Barbara recorded in her diary that she thought its front cover, which featured an elderly man dozing on a sofa, clearly the worse for several glasses of wine and being propositioned by one of the house residents, was 'very arresting and original'. The book was released in the United States during the same year, where it was warmly praised, and in November *Who was Changed and Who was Dead* was serialized as Radio 4's 'Book at Bedtime'. Book Club Associates bought a thousand copies of the novel and the publishing firm Icaria Editorial, based in Barcelona, offered an advance of £800 (about £2,400 today) prior to its publication in Spain.

Despite all this good news about her work, Barbara was becoming increasingly depressed by her physical frailty and was aware that she was growing more absent-minded. Her anxiety, which had been steadily getting worse over the previous two years, was now casting a shadow over her life. Some of her worries related to family problems and were quite justified. Mariquita wrote to say that she and her baby were miserable and starving in The Hague: 'This makes me very sad', Barbara wrote in her diary in April. She was also worried about her grandson Nicholas, who was undergoing treatment for alcoholism, although when Julian took her to visit him at a residential clinic in May, she was relieved to see that the house and grounds were very beautiful and that he was not unhappy there. (The treatment was successful and Nicholas gradually overcame his drinking problems.)

Other anxieties were irrational and augured the onset of dementia. During 1989 she had frequently felt 'on edge' and was beginning to behave oddly: in August she went to the bank and told the cashier that she did not want a cheque card: 'I think them very dangerous and get in other people's hands. The bank girl says I will love it. I have put the cheque card in a book *Our*

310   *Barbara Comyns*

Mutual Friend (Dickens). No one must know', she wrote in her diary. When they visited 65 Hamilton Road, Julian and Sally noticed that Barbara was using sour milk and that the house was starting to smell of cats' pee because she had taken to feeding so many stray cats in her home and would forget to let them out (her own had all died by now). She found filling in forms for agents and publishers difficult and she constantly lost things; in September 1989 she confessed to her diary that she had spent an entire day 'looking for an important Bank paper. Had the contents of 6 drawers all over the floor but at about 8 in the evening found a grubby paper which may be what I want.' She started work on revising *Waiting* in March 1990 but quickly grew impatient with it: 'It is better than I remembered but depressing and dangerous – too many real characters and I don't like the heroine much', she noted gloomily in her diary.

The situation grew steadily worse: by the early summer of 1990 Barbara had begun to develop symptoms of paranoia. At first she was aware that she was being irrational at times, writing in her diary in May: 'See things all wrong. Feel very strange; thought Julian was doing bad things when he was only being kind.' But very quickly she began to have delusions, imagining that Julian was having an affair with one of her neighbours and that her sister Nan (who had died in 1984) had bought the house next door. She thought she heard noises upstairs and seemed to think that her daughter was treating her badly: 'Felt sad and lonely, felt very hurt by Caroline who has treated me like a tramp', she confided to her diary. Realizing that Barbara needed support, Julian arranged for his secretary to drive her to a supermarket once a week to stock up with food, and in May he made an appointment for her to be examined at the local hospital. The paranoia grew worse, however: in June she imagined she was being followed by two young people, writing in her diary: 'They hung about so that they could see me through holes they had made in the walls. The police came about it. They haven't questioned me yet. It has done a lot of harm to the wood.' She also felt persecuted by a 'horrible rude woman' who 'wants to be given the house for nothing. It worries me very much.' Barbara's diary for 1990 finishes abruptly in July and there are only three entries in her 1991 diary: 'Friday 25 January: Very nervous and upset; Tuesday 5 February: Alone in the house, very cold; Friday 8 February: Still this deep snow and most of my plants are dead.' Their brevity and bleakness indicate something of the inner desolation she felt at this time.

Family members and close friends such as Ursula Holden realized that Barbara was moving from confusion into dementia. The situation came to a head when a young man found her wandering in Twickenham in her nightdress at 4 o'clock in the morning. He took her to the local hospital where she was admitted for a few days, and the staff contacted family members. Julian and Sally were first there and Nuria arrived soon after, having driven down from Shropshire. Barbara's behaviour was now alarming her relatives and it was clear that she could no longer live on her own. In a spontaneous and generous gesture, Nuria offered to take her back to Shropshire and look after her in her mother's cottage, where she was now living. On the journey northwards in May, Barbara declaimed loudly that she hated 'the fucking countryside' and certainly didn't want to live in it. But, once settled in the cottage in Stanton upon Hine Heath, she calmed down. Nuria was a good cook and Barbara's health improved once she started eating properly; she also enjoyed talking to Stuart Phillips, Nuria's new partner, a wood turner and a gentle, patient man. Nuria fetched some of Barbara's furniture and books from 65 Hamilton Road so that she would have the comfort of her own things around her, and Barbara gradually settled into her new way of life. Caroline, now living with a new partner in a cottage in north Wales, frequently came over to spend time with her mother and help out. Barbara paid a woman in the village to wash her clothes and, having developed a sweet tooth in old age, enjoyed trips with Nuria and William to the Safeway supermarket in the nearby village of Wem, where she would study intently the confectionery and biscuit shelves before making her choice, often with interference from William, who wished to have a say in the matter. Seeing Barbara's trolley laden with enough packets of sweets and biscuits to last months, Nuria would smuggle some back on to the shelves before joining the checkout queue.

Like her grandmother, Nuria enjoyed having birds and animals around her: at Stanton upon Hine Heath she kept chickens and Barbara found great pleasure in sitting on a low chair with a white chicken on her lap, stroking its feathers and speaking to it softly. She had lucid intervals when she liked to scribble ideas down and was able to write letters. She wrote to Ursula Holden that she was fond of the hens – 'they are beautiful birds and so loving' – and she liked to watch the cows passing the house twice daily, even though she knew they were 'doomed'.[21] On sunny days she would sit on the empty beehive in the garden, chatting to Stuart while he worked at his woodturning.

In the summer of 1991 Stuart's father died, leaving Upper Harcourt, a detached Georgian stone house situated on a hill above Stanton upon Hine Heath, to Stuart and his siblings. In September 1991 he and Nuria moved there temporarily. Upper Harcourt, a large house surrounded by trees and agricultural land, had fine views; it was approached by a long drive and the rather grand front door was framed by a portico with stone pillars. Barbara felt happy and secure there, perhaps because the proportions of the house reminded her of Milborne Grove, her home in London many years before. The chickens came too, joining the other animals already in the house – two puppies and several cats. Barbara had her own room, a large guest bedroom with a handsome fireplace, in which Nuria or Stuart would light a fire on cold winter days. She felt at home in Upper Harcourt, to the extent of complaining to Stuart about 'those two awful maids' in the house. The 'maids' were Caroline and Nuria, who were laughing and chatting in the next room. She was sometimes to be found wandering round the hall in the early morning, announcing that she had just cycled from Birmingham. Perhaps she thought she was back in Bell Court again, her childhood home, which was an hour's ride away from that city. She also claimed to see Stuart's father with his dog and described him accurately, despite the fact she had never met him and he had died some months previously – but then she had several times in her life 'seen' dead people alive.[22]

In January 1992 Nuria and Stewart returned with Barbara to the cottage in Stanton upon Hine Heath because Upper Harcourt had been sold. Barbara's dementia was worsening and she would hide money in odd places, pushing pound notes into the plughole in her bedroom sink and into the phone socket downstairs. By this time, Caroline was dealing with all correspondence from Barbara's publishers and her agent. When Julian visited his mother with Sally and their daughter Lucy, they saw a marked deterioration. Lucy, now 12, was upset that her lively grandmother had become so withdrawn and distant and she did not know how to respond when Barbara pleaded with her the next morning to stay, saying 'Don't leave me.' Barbara still wrote to Ursula Holden but her letters were now laboured and incoherent: 'I am very weak and can hardly walk and have trouble speaking, in fact I have trouble with everything I try to do.' Her last, almost illegible letter ended, 'Don't let anyone read this.'[23] In the spring Barbara fell ill, and Nuria called the local doctor, who casually examined his elderly patient and declared that she had pneumonia. He suggested that, as she was not much more than skin and bone, she should be allowed to die. Furious, Nuria told him in no uncertain terms that this 'old lady' was not only her grandmother, but the famous author Barbara Comyns. The doctor rapidly backtracked and arranged for Barbara to be taken to Shrewsbury hospital where she was cared for in the geriatric ward.

Nuria and Stewart were expecting a child, and their baby was born on 18 June in the maternity wing of the same hospital, which was housed in a different building. She was named Chloe. Against all the rules, Nuria pushed her in a neo-natal cot to the geriatric ward across the road so that Barbara could see her great-granddaughter. She was too weak to hold the baby but she smiled at Nuria and her child. It was as if she had held on to life so that she could see the baby before she died. Soon afterwards, when it became evident that she was fading, Caroline brought her back to the cottage in Stanton upon Hine Heath so that she and Nuria could look after her there. Barbara died in Stanton upon Hine Heath on 14 July 1992. Her death certificate stated that a stroke and Parkinson's disease had caused her death.

When Ursula Holden and Barbara met for their last meal together in Twickenham, before Nuria took Barbara to Shropshire, they had talked about death. Ursula said that she would hate it when her friend died: 'Well, I've got to do it, haven't I?', Barbara had replied somewhat acerbically, without a shred of self-pity.[24] She had several times remarked to her family over the years that she would like to be taken to her grave in a coach drawn by four white horses, their heads adorned with black plumes. As the graveyard of St Andrew's Church in the village was only half a mile from the cottage where Barbara died, the family decided this wish was too expensive and extravagant to honour. Instead, they offered their remarkable relative a libation by pouring a gin and tonic on her simple grave after the funeral ceremony, in memory of Barbara's habit of holding that drink in her left hand while she stirred cake mixture with a wooden spoon held in her right. This ritual is still repeated whenever a family wedding or funeral takes place at the church of St Andrews, as it was after Nuria's wedding to Michael Leighton in 2002, and after Caroline's funeral in 2013. Each Christmas Eve, Nuria places a small Christmas tree on her grandmother's grave – Barbara loved Christmas – together with a lighted candle.

Barbara Comyns died a relatively wealthy woman. On her death, the net value of her estate was £241,848, a sum worth about £620,000 today. She left her house in Hamilton Road and all her antique furniture to be shared between her son Julian and her daughter Caroline. She also left the royalties and profits accruing to her books to Caroline, as well as her jewellery and silverware. To Julian she left her money in the Halifax Building Society, all her paintings and three drawings by Edward Burne-Jones. To Sally and to her grandchildren, Nuria, Nicholas, George and Lucy, she left £1,000 each (about £2,550 today).[25] Through talent and determination, Barbara had managed to conquer the spectre of poverty that had haunted her for much of her life. She also left a remarkable legacy of extraordinary fiction which has the power to entertain and to disturb in equal measure.

Afterword

Barbara Comyns' life spanned most of the twentieth century, but apart from references to the Second World War in *A Touch of Mistletoe* and *Mr Fox*, her novels give little indication of world events or political change. They focus instead on the dynamics of relationships and of family life and, in particular, how they affect girls and women. Her female characters usually struggle to make ends meet and we see how terrifyingly quickly their lives can drop into poverty. She was well aware of the challenges facing a woman who wishes to combine writing with bringing up a family; her friend Ursula Holden observed that 'She had no illusions about the pitfalls of a woman writer's life.'[1] Barbara experienced many difficulties – including those of juggling a writing life with family commitments – but she managed to overcome them through resilience and sheer determination. Diana Brinton Lee's description of her in 1944 as 'one of those wide-eyed wiry little sea-daisies, sort of innocent and fragile and yet tough', was very perceptive.

Despite her focus on women and her use of female narrators, Barbara Comyns never thought of herself as a feminist writer and she had no interest in feminism as a movement.[2] Nor did she idealize or sentimentalize women; she was well aware that they could be as emotionally cruel and as controlling as men. In *The Juniper Tree* Bella's narcissistic mother continually and deliberately undermines her daughter's confidence, and the grandmother in *Who was Changed and Who was Dead* is a formidable figure who terrorizes her family. Rather, Barbara's strength lies in a narrative perspective that offers a candid and irreverent view of human relationships in the home and at work; a perspective that enabled her to describe vividly all the small cruelties, humiliations and absurdities that take place behind closed doors. She was also acutely aware of the compromises many women had to make in order to stay financially solvent. In a climate of economic gloom, Victoria Green of *A Touch of Mistletoe* grimly hangs on to her job in a commercial studio in Pimlico, despite the long hours and the behaviour of the bald-headed sleeping partner who tries to give her 'awful sucking kisses'. Twenty-first-century readers will be more aware of the sinister implications of such unwanted advances than the novel's first readers in 1967. At that time, most women simply regarded such behaviour as an inevitable hazard of the workplace. As she grew older, Barbara became alert to how such manipulations could transmute into a darker cruelty. The apparent artlessness of her first few books was gradually replaced by carefully structured plots and a more subtle use of the faux-naïve narrator. The small humiliations and rejections within the home evident in earlier works become abuse writ large in *The Vet's Daughter*, *The Skin Chairs* and *The Juniper Tree*. They are classics of domestic gothic, written before the phrase was coined. She was innovative in other ways too, experimenting with magical realist effects before Angela Carter published her first novel.

Sometimes the comic effects in her books derive from a Dickensian tendency to exaggerate human characteristics and foibles; sometimes from a surreal juxtaposition of the bizarre and the everyday; and sometimes from a faux-naïve view of the world as a slightly mad and challenging place over which one has little control. The humour in her books moderates the suffering of her female characters and prevents it from dropping into mawkishness or morbidity. Their plight is never sentimentalized but presented simply as the mundane outcome of having no money, no power and little independence. Her novels are about survival – there is invariably a vulnerable girl or a woman at risk in them – but despite their dark subject matter, they are not gloomy or bleak. With the exception of *The Vet's Daughter*, in which cruelty triumphs, her work shows how resourcefulness and endurance can win the day, as indeed they did in Barbara's own life.

Soon after Barbara Comyns died in 1992 several obituaries appeared in the national press. In the *Independent*, Ursula Holden praised her as 'a true original' whose death marked 'a loss to English writing'.[3] Teresa Grimes thought her work 'unique' and suggested that Barbara's special talent lay in her ability to portray vividly the 'bizarre nature of "ordinary" life and the comic madness of families'.[4] Jane Gardam described her novels in the *Guardian* as 'idiosyncratic, episodic, vivid, funny, slightly sinister', and suggested that she shared with Graham Greene a 'sense of wreckage and of evil in the air'.[5]

After a short flurry of appreciation prompted by her obituaries, her reputation dwindled in the 1990s apart from a few brief entries in reference books, in one of which her novels were likened to those of Ivy Compton-Burnett.[6] However, the tide turned at the millennium. In June 2000 Elizabeth Jane Howard described *The Vet's Daughter* in the *Sunday Telegraph* as 'a small, near-perfect work of art' that had haunted her ever since she first read it in 1959.[7] The following year the commissioning editor for Virago Modern Classics wrote, 'She was a contemporary of Barbara Pym, Elizabeth Bowen and Elizabeth Taylor but no one else wrote with the same wilful craziness and breezy insouciance.'[8] Recently, contemporary writers such as Maggie O'Farrell, Helen Oyeyemi and Kate Hamer have discovered her books and have been quick to praise their originality and imaginative power. Academics have also begun rather belatedly to take an interest in her novels.[9]

New editions of the most popular books began to appear from 2000, when Virago reissued *Sisters by a River*, *Our Spoons Came from Woolworths* and *The Vet's Daughter* – and the company reissued them again, with fresh introductions, in 2013. Barbara's novels have also been reissued by New York Review Books, the Dorothy Project, Capuchin Classics, Turnpike Books and Daunt Books.[10] Each time one of them is reprinted, it prompts a reassessment. Reviewers have praised her ability to combine 'dispassion, levity and veiled ferocity', and she has even been described as 'a neglected genius' and as 'the unrecognized British Nabokov'.[11] Writing about the New York Review Books edition of *The Juniper Tree*, published in the States in January 2018, Marina Warner suggested that her work 'touches blazing questions about stepfamilies, children's survival, parental damage, male charisma and female surrender'.[12] Later the same year, Sarah Waters described *The Vet's Daughter* as 'a perfect novel, a masterpiece of domestic gothic'.[13] In 2021 Christopher Shrimpton enthusiastically reviewed three of her reissued books in the *Times Literary Supplement*, suggesting that 'As well as a somewhat wide-eyed alertness to the wonderful and monstrous, there is a certain cut-throat logic' to her work.[14] The editor of that issue of the *Times Literary Supplement*, which also contained an article on the friendship between Graham Greene and Barbara Comyns, suggested that 'The novels of Barbara Comyns are [...] enjoying a revival.'[15] This biography will, I hope, help that revival.

Acknowledgements

When, in 2015, I decided to write a biography of Barbara Comyns, I contacted her son, Julian Pemberton, and her granddaughter, Nuria Leighton. I was astonished to find that they had both carefully kept boxes and boxes of letters, some of them dating back to the 1930s, to which they allowed me free access. Writing this book would have been impossible without their help. They both warmly welcomed me into their homes and generously spent much time answering my many questions. They also confirmed which episodes in Barbara's books drew on actual events or relationships and so helped me negotiate the difficult tightrope between fact and fiction. Other relatives and friends of Barbara's family who have provided useful information include William Gray, Nicola Howard Jones, Michael Leighton, Sally Fletcher Pemberton, Lucy Pemberton, Nicholas Pemberton, Chloe Phillips, Stewart Phillips and Mariquita Urbano. Adrian Darby, whose grandfather was the brother of Barbara's maternal grandmother, advised on the genealogy of the Darby family line in England and kindly shared his family memorabilia with me. The Estate of Barbara Comyns was extremely helpful throughout.

For help in researching the life of Diana Brinton Lee, I am greatly indebted to Denys J. Wilcox, who loaned me the Diana Brinton Lee Archive, currently a private collection, and to John Pilling, nephew of Diana Brinton Lee, who gave me permission to quote from his aunt's letters in that archive. I am also grateful to John Pilling, Joanna Box and the late Julian Clist for providing additional information about their aunt 'Dinnie'.

I am much indebted to Hannah McSorley (née Stoneham) who, unable to complete the biography of Barbara Comyns she started some years ago, very generously shared her research with me.

Other individuals who helped and advised include Kate Aubury (Administrator, Kemerton Estate); Carlota María Melguizo Barrachina; Gill Bennett (Former Chief Historian at the Foreign Office); Celia Brayfield; Veronica Brendon; the late Carmen Callil; Anthony Nicholas d'Esterre Darby; Penelope Durie; Teresa Grimes; the late Ursula Holden and her daughter, Kathy

Dixon; Elsbeth Lindner; Mark Shaddick (Chair of Bidford Historical Society); and Elizabeth Velluet of the Richmond Local History Society.

I am grateful to librarians and archivists at the following institutions for their help and expertise: the British Library and the Newsroom at the British Library; The National Archives at Kew; the Victoria and Albert Museum, Archive of Art and Design; the Shakespeare Birthplace Trust, Stratford-upon-Avon; the University of Sussex Special Collections; Samantha Blake at the BBC Written Archives; Stephen Bartley at the Heatherley School of Fine Art; John J. Burns Library, Massachusetts; Robin Bray at Independent Television (ITV) (Programme Copy Sales); Matthew J. Geoghegan at the Irish Film Classification Office, Dublin; Kirby Smith and Thomas Charles Birkhead at Penguin Random House UK Archive and Library, Rushden, Northamptonshire; and Stephen Witkowski at the British Council (Records and Archives). The British Newspaper Archive has also been an invaluable online resource.

Thanks for permissions are due to Kathy Dixon, on behalf of her late mother, Ursula Holden, for permission to quote from the unpublished article 'Barbara Comyns (1909–1992)', written in 1997; ITV for permission to quote from the 1984 Channel Four 'Book Four' programme 'Neglected Authors'; and also to the Estate of Graham Greene for permission to quote from several unpublished letters.

Several people were kind enough to read this biography before it was published. I owe them all immense gratitude for their keen observations and their continued interest. They include Norah Perkins and Becky Brown who suggested several improvements and offered much support; Sue Zlosnik, who introduced me to Barbara Comyns' books many years ago and who has been a source of encouragement throughout; Frances White, whose sharp eyes spotted many small errors; Helen Taylor who offered valuable observations and editorial suggestions; Janet Beer, who showed continued interest and made helpful comments on the final draft; and Anne Rowe, who read every chapter as soon as it was finished and whose detailed comments on style and content resulted in the book being more readable.

I owe Ed Wilson, my agent, many heartfelt thanks for his patience and encouragement and for providing access to material held by Johnson & Alcock.

I also owe Matthew Frost of Manchester University Press a huge debt of gratitude for his belief in *Barbara Comyns: A Savage Innocence*. Thanks also to the anonymous readers who offered valuable suggestions about the book's early chapters.

Finally, I must record a very warm debt of gratitude to my family, especially my husband Howard who cheerfully put up with my distracted states throughout the seven years it took me to write this book, offering cups of tea and coffee, glasses of wine and encouragement throughout. He also used his family history skills to track Barbara's ancestry and the family trees of other people who were important to her. Finally, I wish to thank our three sons, Laurie, Joel and Daniel, and our daughters-in-law, Jen, Sarah and Michelle, for their continued interest. I could not have written this book without the love and support of them all.

Illustrations

Every effort has been made to obtain permission to reproduce copyright material, and the publisher will be pleased to be informed of any errors and omissions for correction in future editions.

Novels by Barbara Comyns

Notes

Abbreviations

BC   Barbara Comyns
DBL   Diana Brinton Lee
RCC   Richard Comyns Carr

Introduction

1 BC to Andrew Hewson, letter dated 11 June 1979, courtesy of Nuria Leighton.
2 David Auerbach, *The Quarterly Conversation*, 24, 6 June 2011, http://quarterlyconversation.com/who-was-changed-and-who-was-dead-by-barbara-comyns, accessed 15 September 2016.
3 This quotation from Serge Doubrovsky's work was used by Alex Clark in her article 'Drawn from Life: Why Have Novelists Stopped Making Things Up?', *The Guardian*, 23 June 2018.

1 From Bell Court to Amsterdam

1 I owe this family memory, and much of the information in this and the following chapters, to conversations with Julian Pemberton that took place between 2015 and 2022.
2 Rodney Crompton, Mike Gerrard, Roger Leese, Sandra Parker, Mark Shaddick and Wendy Shaddick, *Yesterday's Children: Bidford-on-Avon Remembered* (Bidford: Bidford Publications, 2013), 44.
3 BC, *Sisters by a River* (1947; London: Virago, 2013), 44, 37.
4 I owe this information to Nuria Leighton, Barbara's granddaughter.
5 BC, *Sisters by a River*, 175.
6 BC, Introduction to *The Vet's Daughter* (1959; London: Virago, 2013), xi.
7 BC, *The Juniper Tree* (1985; New York: New York Review Books, 2018), 168.
8 BC, *Sisters by a River*, 13.
9 Ursula Holden, 'A Singular Woman', *The Oldie*, January 2012, 20.
10 'Biography of John Darby (1857–1943)', *British Hunts and Huntsmen (The South East, East and Eastern Midlands of England)* (London: The Biographical

Press, 1909), 243. In this brief biography it is claimed that George's father, John Darby (b. 1786), was a Master of the Hounds and hunted with his own pack in Ireland before he became a horse-dealer in England.

11 *Baily's Monthly Magazine of Sports and Pastimes*, November 1904, 393.

12 I owe this fact, and much of the information about the Darby family in this chapter, to a conversation with Adrian Darby, 8 August 2016.

13 I am grateful to Adrian Darby for showing me this painting.

14 Ursula Holden, 'Barbara Comyns 1909–1992' [*sic*], 5. This article was written for *The London Magazine* in 1997 but, according to Julie Hearn, author of an article on Barbara Comyns' work, it was 'rejected on the grounds that Barbara Comyns was not that important a novelist'. It remains unpublished and is held by the literary agency Johnson & Alcock.

15 Letter to DBL, Diana Brinton Lee Archive, private collection.

16 BC, *Sisters by a River*, 180.

17 BC, *Sisters by a River*, 20–1.

18 From an unpublished and unpaginated memoir written by Caroline Urbano (née Pemberton), Barbara's daughter, courtesy of Nuria Leighton. The furniture is now owned by Barbara's descendants.

19 See Marigold Freeman-Attwood, *Leap Castle: A Place and its People* (Norwich: Michael Russell Publishing, 2001), which includes several versions of how the marriage came about and also provides a more accurate historical account of how the castle passed from the O'Carrolls to the Darby family.

20 Extract from 'Kilman Castle, the House of Horror' by Mildred Darby, quoted in Freeman-Attwood, *Leap Castle*, 115.

21 Extract from 'Something to Celebrate', courtesy of Nuria Leighton.

22 See back cover, inside flap of first edition (hardback) of *The Vet's Daughter* (London: Heinemann, 1959) and Introduction by BC to the Virago Press edition of *The Vet's Daughter* (1981; 2013), xii.

23 From an interview with Kate Saunders, who then wrote the review article, 'Mad Hatter's Tea Party', *Books*, June 1987, 6.

24 Present-day cash equivalents have been calculated using the historical inflation calculator on the This is Money website, https://www.thisismoney.co.uk/money/bills/article-1633409/Historic-inflation-calculator-value-money-changed-1900.html, accessed 31 July 2023.

25 Courtesy of the British Newspaper Archive.

26 Letter to George Brendon, 15 May 1967, courtesy of Veronica Brendon.

27 Extract from letter courtesy of Nuria Leighton.

2 Portrait of the artist as a young woman

1 Rosa Eva, 'Heatherleys: An Assessment', *The Heatherley School of Fine Art: 150th Exhibition* (exh. cat.) (London: Heatherley School of Fine Art, 1995), 25.

2 The school premises were bombed during the Second World War and Heatherleys was closed for a period. It is now an independent art college in Chelsea.

3 'Henry and Gertrude Massey: A Life's Class at Heatherleys' by Andrew Sim, www.simfineart.com/pdf_bin/Massey%20Collection.pdf, accessed 2 August 2016. This website offers a useful profile of Massey and his influence on Heatherleys.

4 Gertrude Massey, *Kings, Commoners and Me* (London: Blackie, 1934), 150.

5 I owe this information to Stephen Bartley, Trustee and Archivist at the Heatherley School of Fine Art, 8 September 2016.

6 Massey, *Kings, Commoners and Me*, 150–1.

7 BC, Introduction to *The Vet's Daughter* (1959; London: Virago, 2013), xiii. Charles Dickens lived at 29 Johnson Street – now Cranleigh Street – between 1824 and 1827.

8 BC, Introduction to *The Vet's Daughter*, xii.

9 BC, *Sisters by a River* (1947; London: Virago, 2013), 158.

10 Ethel Mannin, *Ragged Banners – A Novel with an Index* (London: Jarrolds, 1931); as quoted in Virginia Nicholson, *Among the Bohemians: Experiments in Living 1900–1939* (2002; Harmondsworth: Penguin, 2003), 106.

11 The book was translated by Herbert Garland and published by John Garland in 1925. The copy John bought Barbara is now owned by their son, Julian Pemberton.

12 BC, Introduction to *The Vet's Daughter*, xiii.

13 I owe the confirmation of what Barbara wore to her wedding, and much of the information in this chapter – particularly about the artists Barbara knew in London and about her marriage to John Pemberton – to conversations with Julian Pemberton.

14 BC, *A Touch of Mistletoe* (1967; London: Daunt Books, 2021), 135.

15 Michel Remy, *Surrealism in Britain* (Aldershot: Ashgate, 1999), 81.

16 Nicholson, *Among the Bohemians*, xv–xvi.

17 See Guy Deghy and Keith Waterhouse, *Café Royal – Ninety Years of Bohemia* (London: Hutchinson, 1955), and Nicholson, *Among the Bohemians*, 268–9

18 Nicholson, *Among the Bohemians*, 185.

19 Letter to DBL, Diana Brinton Lee Archive, private collection.

20 Now Central Saint Martins and a constituent college of the University of the Arts London.

21 The Beggarstaffs, aka J. & W. Beggarstaff, was the name under which William Nicholson and James Pryde worked as partners designing posters and other graphic products between 1893 and 1899. Their work had a profound influence on graphic design for some years.

22 Louise Welsh, 'James Pryde: The Edgar Allen [*sic*] Poe of Painting', *The Bottle Imp*, issue 6, November 2009, www.thebottleimp.org.uk/wp-content/uploads/2017/08/TBI2009-Issue-6-James-Pryde-The-Edgar-Allen-Poe-of-Painting-Louise-Welsh.pdf, accessed 3 September 2016.

23 See Nicholson, *Among the Bohemians*, 1–31, for a highly entertaining and informative chapter on poverty and borrowing in bohemian London.

24 BC, *Our Spoons Came from Woolworths* (1950; London: Virago, 2014), 26.

25 BC, *Our Spoons Came from Woolworths*, 61.

26 From an interview between Hermione Lee and BC for the programme 'Neglected Authors', 'Book Four', Channel Four, broadcast 27 May 1984.

27 Elizabeth ('Buffy') Pemberton, letter to Hannah Stoneham dated 2 December 2005, courtesy of Hannah McSorley (née Stoneham).

28 Evelyn Waugh, *Vile Bodies* (1930; Harmondsworth: Penguin, 1967), 123.

29 'Mapping the Practice and Profession of Sculpture in Britain and Ireland, 1851–1951', http://sculpture.gla.ac.uk/view/person.php?id=msib2_1217338986, accessed 7 September 2016.

3 Lovers and others

1 Letter to DBL, written probably in November 1936, Diana Brinton Lee Archive, private collection.

2 Virginia Nicholson, *Among the Bohemians: Experiments in Living 1900–1939* (2002; Harmondsworth: Penguin, 2003), 59.

3 BC, *Our Spoons Came from Woolworths* (1950; London: Virago, 2013), 99; BC, *A Touch of Mistletoe* (1967; London: Daunt Books, 2021), 284.

4 André Salmon, 'Negro Art', *The Burlington Magazine*, 36.205 (April 1920), 164–72.

5 I owe this fact and much of the information in this chapter to Julian Pemberton's unpublished memoir.

6 I owe this information to Denys J. Wilcox.

7 David Aaronovitch, *Party Animals: My Family and Other Communists* (2016; London: Vintage, 2017), 52.

8 Paul Nash, *Outline: An Autobiography* (1949; London: Lund Humphries, 2016), 85.

9 Rupert Lee, *The First Forty Years*, unpublished typescript (the Artist's Estate), 81; quoted in Denys J. Wilcox, *Rupert Lee: Painter, Sculptor, Printmaker* (Bristol: Sansom, 2010), 21.

10 Nash, *Outline*, 85.

11 Wilcox, *Rupert Lee*, 25.

12 Nash, *Outline*, 118.

13 From Lee, *The First Forty Years,* unpublished typescript, quoted in Wilcox, *Rupert Lee*, 81.

14 The painting is reproduced on page 58 of Wilcox, *Rupert Lee*, from which much of the information in this paragraph is taken.

15 Denys J. Wilcox, *The London Group 1913–1939: The Artists and their Works* (Aldershot: The Scolar Press, 1995), 5. Much of the information about the London Group in this paragraph is drawn from Wilcox's book, which gives a full account of the group's history.

16 M. M. Kaye, *The Sun in the Morning* (London: Viking, 1990), 376.

17 Denys J. Wilcox, 'Vision and Leadership: The Recently Discovered Diana Brinton Lee Archive and the Crucial Role of the Individuals who Shaped the London Group's Formative Years', in *Uproar: The First 50 Years of the London Group 1913–63*, ed. Sarah Macdougall and Rachel Dickson (Farnham: Lund Humphries, 2013), 58.

18 I owe this information to Joanna Box, Diana Brinton Lee's niece.

19 Wilcox, *Rupert Lee*, 90.

20 These photographs can be found on page 102 of Wilcox, *Rupert Lee*.

21 The Westminster School anecdote and the lines of poetry are taken from 'Biographical notes', compiled by Joanna Box, Diana Brinton Lee's niece; Rupert Lee Archive, File AAD/2001/11/27: Archive of Art and Design, Victoria and Albert Museum.

22 BC, *Our Spoons Came from Woolworths*, 5–6.

23 Diana Brinton Lee, 'Synopsis: New Readers Start Here', Diana Brinton Lee Archive, private collection.

24 Wilcox, *Rupert Lee*, 105.

25 Elizabeth Japp (b. 1908) later married and became Elizabeth Fowler. Under that name she wrote an extraordinary book entitled *Standing Room Only*, about being the only woman among 35 passengers on a lifeboat in the Atlantic Ocean for ten days during the Second World War. She spent most of her adult life thereafter in the United States and died in New Jersey in 2003. I am grateful to Denys J. Wilcox for providing this information.

26 Most of the information in this paragraph, including Rupert Lee's words 'our life together is planned and nothing else will be', is taken from Brinton Lee, 'Synopsis: New Readers Start Here'.

27 This quotation is taken from notes made by Hannah McSorley, who (as Hannah Stoneham) had access to some private papers of Diana Brinton Lee, since lost.

28 Anne de Courcy, *The Fishing Fleet: Husband-Hunting in the Raj* (2012; London: Phoenix, 2013), 26. This book offers a fascinating study of the 'fishing fleet' women and their subsequent lives in India.

29 de Courcy, *The Fishing Fleet*, 99.

30 At this time, disposing of human faeces was a task that fell to the 'dalits' or 'untouchables'.

31 I owe this information to Nuria Leighton, 16 August 2016.

32 Letter from BC to DBL, dated 9 November 1936, Diana Brinton Lee Archive, private collection.

33 BC, *Our Spoons Came from Woolworths*, 82.

34 Nicholson, *Among the Bohemians*, 74.

35 Brinton Lee, 'Synopsis: New Readers Start Here'.

4 Desperate measures

1 Denys J. Wilcox, *Rupert Lee: Painter, Sculptor, Printmaker* (Bristol: Sansom, 2010), 107.

2 Letter to DBL, undated. All quotations from letters in this chapter, unless stated otherwise, are from the Diana Brinton Lee Archive, private collection.

3 Julian Pemberton, unpublished memoir. This chapter draws on this memoir elsewhere.

4 BC, *Our Spoons Came from Woolworths* (1950; London: Virago, 2013), 135.

5 These photographs are now owned by Barbara's granddaughter, Nuria Leighton. One of them is dated '1936'.

6 Wilcox, *Rupert Lee*, 108.
7 David Redfern, *The London Group: A History, 1913–2013* (London: The London Group, 2013), 114.
8 Michel Remy, *Surrealism in Britain* (Aldershot: Ashgate, 1999), 73–4.
9 Wilcox, *Rupert Lee*, 110.
10 Wilcox, *Rupert Lee*, 115.
11 Remy, *Surrealism in Britain*, 76.
12 Wilcox, *Rupert Lee*, 113.
13 Remy, *Surrealism in Britain*, 77–8.
14 BC, *A Touch of Mistletoe* (1967; London: Daunt Books, 2021), 211.
15 Ian Walker, *So Exotic, So Homemade: Surrealism, Englishness and Documentary Photography* (Manchester: Manchester University Press, 2007), 10.
16 I am grateful to Denys J. Wilcox and Hannah McSorley for this information.
17 Some of the information in this paragraph is taken from a letter written by BC to DBL in October 1936.
18 The National Archives at Kew show that John filed for divorce in August 1936. There can be little doubt that he took this action at the bidding of his parents. The petition was withdrawn quickly and never resubmitted for the reasons given later in this chapter.
19 BC, *The Juniper Tree* (1985; New York: New York Review Books, 2018), 155.
20 Mr Rudolph Stulik, a Viennese Jew who had bought the restaurant in 1910, was renowned for his generosity and for allowing his patrons endless credit. He no doubt would have allowed Barbara to stay there without paying for a while – he was remarkably casual about his clients' debts and once allowed Dylan Thomas to run up the cost of a fortnight's stay on the sole assurance that Augustus John would pay for it (which he did). Perhaps not surprisingly, the Eiffel Tower restaurant closed and Rudolph Stulik was declared bankrupt in 1938. See Virginia Nicholson, *Among the Bohemians: Experiments in Living 1900–1939* (2002; Harmondsworth: Penguin, 2003), 268, 183–4, 310, 269.
21 Report 'Private and Confidential', dated 10 September 1936, Diana Brinton Lee Archive, private collection.
22 BC, *The Juniper Tree*, 164.

5 The Pemberton persecution

1 The Shakespeare Centre now stands on the site of the Custodian's House.
2 Letter written by BC to DBL from Henley Street, Stratford-upon-Avon, dated 4 October 1936, in which she quotes the words 'an adulteress and a wicked woman' and 'that dreadful woman his mother' from Guy Pemberton's letter. Diana Brinton Lee Archive, private collection. Unless stated otherwise, all quotations from letters in this chapter are from this archive.
3 BC, *Our Spoons Came from Woolworths* (1950; London: Virago, 2013), 143–4.
4 Alec Waugh, *My Brother Evelyn and Other Profiles* (London: Cassell, 1967), 233, 232. This paragraph also draws on the entry on Haynes by S. M. Cretney

in *The Oxford Dictionary of National Biography*, ed. H. C. G. Matthew and Brian Harrison (Oxford: Oxford University Press, 2004), vol. 26, 60–1.

5 Information taken from draft of a letter from DBL to Frank Slater, dated 2 September, 1936.

6 The Matrimonial Causes Act became law on 1 January 1938. It allowed three further grounds for divorce: cruelty, desertion for at least three years and incurable insanity – but the emphasis was still on proving a matrimonial offence by the respondent (except in the case of insanity). There was also a bar on any divorce within the first three years of marriage. However, the cost of obtaining a divorce, at £50 (about £4,050 today), remained prohibitively expensive for many.

7 Denys J. Wilcox, *Rupert Lee: Painter, Sculptor, Printmaker* (Bristol: Sansom, 2010), 115–16.

8 Diana Brinton Lee, 'Answers to questions on Mass Observation; 0.21' (1937), Mass Observation Archive, University of Sussex Special Collections.

9 Quotations taken from two letters written by Rupert Lee early in 1937. Both letters are owned by Joanna Box, Diana Brinton Lee's niece, who kindly gave me permission to quote from them.

10 By way of comparison, an agricultural labourer earned about thirty shillings a week at this time.

11 Celia Brayfield, Introduction to *Our Spoons Came from Woolworths*, 5.

12 See https://brentwoodreflections.blogspot.co.uk/2011/07/how-they-treated-scarlet-fever-in-1937.html, accessed 7 August 2017.

13 The exhibition was briefly reported in the *Daily Sketch* on 22 July 1937. John was described in the article as spending 'the small hours tracking down unusual coloured types in London's Harlem, in Soho. His "bag" includes dancers, boxers, waitresses, musicians, chefs and club "chuckers out".'

6 Mr Fox

1 For information about Price I have drawn on Julian Pemberton's unpublished memoir and also on Merchant Navy documentation, the sailing list of the *Grantully Castle* and the National Census for 1911.

2 See Juliet Gardiner, *The Thirties: An Intimate History* (2010; London: Harper Press, 2011), 679, 685.

3 http://hidden-london.com/gazetteer/warren-street/, accessed 28 September 2017.

4 BC, *Mr Fox* (London: Turnpike Books, 2020), 8.

5 BC, *Mr Fox*, 36.

6 The crash was reported in the *Cheltenham Chronicle and Gloucestershire Graphic*, 14 August 1937, p. 7, British Newspapers Archive.

7 Unless stated otherwise, all quotations in this chapter from notes and letters between DBL, BC, E. S. P. Haynes and Arthur Price are from the Diana Brinton Lee Archive, private collection.

8 BC, *Mr Fox*, 44–53.

9 Diana Brinton Lee, 'The Uniform State', *Time and Tide*, 23 April 1938, 566–7, courtesy of Denys J. Wilcox.

10 BC, *Mr Fox*, 31–5.

11 BC, *Mr Fox*, 57.

12 Gardiner, *The Thirties: An Intimate History*, 751, and Juliet Gardiner, *Wartime Britain 1939–1945* (London: Headline, 2004), 78–9.

13 John Pemberton was registered 'at Flat 231, 28–33 Shaftesbury Avenue, Holborn on 1ˢᵗ May 1939 (Listings for 1939). Royal Artillery: Attestation Year 1940', www.findmypast.co.uk, accessed 10 November 2017.

14 Gardiner, *Wartime: Britain 1939–1945*, 65.

15 BC, *A Touch of Mistletoe* (1967; London: Daunt Books, 2021), 248.

16 Imperial War Museum website, https://www.iwm.org.uk/history/the-evacuated-children-of-the-second-world-war, accessed 7 January 2019.

17 BC, *A Touch of Mistletoe*, 248.

7 Becoming a writer

1 BC, *Mr Fox* (1987; London: Turnpike Books, 2020), 59.

2 George Orwell, letter to Eleanor Jacques of 14(?) June 1932, in *The Collected Essays, Journalism and Letters of George Orwell, Volume 1: An Age Like This* (1945; Harmondsworth: Penguin, 1970), 105.

3 BC, *Mr Fox*, 60, 61.

4 BC, *Mr Fox*, 69.

5 BC, *Mr Fox*, 67.

6 Juliet Gardiner, *Wartime Britain 1939–1945* (London: Headline, 2004), 382.

7 Much of the detail in this paragraph is taken from Julian Pemberton's unpublished memoir. In this chapter I also draw heavily on conversations with Julian Pemberton and on Caroline Urbano's unpublished memoir.

8 Donald Thomas, *An Underworld at War: Spivs, Deserters, Racketeers and Civilians in the Second World War* (London: John Murray, 2003), xiv.

9 BC, *Mr Fox*, 86.

10 BC, *Mr Fox*, 103.

11 Gardiner, *Wartime Britain*, 484–7.

12 Urbano, unpublished memoir.

13 Diana Brinton Lee's wartime diary, written 1940–1 and entitled *It Happened Like This: A Housewife's Diary of the Blitz* is held in the Archive of Mass-Observation, The Keep, University of Sussex Special Collections, ref. SxMOA32/13/4.

14 Denys J. Wilcox, *Rupert Lee: Painter, Sculptor, Printmaker* (Bristol: Sansom, 2010), 121.

15 Recorded interview with Francis Codd held by the Imperial War Museum, www.iwm.org.uk/collections/search?query=Francis+Codd&items_per_page=10, accessed 15 November 2016.

16 BC, *A Touch of Mistletoe* (1967; London: Daunt Books, 2021), 256.

17 Malcolm Muggeridge, *Chronicles of Wasted Time: The Infernal Grove* (London: Collins, 1973), 4–5, quoted in Richard Davenport-Hines, *Enemies Within: Communists, The Cambridge Spies and the Making of Modern Britain* (London: William Collins, 2018), 292.

18 School reports for Julian Pemberton for the years 1940–42. Courtesy of Julian Pemberton.

19 Ursula Holden, 'Barbara Comyns 1909–1992', 7, courtesy of Johnson & Alcock.

20 BC, *Our Spoons Came from Woolworths* (1950; London: Virago, 2013), 158.

21 All quotations from letters between BC and DBL in this chapter, unless stated otherwise, are from the Diana Brinton Lee Archive, private collection.

22 BC, *Our Spoons Came from Woolworths*, 163.

23 BC, *A Touch of Mistletoe*, 257.

24 BC, *The Vet's Daughter* (1959; London: Virago, 2013), 13, 43.

25 Urbano, unpublished memoir. Information about John Pemberton's desertion is taken from Royal Artillery record: 'Attestation Year 1940. Registered as Deserted 11/9/1941', www.findmypast.com/, accessed 14 October 2016.

26 Thomas, *An Underworld at War*, 10.

27 Gardiner, *Wartime Britain*, 607–8.

28 From an interview with Ursula Holden by Hannah McSorley (then Hannah Stoneham). Courtesy of Hannah McSorley.

29 BC, *Sisters by a River* (1947; London: Virago, 2013), 19.

30 BC, *Sisters by a River*, 13.

31 BC, *Sisters by a River*, 67.

32 Ursula Holden, Introduction to *Sisters by a River* (London: Virago, 1985), vi, and Barbara Trapido, Introduction to *Sisters by a River* (London: Virago, 2013), x.

33 In fact, over sixty men from Bidford on Avon died fighting for their country between 1914 and 1918. Barbara's mother would regularly send food parcels to her 20-year-old cousin Cyril Darby when he was fighting in France – as is clear from a letter he wrote to her dated 17 January 1917, thanking his 'aunt Margie' for the parcel. The letter is owned by Adrian Darby, son of Cyril Darby.

34 BC, *Sisters by a River*, 135–6.

35 BC, *Sisters by a River*, 90.

36 BC, *Sisters by a River*, 92, 114, 148.

37 BC, *Sisters by a River*, 193.

38 Unpublished document entitled 'How I write'; undated but possibly written during the 1950s. Courtesy of Nuria Leighton.

8 Becoming Comyns

1 Two high explosive bombs fell on Abbey Road during the Blitz. See 'Bomb Sight: Mapping the World War Two Bomb Census', National Archives website, http://www.bombsight.org/#16/51.5413/-0.1941, accessed 20 January 2018.

2 BC, *Mr Fox* (1987; London: Turnpike Books, 2020), 116–17.

3 BC, *Mr Fox*, 121.

4 Much of the detail in this paragraph and elsewhere is taken from Julian Pemberton's unpublished memoir.

5 Juliet Gardiner, *Wartime Britain 1939–1945* (London: Headline, 2004), 598.

6 Donald Thomas, *An Underworld at War: Spivs, Deserters, Racketeers and Civilians in the Second World War* (London: John Murray, 2003), 12, 34.

7 Letter written by BC to DBL in January 1943, Diana Brinton Lee Archive, private collection. All quotations from letters between BC and DBL in this chapter are from this archive unless stated otherwise.

8 BC, *Mr Fox*, 124.

9 Possibly Wilson's MOR, which was tinned cured pork shoulder meat imported from the USA.

10 BC, *Mr Fox*, 149.

11 Thomas, *An Underworld at War*, 93.

12 BC, *Mr Fox*, 129.

13 BC, *A Touch of Mistletoe* (1967; London: Daunt Books, 2021), 173.

14 Letter from RCC to BC, dated 8 June 1944, courtesy of Nuria Leighton. All quotations from letters between BC and RCC in this chapter are from correspondence held by Nuria Leighton unless otherwise stated.

15 Urbano, unpublished memoir.

16 Richard Comyns Carr (ed.), *Red Rags: Essays of Hate from Oxford with an Epilogue by Mr. Justice McCardie* (London: Chapman and Hall, 1933).

17 BBC Written Archives, Caversham Park, Reading.

18 Richard Davenport-Hines, *Enemies Within: Communists, the Cambridge Spies and the Making of Modern Britain* (London: William Collins: 2018), 78.

19 Nigel West and Oleg Tsarev (eds), *Triplex: Secrets from the Cambridge Five* (New Haven, CT: Yale University Press, 2009), 117.

20 Graham Greene, Introduction to Kim Philby, *My Silent War* (1968; London: Panther, 1973), 8.

21 Norman Sherry, *The Life of Graham Greene, Volume Two: 1939–1955* (London: Jonathan Cape, 1994), 211.

22 Sherry, *The Life of Graham Greene, Volume Two*, 174.

23 Sherry, *The Life of Graham Greene, Volume Two*, 175; Andrew Biswell, *The Real Life of Anthony Burgess* (2005; London: Picador, 2006), 94–5.

24 'Alan Watkins reports that Muggeridge continued to work part time for MI6. Not unnaturally, some of Muggeridge's friends in this period were former colleagues in Section V, MI6 officers such as Richard Comyns Carr and Graham Greene.' Stephen Dorril, *MI6: Fifty Years of Special Operations* (2000, London: Fourth Estate, 2001), 843.

25 Ben Macintyre, *A Spy Among Friends: Philby and the Great Betrayal* (2014; London: Bloomsbury, 2015), 29.

26 West and Tsarev (eds), *Triplex*, 115.

27 West and Tsarev (eds), *Triplex*, 117.

28 BBC Written Archives, Caversham Park, Reading.

29 Keith Jeffery, *MI6: The History of the Secret Intelligence Service 1909–1949* (London: Bloomsbury, 2010), 156–7, 479. See also Davenport-Hines, *Enemies Within*, 68: 'Few men could live on the sums offered unless they had other income'.

30 Denys J. Wilcox, *Rupert Lee: Painter, Sculptor, Printmaker* (Bristol: Sansom, 2010), 121.

31 Diana Brinton Lee Archive, private collection. This letter is a draft version of the letter that was finally sent (now lost). It suggests that Diana took considerable care in writing the letter before sending it.

32 Letter written from RCC to BC dated 23 August 1944, Diana Brinton Lee Archive, private collection.

33 BC, *Mr Fox*, 166–7.

34 BC, *Mr Fox*, 167.

35 Quotations from the unpublished story are courtesy of Nuria Leighton.

36 BC, unpaginated Introduction to *The Vet's Daughter* (1959; London: Virago, 1981). In the Virago 2013 edition of the novel, the quotation can be found on page xiv.

37 Quotations from this letter are courtesy of Nuria Leighton.

38 Quotation from letter from BC to Carmen Callil of Virago Press, dated 14 September 1982, in which she asked whether the spellings should be corrected for the forthcoming Virago edition. In the same letter she quoted Tom Hopkinson's words about *Sisters by a River*, before it was published in *Lilliput*, advising her not to correct the misspellings. Courtesy of Nuria Leighton.

39 The months in which Barbara's work was published in *Lilliput* were May, July, September and November 1945 and August 1946. These magazines can be read in the British Library, which holds *Lilliput* issues published between July 1937 and July 1960. There are some minor differences between the *Lilliput* extracts and the corresponding chapters in *Sisters by a River*: a few paragraphs appear in different places and 'Constance' and 'Nan' become 'Mary' and 'Beatrix' in the novel version.

40 Quotations from this letter are courtesy of Nuria Leighton.

41 Sherry, *The Life of Graham Green, Volume Two*, 213.

9 Spies, lies and fictions

1 Introduction to *The Vet's Daughter* (1959; London: Virago, 2013), xiv.

2 Undated letter from Caroline Urbano to Andrew Hewson, courtesy of Johnson & Alcock. Courtesy of Nuria Leighton.

3 BC, *Our Spoons Came from Woolworths* (1950; London: Virago, 2013), 170–1, 193.

4 Duties described by Tim Milne in *Kim Philby: A Story of Friendship and Betrayal* (London: Biteback Publishing, 2014), 198.

5 Sue Smithson, *The Story of Long Dene School* (London: New European Publications, 1999), 25–6.

6 I owe Angela Landels's memories of Barbara to Hannah McSorley who, as Hannah Stoneham, interviewed her some years ago. Angela Landels was later to provide the cover illustration for the Capuchin Classics edition of *The Juniper Tree*.

7 BC, *Mr Fox* (1987; London: Turnpike Books, 2020), 172.

8 Norman Sherry, *The Life of Graham Greene, Volume Two: 1939–1955* (London: Jonathan Cape, 1994), 187.

9 Sherry, *The Life of Graham Greene, Volume Two*, 188.

10 Letter from Katherine Clutton to BC, dated 3 July 1946, courtesy of Nuria Leighton. All quotations from letters included in this chapter, including those between BC and RCC, are courtesy of Nuria Leighton unless stated otherwise.

11 Sherry, *The Life of Graham Greene, Volume Two*, 183. But see also Richard Greene (no relation), who has more recently claimed that the offer of a lucrative scriptwriting contract with MGM prompted Greene's resignation: *Russian Roulette: The Life and Times of Graham Greene* (London: Little, Brown, 2020), 156.

12 Greene, *Russian Roulette*, 279, 328.

13 Letter from Tony Gishford to Rupert Lee, dated 10 December 1945, Diana Brinton Lee Archive, private collection.

14 Letter from BC to DBL, dated 29 May 1947. Diana Brinton Lee Archive, private collection. All further quotations from correspondence between BC and DBL and between RCC and DBL in this chapter derive from this source unless stated otherwise.

15 Urbano, unpublished memoir.

16 Letter to Molly, the sister of Julian Pemberton's third wife, Sally; written from 64 The Green, Twickenham, dated 21 June 1985; courtesy of Sally Fletcher Pemberton.

17 BC, *Birds in Tiny Cages* (London: Heinemann, 1964), 23, 24.

18 David Kynaston, *Austerity Britain, 1945–51* (London: Bloomsbury, 2007), 226–7.

19 Letter to DBL, dated 3 September 1947; other information in this paragraph is taken from letters written by BC to DBL, dated 26 June, 12 July and 5 August 1947.

20 *Harper's Bazaar*, October 1947; *The Tatler and Bystander*, 19 November 1947.

21 'Questing Imagination', *Times Literary Supplement*, 15 November 1947; *The Listener*, 27 November 1947.

22 Letter from Julian MacLaren-Ross, dated 12 December 1947, and letter from John Heygate, dated 3 January 1948, both courtesy of Nuria Leighton.

23 Diary entry, 1 January 1948. Barbara kept a diary haphazardly; any diaries before 1948 have been lost and there are no diaries for 1949 or 1950. Entries in her early diaries are often confined to a line a day that simply records a factual event.

24 Letter from Ruby Millar to BC, dated 16 March 1948, courtesy of Nuria Leighton.

25 BC, *Mr Fox*, 175.

26 See Keith Jeffery, *MI6: The History of the Secret Intelligence Service, 1909–1949* (London: Bloomsbury, 2010), 'Part Six: From Hot to Cold War', 619–721.

27 Richard Davenport-Hines, *Enemies Within: Communists, the Cambridge Spies and the Making of Modern Britain* (London: William Collins, 2018), xvi.

28 Although Caroline had strong suspicions that John Pemberton was not her real father and that Rupert Lee might be, it was only in 2010 when she was 75 years old that a retrospective exhibition of Lee's work included letters that confirmed that she was his daughter.

29 BC, *Our Spoons Came from Woolworths*, 96.

30 BC, *Our Spoons Came from Woolworths*, 89–90.

31 BC, *Our Spoons Came from Woolworths*, 118.

32 BC, *Our Spoons Came from Woolworths*, 105–6.

33 Ursula Holden, 'Barbara Comyns 1909–1992', 8, courtesy of Johnson & Alcock.

34 Introduction to *Our Spoons Came from Woolworths*, viii.

35 Julian MacLaren-Ross, 'Points of View', *Times Literary Supplement*, 28 July 1950; Lionel Hale, *The Observer*, 23 July 1950; 'B.W', *The Irish Times*, 22 July 1950; Eric Young, *Sheffield Daily Telegraph*, 4 August 1950.

36 Richard Blakesley, 'Simple Story of Girl's Life in Slums', *Chicago Tribune* (date unavailable); anonymous reviewer, *Buffalo Courier-Express*, 11 February 1951; anonymous reviewer, *New Yorker*, 24 February 1951.

37 RCC, diary entry for 9 July 1951, courtesy of Nuria Leighton.

38 Diary entry, 7 July 1951. All quotations from Barbara's diaries are courtesy of Nuria Leighton.

39 Andrew Lownie, *Stalin's Englishman: The Lives of Guy Burgess* (London: Hodder and Stoughton, 2015), 217–21.

40 The National Archives, KV4/473, 1951 Volume 20; diary entry for 29 May 1951. 'Watchers' were people who physically trailed MI5 or MI6 staff suspected of being double agents.

41 Lownie, *Stalin's Englishman*, 51–6.

42 Philby's words to the press in October 1955 are taken from Anthony Cave Brown, *Treason in the Blood: H. St. John Philby, Kim Philby and the Spy Case of the Century* (Boston: Houghton Mifflin, 1994), 459.

43 Stephen Dorril, *MI6: Fifty Years of Special Operations* (London: Fourth Estate, 2000), 79–80.

44 This statement appeared in the *Sunderland Daily Echo and Shipping Gazette* and was repeated in the *Belfast News-Letter* and the *Northern Whig*, all published on 29 August 1951.

45 *Northern Whig*, 29 August 1951.

46 RCC, diary entries for 9 and 20 August and 14 September, 1951.

47 Letter from Graham Greene to Alexander Frere, president of Heinemann Publishers, dated 11 April 1958, recounting his support for *Leigh Hunt in Italy* some years earlier. Heinemann files, Penguin Random House Archive and Library, Rushden, Northants.

48 Letter from John Johnson to BC, dated 3 April 1952, courtesy of Nuria Leighton.

49 Dorrill, *MI6: Fifty Years of Special Operations*, 59.

50 BC, *Who was Changed and Who was Dead* (1954; London: Daunt Books, 2021), 5. All quotations are from this edition of the novel.

51 BC, *Who was Changed and Who was Dead*, 57.

52 BC, *Who was Changed and Who was Dead*, 77.

53 BC, *Who was Changed and Who was Dead*, 117–18.

54 BC, *Who was Changed and Who was Dead*, 127.

55 See Nick Turner, 'Barbara Comyns and New Directions in Women's Writing', in Sue Kennedy and Jane Thomas (eds), *British Women's Writing 1930–1960: Between the Waves* (Liverpool: Liverpool University Press, 2020), 207.

56 From an undated note written by BC, courtesy of Nuria Leighton.
57 Letter from John Johnson of E. P. Lewin & Partners to BC, dated 21 May 1953, courtesy of Nuria Leighton.
58 George D. Painter, 'New Novels', *The Listener*, 25 November 1954; W.L.W, 'Recent Novels', *Irish Times*, 11 December 1954; John Connell, 'George Millar Finds Himself', *Evening News*, 4 December 1954.
59 John Betjeman, *Daily Telegraph*, 12 November 1954; Margaret Willy, 'New Novels', *Birmingham Post*, 16 November 1954.
60 This letter is included courtesy of Nuria Leighton.

10 Ibiza

1 Jane Gardam, 'Novelist Levitated', *The Guardian*, 4 August 1992.
2 Jane Gardam, *The Spectator*, 6 July 2013.
3 Anthony Cave Brown, *Treason in the Blood: H. St. John Philby, Kim Philby and the Spy Case of the Century* (Boston: Houghton Mifflin, 1994), 457.
4 James Hanning, *Love and Deception: Philby in Beirut* (London: Corsair, 2021), 37.
5 Hanning, *Love and Deception*, 152.
6 Cave Brown, *Treason in the Blood*, 463.
7 'a close friend': Richard Greene, *Russian Roulette: The Life and Times of Graham Greene* (London: Little Brown, 2020), 142; 'knew David Astor': Ben Macintyre, *A Spy Among Friends: Philby and the Great Betrayal* (London: Bloomsbury, 2014), 204.
8 Greene, *Russian Roulette*, 350.
9 Letter to Andrew Hewson, who later replaced John Johnson as Barbara's agent, dated 11 June 1979, courtesy of Nuria Leighton.
10 BC, *Out of the Red, Into the Blue* (London: Heinemann, 1960), 20.
11 BC, *Out of the Red*, 5.
12 RCC, private papers, courtesy of Nuria Leighton.
13 BBC Written Archives, Caversham, Reading.
14 See 'The Vetting Files: How the BBC kept out "subversives"', www.bbc.co.uk/news/stories-43754737, accessed 25 April 2018.
15 Conversation with Julian Pemberton, 3 December 2018. I owe much of the detail in this chapter to Julian Pemberton's unpublished memoir.
16 Teresa Grimes (granddaughter of Leslie Grimes), 'Obituary: Barbara Comyns', *The Independent*, 24 August 1992.
17 Postcard from BC to RCC, undated, courtesy of Nuria Leighton. All further quotations from letters between BC and RCC in this chapter are from correspondence held by Nuria Leighton unless stated otherwise.
18 Letter dated 25 June (probably 1958), Box 15, Folder 3, Graham Greene Papers; MS1995–003, John J. Burns Library, Boston College.
19 BC, *Out of the Red*, 87.
20 BC, *Out of the Red*, 90.

21 Walham Green was a former working-class area in what is now Fulham Broadway in London.

22 BC, *Out of the Red*, 106–7.

23 Letter dated 1 May (probably 1958), Box 15, Folder 3, Graham Greene Papers; MS1995–003, John J. Burns Library, Boston College.

24 BC, *Out of the Red*, 114.

25 'Barbara Comyns Writes': a short autobiographical profile written as publicity material prior to the publication of *The Vet's Daughter*. It is held in the Heinemann files in the Penguin Random House Archive and Library, Rushden, Northants.

26 The contract for the book, held in Heinemann files in the Penguin Random House Archive and Library, Rushden, Northants, is dated 27 January 1959 and carries the title *The Way We Live Now* crossed through and replaced by *Out of the Red, Into the Blue*.

27 BC, *Out of the Red*, 131.

28 Quotations from 'Something to Celebrate', courtesy of Nuria Leighton.

29 BC, *Out of the Red*, 147.

30 BC, *Out of the Red*, 143.

31 BC, *Out of the Red*, 183.

32 BC, *The Vet's Daughter* (1959; London: Virago, 2013), 77.

33 BC, *The Vet's Daughter*, 68–9.

34 BC, *Out of the Red*, 129.

35 Ursula Holden, 'Barbara Comyns 1909–1992', 8, courtesy of Johnson & Alcock.

36 Norman Sherry, *The Life of Graham Greene, Volume Three: 1955–1991* (London: Jonathan Cape, 2004), 115.

37 Extract from a letter written by Graham Greene to Alexander Frere, dated 11 April 1958, held in the Heinemann files in the Penguin Random House Archive and Library, Rushden, Northants.

38 Hilary Spurling, *Anthony Powell: Dancing to the Music of Time* (London: Hamish Hamilton, 2017), 310.

39 BC, *Out of the Red*, 199.

11 Settling in Barcelona

1 This and the previous two quotations are taken from a letter written by RCC to Graham Greene, dated 24 August 1958. Box 15, Folder 3, Graham Greene Papers; MS1995–003, John J. Burns Library, Boston College.

2 BC, *Birds in Tiny Cages* (London: Heinemann, 1964), 2.

3 BC, *Birds in Tiny Cages*, 25.

4 BC, *Birds in Tiny Cages*, 53.

5 Letter from BC to RCC, undated, courtesy of Nuria Leighton. All further quotations from letters between BC and RCC in this chapter are from correspondence owned by Nuria Leighton unless stated otherwise.

6 Heinemann files, Penguin Random House Archive and Library, Rushden, Northants.

7 Kenneth Allsop, *Daily Mail*, 14 February 1959, 6.

8 Roy Perrott, 'Well-bred Non-conformists', *Manchester Guardian*, 13 February 1959, 6; Enid Bagnold, quoted in a Heinemann advertisement in *The Times*, 12 March 1959, 15; Siriol Hugh-Jones, *Tatler*, 11 March 1959, 492; Richard Church, *The Bookman*, March 1959, 11.

9 Robert Pitman, 'Book Page', *Sunday Express*, 15 February 1959.

10 Brief anonymous review in *Publishers' Circular*, 14 February 1959; John Connell, 'Books', *Evening News*, 26 February 1959; Howard Spring, 'Reviews', *Country Life*, 19 February 1959; John Coleman, 'Effective Chekhov', *The Spectator*, 13 February 1959; Aldous Huxley, 'The Overpopulated World', *Sphere*, 28 February 1959, 342.

11 Stewart Purvis and Jeff Hulbert, *When Reporters Cross the Line: The Heroes, the Villains, the Hackers and the Spies* (London: Biteback Publishing, 2013), 112.

12 Goronwy Rees, 'New Novels', *Listener*, 5 March 1959, 426.

13 BC, *Birds in Tiny Cages*, 141–2.

14 Unpublished fragment from a file marked 'Odds and Ends Very Old', courtesy of Nuria Leighton.

15 BC, *Birds in Tiny Cages*, 51.

16 Letter from BC to DBL, undated but probably written July 1959, Diana Brinton Lee Archive, private collection. All further quotations from letters between BC and DBL in this chapter are from correspondence in this archive unless stated otherwise.

17 Denys J. Wilcox, *Rupert Lee: Painter, Sculptor, Printmaker* (Bristol: Sansom, 2010), 131.

18 Anne Piper, 'Courage and Curiosity', *Sunday Times*, 21 February 1960; Ronald Bryden, *The Spectator*, 29 January 1960, 143; Martin Moore, 'Southward to the Sun', *Daily Telegraph*, 5 August 1960, 15; David Brett, 'Out of the Legend Rides Arthur the Man', *Manchester Evening News*, 25 February 1960; Stella Rodway, 'Balanced Account', *Times Literary Supplement*, 26 February 1960, 131; Penelope Gilliat, 'Basilisk Abroad', *The Observer*, 30 January 1960.

19 Letter from Sir John A. Pilcher to the British Council, dated 27 August 1957, The National Archives BW56; Registry File SP701/3.

20 Conversation with Julian Pemberton, 26 March 2018.

21 Letter from BC to Julian, undated, but probably written in the spring or early summer of 1974, courtesy of Julian Pemberton.

22 'Sounds in the Flat', an unpublished fragment in a file marked 'Odds and Ends Very Old', courtesy of Nuria Leighton.

23 Letter from BC to a Mr Holden at William Heinemann, dated 3 November 1959, courtesy of Nuria Leighton.

24 Letter from BC to Julian, undated but probably written in the spring or early summer of 1961, courtesy of Julian Pemberton.

25 Letter from BC to George Brendon, dated 11 December 1962, courtesy of Veronica Brendon.

26 Reader's Report written by 'J.C.M.', dated 2 October 1961. This document is held in the Heinemann files in the Penguin Random House Archive and Library, Rushden, Northants.

27 Ursula Holden, Introduction to BC, *The Skin Chairs* (1962; London: Virago, 1986), x.

28 BC, *The Skin Chairs*, 87.

29 BC, *The Skin Chairs*, 19.

30 BC, *The Skin Chairs*, 200.

31 RCC, diary entry for January 1961. This and all other entries from Richard's diaries are reproduced courtesy of Nuria Leighton. Barbara's paintings are now owned by her son Julian Pemberton and her granddaughter Nuria Leighton.

32 Letter from BC to George Brendon, dated 11 December 1962, courtesy of Veronica Brendon.

33 Letter from BC to George Brendon, dated 11 December 1962, courtesy of Veronica Brendon.

34 E. D. O'Brien, 'A Literary Lounger', *Illustrated London News*, 29 September 1962; Richard Church, *Country Life*, 30 August 1962; Laurence Meynell, *Express & Star*, 27 August 1962; Anthony Burgess, 'The Innocent Nightmare', *The Observer*, 26 August 1962; Olivia Manning, 'With the Eyes of a Child', *Sunday Times*, 26 August 1962, 20; Susan Chitty, 'Under the Skin', *Sunday Telegraph*, 26 August 1962, 7; Siriol Hugh-Jones, *Tatler*, 19 September 1962.

35 Letter from BC to George Brendon, dated 11 December 1962, courtesy of Veronica Brendon.

36 Letter from BC to George Brendon, dated 11 December 1962, courtesy of Veronica Brendon.

37 Letter from Roderick Cook to BC, dated 8 May 1963, courtesy of Nuria Leighton.

38 BC, *Birds in Tiny Cages*, 46.

39 Letter to George Brendon, dated 10 December 1964, courtesy of Veronica Brendon.

40 Iain Hamilton, 'Mediterranean Cat's Cradle', *Daily Telegraph*, 2 July 1964, 19; E. D. O'Brien, 'A Literary Lounger', *Illustrated London News*, 15 August 1964, 246; R. G. G. Price, 'New Novels', *Punch*, 15 July 1964, 103; Jeremy Rundall, 'Short Reports', *Sunday Times*, 5 July 1964, 38.

41 Letter from BC to George Brendon, dated 10 December 1964, courtesy of Veronica Brendon.

12 The San Roque venture

1 Letter to George Brendon, 29 April 1965, courtesy of Veronica Brendon.

2 Letter to Graham Greene written from Barcelona, dated 6 October 1969, Box 15, Folder 3, Graham Greene Papers; MS1995–003, John J. Burns Library, Boston College.

3 BC, *A Touch of Mistletoe* (1967; London: Daunt Books, 2021), 174.

4 Letter from John Johnson to BC, dated 16 February 1966, courtesy of Johnson & Alcock.

5 Letter from BC to George Brendon, dated 15 May 1967, courtesy of Veronica Brendon.

6 BC, *Birds in Tiny Cages* (London: Heinemann, 1964), 153.

7 BC, *The Skin Chairs* (1962; London: Virago, 1986), 172.

8 BC, *A Touch of Mistletoe*, 308.

9 Letter from BC to RCC, dated 12 August 1966, courtesy of Nuria Leighton. All further quotations from letters between BC and RCC in this chapter are from correspondence owned by Nuria Leighton, unless stated otherwise.

10 BC, unpublished essay entitled 'A Rough Description of having my Appendix removed in a Spanish clinic', courtesy of Nuria Leighton.

11 This paragraph draws on diary entries for the year 1966, courtesy of Nuria Leighton.

12 Letter from John Johnson to BC, dated 19 June 1967, courtesy of Nuria Leighton.

13 Jeremy Rundall, 'Ladies' Nightmare', *The Scotsman*, 20 May 1967; R. G. G. Price, 'New Novels', *Punch*, 10 May 1967; Laurence Meynell, 'Here's Tears and Laughter ... You'll like Vicky', *Express & Star*, 26 May 1967; anonymous reviewer, 'Novels in Brief', *The Observer*, 11 June 1967; anonymous reviewer, *Times Literary Supplement*, 4 May 1967, 383.

14 This report is held in the Heinemann files, Penguin Random House Archive and Library, Rushden, Northants. Edmund Gordon, *The Invention of Angela Carter: A Biography* (London: Chatto and Windus, 2016), 91, wrongly attributes the report to BC.

15 Letter from BC to Patricia Newnham at Heinemann's, dated 23 May 1967, Heinemann files, Penguin Random House Archive and Library, Rushden, Northants.

16 From a letter dated 22 July 1967 written from DBL to BC, courtesy of Nuria Leighton. All further quotations from letters between BC and DBL in this chapter are from correspondence owned by Nuria Leighton unless stated otherwise.

17 Letter from John Johnson to BC, dated 30 October 1967, courtesy of Johnson & Alcock.

18 Letter from John Johnson to BC, dated 21 December 1967, courtesy of Nuria Leighton.

19 Letter from BC to John Johnson, dated 26 December 1967, courtesy of Johnson & Alcock.

20 Letter from BC to John Johnson, dated 10 September 1968, courtesy of Johnson & Alcock.

21 Ursula Holden, 'Barbara Comyns 1909–1992', 7, courtesy of Johnson & Alcock.

22 Diary entry 28 January 1969.

23 Letter to John Johnson, dated 3 October 1968, courtesy of Johnson & Alcock, and diary entries made during 1969 and 1970.

24 Transcription of dream, dated 4 December 1968. One of 25 dreams contained in a file marked 'Barbara's dreams written down by Richard 1968 to 1969', courtesy of Nuria Leighton.

25 Ursula Holden, 'Barbara Comyns 1909–1992', 5.

26 Letter from Graham Greene to BC, dated 26 September 1969, courtesy of Nuria Leighton. All quotations from letters between BC and Graham Greene in this chapter are from top copies owned by Nuria Leighton unless stated

otherwise; carbon copies of several are held by the John J. Burns Library, Boston College.

27 In 1961 the Tilling Group bought Heinemann and discovered that it was 'on the verge of bankruptcy. For all his literary flair and confidence, Frere had squandered the firm's resources through financial fecklessness, long-term mismanagement and over-rapid, under-funded expansion. His job was handed over to executives with no experience of or interest in books. Graham Greene and many other authors moved elsewhere at this point, along with Heinemann's more enterprising staff.' Hilary Spurling, *Anthony Powell: Dancing to the Music of Time* (London: Hamish Hamilton, 2017), 388–9.

28 BC, *The House of Dolls* (1989; London: Turnpike Books, 2020), 17.

29 Letter from John Johnson to BC, dated 26 January 1970, courtesy of Nuria Leighton.

30 Letter from BC to George Brendon, undated but written probably in early 1970, courtesy of Nuria Leighton.

31 Quotations taken from letters from DBL to BC, dated 9 December 1970 and 25 June 1971, courtesy of Nuria Leighton.

32 Letter from BC to John Johnson, dated 30 October 1972, courtesy of Johnson & Alcock.

33 This and the previous quotations are from a letter to George Brendon, dated 30 December 1972, courtesy of Veronica Brendon.

34 Letter dated 3 January; no year given, but probably 1973. This and all subsequent quotations from correspondence between BC and Julian are from letters owned by Julian Pemberton.

35 'Jeanette' and 'Mary' are not their real names.

36 Letter from Jeanette to author, dated 15 October 2018.

37 This and all subsequent quotations from correspondence between BC and Jeanette are from letters owned by Julian Pemberton.

38 Conversation with Nuria Leighton, 9 June 2016.

39 From an undated three-page foolscap document entitled 'Letter to Diana', courtesy of Julian Pemberton. In it BC explains at length why she and RCC have decided to leave El Almendral.

40 Undated unpublished poem written probably sometime in 1974, courtesy of Nuria Leighton.

13 The return to England

1 Letter from BC to DBL, dated 13 November 1974, courtesy of Nuria Leighton.

2 Letter from BC to John Johnson, undated but probably written in early December 1974, courtesy of Johnson & Alcock. All quotations from letters between BC and John Johnson are from correspondence owned by Johnson & Alcock unless stated otherwise.

3 Letter from John Johnson to BC, dated 11 December 1974, courtesy of Nuria Leighton.

4 Letter from BC to RCC, dated 25 June 1977, courtesy of Nuria Leighton.

5 Norman Sherry, *The Life of Graham Green, Volume Three: 1955–1991* (London: Jonathan Cape, 2004), 84.

6 Diary entries for 29 March, 19 September, 30 September and 15 October 1975.

7 BC, extract from her first draft of the Introduction to the Virago 1981 edition of *The Vet's Daughter*; these words were not included in the final published version. Courtesy of Nuria Leighton

8 BC, *The Juniper Tree* (New York: New York Review of Books, 2018), 62.

9 Letter from Shirley Gee to BC, dated 25 April 1976, courtesy of Nuria Leighton.

10 Letter to Anna Cooper, John Johnson Ltd, dated 12 April 1976, courtesy of Johnson & Alcock.

11 This paragraph draws on conversations with Julian, 23 August 2018, and with Nicola, 4 and 10 February 2019.

12 Letter written from 221 Ashburham Road, undated but probably written in early April 1978, courtesy of Julian Pemberton.

13 Letter dated 14 April 1978, courtesy of Julian Pemberton.

14 Nicholas de Jongh, 'The Clapham Wonder', *The Guardian*, 27 April 1978; Irving Wardle, *The Times*, 27 April 1978; and Eric Shorter, 'Comedy of Levitation Stays on the Ground', *Daily Telegraph*, 28 April 1978, 15.

15 'PHS', 'A Perfect Ending to a Rotten Show', *The Times*, 14 October 1978, 14.

16 Letter from John Johnson to BC, dated 14 April 1979, courtesy of Nuria Leighton.

17 A copy of the agreement can be seen in the Virago Archive held in the British Library, 'Barbara Comyns', File Ms 88904/1/81.

18 Norman Sherry, *The Life of Graham Greene, Volume Two: 1939–1955* (London: Jonathan Cape, 1994), 187; Jane Dunn, *Antonia White: A Life* (London: Jonathan Cape, 1998), 282.

19 Letter from Graham Greene to Carmen Callil, courtesy of Nuria Leighton.

20 Letter from Carmen Callil to Graham Greene, dated 2 October 1980, courtesy of Nuria Leighton.

21 Letter from BC to Andrew Hewson, dated 11 June 1979, courtesy of Nuria Leighton.

22 Letter from James Michie to John Johnson, dated 16 October 1979, courtesy of Johnson & Alcock.

23 Dunn, *Antonia White: A Life*, 417–18.

24 Letter from BC to Carmen Callil, dated 8 October 1980, courtesy of Nuria Leighton.

25 Draft of letter from BC to Graham Greene, dated 9 October 1980, courtesy of Nuria Leighton.

26 Letter from Graham Greene to BC, dated 16 October 1980, courtesy of Nuria Leighton.

27 Caroline Moorehead, 'Afloat, with a down-to-earth girl called Alice', *The Times*, 28 January 1981, 9.

28 *Manchester Evening News* (undated); Jean Blackburn, 'Living "wasted days"', *Morning Star*, 3 March 1981; Gillian Somerville-Large, 'Bleak Times', *Irish Times*, 7 March 1981; Alan Hollinghurst, 'Wordy Wisdom', *New Statesman*, 30 January 1981; Pat Raine, *Times Literary Supplement*, 3 April 1981; Stephen Brook, 'Three Women', *Spectator* (date unknown), 22.

14 Hauntings

1 In 2006 the property was sold with partial planning permission to local developers who built some terraced houses on the land. Email from John Pilling, 27 January 2020.

2 Letter from Carmen Callil to BC, dated 25 September 1982, courtesy of Nuria Leighton. All quotations from letters in this chapter are from correspondence owned by Nuria Leighton unless stated otherwise.

3 Letter to Andrew Hewson, dated 2 November 1982, courtesy of Johnson & Alcock.

4 Moonlighter Productions, 'Proposal: *The Vet's Daughter*', undated but probably collated in August 1982, courtesy of Johnson & Alcock.

5 Jenny Scott, 'Barbara's Macabre Plots', *Richmond and Twickenham Times*, courtesy of Nuria Leighton. (The clipping carries no page number or date.)

6 Patricia Craig, 'Paperback Fiction in Brief', *Times Literary Supplement*, 29 July 1983, 820.

7 From an interview between Hermione Lee and BC for the programme 'Neglected Authors', 'Book Four', Channel Four, broadcast 27 May 1984.

8 Letter from Virago Press to Andrew Hewson, dated 23 January 1984.

9 Letter from Andrew Hewson to BC, dated 27 January 1984.

10 Conversation with Lucy Pemberton, 28 August 2018.

11 Email to the author from Elsbeth Lindner, 11 December 2018.

12 Draft letter from BC to Elsbeth Lindner, 14 October 1984.

13 From the programme 'Neglected Authors', 'Book Four', Channel Four, broadcast 27 May 1984.

14 BC, *The Juniper Tree* (New York: New York Review Books, 2018), 13. All quotations from the novel are from this edition.

15 BC, *The Juniper Tree*, 19.

16 BC, *The Juniper Tree*, 127.

17 BC, *The Juniper Tree*, 176.

18 BC, *The Juniper Tree*, 14.

19 BC, *The Juniper Tree*, 155.

20 BC, *The Juniper Tree*, 48, 94.

21 Margaret Drabble, Introduction to BC, *The Juniper Tree* (London: Capuchin Classics, 2011), 9.

22 The typescript is marked with many corrections, and the word 'rewrite' is sprinkled liberally across it. The document is owned by Nuria Leighton, Barbara's granddaughter. BC wrote 'To be distroyed' [*sic*] at the top of the first page but Nuria Leighton and Julian Pemberton, who have confirmed that 'Rough Ideas' draws on the last months of RCC's life, kindly granted me permission to include parts of it in this chapter.

23 Letter from Desmond Pakenham, dated 13 February 1985, courtesy of Nuria Leighton.

24 Ursula Holden, 'Barbara Comyns 1909–1992', 10, courtesy of Johnson & Alcock.

25 Diary entries, 13 February and 2 November 1985.

26 Diary entry, 18 October 1985.

27 Draft of a letter from BC to Joanna Hansen, undated, but probably written in late February or early March 1985.
28 Katya Watter, *Times Educational Supplement*, 30 August 1985; anonymous reviewer, *Irish Press*, 23 March 1985; Patricia Craig, 'In Brief', *Times Literary Supplement*, 26 April 1985, 479; David Holloway, 'Paperback', *Sunday Telegraph*, 27 January 1985, 20.
29 Hinde Thomas, 'Forster Country', *Sunday Telegraph*, 14 April 1985, 14; Isabel Quigly, *Financial Times*, 13 April, 1985; Ruth Baumgarten, 'Beauty and the Beasts', *City Limits*, 9 May 1985; Selina Hastings, 'Recent Fiction', *Daily Telegraph*, 26 April 1985; Miranda Seymour, 'Perfect Happiness', *Books and Bookmen*, July 1985; Patricia Craig, 'The White and the Red', *Times Literary Supplement*, 10 May 1985, 529
30 Probably Joan Prats (1891–1970), an artist from Barcelona whose family sold hats. He was a good friend of Joan Miró and organized exhibitions for Dali and Picasso. Miró painted a picture of hats and strange figures entitled *Homage to Joan Prats* in 1934, now in the Fundació Joan Miró, Barcelona.

15 Legacies

1 Kathy Page, *City Limits*, 31 July 1986; Patricia Craig, 'In Brief', *Times Literary Supplement*, 19 December 1986.
2 'The painter Rousseau had of course influenced her in the making of her gardens': Ursula Holden, 'Barbara Comyns: 1909–1992', courtesy of Johnson & Alcock.
3 Ursula Holden, Introduction to BC, *Who was Changed and Who was Dead* (London: Virago, 1987), viii.
4 Patricia Craig, 'Paperback Fiction', *Times Literary Supplement*, 18 September 1987.
5 Rosemary Hill, 'Ethel in Wartime', *Literary Review*, May 1987, 17; Kirsty Milne, 'Nature Reserve', *The Observer*, 7 June 1987.
6 Patricia Craig, 'Everyday Employments', *Times Literary Supplement*, 5 June 1987, 610; Nina Bawden, 'What a Stupid Husband', *Daily Telegraph*, 5 June 1987; Shaun Usher, 'Candid Caroline Wins Through', *Daily Mail*, 11 June 1987; Mary Wesley, 'Bliss Among the Bombs', *Daily London News*, 17 June 1987.
7 Kate Saunders, 'Being Funny on Purpose', *Books*, no. 2, May 1987, 2.
8 Kate Saunders, 'Mad Hatter's Tea Party', *Books*, no. 3, June 1987, 6.
9 Letter from Teresa Grimes on notepaper headed 'Cinewomen Productions', dated 7 October 1987, courtesy of Nuria Leighton. All quotations from letters in this chapter are from correspondence owned by Nuria Leighton unless stated otherwise.
10 This and the previous quotation are taken from Teresa Grimes, 'Obituary: Barbara Comyns', *The Independent*, 24 August 1992.
11 Letter from Teresa Grimes to BC, dated 7 June 1991, written on notepaper headed 'Paintbrush Productions'.
12 Draft of a letter to Andrew Vores, dated 20 May 1988.
13 Ursula Holden, 'Barbara Comyns 1909–1992', 10, courtesy of Johnson & Alcock.

14 Patricia Craig, Introduction to BC, *A Touch of Mistletoe* (London: Virago, 1989), v.

15 Anonymous reviewer, *Daily Telegraph*, 13 March 1989; Brian Fallon, 'Paperbacks', *Irish Times*, 25 March 1989.

16 Hazel Leslie, 'Vices and Virtues', *Mail on Sunday*, 5 March 1989; Nicholas Best, 'Biggleswade Bounder', *Financial Times*, 11 March 1989.

17 J. Alice Thompson, 'Family Fished from its Water', *Hampstead and Highgate Express*, 10 March 1989; Kate Saunders, 'Comyns Land: Kind Tarts and Lunatics', *The Independent*, 11 March 1989; Justin Lovell, 'Still Possible at Eighty', *Literary Review*, March 1989, 27–8.

18 Letter from Monica Dickens to BC, dated 1 July 1989.

19 Letter from Monica Dickens to BC, 29 July 1989.

20 Two letters from Molly to BC, undated but found in BC's diary for 1989 so presumably written during that year.

21 Ursula Holden, 'Barbara Comyns: 1909–1992', 11.

22 This paragraph owes much to a conversation with Stuart Phillips that took place on 12 September 2018.

23 Ursula Holden, 'Barbara Comyns: 1909–1992' , 11.

24 Ursula Holden, 'A Singular Woman', *The Oldie*, January 2012, 21.

25 This information is taken from the last will and testament of BC. She did not leave Eduardo or Mariquita anything in her will as she had already given them money from the account she held in Spain.

Afterword

1 Ursula Holden, 'Barbara Comyns: 1909–1992', 4, courtesy of Johnson & Alcock.

2 Conversation with Sally Fletcher Pemberton, 28 August 2018.

3 Ursula Holden, 'Obituary: Barbara Comyns', *The Independent*, 16 July 1992.

4 Teresa Grimes, 'Obituary: Barbara Comyns', *The Independent*, 24 July 1992.

5 Jane Gardam, 'Novelist Levitated', *The Guardian*, 4 August 1992, 31.

6 *Oxford Companion to Twentieth-Century Literature in English*, ed. Jenny Stringer (Oxford: Oxford University Press, 1996), 135.

7 Elizabeth Jane Howard, 'Revised Editions', *Sunday Telegraph*, 11 June 2000, 13.

8 Email from Jill Foulston to Julie Hearn, 15 December 2001, Virago Archive, Barbara Comyns file, British Library.

9 Academic essays include Julie Hearn, 'Barbara Comyns (1907–1992)', in Jay Parini (ed.), *British Writers: Supplement VIII* (New York: Scribner's, 2003), 53–66; Avril Horner and Sue Zlosnik, 'Skin Chairs and Other Domestic Horrors', *Gothic Studies*, 6.1 (2004), 90–102; and Nick Turner, 'Barbara Comyns and New Directions in Women's Writing', in Sue Kennedy and Jane Thomas (eds), *British Women's Writing 1930–1960: Between the Waves* (Liverpool: Liverpool University Press, 2020), 197–213.

10 Virago reprinted three of her novels with fresh introductions in 2013: *Sisters by a River* introduced by Barbara Trapido, *Our Spoons Came from Woolworths*

introduced by Maggie O'Farrell, and *The Vet's Daughter* introduced by Jane Gardam. The independent Dorothy Project reprinted *Who was Changed and Who was Dead* with an introduction by Brian Evenson in 2010, and Capuchin Classics reissued *The Juniper Tree* with an introduction by Margaret Drabble in 2011. New York Review Books brought out fresh editions of *The Vet's Daughter* in 2003 introduced by Kathryn Davis, *Our Spoons Came from Woolworths* in 2015 introduced by Emily Gould, and *The Juniper Tree* in 2018 introduced by Sadie Stein. Turnpike Books reissued *Mr Fox* and *The House of Dolls* in October 2020, and Daunt Books reprinted *Who was Changed and Who was Dead* and *A Touch of Mistletoe* in 2021.

11 Amy Gentry, 'Love, Marriage and the Mess that Came After', *Chicago Tribune*, 22 November 2015; Lucy Scholes, '*Sisters by a River; Our Spoons Came from Woolworths; The Vet's Daughter* by Barbara Comyns – Review', *The Guardian*, 28 July 2013; Camilla Grudova, review of *A Touch of Mistletoe*, *Granta*, 29 December 2016.

12 Marina Warner, 'Evil Stepmother; Reimagined', *New York Times*, 2 February 2018.

13 Sarah Waters, 'The Books that Made Me', *The Guardian*, 1 December 2018.

14 Christopher Shrimpton, 'Hard not to be a Criminal: Reviving Barbara Comyns', *Times Literary Supplement*, 5 February 2021, 12.

15 Avril Horner, 'The Legend and the Crazy Novelist: Graham Greene's Role in Barbara Comyns's Writing Career', and Martin Ivens, 'In this Issue', *Times Literary Supplement*, 5 February 2021, 10–12, 2.

Index

EU authorised representative for GPSR:
Easy Access System Europe, Mustamäe tee 50,
10621 Tallinn, Estonia
gpsr.requests@easproject.com